Okewood of the Secret Service

Valentine Williams

Table of Contents

Okewood of the Secret Service

Valentine Williams

CHAPTER I. THE DEPUTY TURN

Mr. Arthur Mackwayte slipped noiselessly into the dining–room and took his place at the table. He always moved quietly, a look of gentle deprecation on his face as much as to say: "Really, you know, I can't help being here: if you will just overlook me this time, by and by you won't notice I'm there at all!" That was how he went through life, a shy, retiring little man, quiet as a mouse, gentle as a dove, modesty personified.

That is, at least, how Mr. Arthur Mackwayte struck his friends in private life. Once a week, however, he fairly screamed at the public from the advertisement columns of "The Referee": "Mackwayte, in his Celebrated Kerbstone Sketches. Wit! Pathos! Tragedy!!! The Epitome of London Life. Universally Acclaimed as the Greatest Portrayer of London Characters since the late Chas. Dickens. In Tremendous Demand for Public Dinners. The Popular Favorite. A Few Dates still Vacant. 23, Laleham Villas, Seven Kings. 'Phone" and so on.

But only professionally did Mr. Mackwayte thus blow his own trumpet, and then in print alone. For the rest, he had nothing great about him but his heart. A long and bitter struggle for existence had left no hardness in his smooth–shaven flexible face, only wrinkles. His eyes were gray and keen and honest, his mouth as tender as a woman's.

His daughter, Barbara, was already at table pouring out the tea—high tea is still an institution in music–hall circles. Mr. Mackwayte always gazed on this tall, handsome daughter of his with amazement as the great miracle of his life. He looked at her now fondly and thought how.... how distinguished, yes, that was the word, she looked in the trim blue serge suit in which she went daily to her work at the War Office.

"Rations a bit slender to–night, daddy, she said, handing him his cup of tea, "only sardines and bread and butter and cheese. Our meatless day, eh?"

"It'll do very well for me, Barbara, my dear," he answered in his gentle voice, "there have been times when your old dad was glad enough to get a cup of tea and a bite of bread and butter for his supper. And there's many a one worse off than we are today!"

"Any luck at the agent's, daddy?"

Mr. Mackwayte shook his head.

"These revues are fair killing the trade, my dear, and that's a fact. They don't want art to–day, only rag–time and legs and all that. Our people are being cruelly hit by it and that's a fact. Why, who do you think I ran into at Harris' this morning? Why, Barney who used to work with the great Charles, you know, my dear. For years he drew his ten pound a week regular. Yet there he was, looking for a job the same as the rest of us. Poor fellow, he was down on his luck!"

Barbara looked up quickly.

"Daddy, you lent him money...."

Mr. Mackwayte looped extremely uncomfortable.

"Only a trifle, my dear, just a few shillings.... to take him over the week–end.... he's getting something.... he'll repay me, I feel sure...."

"It's too bad of you, daddy," his daughter said severely. "I gave you that ten shillings to buy yourself a bottle of whiskey. You know he won't pay you back. That Barney's a bad egg!"

"Things are going bad with the profession, replied Mr. Mackwayte. "They don't seem to want any of us old stagers today, Barbara!"

"Now, daddy, you know I don't allow you to talk like that. Why, you are only just finished working.... the Samuel Circuit, too!"

Barbara looked up at the old man quickly.

"Only, four weeks' trial, my dear.... they didn't want me, else they would have given me the full forty weeks. No, I expect I am getting past my work. But it's hard on you child...."

Barbara sprang up and placed her hand across her father's mouth.

"I won't have you talk like that, Mac"—that was her pet name for him—"you've worked hard all your life and now it's my turn. Men have had it all their own way before this war came along: now women are going to have a look in. Presently' when I get to be supervisor of my section and they raise my pay again, you will be able to refuse all offers of work. You can go down to Harris with a big cigar in your mouth and patronize him, daddy..."

The telephone standing on the desk in the corner of the cheap little room tingled out sharply. Barbara rose and went across to the desk. Mr. Mackwayte thought how singularly graceful she looked as she stood, very slim, looking at him whimsically across the dinner–table, the receiver in her hand.

Then a strange thing happened. Barbara quickly put the receiver down on the desk and clasped her hands together, her eyes opened wide in amazement.

"Daddy," she cried, "it's the Palaceum... the manager's office... they want you urgently! Oh, daddy, I believe it is an engagement!"

Mr. Mackwayte rose to his feet in agitation, a touch of color creeping into his gray cheeks.

"Nonsense, my dear!" he answered, "at this time of night! Why, it's past eight... their first house is just finishing... they don't go engaging people at this time of day... they've got other things to think of!"

3

He went over to the desk and picked up the receiver.

"Mackwayte speaking!" he said, with a touch of stage majesty in his voice.

Instantly a voice broke in on the other end of the wire, a perfect torrent of words.

"Mackwayte? Ah! I'm glad I caught you at home. Got your props there? Good. Hickie of Hickie and Flanagan broke his ankle during their turn at the first house just now, and I want you to take their place at the second house. Your turn's at 9.40: it's a quarter past eight now: I'll have a car for you at your place at ten to nine sharp. Bring your band parts and lighting directions with you... don't forget! You get twenty minutes, on! Right! Goodbye!"

"The Palaceum want me to deputize for Hickie and Flanagan, my dear," he said a little tremulously' "9.40... the second house... it's... it's very unexpected!"

Barbara ran up and throwing her arms about his neck, kissed him.

"How splendid!" she exclaimed, "the Palaceum, daddy! You've never had an engagement like this before... the biggest hall in London...!!

"Only for a night, my dear"' said Mr. Mackwayte modestly.

"But if they like you, daddy, if it goes down... what will you give them, daddy?"

Mr. Mackwayte scratched his chin.

"It's the biggest theatre in London"' he mused, "It'll have to be broad effects... and they'll want something slap up modern, my dear, I'm thinking..."

"No, no, daddy" his daughter broke in vehemently "they want the best. This is a London audience, remember, not a half−baked provincial house. This is London, Mac, not Wigan! And Londoners love their London! You'll give 'em the old London horse bus driver, the sporting cabby, and I believe you'll have time to squeeze in the hot potato man..."

"Well, like your poor dear mother, I expect you know what's the best I've got" replied Mr. Mackwayte, "but it'll be a bit awkward with a strange dresser... I can't get hold of Potter at this time, of night... and a stranger is sure to mix up my, wigs and things..."

"Why, daddy, I'm going with you to put out your things..."

"But a lady clerk in the War Office, Barbara... a Government official, as you might say... go behind at a music—hall... it don't seem proper right. my dear!"

"Nonsense, Mac. Where Is your theatre? Come along. We'll have to try and get a taxi!"

"They're sending a car at ten to nine, my dear!"

"Good gracious! what swells we are! And it's half—past eight already! Who is on the bill with you?"

"My dear, I haven't an idea... I'm not very well up in the London programmes' I'm afraid... but it is sure to be a good programme. The Palaceum is the only house that's had the courage to break away from this rotten revue craze!"

Barbara was in the hall now, her arms plunged to the shoulder in a great basket trunk that smelt faintly of cocoa—butter. Right and left she flung coats and hats and trousers and band parts, selecting with a sure eye the properties which Mr. Mackwayte would require for the sketches he would play that evening. In the middle of it all the throbbing of a car echoed down the quiet road outside. Then there came a ring at the front door.

* * * * * *

At half—past nine that night, Barbara found herself standing beside her father in the wings of the vast Palaceum stage. Just at her back was the little screened—off recess where Mr. Mackwayte was to make the quick changes that came in the course of his turn. Here, since her arrival in the theatre, Barbara had been busy laying out coats and hats and rigs and grease—paints on the little table below the mirror with its two brilliant electric bulbs, whilst Mr. Mackwayte was in his dressing—room upstairs changing into his first costume.

Now, old Mackwayte stood at her elbow in his rig-out as an old London bus-driver in the identical, characteristic clothes which he had worn for this turn for the past 25 years. He was far too old a hand to show any nervousness he might feel at the ordeal before him. He was chatting in undertones in his gentle, confidential way to the stage manager.

All around them was that curious preoccupied stillness hush of the power-house which makes the false world of the stage so singularly unreal by contrast when watched from the back. The house was packed from floor to ceiling, for the Palaceum's policy of breaking away from revue and going back to Mr. Mackwayte called "straight vaudeville" was triumphantly justifying itself.

Standing in the wings, Barbara could almost feel the electric current running between the audience and the comedian who, with the quiet deliberation of the finished artist, was going through his business on the stage. As he made each of his carefully studied points, he paused, confident of the vast rustle of laughter swelling into a hurricane of applause which never failed to come from the towering tiers of humanity before him, stretching away into the roof where the limelights blazed and spluttered. Save for the low murmur of voices at her side, the silence behind the scenes was absolute. No one was idle. Everyone was at his post, his attention concentrated on that diminutive little figure in the ridiculous clothes which the spot-lights tracked about the stage.

It was the high-water mark of modern music-hall development. The perfect smoothness of the organization gave Barbara a great feeling of contentment for she knew how happy her father must be. Everyone had been so kind to him. "I shall feel a stranger amongst the top-liners of today, my dear," he had said to her in the car on their way to the hall. She had had no answer ready for she had feared he spoke the truth.

Yet everyone they had met had tried to show them that Arthur Mackwayte was not forgotten. The stage-door keeper had known him in the days of the old Aquarium and welcomed him by name. The comedian who preceded Mr. Mackwayte and who was on the stage at that moment had said, "Hullo, Mac! Come to give us young 'uns some tips?" And even now the stage manager was talking over old days with her father.

"You had a rough but good schooling, Mac," he was saying, "but, by Jove, it gave us finished artists. If you saw the penny reading line that comes trying to get a job here... and gets it, by Gad!... it'd make you sick. I tell you I have my work cut out staving them

6

off! It's a pretty good show this week, though, and I've given you a good place, Mac...
you're in front of Nur–el–Din!"

"Nur–el–Din?" repeated Mr. Mackwayte' "what is it, Fletcher? A conjurer?"

"Good Lord' man' where have you been living?" replied Fletcher. "Nur–el–Din is the
greatest vaudeville proposition since Lottie Collins. Conjurer! That's what she is, too, by
Jove! She's the newest thing in Oriental dancers... Spaniard or something... wonderful
clothes, what there is of 'em... and jewelry... wait till you see her!"

"Dear me"' said Mr. Mackwayte' "I'm afraid I'm a bit behind the times. Has she been
appearing here long?"

"First appearance in London, old man' and she's made good from the word 'Go!' She's
been in Paris and all over the Continent, and America, too, I believe, but she had to come
to me to soar to the top of the bill. I saw at once where she belonged! She's a real artiste,
temperament, style and all that sort of thing and a damn good producer into the bargain!
But the worst devil that ever escaped out of hell never had a wickeder temper! She and I
fight all the time! Not a show, but she doesn't keep the stage waiting! But I won! I won't
have her prima donna tricks in this theatre and so I've told her! Hullo, Georgie's he's
finishing..."

The great curtain switched down suddenly, drowning a cascade of applause, and a bundle
of old clothes, twitching nerves, liquid perspiration and grease paint hopped off the stage
into the centre of the group. An electric bell trilled, the limelights shut off, with a jerk that
made the eyes ache, a back–cloth soared aloft and another glided down into its place, the
comedian took two, three, four calls, then vanished into a horde of dim figures scuttling
about in the gloom.

An electric bell trilled again and deep silence fell once more, broken only by the hissing
of the lights.

"You ought to stop behind after your turn and see her, Mac," the stage manager's voice
went on evenly. "All right, Jackson! On you go, Mac!"

Barbara felt her heart jump. Now for it, daddy!

The great curtain mounted majestically and Arthur Mackwayte, deputy turn, stumped serenely on to the stage.

CHAPTER II. CAPTAIN STRANGWISE ENTERTAINS A GUEST

It was the slack hour at the Nineveh Hotel. The last groups about the tea–tables in the Palm Court had broken up, the Tzigane orchestra had stacked its instruments together on its little platform and gone home, and a gentle calm rested over the great hotel as the forerunner of the coming dinner storm.

The pre–dinner hour is the uncomfortable hour of the modern hotel de luxe. The rooms seem uncomfortably hot, the evening paper palls, it is too early to dress for dinner, so one sits yawning over the fire, longing for a fireside of one's own. At least that is how it strikes one from the bachelor standpoint, and that is how it appeared to affect a man who was sitting hunched up in a big arm–chair in the vestibule of the Ninevah Hotel on this winter afternoon.

His posture spoke of utter boredom. He sprawled length in his chair, his long legs stretched out in front of him, his, eyes half–closed, various editions of evening papers strewn about the ground at his feet. He was a tall, well–groomed man, and his lithe, athletic figure looked very well in its neat uniform.

A pretty little woman who sat at one of the writing desks in the vestibule glanced at him more once. He was the sort of man that women look at with interest. He had a long, shrewd, narrow head, the hair dark and close–cropped, a big, bold, aquiline nose, and a firm masterful chin, dominated by a determined line of mouth emphasised by a thin line of moustache. He would have been very handsome but for his eyes, which, the woman decided as she glanced at him, were set rather too close together. She thought she would prefer him as he was now, with his eyes glittering in the fire–light through their long lashes.

But what was most apparent was the magnificent physical fitness of the man. His was the frame of the pioneer, the man of the earth's open spaces and uncharted wilds. He looked as hard as nails, and the woman murmured to herself, as she went on with her note, "On leave from the front."

Presently, the man stirred, stretched himself and finally sat up. Then he started, sprang to his feet, and strode easily across the vestibule to the reception desk. An officer was standing there in a worn uniform, a very shabby kit–bag by his side, a dirty old Burberry over his arm.

"Okewood!" said the young man and touched the other on the shoulder, "isn't it Desmond Okewood? By Jove, I am glad to see you!"

The new–comer turned quickly.

"Why, hullo," he said, "if it isn't Maurice Strangwise! But, good heavens, man, surely I saw your name in the casualty list... missing, wasn't it?"

"Yep!" replied the other smiling, "that's so! It's a long story and it'll keep! But tell me about yourself... this," he kicked the kit–bag with the toe of his boot, looks like a little leave! Just in from France?"

He smiled again, baring his firm, white teeth, and looking at him Desmond suddenly remembered, as one recalls a trifle, his trick of smiling. It was a frank enough smile but... well, some people smile too much.

"Got in just now by the leave train," answered Desmond.

"How much leave have you got?" asked Strangwise.

"Well," said the other, "it's a funny thing, but I don't know!"

"Say, are they giving unlimited leave over there now?"

Desmond laughed.

"Hardly," he replied. "But the War Office just applied for me to come over and here I am! What they want me for, whether it's to advise the War Council or to act as Quartermaster to the Jewish Battalion I can't tell you! I shan't know until tomorrow morning! In the meantime I'm going to forget the war for this evening!"

"What are you going to do to-night?" asked Strangwise.

Desmond began to check off on his fingers.

"Firstly, I'm going to fill the biggest bath in this hotel with hot water, get the biggest piece of Pears' soap in London, and jump in: Then, if my tailor hasn't betrayed me, I'm going to put on dress clothes, and whilst I am dressing summon Julien (if he's maitre d'hotel here) to a conference, then I'm going to eat the best dinner that this pub can provide. Then..."

Strangwise interrupted him.

"The bath is on you, if you like," he said, "but the dinner's on me and a show afterwards. I'm at a loose end, old man, and so are you, so we'll hit up together! We'll dine in the restaurant here 7.30, and Julien shall come up to your room so this you can order the dinner. Is it a go?"

"Rather," laughed Desmond, "I'll eat your dinner, Maurice, and you shall tell me how you managed; to break out of the casualty list into the Nineveh Hotel. But what do all these anxious- looking gentry want?"

The two officers turned to confront a group of four men who were surveying them closely. One of them, a fat, comfortable looking party with grizzled hair, on seeing Desmond, walked up to him.

"Hullo!" said Desmond, "it's Tommy Spencer! How are you, Spencer? What's the betting in Fleet Street on the war lasting another five years? Have you come to interview me?"

The tubby little man beamed and shook hands effusively.

"Glad to see you looking so well, Major," he said, "It's your friend we want..."

"What? Strangwise? Here, Maurice, come meet my friend Tommy Spencer of the "Daily Record," whom I haven't seen since we went on manoeuvres together down at Aldershot!

Captain Strangwise, Tommy Spencer! Now, then, fire away; Spencer!"

Strangwise smiled and shook his head.

"I'm very pleased to know your friend, Desmond," he said, "but, you know, I can't talk! I had the strictest orders from the War Office... It's on account of the other fellows, you know..."

Desmond looked blankly at him. Then he—turned to Spencer.

"You must let me into this, Spencer," he said, "what's old Maurice been up to? Has he been cashiered for wearing shoes or what?"

Spencer's manner became a trifle formal.

"Captain Strangwise has escaped from a prisoners' of war camp in Germany, Major," he said, "we've been trying to get hold of him for days! He's the talk of London!"

Desmond turned like a shot.

"Maurice!" he cried, "'pon my soul, I'm going to have an interesting evening... why, of course, you are just the sort of fellow to do a thing like that. But, Spencer, you know, it won't do... fellows are never allowed to talk to the newspaper men about matters of this kind. And if you're a good fellow, Spencer, you won't even say that you have seen Strangwise here... you'll only get him into trouble!"

The little man looked rather rueful.

"Oh, of course, Major, if you put it that way," he said.

"... And you'll use your influence to make those other fellows with you drop it, will you, Spencer? And then come along to the bar and we'll haven a drink for old times' sake!"

Spencer seemed doubtful about the success of his representations to his colleagues but he obediently trotted away. Apparently, he succeeded in his mission for presently he joined the two officers alone in the American Bar.

"I haven't seen Strangwise for six months, Spencer," said Desmond over his second cocktail. "Seeing him reminds me how astonishing it is the way fellows drop apart in war. Old Maurice was attached to the Brigade of which I am the Brigade Major as gunner officer, and we lived together for the best part of three months, wasn't it, Maurice? Then he goes back to his battery and the, next thing I hear of him is that he is missing. And then I'm damned if he doesn't turn up here!"

Spencer cocked an eye at Strangwise over him Martini.

"I'd like to hear your story, despite the restrictions," he said.

Strangwise looked a trifle embarrassed.

"Maybe I'll tell you one day," he replied in his quiet way, "though, honestly, there's precious little to tell..."

Desmond marked his confusion and respected him for it. He rushed in to the rescue.

"Spencer," he said abruptly, "what's worth seeing in London? We are going to a show to−night. I want to be amused, mark you, not elevated!"

"Nur−el−Din at the Palaceum," replied the reporter.

"By Jove, we'll go there," said Desmond, turning to Maurice. "Have you ever seen her? I'm told she's perfectly marvelous..."

"It's an extraordinarily artistic turn," said Spencer, "and they're doing wonderful business at the Palaceum. You'd better go and see the show soon, though, for they tell me the lady is leaving the programme."

"No!" exclaimed Strangwise so suddenly that Desmond turned round and stared at him. "I thought she was there for months yet..."

"They don't want her to go," answered Spencer, "she's a perfect gold−mine to them but I gather the lady is difficult... in fact, to put it bluntly she's making such a damn nuisance of herself with her artistic temperament that they can't get on with her at all."

"Do you know this lady of the artistic temperament, Maurice?" asked Desmond.

Strangwise hesitated a moment.

"I met her in Canada a few years ago," he said slowly, "she was a very small star then. She's a very handsome and attractive girl, in spite of our friend's unfavorable verdict. There's something curiously real about her dancing, too, that you don't find in this sort of show as a rule!"

He stopped a moment, then added abruptly:

"We'll go along to the Palaceum to–night, if you like, Desmond," and Desmond joyfully acquiesced. To one who has been living for weeks in an ill–ventilated pill–box on the Passchendaele Ridge, the lights and music and color of a music–hall seem as a foretaste of Paradise.

And that was what Desmond Okewood thought as a few hours later he found himself with Maurice Strangwise in the stalls of the vast Palaceum auditorium. In the unwonted luxury of evening clothes he felt clean and comfortable, and the cigar he way smoking was the climax of one of Julien's most esoteric efforts.

The cards on either side of the proscenium opening bore the words: "Deputy Turn." On the stage wad a gnarled old man with ruddy cheeks and a muffler a seedy top hat on his head, a coaching whip in his hand, the old horse bus–driver of London in his habit as he had lived. The old fellow stood there and just talked to the audience of a fine sporting class of men that petrol has driven from the streets, without exaggerated humor or pathos. Desmond, himself a born Cockney, at once fell under the actor's spell and found all memories of the front slipping away from him as the old London street characters succeeded one another on the stage. Then the orchestra blared out, the curtain descended, and the house broke into a great flutter of applause.

Desmond, luxuriating in his comfortable stall puffed at his cigar and fell into a pleasant reverie.

He was contrasting the ghastly nightmare of mud and horrors from which he had only just emerged with the scene of elegance, of civilization; around him.

Suddenly, his attention became riveted on the stage. The atmosphere of the theatre had changed. Always quick at picking up "influences," Desmond instantly sensed a new mood in the throngs around him. A presence was in the theatre, an instinct–awakening, a material influence. The great audience was strangely hushed. The air was heavy with the tent of incense. The stringed instruments and oboes in the orchestra were wandering into rhythmic dropped,

Maurice touched his elbow.

"There she is!" he said.

Desmond felt inclined to shake him off roughly. The interruption jarred on him. For he was looking at this strangely beautiful girl with her skin showing very brown beneath a wonderful silver tiara–like headdress, and in the broad interstices of a cloth–of–silver robe with short, stiffly wired–out skirt. She was seated, an idol, on a glittering black throne, at her feet with their tapering dyed nails a fantastically attired throng of worshipers.

The idol stirred into life, the music of the orchestra died away. Then a tom–tom began to beat its nervous pulse–stirring throb, the strident notes of a reed–pipe joined in and the dancer, raised on her toes on the dais, began to sway languorously to and fro. And so she swayed and swayed with sinuously curving limbs while the drums throbbed out faster with ever–shortening beats, with now and then a clash of brazen cymbals that was torture to overwrought nerves.

The dancer was the perfection of grace. Her figure was lithe and supple as a boy's. There was a suggestion of fire and strength and agility about her that made one think of a panther as she postured there against a background of barbaric color. The grace of her movements, the exquisite blending of the colors on the stage, the skillful grouping of the throng of worshipers, made up a picture which held the audience spellbound and in silence until the curtain dropped.

Desmond turned to find Strangwise standing up.

"I thought of just running round behind the scenes for a few minutes," he said carelessly.

"What, to see Nur–el–Din? By Jove, I'm coming, too!" promptly exclaimed Desmond.

Strangwise demurred. He didn't quite know if he could take him: there might be difficulties: another time... But Desmond got up resolutely.

"I'11 be damned if you leave me behind, Maurice," he laughed, "of course I'm coming, too! She's the most delightful creature I've ever set eyes on!"

And so it ended by them going through the pass–door together.

CHAPTER III. MR. MACKWAYTE MEETS AN OLD FRIEND

That night Nur–el–Din kept the stage waiting for five minutes. It was a climax of a long series of similar unpardonable crimes in the music–hall code. The result was that Mr. Mackwayte, after taking four enthusiastic "curtains," stepped off the stage into a perfect pandemonium.

He found Fletcher, the stage manager, livid with rage, surrounded by the greater part of the large suite with which the dancer traveled. There was Madame's maid, a trim Frenchwoman, Madame's business manager, a fat, voluble Italian, Madame's secretary, an olive–skinned South American youth in an evening coat with velvet collar, and Madame's principal male dancer in a scanty Egyptian dress with grotesquely painted face. They were all talking at the same time, and at intervals Fletcher muttered hotly: "This time she leaves the bill or I walk out of the theatre!"

Then a clear voice cried:

"Me voila!" and a dainty apparition in an ermine wrap tripped into the centre of the group, tapped the manager lightly on the shoulder and said:

"Allons! I am ready!"

Mr. Mackwayte's face creased its mask of paint into a thousand wrinkles. For, on seeing him, the dancer's face lighted up, and, running to him with hands outstretched, she cried:

"Tiens! Monsieur Arthur!" while he ejaculated:

"Why, it's little Marcelle!"

But now the stage manager interposed. He whisked Madame's wrap off her with one hand and with the other, firmly propelled her on to the stage. She let him have his way with a merry smile, dark eyes and white teeth flashing, but as she went she said to Mr. Mackwayte:

"My friend, wait for me! Et puis nous causerons! We will 'ave a talk, nest−ce pas?"

"A very old friend of mine, my dear," Mr. Mackwayte said to Barbara when, dressed in his street clothes, he rejoined her in the wings where she stood watching Nur−el−Din dancing. "She was an acrobat in the Seven Duponts, a turn that earned big money in the old days. It must be... let's see... getting on for twenty years since I last set eyes on her. She was a pretty kid in those days! God bless my soul! Little Marcelle a big star! It's really most amazing!"

Directly she was off the stage, Nur−el−Din cams straight to Mr. Mackwayte, pushing aside her maid who was waiting with her wrap.

"My friend," she cooed in her pretty broken English, "I am so glad, so glad to see you. And this is your girl... ah! she 'as your eyes, Monsieur Arthur, your nice English gray eyes! Such a big girl... ah! but she make me feel old!"

She laughed, a pretty gurgling laugh, throwing back her head so that the diamond collar she was wearing heaved and flashed.

"But you will come to my room, hein?" she went on. "Marie, my wrap!" and she led the way to the lift.

Nur−el−Din's spacious dressing−room seemed to be full of people and flowers. All her little court was assembled amid a perfect bower of hot−house blooms and plants". Head and shoulders above everybody else in the room towered the figure of an officer in uniform, with him another palpable Englishman in evening dress.

16

Okewood of the Secret Service

Desmond Okewood thought he had never seen anything in his life more charming than the picture the dancer made as she came into the room. Her wrap had fallen open and beneath the broad bars of her cloth-of-silver dress her bosom yet rose and fell after the exertions of her dance. A jet black curl had strayed out from beneath her lofty silver head-dress, and she thrust it back in its place with one little brown bejeweled hand whilst she extended the other to Strangwise.

"Tiens, mon capitaine!" she said. Desmond was watching her closely, fascinated by her beauty, but noticed an unwilling, almost a hostile tone, in her voice.

Strangwise was speaking in his deep voice.

"Marcelle," he said, "I've brought a friend who is anxious to meet you. Major Desmond Okewood! He and I soldiered together in France!" The dancer turned her big black eyes full on Desmond as she held out her hand to him.

"Old friends, new friends," she cried, clapping, her hands like a child, "I love friends. Captaine, here is a very old friend," she said to Strangwise as Mr. Mackwayte and Barbara came into the rooms, "Monsieur Arthur Mackwayte and 'is daughter. I 'ave know Monsieur Arthur almos' all my life. And, Mademoiselle, permit me? I introduce le Captaine Strangwise and 'is friend... what is the name? Ah, Major Okewood!"

Nur-el-Din sank into a bergere chair beside her great mirror.

"There are too many in this room," she cried, "there is no air! Lazarro, Ramiro, all of you, go outside, my friends!"

As Madame's entourage surged out, Strangwise said:

"I hear you are leaving the Palaceum, Marcelle!"

He spoke so low that Mr. Mackwayte and Barbara, who were talking to Desmond, did not hear. Marcelle, taking off her heavy head-dress, answered quickly:

"Who told you that?"

"Never mind," replied Strangwise. "But you never told me you were going. Why didn't you?"

His voice was stern and hard now, very different from his usual quiet and mellow tones. But he was smiling.

Marcelle cast a glance over her shoulder. Barbara was looking round the room and caught the reflection of the dancer's face in a mirror hanging on the wall. To her intense astonishment, she saw a look of despair, almost of terror, in Nur-el-Din's dark eyes. It was like the frightened stare of some hunted beast. Barbara was so much taken aback that she instinctively glanced over her shoulder at the door, thinking that the dancer had seen something there to frighten her. But the door was shut. When Barbara looked into the mirror again, she saw only the reflection of Nur-el-Din's pretty neck and shoulders. The dancer was talking again in low tones to Strangwise.

But Barbara swiftly forgot that glimpse of the dancer's face in the glass. For she was very happy. Happiness, like high spirits, is eminently contagious, and the two men at her side were supremely content.

Her father's eyes were shining with his little success fit, of the evening: on the way upstairs Fletcher had held out hopes to him of a long engagement at the Palaceum while as for the other, he was radiant with the excitement of his first night in town after long months of campaigning.

He was thinking that his leave had started most propitiously. After a man has been isolated for months amongst muddy masculinity, the homeliest woman will find favor in his eyes. And to neither of these women, in whose presence he so unexpected found himself within a few hours of landing in England, could the epithet "homely" be applied. Each represented a distinct type of beauty in herself, and Desmond, as he chatted with Barbara, was mentally contrasting the two women. Barbara, tall and slim and very healthy, with her braided brown hair, creamy complexion and gray eyes, was essentially English. She was the typical woman of England, of England of the broad green valleys and rolling downs and snuggling hamlets, of England of the white cliffs gnawed by the restless ocean, The other was equally essentially a woman of the South. Her dark eyes, her upper lip just baring her firm white teeth, spoke of hot Latin or gypsy blood surging in her veins. Hers was the beauty of the East, sensous, arresting, conjuring up pictures of warm, perfumed nights, the thrumming of guitars, a great yellow moon hanging low behind the palms.

"Barbara!" called Nur-el-Din from the dressing table. Mr. Mackwayte had joined her there and was chatting to Strangwise.

"You will stay and talk to me while I change n'est-ce pas? Your papa and these gentlemen are going to drink a whiskey-soda with that animal Fletcher... quel homme terrible... and you shall join them presently."

The men went out, leaving Barbara alone with the dancer. Barbara noticed how tired Nur-el-Din was looking. Heir pretty, childish ways seemed to have evaporated with her high spirits. Her face was heavy and listless. There were lines round heir eyes, and her mouth had a hard, drawn look.

"Child," she said, "give me, please, my peignoir... it is behind the door,... and, I will get this paint off my face!"

Barbara fetched the wrapper and sat down beside the dancer. But Nur-el-Din did not move. She seemed to be thinking. Barbara saw the hunted look she had already observed in her that evening creeping over her face again.

"It is a hard life; this life of ours, a life of change, ma petite! A great artiste has no country, no home, no fireside! For the past five years I have been roaming about the world! Often I think I will settle down, but the life holds me!"

She took up from her dressing-table a little oblong plain silver box.

"I want to ask you a favor, ma petite Barbara!" she said. "This little box is a family possession of mine: I have had it for many years. The world is so disturbed to-day that life is not safe for anybody who travels as much as I do! You have a home, a safe home with your dear father! He was telling me about it! Will you take this little box and keep it safely for me until... until... the war is over... until I ask you for it?"

"Yes, of course," said Barbara, "if you wish it, though, what with these air raids, I don't know that London is particularly safe, either."

"Ah! that is good of you," cried Nur–el–Din, "anyhow, the little box is safer with you than with me. See, I will wrap it up and seal it, and then you will take it home with you, n'est–ce pas?"

She opened a drawer and swiftly hunting among its contents produced a sheet, of white paper, and some sealing–wax. She wrapped the box in the paper and sealed it up, stamping the seals with a camel signet ring she drew off her finger. Then she handed the package to Barbara.

There was a knock at the door. The maid, noiselessly arranging Madame's dresses in the corner opened it.

"You will take care of it well for me," the dancer said to Barbara, and her voice vibrated with a surprising eagerness, "you will guard it preciously until I come for it..." She laughed and added carelessly: "Because it is a family treasure, a life mascotte of mine, hein?"

Then they heard Strangwise's deep voice outside.

Nur–el–Din started.

"Le Captaine is there, Madame," said the French maid, "'e say Monsieur Mackwayte ask for Mademoiselle!"

The dancer thrust a little hand from the folds of her silken kimono.

"Au revoir, ma petite," she said, "we shall meet again. You will come and see me, nest–ce pas? And say nothing to anybody about..." she pointed to Barbara's bag where the little package was reposing, "it shall be a secret between us, hein? Promise me this, mon enfant!"

"Of course, I promise, if you like!" said Barbara, wonderingly.

At half–past eight the next morning Desmond Okewood found himself in the ante–room of the Chief of the Secret Service in a cross and puzzled mood. The telephone at his bedside had roused him at 8 a.m. from the first sleep he had had in a real bed for two months. In a drowsy voice he had protested that he had an appointment at the War Office at 10 o'clock, but a curt voice had bidden him dress himself and come to the Chief forthwith. Here he was, accordingly, breakfastless, his chin smarting from a hasty shave. What the devil did the Chief want with him anyhow? He wasn't in the Secret Service, though his brother, Francis, was.

A voice broke in upon his angry musing.

"Come in, Okewood!" it said.

The Chief stood at the door of his room, a broad–shouldered figure in a plain jacket suit. Desmond had met him before. He knew him for a man of many questions but of few confidences, yet his recollection of him was of a suave, imperturbable personality. To–day, however, the Chief seemed strangely preoccupied. There was a deep line between his bushy eyebrows as he bent them at Desmond, motioning him to a chair. When he spoke, his manner was very curt.

"What time did you part from the Mackwaytes at the theatre last night?"

Desmond was dumbfounded. How on earth did the Chief know about his visit to the Palaceum? Still, he was used to the omniscience of the British Intelligence, so he answered promptly:

"It was latish, sir; about midnight, I think!"

"They went home to Seven Kings alone!"

"Yes, sir, in a taxi!" Desmond replied.

The Chief contemplated his blotting–pad gloomily. Desmond knew it for a trick of his when worried.

"Did you have a good night?" he said to Desmond, suddenly.

"Yes," he said, not in the least understanding the drift of the question. "... though I didn't mean to get up quite so early!"

The Chief ignored this sally.

"Nothing out of the ordinary happened during the night, I suppose?" he asked again.

Desmond shook his head.

"Nothing that I know of, sir," he said.

"Seen Strangwise this morning?"

Desmond gasped for breath. So the Chief knew about him meeting Strangwise, too!

"No, sir!"

A clerk put his head in at the door.

"Well, Matthews!"

"Captain Strangwise will be along very shortly, sir," he said.

The Chief looked up quickly.

"Ah, he's all right then! Good."

"And, sir," Matthews added, "Scotland Yard telephoned to say that the doctor is with Miss Mackwayte now."

Desmond started up.

"Is Miss Mackwayte ill?" he exclaimed.

The Chief answered slowly, as Matthew s withdrew: "Mr. Mackwayte was found murdered at his house early this morning!"

CHAPTER IV. MAJOR OKEWOOD ENCOUNTERS A NEW TYPE

There is a sinister ring about the word "murder," which reacts upon even the most hardened sensibility. Edgar Allan Poe, who was a master of the suggestive use of words, realized this when he called the greatest detective story ever written "The Murders in the Rue Morgue." From the very beginning of the war, Desmond had seen death in all its forms but that word "murdered," spoken with slow emphasis in the quiet room, gave him an ugly chill feeling round the heart that he had never experienced on the battlefield.

"Murdered!" Desmond repeated dully and sat down. He felt stunned. He was not thinking of the gentle old man cruelly done to death or of the pretty Barbara prostrate with grief. He was overawed by the curious fatality that had plucked him from the horrors of Flanders only to plunge him into a tragedy at home.

"Yes," said the Chief bluntly, "by a burglar apparently—the house was ransacked!"

"Chief," he broke out, "you must explain. I'm all at sea! Why did you send for me? What have you got to do with criminal cases, anyway? Surely, this is a Scotland Yard matter!"

The Chief shook his head.

"I sent for you in default of your brother, Okewood!" he said. "You once refused an offer of mine to take you into my service, but this time I had to have you, so I got the War Office to wire..."

"Then my appointment for ten o'clock to–day was with you?" Desmond exclaimed in astonishment.

The Chief nodded.

"It was," he said curtly.

"But," protested Desmond feebly, "did you know about this murder beforehand!"

The Chief threw back his head and laughed.

"My dear fellow," he said; "I'm not quite so deep as all that. I haven't second sight, you know!"

"You've got something devilish like it, sir!" said Desmond. "How on earth did you know that I was at the Palaceum last night?"

The Chief smiled grimly.

"Oh, that's very simple," he said. "Shall I tell you some more about yourself? You sat..." he glanced down at the desk in front of him,"... in Stall E 52 and, after Nur–el–Din's turn, Strangwise took you round and introduced you to the lady. In her dressing–room you met Mr. Mackwayte and his daughter. After that..."

"But," Desmond interrupted quickly, "I must have been followed by one of your men. Still, I can't see why my movements should interest the Secret Service, sir!"

The Chief remained silent for a moment. Then he said:

"Fate often unexpectedly takes a hand in this game of ours, Okewood. I sent for you to come back from France but old man Destiny wouldn't leave it at that. Almost as soon as you landed he switched you straight on to a trail that I have been patiently following up for months past. That trail is..."

The telephone on the desk rang sharply.

"Whose trail?" Desmond could not forbear to ask as the Chief took off the receiver.

"Just a minute," the Chief said. Then he spoke into the telephone:

"Marigold? Yes. Really? Very well, I'll come straight along now... I'll be with you in twenty minutes. Good–bye!"

He put down the receiver and rose to his feet.

"Okewood," he cried gaily, "what do you say to a little detective work? That was Marigold of the Criminal Investigation Department... he's down at Seven Kings handling this murder case. I asked him to let me know when it would be convenient for me to come along and have a look round, and he wants me to go now. Two heads are better than one. You'd better come along!"

He pressed a button on the desk.

The swift and silent Matthews appeared.

"Matthews," he said, "when Captain Strangwise comes, please tell him I've been called away and ask him to call back here at two o'clock to see me."

He paused and laid a lean finger reflectively along his nose.

"Are you lunching anywhere, Okewood?" he 'said. Desmond shook his head.

"Then you will lunch with me, eh? Right. Come along and we'll try to find the way to Seven Kings."

The two men threaded the busy corridors to the lift which deposited them at the main entrance. A few minutes later the Chief was dexterously guiding his Vauxhall car through the crowded traffic of the Strand, Desmond beside him on the front seat.

Desmond was completely fogged in his mind. He couldn't see light anywhere. He asked himself in vain what possible connection could exist between this murder in an obscure quarter of London and the man at his side who, he knew, held in his firm hands lines that stretched to the uttermost ends of the earth? What kind of an affair was this, seemingly so commonplace that could take the Chief's attention from the hundred urgent matters of national security that occupied him?

The Chief seemed absorbed in his driving and Desmond felt it would be useless to attempt to draw him out. They wended their way through the city and out into the squalid length of the Mile End Road. Then the Chief began to talk.

"I hate driving through the City," he exclaimed, "but I always think it's good for the nerves. Still, I have a feeling that I shall smash this old car up some day. That friend of yours, Strangwise, now he's a remarkable man!" Do you know his story?"

"About his escape from Germany?" asked Desmond.

The Chief nodded.

He told me something about it at dinner last night," said Desmond, "but he's such a modest chap he doesn't seem to like talking about it!"

"He must have a cool nerve," replied the Chief, "he doesn't know a word of German, except a few scraps he picked up in camp. Yet, after he got free, he made his way alone from somewhere in Hanover clear to the Dutch frontier. And I tell you he kept his eyes and ears open!"

"Was he able to tell you anything good" asked Desmond.

"The man's just full of information. He couldn't take a note of any kind, of course, but he seems to have a wonderful memory. He was able to give us the names of almost every unit of troops he came across."

He stopped to skirt a tram, then added suddenly:

"Do you know him well, Okewood?"

"Yes, I think I do," said Desmond. "I lived with him for about three months in France, and we got on top-hole together. He's a man absolutely without fear."

"Yes," agreed the Chief. "But what about his judgment? Would you call him a well-balanced fellow? Or is he one of these harum-scarum soldier of fortune sort of chaps?"

"I should say he was devilish shrewd," replied the other. "Strangwise is a very able fellow and a fine soldier. The Brigadier thought a lot of him. There's very little about artillery work that Strangwise doesn't know. Our Brigadier's a good judge, too... he was a gunner himself once, you know."

"I'm glad to hear you say that," answered the Chief, "because there are some things he has told us, about the movements of troops, particularly, that don't agree in the least with our own Intelligence reports. I am an old enough hand at my job to know that very often one man may be right where fifty independent witnesses are dead wrong. Yet our reports from Germany have been wonderfully accurate on the whole."

He stopped.

"Tell me," he asked suddenly, "is Strangwise a liar, do you think?"

Desmond laughed. The question was so very unexpected.

"Let me explain what I mean," said the Chief. "There is a type of man who is quite incapable of telling the plain, unvarnished truth. That type of fellow might have the most extraordinary adventure happen to him and yet be unable to let it stand on its merits. When he narrates it, he trims it up with all kinds of embroidery. Is Strangwise that type?"

Desmond thought a moment.

"Your silence is very eloquent," said the Chief drily.

Desmond laughed.

"It's not the silence of consent," he said, "but if you want me to be quite frank about Strangwise, Chief, I don't mind telling you I don't like him overmuch. We were very intimate in France. We were in some very tight corners together and he never let me down. He showed himself to be a very fine fellow, indeed. There are points about him I admire immensely. I love his fine physique, his manliness. I'm sure he's got great strength of character, too. It's because I admire all this about him that I think perhaps it's just jealousy on my part when I feel..."

"What?" said the Chief.

"Well," said Desmond slowly, "I feel myself trying to like something below the surface in the man. And then I am balked. There seems to be something abysmally deep behind the facade, if you know what I mean. If I think about it much, it seems to me that there is too much surface about Strangwise and not enough foundation! And he smiles... Well, rather often, doesn't he?"

"I know what you mean," said the Chief. "I always tell my young men to be wary when a man smiles too much. Smiles are sometimes camouflage, to cover up something that mustn't be seen underneath! Strangwise is a Canadian, isn't he?"

"I think so," answered Desmond, "anyhow, he has lived there. But he got his commission over here. He came over some time in 1915, I believe, and joined up."

"Ah, here we are!" cried the Chief, steering the car down a turning marked "Laleham Villas."

Laleham Villas proved to be an immensely long terrace of small two—story houses, each one exactly like the other, the only difference between them lying in the color of the front doors and the arrangement of the small strip of garden in front of each. The houses stretched away on either side in a vista of smoke—discolored yellow brick. The road was perfectly straight and, in the dull yellow atmosphere of the winter morning, unspeakably depressing.

The abode of small clerks and employees, Laleham Villas had rendered up, an hour before, its daily tribute of humanity to the City—bound trains of the Great Eastern Railway. The Mackwayte's house was plainly indicated, about 200 yards down on the right—hand side, by a knot of errand boys and bareheaded women grouped on the side—walk. A large, phlegmatic policeman stood at the gate.

"You'll like Marigold," said the Chief to Desmond as they got out of the car, "quite a remarkable man and very sound at his work!"

British officers don't number detective inspectors among their habitual acquaintances, and the man that came out of the house to meet them was actually the first detective that Desmond had ever met. Ever since the Chief had mentioned his name, Desmond had been wondering whether Mr. Marigold would be lean and pale and bewildering like Mr.

Sherlock Holmes or breezy and wiry like the detectives in American crook plays.

The man before him did not bear the faintest resemblance to either type. He was a well–set up, broad–shouldered person of about forty–five, very carefully dressed in a blue serge suit and black overcoat, with a large, even–tempered countenance, which sloped into a high forehead. The neatly brushed but thinning locks carefully arranged across the top of the head testified to the fact that Mr. Marigold had sacrificed most of his hair to the vicissitudes of his profession. When it is added that the detective had a small, yellow moustache and a pleasant, cultivated voice, there remains nothing further to say about Mr. Marigold's external appearance. But there was something so patent about the man, his air of reserve, his careful courtesy, his shrewd eyes, that Desmond at once recognized him for a type, a cast from a certain specific mould. All services shape men to their own fashion. There is the type of Guardsman, the type of airman, the type of naval officer. And Desmond decided that Mr. Marigold must be the type of detective, though, as I have said, he was totally unacquainted with the genus.

"Major Okewood, Marigold," said the Chief, "a friend of mine!"

Mr. Marigold mustered Desmond in one swift, comprehensive look.

"I won't give you my hand, Major," the detective said, looking down at Desmond's proffered one, "for I'm in a filthy mess and no error. But won't you come in, sir?" he said to the Chief and led the way across the mosaic tile pathway to the front door which stood open.

"I don't think this is anything in your line, sir," said Mr. Marigold to the Chief as the three men entered the house, "it's nothing but just a common burglary. The old man evidently heard a noise and coming down, surprised the burglar who lost his head and killed him. The only novel thing about the whole case is that the old party was shot with a pistol and not bludgeoned, as is usually the case in affairs of this kind. And I shouldn't have thought that the man who did it was the sort that carries a gun..."

"Then you know who did it?" asked the Chief quietly.

"I think I can safely say I do, sir," said Mr. Marigold with the reluctant air of one who seldom admits anything to be a fact, "I think I can go as far as that! And we've got our man under lock and key!"

"That's a smart piece of work, Marigold," said the Chief.

"No, sir," replied the other, "you could hardly call it that. He just walked into the arms of a constable over there near Goodmayes Station with the swag on him. He's an old hand... we've known him for a receiver for years!

"Who is it?" asked the Chief, "not one of my little friends, I suppose, eh, Marigold!"

"Dear me, no, sir," answered Mr. Marigold, chuckling, "it's one of old Mackwayte's music–hall pals, name o' Barney!"

CHAPTER V. THE MURDER AT SEVEN KINGS

"This is Mrs. Chugg, sir," said Mr. Marigold, "the charwoman who found the body!"

The Chief and Desmond stood at the detective's side in the Mackwaytes' little dining–room. The room was in considerable disorder. There was a litter of paper, empty bottles, overturned cruets and other debris on the floor, evidence of the thoroughness with which the burglar had overhauled the cheap fumed oak sideboard which stood against the wall with doors and drawers open. In the corner, the little roll–top desk showed a great gash in the wood round the lock where it had been forced. The remains of a meal still stood on the table.

Mrs. Chugg, a diminutive, white–haired, bespectacled woman in a rusty black cape and skirt, was enthroned in the midst of this scene of desolation. She sat in an armchair by the fire, her hands in her lap, obviously supremely content with the position of importance she enjoyed. At the sound of Mr. Marigold's voice, she bobbed up and regarded the newcomers with the air of a tragedy queen.

"Yus mister," she said with the slow deliberation of one who thoroughly enjoys repeating an oft–told tale, "I found the pore man and a horrid turn it give me, too, I declare! I come in early this morning a–purpose to turn out these two rooms, the dining–room and the droring–room, same as I always do of a Saturday, along of the lidy's horders and wishes.

I come in 'ere fust, to pull up the blinds and that, and d'reckly I switches on the light 'Burglars!' I sez to meself, 'Burglars! That's wot it is!' seeing the nasty mess the place was in. Up I nips to Miss Mackwayte's room on the first floor and in I bursts. 'Miss,' sez I, 'Miss, there's been burglars in the house!' and then I sees the pore lamb all tied up there on 'er blessed bed! Lor, mister, the turn it give me and I ain't telling you no lies! She was strapped up that tight with a towel crammed in 'er mouth she couldn't 'ardly dror 'er breath! I undid 'er pretty quick and the fust thing she sez w'en I gets the towl out of her mouth, the pore dear, is 'Mrs. Chugg,' she sez all of a tremble as you might say, 'Mrs. Chugg' sez she, 'my father!' my father!' sez she. With that up she jumps but she 'adn't put foot to the floor w'en down she drops! It was along of 'er being tied up orl that time, dyer see, mister! I gets 'er back on the bed. 'You lie still, Miss,' says I, 'and I'll pop in and tell your pa to come in to you!' Well; I went to the old genelmun's room. Empty!"

Mrs. Chugg paused to give her narrative dramatic effect.

"And where did you find Mr. Mackwayte?" asked the Chief in such a placid voice that Mrs. Chugg cast an indignant glance at him.

"I was jes' going downstairs to see if 'e was in the kitching or out at the back," she continued, unheeding the interruption, "when there on the landing I sees a foot asticking out from under the curting. I pulls back the curting and oh, Lor! oh, dear, oh, dear, the pore genelmun, 'im as never did a bad turn to no one!"

"Come, come, Mrs. Chugg!" said the detective.

The charwoman wiped her eyes and resumed.

"'E was a–lying on his back in 'is dressing–gown, 'is face all burnt black, like, and a fair smother o' blood. Under 'is hed there was a pool o' blood, mister, yer may believe me or not..."

Mr. Marigold cut in decisively.

"Do you wish to see the body, sir?" the detective asked the Chief, "they're upstairs photographing it!"

31

The Chief nodded. He and Desmond followed the detective upstairs, whilst Mrs. Chugg resentfully resumed her seat by the fire. On her face was the look of one who has cast pearls before swine.

"Any finger-prints?" asked the Chief in the hall.

"Oh, no," he said, "Barney's far too old a hand for that sort o' thing!"

The landing proved to be a small space, covered with oilcloth and raised by a step from the bend made by the staircase leading to the first story. On the left-hand side was a window looking on a narrow passage separating the Mackwayte house from its neighbors and leading to the back-door. By the window stood a small wicker-work table with a plant on it. At the back of the landing was a partition, glazed half-way up and a door—obviously the bath-room.

The curtain had been looped right over its brass rod. The body lay on its back at the foot of the table, arms flung outward, one leg doubled up, the other with the foot just jutting out over the step leading down to the staircase. The head pointed towards the bath-room door. Over the right eye the skin of the face was blackened in a great patch and there was a large blue swelling, like a bruise, in the centre. There was a good deal of blood on the face which obscured the hole made by the entrance of the bullet. The eyes were half-closed. A big camera, pointed downwards, was mounted on a high double ladder straddling the body and was operated by a young man in a bowler hat who went on with his work without taking the slightest notice of the detective and his companions.

"Close range," murmured Desmond, after glancing at the dead man's face, "a large calibre automatic pistol, I should think!"

"Why do you think it was a large calibre pistol, Major?" asked Mr. Marigold attentively.

"I've seen plenty of men killed at close range by revolver and rifle bullets out at the front," replied Desmond, "but I never saw a man's face messed up like this. In a raid once I shot a German at point blank range with my revolver, the ordinary Army issue pattern, and I looked him over after. But it wasn't anything like this. The only thing I've seen approaching it was one of our sergeants who was killed out on patrol by a Hun officer who put his gun right in our man's face. That sergeant was pretty badly marked, but..."

He shook his head. Then he added, addressing the detective: "Let's see the gun! Have you got it?"

Mr. Marigold shook his head.

"He hadn't got it on him," he answered, "he swears he never had a gun. I expect he chucked it away somewhere. It'll be our business to find it for him!"

He smiled rather grimly, then added:

"Perhaps you'd care to have a look at Miss Mackwayte's room, sir!"

"Is Miss Mackwayte there" asked the Chief.

"I got her out of this quick," replied Mr. Marigold, "she's had a bad shock, poor girl, though she gave her evidence clearly enough for all that... as far as it goes and that's not much. Some friends near by have taken her in! The doctor has given her some bromide and says she's got to be kept quiet..."

"What's her story!" queried the Chief.

"She can't throw much light on the business. She and her father reached home from the theatre about a quarter past twelve, had a bit of supper in the dining−room and went up to bed before one o'clock. Miss Mackwayte saw her father go into his room, which is next to hers, and shut the door. The next thing she knows is that she woke up suddenly with some kind of a loud noise in her ears... that was the report of the pistol, I've no doubt... she thought for a minute it was an air raid. Then suddenly a hand was pressed over her mouth, something was crammed into her mouth and she was firmly strapped down to the bed."

"Did she see the man?" asked Desmond.

"She didn't see anything from first to last," answered the detective, "as far as she is concerned it might have been a woman or a black man who trussed her up. It was quite dark in her bedroom and this burglar fellow, after binding and gagging her, fastened a bandage across her eyes into the bargain. She says she heard him moving about her room and then creep out very softly. The next thing she knew was Mrs. Chugg arriving at her bedside this morning."

"What time did this attack take place?" asked the Chief.

"She has no idea," answered the detective. "She couldn't see her watch and they haven't got a striking clock in the house."

"But can she make no guess!"

"Well, she says she thinks it was several hours before Mrs. Chugg arrived in the morning... as much as three hours, she thinks!"

A"nd what time did Mrs. Chugg arrive!"

"At half–past six!"

"About Mackwayte... how long was he dead when they found him? What does the doctor say?"

"About three hours approximately, but you know, they can't always tell to an hour or so!"

"Well," said the Chief slowly, "it looks as if one might figure the murder as having been committed some time between 3 and 3.30 a.m."

"My idea exactly," said Mr. Marigold. "Shall we go upstairs?"

He conducted the Chief and Desmond up the short flight of stairs to the first story. He pushed open the first door he came to.

"Mackwayte's room, on the back," he said, "bed slept in, as you see, old gentleman's clothes on a chair—obviously he was disturbed by some noise made by the burglar and came out to see what was doing! And here," he indicated a door adjoining, Mis Miss Mackwayte's room, on the front; as you observe. They don't use the two rooms on the second floor, except for box–rooms... one's full of old Mackwayte's theatre trunks and stuff. They keep no servant; Mrs. Chugg comes in each morning and stays all day. She

34

goes away after supper every evening."

Desmond found himself looking into a plainly furnished but dainty bedroom with white furniture and a good deal of chintz about. There were some photographs and pictures hanging on the walls. The room was spotlessly clean and very tidy.

Desmond remarked on this, asking if the police had put the room straight.

Mr. Marigold looked quite shocked.

"Oh, no, everything is just as it was when Mrs. Chugg found Miss Mackwayte this morning. There's Miss Mackwayte's gloves and handbag on the toilet–table just as she left 'em last night. I wouldn't let her touch her clothes even. She went over to Mrs. Appleby's in her dressing–gown, in a taxi."

"Then Master Burglar didn't burgle this room?" asked the Chief.

"Nothing touched, not even the girl's money," replied Marigold.

"Then why did he come up here at all?" asked Desmond.

"Obviously, the old gentleman disturbed him," was the detective's reply. "Barney got scared and shot the old gentleman, then came up here to make sure that the daughter would not give him away before he could make his escape. He must have known the report of the gun would wake her up."

"But are there no clues or finger–prints or anything of that kind here, Marigold?" asked the Chief.

"Not a finger–print anywhere," responded the other, "men like Barney are born wise to the fingerprint business, sir."

He dipped a finger and thumb into his waistcoat pocket.

"Clues? Well, I've got one little souvenir here which I daresay a writer of detective stories would make a good bit of."

He held in his hand a piece of paper folded flat. He unfolded it and disclosed a loop of dark hair.

"There!" he said mockingly, straightening out the hair and holding it up in the light. "That's calculated to set one's thoughts running all over the place, isn't it? That piece of hair was caught in the buckle of one of the straps with which Miss Mackwayte was bound to the bed. Miss Mackwayte, I would point out, has brown hair. Whose hair do you think that is?"

Desmond looked closely at the strand of hair in the detective's fingers. It was long and fine and glossy and jetblack.

The Chief laughed and shook his head.

"Haven't an idea, Marigold," he answered, "Barney's, I should imagine, that is, if he goes about with black ringlets falling round his shoulders

"Barney?" echoed the detective. "Barney's as bald as I am. Besides, if you saw his sheet, you'd realize that he has got into the habit of wearing his hair short!"

He carefully rolled the strand of hair up, replaced it in its paper and stowed it in his waistcoat pocket.

"It just shows how easily one is misled in a matter of this kind," he went on. "Supposing Barney hadn't got himself nabbed, supposing I hadn't been able to find out from Miss Mackwayte her movements on the night previous to the murder, that strand of hair might have led me on a fine wild goose chase!"

"But, damn it, Marigold," exclaimed the Chief, laughing, "you haven't told us whose hair it is?"

"Why, Nur—el—Din's, of course!"

The smile froze on the Chief's lips, the laughter died out of his eyes. Desmond was amazed at the change in the man. The languid interest he had taken in the different details of the crime vanished. Something seemed to tighten up suddenly in his face and manner.

"Why Nur—el—Din?" he asked curtly.

Mr. Marigold glanced quickly at him. Desmond remarked that the detective was sensible of the change too.

"Simply because Miss Mackwayte spent some time in the dancer's dressing—room last night, sir," he replied quietly, "she probably sat at her dressing—table and picked up this hair in hers or in her veil or something and it dropped on the bed where one of Master Barney's buckles caught it up."

He spoke carelessly but Desmond noticed that he kept a watchful eye on the other.

The Chief did not answer. He seemed to have relapsed into the preoccupied mood in which Desmond had found him that morning.

"I was going to suggest, sir," said Mr. Marigold diffidently, "if you had the time, you might care to look in at the Yard, and see the prisoner. I don't mind telling you that he is swearing by all the tribes of Judah that he's innocent of the murder of old Mackwayte. He's got an amazing yarn... perhaps you'd like to hear it!"

Mr. Marigold suddenly began to interest Desmond. His proposal was put forward so modestly that one would have thought the last thing he believed possible was that the Chief should acquiesce in his suggestion. Yet Desmond had the feeling that the detective was far from being so disinterested as he wished to seem. It struck Desmond that the case was more complicated than Mr. Marigold admitted and that the detective knew it. Had Mr. Marigold discovered that the Chief knew a great deal more about this mysterious affair than the detective knew himself? And was not his attitude of having already solved the problem of the murder, his treatment of the Chief as a dilettante criminologist simply an elaborate pose, to extract from the Chief information which had not been proffered?

The Chief glanced at his watch.

"Right," he said, "I think I'd like to go along."

"I have a good deal to do here still," observed Mr. Marigold, "so, if you don't mind, I won't accompany you. But perhaps, sir, you would like to see me this afternoon?"

The Chief swung round on his heel and fairly searched Mr. Marigold with a glance from beneath his bushy eyebrows. The detective returned his gaze with an expression of supreme innocence.

"Why, Marigold," answered the Chief, "I believe I should. Six o'clock suit you?"

"Certainly, sir," said Mr. Marigold.

Desmond stood by the door, vastly amused by this duel of wits. The Chief and Mr. Marigold made a move towards the door, Desmond turned to open it and came face to face with a large framed photograph of the Chief hanging on the wall of Miss Mackwayte's bedroom.

"Why, Chief," he cried, "you never told me you knew Miss Mackwayte!"

The Chief professed to be very taken aback by this question. "Dear me, didn't I, Okewood?" he answered with eyes laughing, "she's my secretary!"

CHAPTER VI. "NAME O'BARNEY"

"Miss Mackwayte telephoned to ask if I could go and see, her," said the Chief to Desmond as they motored back to White hall, Marigold gave me the message just as we were coming out. She asked if I could come this afternoon. I'm going to send you in my place, Okewood. I've got a conference with the head of the French Intelligence at three, and the Lord knows when I shall get away. I've a notion that you and Miss Mackwayte will work very well together."

"Certainly," said Desmond, "she struck me as being a very charming and clever girl. Now I know the source of your information about my movements last night!"

"That you certainly don't!" answered the Chief promptly, " if I thought you did Duff and No.39 should be sacked on the spot!"

"Then it wasn't Miss Mackwayte who told you?"

"I haven't seen or heard from Miss Mackwayte since she left my office yesterday evening. You were followed!"

"But why?"

"I'll tell you all about it at, lunch!"

Bated once more, Desmond retired into his shell. By this he was convinced of the utter impossibility of making the Chief vouchsafe any information except voluntarily.

Mr. Marigold had evidently announced their coming to Scotland Yard, for a very urbane and delightful official met them at the entrance and conducted them to a room where the prisoner was already awaiting them in charge of a plain clothes man. There the official excused himself and retired, leaving them alone with the prisoner and his escort.

Barney proved to be a squat, podgy, middle–aged Jew of the familiar East End Polish or Russian type. He had little black beady eyes, a round fat white face, and a broad squabby Mongol nose. His clothes were exceedingly seedy, and the police had confiscated his collar and tie. This absence of neckwear, coupled with the fact that the lower part of his face was sprouting with a heavy growth of beard, gave him a peculiarly villainous appearance:

He was seated on a chair, his head sunk on his breast. His eyes were hollow, and his face overspread with a horrible sickly greenish pallor, the hue of the last stage of fear. His hands, resting on his knees, twisted and fiddled continually. Every now and then convulsive shudders shook him. The man was quite obviously on the verge of a collapse.

As the Chief and Desmond advanced into the room, the Jew looked up in panic. Then he sprang to his feet with a scream and flung himself on his knees, crying:

"Ah, no! Don't take me away! I ain't done no 'arm, gentlemen! S'welp me, gentlemen, I ain't a murderer! I swear..."

"Get him up!" said the Chief in disgust, "and, look here, can't you give him a drink? I want to speak to him. He's not fit to talk rationally in this state!"

The detective pushed a bell in the wall, a policeman answered it, and presently the prisoner was handed a stiff glass of whiskey and water.

After Barney had swallowed it, the Chief said:

"Now, look here, my man, I want you to tell me exactly what happened last night. No fairy tales, remember! I know what you told the police, and if I catch you spinning me any yarns on to it, well, it'll only be the worse for you. I don't mind telling you, you're in a pretty bad mess!"

The prisoner put down the glass wearily and wiped his forehead with the back of his hand. Though the room was bitterly cold, the perspiration stood out in beads on his brow.

"I have told the trewth, sir," he said hoarsely, "and it goes against me, don't it? Hafen't I not gif myself op to the policeman? Couldn't I not haf drop the svag and ron away? For sure! And vy didn't I not do it? For vy, because of vot I seen in that house. I've 'ad my bit of trobble mit the police and vy should I tell them how I vos op to a game last night if I vas not a–telling the trewth, eh! I've been on the crook, gentlemen, I say it, ja, but I ain't no murderer, God choke me I ain't!"

"I've earned gut monney in my time on the 'alls but life is very 'ardt, and I've been alvays hongry these days. Yesterday I meet old Mac wot I used to meet about the 'alls I vos workin' along o' my boss... at the agent's it vos were I vos lookin' for a shop! The perfesh always makes a splash about its salaries, gentlemen, and Mac 'e vos telling me vot a lot o' monney he make on the Samuel Circuit and 'ow 'e 'ad it at home all ready to put into var savings certif'kits. I never done a job like this von before, gentlemen, but I vos hardt pushed for money, s'welp me I vos!"

"I left it till late last night because of these air raids... I vanted to be sure that ole Mac and 'is daughter should be asleep. I god in from the back of the louse, oi, oi, bot it vos dead easy! through the scollery vindow. I cleared op a bagful of stuff in the dining–room... there vosn't, anything vorth snatching outer the parlor... and sixty–five quid out of an old cigar–box in the desk. The police 'as got it... I give it all back! I say I haf stolen, but murder? No!" He paused.

"Go on," said the Chief.

The prisoner looked about him in a frightened way.

"I vos jus' thinking I had better be getting avay, he continued in his hoarse, gutteral voice, 'ven snick.!... I hears a key in the front door. I vos, standing by the staircase... I had no time to get out by the vay I had kom so I vent opstairs to the landing vere there vos a curtain. I shlip behind the curtain and vait! I dare not look out but I listen, I listen.. I hear some one go into the dining–room and move about. I open the curtain a little way... so!... because I think I vill shlip downstairs vile the other party is in the dining–room... and there I sees ole Mac in his dressing–gown just coming down from the first floor. The same moment I hear a step in the front hall.

"I see ole Mac start but he does not stop. He kom right downstairs, and I step back behind the curtain ontil I find a door vich I push. I dare not svitch on my light but presently I feel the cold edge of a bath with my hands. I stay there and vait. Oi, oi, oi, how shall you belief vot I tell?"

He broke off trembling.

"Go on, Barney," said the detective, "can't you see the gentlemen are waiting?"

The Jew resumed, his voice sinking almost to a whisper.

"It vos quite dark behind the curtain but from the bathroom, through the open door, I could just see ole Mac standing with his back to me, a–holding the curtain. He must haf shlip in there to watch the other who vos komming opstairs. Then... then... I hear a step on the stair... a little, soft step... then ole Mac he open the curtain and cry 'Who are you?' Bang! the... the... other on the stairs he fire a shot. I see the red flash and I smell the... the powder not? The other, he does not vait... he just go on opstairs and ole Mac is lying there on his back with the blood a–trickling out on the oil–cloth. And I, vith my bag on my back, I creep downstair and out by the back again, and I ron and ron and then I valks. Gott! how I haf walked! I vos so frightened! And then, at last, I go to a policeman and gif 'myself op!"

Barney stopped. The tears burst from his eyes and laying his grimy face on his arm, he sobbed.

The detective patted him on the back.

"Pull yourself together, man!" he said encouragingly.

"This man on the stairs," queried the Chief, "did you see him?"

"Ach was!" replied the prisoner, turning a tearstained face towards him, "I haf seen nothing, except old Mac's back vich vos right in vront of me, it vos so dark!"

"But couldn't you see the other person at all, not even the outline" persisted the Chief.

The prisoner made a gesture of despair.

"It vos so dark, I say! Nothing haf I seen! I haf heard only his step!"

"What sort of step I Pas it heavy or light or what? Did this person seem in a hurry?"

"A little light tread... so! won, two! won, two! , and qvick like 'e think 'e sneak opstairs vithout nobody seeing!"

"Did he make much noise"

"Ach was! hardly at all... the tread, 'e vos so light like a woman's..."

"Like a woman's, eh!", repeated the Chief, as if talking to himself, "Why do you think that?"

"Because for vy it vos so gentle! The' staircase, she haf not sqveak as she haf sqveak when I haf creep away!"

The Chief turned to the plain clothes man.

"You can take him away now, officer," he said.

Barney sprang up trembling.

"Not back to the cell," he cried imploringly, "I cannot be alone. Oh, gentlemen, you vill speak for me! I haf not had trobble vith the police this long time! My vife's cousin, he is an elder of the Shool he vill tell you 'ow poor ve haf been..."

But the Chief crossed the room to the door rind the detective hustled the prisoner away,

Then the official whom they had seen before came in.

"Glad I caught you," he said. "I thought you would care to see the post mortem report. The doctor has just handed it in."

The chief waved him off.

"I don't think there's any doubt about the cause of death," he replied, "we saw the body ourselves..."

"Quite so," replied the other, "but there is something interesting about this report all the, same. They were able to extract the bullet!"

"Oh," said the Chief, "that ought to tell us something!"

"It does," answered the official. "We've submitted it to our small arms expert, and he pronounces it to be a bullet fired by an automatic pistol of unusually large calibre."

The Chief looked at Desmond.

"You were right there," he said.

"And," the official went on, "our man says, further, that, as far as he knows, there is only one type of automatic pistol that fires a bullet as big as this one!"

"And that is?" asked the Chief.

"An improved pattern of the German Mauser pistol," was the other's startling reply.

The Chief tapped a cigarette meditatively on the back of his hand.

Okewood of the Secret Service

"Okewood," he said, "you are the very model of discretion. I have put your reticence to a pretty severe test this morning, and you have stood it very well. But I can see that you are bristling with questions like a porcupine with quills. Zero hour has arrived. You may fire away!"

They were sitting in the smoking-room of the United Service Club. "The Senior," as men call it, is the very parliament of Britain's professional navy and army. Even in these days when war has flung wide the portals of the two services to all-comers, it retains a touch of rigidity. Famous generals and admirals look down from the lofty walls in silent testimony of wars that have been. Of the war that is, you will hear in every cluster of men round the little tables. Every day in the hour after luncheon battles are fought over again, personalities criticized, and decisions weighed with all the vigorous freedom of ward-room or the mess ante-room.

And so to-day, as he sat in his padded leather chair, surveying the Chief's quizzing face across the little table where their coffee was steaming, Desmond felt the oddness of the contrast between the direct, matter-of-fact personalities all around them, and the extraordinary web of intrigue which seemed to have spun itself round the little house at Seven Kings.

Before he answered the Chief's question, he studied him for a moment under cover of lighting a cigarette. How very little, to be sure, escaped that swift and silent mind! At luncheon the Chief had scrupulously avoided making, the slightest allusion to the thoughts with which Desmond's mind was seething. Instead he had told, with the gusto of the born raconteur, a string of extremely droll yarns about "double crosses," that is, obliging gentlemen who will spy for both sides simultaneously, he had come into contact with during his long and varied career. Desmond had played up to him and repressed the questions which kept rising to his lips. Hence the Chief's unexpected tribute to him in the smoking room,

"Well," said Desmond slowly, "there are one or two things I should like to know. What am I here for? Why did you have me followed last night? How did you know, before we ever went to Seven Kings, that Barney did not murder old Mackwayte? And lastly..."

He paused, fearing to be rash; then he risked it:

"And lastly, Nur–el–Din?"

The Chief leant back in his chair and laughed.

"I'm sure you feel much better now," he said. Then his face grew grave and he added:

"Your last question answers all the others!"

"Meaning Nur–el–Din?" asked Desmond.

The Chief nodded.

"Nur–el–Din," he repeated. "That's why you're here, that's why I had you followed last night, that's why I..." he hesitated for the word, "let's say, presumed (one knows for certain so little in our work) that our friend Barney had nothing to do with the violent death of poor old Mackwayte. Nur–el–Din in the center, the kernel, the hub of everything!"

The Chief leant across the table and Desmond pulled his chair closer.

"There's only one other man in the world can handle this job, except you," he began, "and that's your brother Francis. Do you know where he is, Okewood?"

"He wrote to me last from Athens," answered Desmond, "but that must be nearly two months ago."

The Chief laughed.

"His present address is not Athens," he said, "if you want to know, he's serving on a German Staff somewhere at the back of Jerusalem the Golden. Frankly, I know you don't care about our work, and I did my best to get your brother. He has had his instructions and as soon as he can get away he will. That was not soon enough for me. It had to be him or you. So I sent for you."

He stopped and cleared his throat. Desmond stared at him. He could hardly believe his eyes. This quiet, deliberate man was actually embarrassed.

45

"Okewood," the Chief went on, "you know I like plain speaking, and therefore you won't make the mistake of thinking I'm trying to flatter you."

Desmond made a gesture.

"Wait a moment and hear me out," the Chief went on. "What is required for this job is a man of great courage and steady nerve. Yes, we have plenty of fellows like that. But the man I am looking for must, in addition to possessing those qualities, know German and the Germans thoroughly, and when I say thoroughly I mean to the very core so that, if needs be, he may be a German, think German, act German. I have men in my service who know German perfectly and can get themselves up to look the part to the life. But they have never been put to the real, the searching test. Not one of them has done what you and your brother successfully accomplished. The first time I came across you, you had just come out of Germany after fetching your brother away. To have lived for weeks in Germany in wartime and to have got clear away is a feat which shows that both you and he can be trusted to make a success of one of the most difficult and critical missions I have ever had to propose. Francis is not here. That's why I want you."

The Chief paused as if weighing something in his mind.

"It's not the custom of either service, Okewood," he said, "to send a man to certain death. You're not in this creepy, crawly business of ours. You're a pukka soldier and keen on your job. So I want you to know that you are free to turn down this offer of mine here and now, and go back to France without my thinking a bit the worse of you."

"Would you tell me something about it?" asked Desmond.

"I'm sorry I can't," replied the other. "There must be only two men in this secret, myself and the fellow who undertakes the mission. Of course, it's not certain death. If you take this thing on, you'll have a sporting chance for your life, but that's all. It's going to be a desperate game played against a desperate opponent. Now do you understand why I didn't want you to think I was flattering you? You've got your head screwed on right, I know, but I should hate to feel afterwards, if anything went wrong, that you thought I had buttered you up in order to entice you into taking the job on!"

Desmond took two or three deep puffs of his cigarette and dropped it into the ash-tray.

"I'll see you!" he said.

The Chief grinned with delight.

"By Jove!" he exclaimed, "I knew you were my man!"

CHAPTER VII. NUR–EL–DIN

The love of romance is merely the, nobler form of curiosity. And there was something in Desmond Okewood's Anglo–Irish parentage that made him fiercely inquisitive after adventure. In him two men were constantly warring, the Irishman, eager for romance yet too indolent to go out in search of it, and the Englishman, cautious yet intensely vital withal, courting danger for danger's sake.

All his ill–humor of the morning at being snatched away from his work in France had evaporated. In the Chief he now saw only the magician who was about to unlock to him the realms of Adventure. Desmond's eyes shone with excitement as the other, obviously simmering with satisfaction, lit another cigarette and began to speak.

"The British public, Okewood," he said, hitching his chair closer, "would like to see espionage in this country rendered impossible. Such an ideal state of things is, unfortunately out of the question. Quite on the contrary, this country of ours is honeycombed with spies. So it will ever be, as long as we have to work with natural means: at present we have no caps of invisibility or magician's carpets available.

"As we cannot hope to kill the danger, we do our best to scotch it. Personally, my modest ambition is to make espionage as difficult as possible for the enemy by knowing as many as possible of his agents and their channels of communication, and by keeping him happy with small results, to prevent him from finding out the really important things, the disclosure of which would inevitably compromise our national safety."

He paused and Desmond nodded.

"The extent of our business," the Chief resumed, "is so large, the issues at stake so vital, that we at the top have to ignore the non–essentials and stick to the essentials. By the nonessentials I mean the little potty spies, actuated by sheer hunger or mere officiousness, the neutral busybody who makes a tip–and–run dash into England, the starving waiter, miserably underpaid by some thieving rogue in a neutral country—or the frank swindler who sends back to the Fatherland and is duly paid for long reports about British naval movements which he has concocted without setting foot outside his Bloomsbury lodgings.

"These folk are dealt with somehow and every now and then one of 'em gets shot, just to show that we aren't asleep, don't you know? But spasmodic reports we can afford to ignore. What we are death on is anything like a regular news service from this country to Germany; and to keep up this steady flow of reliable information is the perpetual striving of the men who run the German Secret Service.

"These fellows, my dear Okewood, move in darkness. Very often we have to grope after 'em in darkness, too. They don't get shot, or hardly ever; they are far too clever for that. Between us and them it is a never–ending series of move and countermove, check and counter–check. Very often we only know of their activities by enemy action based on their reports. Then there is another leak to be caulked, another rat–hole to be nailed up, and so the game goes on. Hitherto I think I may say we have managed to hold our own!"

The Chief stopped to light another cigarette. Then he resumed but in a lower voice.

"During the past month, Okewood," he said, "a new organization has cropped up. The objective of every spy operating in this country is, as you may have surmised, naval matters, the movements of the Fleet, the military transports, and the food convoys. This new organization has proved itself more efficient than any of its predecessors. It specializes in the movement of troops to France, and in the journeys of the hospital ships across the Channel. Its information is very prompt and extremely accurate, as we know too well. There have been some very disquieting incidents in which, for once in a way, luck has been on our side, but as long as this gang can work in the dark there is the danger of a grave catastrophe. With its thousands of miles of sea to patrol, the Navy has to take a chance sometimes, you know! Well, on two occasions lately, when chances were taken, the Hun knew we were taking a chance, and what is more, when and where we were taking it!"

The Chief broke off, then looking Desmond squarely in the eyes, said:

"This is the organization that you're going to beak up!"

Desmond raised his eyebrows.

"Who is at the head of it?" he asked quietly.

The Chief, smiled a little bitterly.

"By George!" he cried, slapping his thigh, "you've rung the bell in one. Okewood, I'm not a rich man, but I would gladly give a year's pay to be able to answer that question. To be perfectly frank with you, I don't know who is at the back of this crowd, but..." his mouth set in a grim line, "I'm going to know!"

He added whimsically:

"What's more, you're going to find out for me!"

Desmond smiled at the note of assurance in his voice.

"I suppose you've got something to go on?" he asked. "There's Nur–el–Din, for instance. What about her?"

"That young person," replied the Chief, "is to be your particular study. If she is not the center of the whole conspiracy, she is, at any rate, in the thick of it. It will be part of your job to ascertain the exact role she is playing."

"But what is there against her?" queried Desmond.

"What is there against her? The bad company she keeps is against her. 'Tell me who your friends are and I'll tell you who you are' is a maxim that we have to go on in our profession, Okewood. You have met the lady. Did you see any of her entourage? Her business manager, a fat Italian who calls himself Lazarro, did you notice him? Would you be surprised to hear that Lazarro alias Sacchetti alias Le Tardenois is a very notorious international spy who after working in the Italian Secret Service in the pay of the Germans was unmasked and kicked out of Italy... that was before the war? This pleasant gentleman subsequently did five years in the French penal settlements in New Caledonia for robbery with violence at Aix−les−Bains... oh, we know a whole lot about him! And this woman's other friends! Do you know, for instance, where she often spends the week−end? At the country−place of one Bryan Mowbury, whose name used to be Bernhard Marburg, a very old hand indeed in the German Secret Service. She has identified herself right and left with the German espionage service in this country. One day she lunches with a woman spy, whose lover was caught and shot by the French. Then she goes out motoring with..."

"But why in Heaven's name are all these people allowed to run loose?" broke in Desmond. "Do you mean to say you can't arrest them?"

"Arrest 'em? Arrest 'em? Of course, we can arrest 'em. But what's the use? They're all small fry, and we have to keep out a few lines baited with minnows to catch the Tritons. None of 'em can do any harm: we watch 'em much too closely for that. Once you've located your spy, the battle's won. It's when he—or it may be a she—is running loose, that I get peeved!"

The Chief sprang impatiently to his feet and strode across the smoking−room, which was all but empty by this time, to get a match from a table. He resumed his seat with a grunt of exasperation.

"I can't see light, Okewood!" he sighed, shaking his head.

"But is this all you've got against Nur−el−Din?" asked Desmond.

"No," answered the other slowly, "it isn't. If it were, I need not have called you in. We would have interned or deported her. No, we've traced back to her a line leading straight from the only member of the new organization we have been able to lay by the heels."

"Then you've made an arrest?"

The Chief nodded.

"A fortnight ago... a respectable, retired English business man, by name of Basil Bellward... taken with the goods on him, as the saying is..."

"An Englishman, by Jove!"

"It's hardly correct to call him an Englishman, though he's posed as an English business man for so long that one is almost justified in doing so. As ,a matter of fact, the fellow is a German named Wolfgang Bruhl and it is my belief that he was planted in this country at least a dozen years ago solely for the purpose of furnishing him with good, respectable credentials for an emergency like this."

"But sorely if you found evidence of his connection with this gang of spies, it should be easy to get a clue to the rest of the crowd?"

"Not so easy as you think," the Chief replied. "The man who organized this system of espionage is a master at his craft. He has been careful to seal both ends of every connection, that is to say, though we found evidence of Master Bellward–Bruhl being in possession of highly confidential information relating to the movements of troops, we discovered nothing to show whence he received it or how or where he was going to forward it. But we did find a direct thread leading straight back to Nur–el–Din."

"Really," said Desmond, "that rather complicates things for her, doesn't it?"

"It was in the shape of a letter of introduction, in French, without date or address, warmly recommending the dancer to our friend, Bellward."

"Who is this letter from?"

"It is simply signed 'P.', but you shall see it for yourself when you get the other documents in the case."

"But surely, sir, such a letter might be presented in perfectly good faith..."

"It might, but not this one. This letter, as an expert has ascertained beyond all doubt, is written on German manufactured note–paper of a very superior quality;, the writing is stiff and angular and not French: and lastly, the French in which it is phrased, while correct, is unusually pompous and elaborate."

"Then..."

"The letter was, in all probability, written by a German!"

There was a moment's silence. Desmond was thinking despairingly of the seeming hopelessness of untangling this intricate webwork of tangled threads.

"And this murder, sir," he began.

The Chief shrugged his shoulders.

"The motive, Okewood, I am searching for the motive. I can see none except the highly improbable one of Miss Mackwayte being my confidential secretary. In that case why murder the father, a harmless old man who didn't even know that his daughter is in my service, why kill him, I ask you, and spare the girl? On the other hand, I believe the man Barney's story, and can see that Marigold does, too. When I first heard the news of the murder over the telephone this morning, I had a kind of intuition that we should discover in it a thread leading back to this mesh of espionage. Is it merely a coincidence that a hair, resembling Nur–el–Din's, is found adhering to the straps with which Barbara Mackwayte was bound? I can't think so... and yet..."

"But do you believe then, that Nur–el–Din murdered–old Mackwayte? My dear Chief, the idea is preposterous..."

The Chief rose from his chair with a sigh.

"Nothing is preposterous in our work, Okewood," he replied. "But it's 3.25, and my French colleague hates to be kept waiting."

"I thought you were seeing Strangwise, at two?" asked Desmond.

"I put him off until six o'clock," replied the Chief, "he knows Nur–el–Din, and he may be able to give Marigold some pointers about this affair. You're off to see Miss Mackwayte now, I suppose. You know where she's staying? Good. Well, I'll say good–bye, Okewood. I shan't see you again..."

"You won't see me again? How do you mean, sir?"

"Because you're going back to France!"

"Going back to France? When?"

"By the leave–boat to–night!"

Desmond smiled resignedly.

"My dear Chief," he said, "you must be more explicit. What am I going back to France for?"

"Why, now I come to think of it," replied the Chief, "I never told you. You're going back to France to be killed, of course!"

"To be killed!"

Desmond looked blankly at the other's blandly smiling face.

"Two or three days from now," said the Chief, "you will be killed in action in France. I thought of making it a shell. But we'll have it a machine gun bullet if you like. Whichever you prefer; it's all the same to me!"

He laughed at the dawn of enlightenment in Desmond's eyes.

"I see," said Desmond.

"I hope you don't mind," the Chief went on more seriously, "but I know you have no people to consider except your brother and his wife. She's in America, and Francis can't possibly hear about it. So you needn't worry on that score. Or do you?"

Desmond laughed.

"No–o–o!" he said slowly, "but I'm rather young to die. Is it absolutely necessary for me to disappear?"

"Absolutely!" responded the Chief firmly.

"But how will we manage it?" asked Desmond.

"Catch the leave–boat to–night and don't worry. You will receive your instructions in due course."

"But whey shall I see you again?"

The Chief chuckled.

"Depends entirely on yourself, Okewood," he retorted. "When you're through with your job, I expect. In the meantime, Miss Mackwayte will act between us. On that point also you will be fully instructed. And now I must fly!"

"But I say, sir," Desmond interposed hastily. "You haven't told me what I am to do. What part am I to play in this business anyway?"

"To–morrow," said the Chief, buttoning up his goat, "you become Mr. Basil Bellward!"

CHAPTER VIII. THE WHITE PAPER PACKAGE

A taxi was waiting in Pall Mall outside the club and Desmond hailed it, though secretly wondering what the driver would think of taking him out to Seven Kings. Rather to his surprise, the man was quite affable, took the address of the house where Barbara was staying with her friends and bade Desmond "hop in." Presently, for the second time that day, he was heading for the Mils End Road.

As they zigzagged in and out of the traffic, Desmond's thoughts were busy with the extraordinary mission entrusted to him. So he was to sink his own identity and don that of an Anglo–German business man, his appearance, accent, habits, everything. The difficulties of the task positively made him cold with fear. The man must have relations, friends, business acquaintances who would be sufficiently familiar with his appearance and manner to penetrate, at any rate in the long run, the most effective disguise. What did Bellward look like? Where did lie live? How was he, Desmond, to disguise himself to resemble him? And, above all, when this knotty problem of make–up had been settled, how was he to proceed? What should be his first step to pick out from among all the millions of London's teeming populace the one obscure individual who headed and directed this gang of spies?

Why hadn't he asked the Chief all these questions? What an annoying man the Chief was to deal with to be sure! All said and done, what had he actually told Desmond? That there was a German Secret service organization spying on the movements of troops to France, that this man, Basil Bellward, who had been arrested, was one of the gang and that the dancer, Nur–el–Din, was in some way implicated in the affair! And that was the extent of his confidence! On the top of all this fog of obscurity rested the dense cloud surrounding the murder of old Mackwayte with the unexplained, the fantastic, clue of that single hair pointing back to Nur–el–Din.

Desmond consoled himself finally by saying that the would be able too get some light on his mission from Barbara Mackwayte, whom he judged to be in the Chief's confidence. But here he was doomed to disappointment. Barbara could tell him practically ;nothing save what he already knew, that they were to work together in this affair. Like him, she was waiting for her instructions.

Barbara received him in a neat little suburban drawing–room in the house of her friends, who lived a few streets away from the Mackwaytes. She was wearing a plainly–made black crepe de chine dress which served to accentuate the extreme pallor of her face, the only outward indication of the great shock she had sustained. She was perfectly calm and collected, otherwise, and she stopped Desmond who would have murmured some phrases of condolence.

"Ah, no, please," she said, "I don't think I can speak about it yet."

She pulled a chair over for him arid began to talk about the Chief.

"There's not the least need for you to worry," she said with a little woeful smile, like a sun–ray piercing a rain–cloud, "if the Chief says 'Go back to France and wait for instructions,' you may be sure that everything is arranged, and you will receive your orders in due course. So shall I. That's the Chief all over. Until you know him, you think he loves mystery for mystery's sake. It isn't that at all. He just doesn't trust us. He trusts nobody!"

"But that hardly semis fair to us..." began Desmond.

"It's merely a precaution," replied Barbara, "the Chief takes no risks. I've not the least doubt that he has decided to tell you nothing whatsoever about your part until you are firmly settled in your new role. I'm perfectly certain that every detail of your part has already been worked out."

"Oh, that's not possible," said Desmond. "Why, he didn't know until an hour ago that I was going to take on this job."

Barbara laughed.

"The Chief has taught me a lot about judging men by their looks," she said: "Personally, if I'd been in the Chief's places I should have gone ahead without consulting you, too."

The girl spoke with such directness that there was not the least suggestion of a compliment in her remark, but Desmond blushed to the roots of his hair. Barbara noticed it and added hastily:

"I'm not trying to pay you a compliment: I'm just judging by your type. I believe I can always tell the man that will take on any job, however dangerous, and carry it through to the end."

Desmond blushed more furiously than ever.

He made haste to divert the conversation into a safer channel.

"Well," he said slowly, "seeing that you and I were intended to work together, it seems to me to be a most extraordinary coincidence our meeting like that last night..."

"It was more than a coincidence," said Barbara, shaking her dark brown head. "Forty–eight hours ago I'd never heard of you, then the Chief gave me a telegram to send to your Divisional General summoning you home, after that he told me that we were to work together, and a few hours later I run into you in Nur–el–Din's dressing–room..."

She broke off suddenly, her gray eyes big with fear. She darted across the room to an ormolu table as which her handbag was lying. With astonishment, Desmond watched her unceremoniously spill out the contents on to the table and rake hastily amongst the collection of articles which a pretty girl carries round in her bag.

Presently she raised herself erect and turning, faced the officer. She was trembling as though with cold and when she spoke, her voice was low and husky.

"Gone!" she whispered.

"Have you lost anything" Desmond asked anxiously.

"How could I have forgotten it?" she went on as though he had not spoken, "how could I have forgotten it? Nearly twelve hours wasted, and it explains everything. What will the Chief think of me!"

Slowly she sank down on the sofa where she had been sitting, then, without any warning, dropped her head into her hands and burst into tears.

Desmond went over to her.

"Please don't cry," he said gently, "you have borne up so bravely against this terrible blow; you must try and not let it overwhelm you."

All her business−like calm had disappeared now she was that most distracting of all pictures of woman, a pretty girl overwhelmed with grief. She crouched curled upon the sofa, with shoulders heaving, sobbing as though her heart would break.

"Perhaps you would like me to leave you?" Desmond asked. "Let me ring for your friends... I am sure you would rather be alone!"

She raised a tear−stained face to his, her long lashes glittering.

"No, no," she said, "don't go, don't go! I want your help. This is such a dark and dreadful business, more than I ever realized. Oh, my poor daddy, my poor daddy!"

Again she hid her face in her hands and cried whilst Desmond stood erect by her aide, compassionate but very helpless.

After a little, she dabbed her eyes with a tiny square of cambric, and sitting up, surveyed the other.

"I must go to the Chief at once," she said, "it is most urgent. Would you ring and ask the maid to telephone for a taxi?"

"I have one outside," answered Desmond. "But won't you tell me what has happened"

"Why," said Barbara, "it has only just dawned on me why our house was broken into last night and poor daddy so cruelly murdered! Whoever robbed the house did not come after our poor little bits of silver or daddy's savings in the desk in the dining room. They came after something that I had!"

"And what was that" asked Desmond.

Then Barbara told him of her talk with Nur—el—Din in the dancer's dressing—room on the previous evening and of the package which Nur—el—Din had entrusted to her care.

"This terrible business put it completely out of my head," said Barbara. "In the presence of the police this morning, I looked over my bedroom and even searched my hand-bag which the police sent back to me this afternoon without finding that the burglars had stolen anything. It was only just now, when we were talking about our meeting in Nur—el—Din's room last night, that her little package suddenly flashed across my mind. And then I looked through my handbag again and convinced myself that it was not there."

"But are you sure the police haven't taken it?"

"Absolutely certain," was the reply. "I remember perfectly what was in my hand—bag this morning when I went through it, and the same things are on that table over there now."

"Do you know what was in this package!" said Desmond.

"Just a small silver box, oblong and quite plain, about so big," she indicated the size with her hands, "about as large as a cigarette-box. Nur-el-Din said it was a treasured family possession of hers, and she was afraid of losing it as she traveled about so much. She asked me to say nothing about it and to keep it until the war was over or until she asked me for it."

"Then," said Desmond, "this clears Nur-el-Din!"

"What do you mean," said Barbara, looking up.

"Simply that she wouldn't have broken into year place and killed your father in order to recover her own package..."

"But why on earth should Nur-el-Din be suspected of such a thing?"

"Have you heard nothing about this young lady from the Chief?"

"Nothing. I had not thought anything about her until daddy discovered an old friend in her last night and introduced me."

The Chief's infernal caution again! thought Desmond, secretly admiring the care with which that remarkable man, in his own phrase, "sealed both ends of every connection."

"If I'm to work with this girl," said Desmond to himself, "I'm going to have all the cards on the table here and now," so forthwith he told her of the Chief's suspicions of the dancer, the letter recommending her to Bellward found when the cheese merchant had been arrested, and lastly of the black hair which had been discovered on the thongs with which Barbara had been fastened.

"And now," Desmond concluded, "the very next thing we must do is to go to the Chief and tell him about this package of Nur-el-Din's that is missing." Barbara interposed quickly.

"It's no use your coming, " she said. "The Chief won't see you. When he has sent a man on his mission, he refuses to see him again until the work has been done. If he wishes to send for you or communicate with you, he will. But it's useless for you to try and see him yourself. You can drop me at the office!"

Desmond was inclined to agree with her on this point and said so.

"There is one thing especially that puzzles me, Miss Mackwayte," Desmond observed as they drove westward again, "and that its, how anyone could have known about your having this box of Nur–el–Din's. Was there anybody else in the room when she gave you the package?"

"No," said Barbara:, "I don't think so. Wait a minute, though, Nur–el–Din's maid must have come in very shortly after for I remember the opened the door when Captain Strangwise came to tell me daddy was waiting to take me home."

"Do you remember if Nur–el–Din actually mentioned the package in the presence of the maid!"

"As far as I can recollect just as the maid opened the door to Captain Strangwise, Nur–el–Din was impressing on me again to take great care of the package. I don't think she actually mentioned the box but I remember her pointing at my bag where I had put the package."

"The maid didn't see Nur–el–Din give you the box?"

"No, I'm sure of that. The room was empty save for us two. It was only just before Captain Strangwise knocked that I noticed Marie arranging Nur–el–Din's dresses. She must have come in afterwards without my seeing her."

"Well then, this girl, Marie, didn't see the dancer give you the box but she heard her refer to it. Is that right?"

"Yes, and, of course, Captain Strangwise..."

"What about him?"

"He must have heard what Nur–el–Din was saying, too!"

60

Desmond rubbed his chin.

"I say, you aren't going to implicate old Strangwise, too, are you?" he asked.

Barbara did not reflect his smile.

"He seems to know Nur—el—Din pretty well," she said, "and I'll tell you something else, that woman's afraid of your friend, the Captain!"

"What do you mean?" asked Desmond.

"I was watching her in the glass last night as he was talking to her while you and I and daddy were chatting in the corner. I don't know what he said to her, but she glanced over her shoulder with a look of terror in her eyes. I was watching her face in the glass. She looked positively hunted!"

The taxi stopped. Desmond jumped out and helped his companion to alight.

"Au revoir." she said to him, "never fear, you and I will meet very soon again!"

With that she was gone. Desmond looked at his watch. It pointed to a quarter to six.

"Now I wonder what time the leave—train starts tonight," he said aloud, one foot on the sideboard of the taxi.

"At 7.45, sir," said a voice.

"Desmond glanced round him. Then he saw it was the taxi—driver who had spoken.

"7.45, eh?" said Desmond. "From Victoria, I suppose?"

"Yes, sir," said the taxi—man.

By Jove, I haven't much time," ejaculated the officer "and there are some things I want to get before I go back across the Channel. And I shall have to see the Railway Transport Officer about my pass."

"That's all right, sir," said the taxi-man, "I have your papers here"; he handed Desmond a couple of slips of paper which he took from his coat-pocket; "those will take yon back to France all right, I think you'll find!"

Desmond looked at the papers: they were quite in order and correctly filled up with his name, rank and regiment, and date.

The taxi-man cut short any further question by saying:

"If you'll get into the cab again, sir, I'll drive you where you want to go, and then wait while you have your dinner and take you to the station. By the way, your dinner's ordered too!"

"But who the devil are you?" asked Desmond in amazement.

"On special service, the same as yon, sir!" said the man with a grin and Desmond understood.

Really, the Chief was extremely thorough.

They went to the stores in the Haymarket, to Fortnum and Mason's, and lastly, to a small, grubby shop at the back of Mayfair where Desmond and his brother had bought their cigarettes for years past. Desmond purchased a hundred of their favored brand, the Dionysus, as a reserve for his journey back to France, and stood chatting over old times with the fat, oily-faced Greek manager as the latter tied up his cigarettes into a clean white paper parcel, neatly sealed up with red sealing wax.

Then Desmond drove back to the Nineveh Hotel where he left his taxi-driving colleague in the courtyard on the understanding that at 7.25 the taxi would be waiting to drive him to the station.

Desmond went straight upstairs to his room to put his kit together. In the strong, firmly woven web spread by the Chief, he felt as helpless as a fly caught in a spider's mesh. He had no idea of what his plans were. He only knew that he was going back to France, and that it was his business to get on the leave-boat that night.

As he passed along the thickly carpeted, silent corridor to his room, he saw the door of Strangwise's room standing ajar. He pushed open the door and walked in unceremoniously. A suitcase stood open on the floor with Strangwise bending over it. At his elbow was a table crowded with various parcels, a case of razors, different articles of kit, and some books. Desmond halted at the door, his box of cigarettes dangling from his finger.

"Hullo, Maurice," he said, "are you off, too?"

Strangwise spun round sharply. The blood had fished to his face, staining it with a dark, angry flush.

"My God, how you startled me!" he exclaimed rather testily. "I never heard you come in!"

He turned rather abruptly and went on with his packing. He struck Desmond as being rather annoyed at the intrusion; the latter had never seen him out of temper before.

"Sorry if I butted in," said Desmond, sliding his box of cigarettes off his finger on to the littered table and sitting down on a chair. "I came in to say good–bye. I'm going back to France to–night!"

Maurice looked round quickly. He appeared to be quite his old self again and was all smiles now.

"So soon?" he said. "Why, I thought you were getting a job at the War Office!"

Desmond shook his head.

"Not good enough," he replied, "it's back to the sandbags for mine. But where are you off to?"

"Got a bit of leave; the Intelligence folk seem to be through with me at last, so they've given me six weeks!"

"Going to the country" asked Desmond.

Strangwise nodded.

"Yep," he said, "down to Essex to see if I can get a few duck or snipe on the fens. I wish you were coming with me!"

"So do I, old man," echoed Desmond heartily. Then he added in a serious voice:

"By the way, I haven't seen you since last night. What a shocking affair this is about old Mackwayte, isn't it? Are there any developments, do you know?"

Strangwise very deliberately fished a cigarette out of his case which was lying open on the table and lit it before replying.

"A very dark affair," he said, blowing out a cloud of smoke and flicking the match into the grate. "You are discreet, I know, Okewood. The Intelligence people had me up this morning... to take my evidence..."

Strangwise's surmise about Desmond's discretion was perfectly correct. With Desmond Okewood discretion was second nature, and therefore he answered with feigned surprise: "Your evidence about what? About our meeting the Mackwaytes last night?"

After he had spoken he realized he had blundered. Surely, after all, the Chief would have told Strangwise about their investigations at Seven Kings. still...

"No," replied Strangwise,, "but about Nur–el–Din!"

The Chief had kept his own counsel about their morning's work. Desmond was glad now that he had dissimulated.

"You see, I know her pretty well," Strangwise continued, "between ourselves, I got rather struck on the lady when she was touring in Canada some years ago, and in fact I spent so much more money that I could afford on her that I had to discontinue the acquaintance. Then I met her here when I got away from Germany a month ago; she was lonely, so I took her about a bit. Okewood, I'm afraid I was rather indiscreet."

"How do you mean?" Desmond asked innocently.

"Well," said Strangwise slowly, contemplating the end of his cigarette, "it appears that the lady is involved in certain activities which considerably interest our Intelligence. But there, I mustn't say any more!"

"But how on earth is Nur–el–what's her name concerned in this murder, Maurice?"

Strangwise shrugged his shoulders.

"Ah, you'd better ask the police. But I tell you she'll be getting into trouble if she's not careful!"

Throughout this conversation Desmond seemed to hear in his ears Barbara's words: "That woman's afraid of your friend!" He divined that for some reason or other, Strangwise wanted to create a bad impression in his mind about the dancer. He scanned Maurice's face narrowly. Its impenetrability was absolute. There was nothing to be gleaned from those careless, smiling features.

"Well," said Desmond, getting up, "nous verrons. I shall have to make a bolt for it now if I don't want to miss my train. Good–bye, Maurice, and I hope you'll get some birds!"

"Thanks, old man. Au revoir, and take care of yourself. My salaams to the General!".

They shook hands warmly, then Desmond grabbed his box of cigarettes in its neat white wrapper with the bold red seals and hurried off to his room.

Strangwise stood for a moment gazing after him. He was no longer the frank, smiling companion of a minute before. His mouth was set hard and his chin stuck out at a defiant angle.

He bent over the table and picked up a white paper package sealed with bold red seals. He poised it for a moment in his hands while a flicker of a smile stole into the narrow eyes and played for an instant round the thin lips. Then, with a quick movement, he thrust the little package into the side pocket of his tunic and buttoned the flap.

Whistling a little tune, he went on with his packing.

CHAPTER IX. METAMORPHOSIS

It was a clear, cold night. A knife-edge icy wind blew from the north-east and kept the lanyards dismally flapping on the flag-mast over the customs house. The leave train lay in the station within a biscuit's throw of the quayside and the black, blank Channel beyond, a long line of cheerfully illuminated windows that to those returning from leave seemed as the last link with home.

The Corporal of Military Police, who stood at the gangway examining the passes, stopped Desmond Okewood as the latter held out his pass into the rays of the man's lantern.

"There was a message for you, sir," said the Corporal. "The captain of the Staff boat would h-esteem it a favor, sir, if you would kindly go to his cabin immediately on h-arriving on board, sir!"

"Very good, Corporal!" answered the officer and passed up the gang plank, enviously regarded by the press of brass-hats and red-tabs who, for the most part, had a cramped berth below or cold quarters on deck to look forward to.

A seaman directed Desmond to the Captain's cabin. It was built out just behind the bridge, a snug, cheery room with bright chintz curtains over the carefully screened portholes, a couple of comfortable benches with leather seats along the walls, a small bunk, and in the middle of the floor a table set out with a bottle of whiskey, a siphon and some glasses together with a box of cigars.

The Captain was sitting there chatting to the pilot, a short, enormously broad man with a magenta face and prodigious hands which were folded round a smoking glass of toddy.

"Pick 'em up? Rescue 'em?" the pilot ejaculated, as Desmond walked in, "I'd let 'em sink, every man Jack o' them, the outrageous murderin' scoundrels. I don't like to hear you a-talking of such nonsense, Cap'en!"

On Desmond's entrance the Captain broke off the conversation. He proved to be a trimly-built man of about fifty with a grizzled beard, and au air of quiet efficiency which is not uncommonly found in seamen. The pilot drained his glass and, scrambling to his feet, nodded to Desmond and stumped out into the cold night air.

"Jawin' about the U boats!" said the Captain, with a jerk of his head towards the cabin door, "I don't know what the feelings of your men in the trenches are towards Fritz, Major, but I tell you that no German will dare set foot in any coast port of the United Kingdom in my life–time or yours, either! Accommodation's a bit narrow on board. I thought maybe you'd care to spend the night up here!"

"Any orders about me?" asked Desmond.

The Captain went a shade deeper mahogany in the face.

"Oh no," he replied, with an elaborate assumption of innocence. "But won't you mix yourself a drink? And try one of my cigars, a present from a skipper friend of mine who sailed into Tilbury from Manila last week."

"Desmond sat in the snug cabin, puffing a most excellent cigar and sipping his whiskey and soda while, amid much shouting of seamen and screaming of windlasses, the staff boat got clear. Presently they were gliding past long low moles and black, inhospitable lighthouses, threading their way through the dark shapes of war craft of all kinds into the open Channel. There was a good deal of swell, but the sea was calm, and the vessel soon steadied down to regular rise and fall.

They had been steaming for nearly an hour when, through the open door of the cabin, Desmond saw a seaman approach the captain on the bridge. He handed the skipper a folded paper.

"From the wireless operator, sir!" Desmond heard him say.

The skipper scanned it. Then the engine telegraph rang sharply, there was the sound of churning water, and the vessel slowed down. The next moment the Captain appeared at the door of the cabin.

"I'm afraid we're going to lose you, Major," he said pleasantly, "a destroyer is coming up to take you off. There was a wireless from the Admiral about you."

"Where are they going to take me, do you know?" asked Desmond.

The Captain shook his head.

"I haven't an idea. I've only got to hand you over!"

He grinned and added:

"Where's your kit?"

"In the hold, I expect!" answered Desmond. "The porter at Victoria told me not to worry about it, and that I should find it on the other side. And, oh damn it!—I've got a hundred cigarettes in my kit, too! I bought them specially for the journey!"

"Well, take some of my cigars," said the skipper hospitably, "for your traps'll have to go to France this trip, Major. There's no time to get 'em up now. I'll pass the word to the Military Landing Officer over there about 'em, if you like. He'll take care of 'em for you. Now will you come with me?"

Desmond scrambled into his coat and followed the Captain down the steps to the deck. A little distance away from the vessel, the long shape of a destroyer was dimly visible tossing to and fro in the heavy swell. A ladder had been let down over the side of the steamer, and at its foot a boat, manned by a number of heavily swathed and muffled forms, was pitching.

A few officers stood by the rail watching the scene with interest. The skipper adroitly piloted Desmond past them and fairly thrust him out on to the ladder.

Desmond took the hint and with a hasty "Good night" to the friendly captain, staggered down the swaying ladder and was helped into the boat. The boat shoved off, the bell of the engine telegraph on the steamer resounded sharply, and the vessel resumed her interrupted voyage whilst the rowing boat was headed towards the destroyer. On board the latter vessel an officer met Desmond at the rail and piloted him to the ward–room. Almost before they got there, the destroyer was under way.

The officer who had welcomed him proved to be the second in command, a joyous person who did the honors of the tiny ward–room with the aplomb of a Commander in a super–Dreadnought. He mixed Desmond a drink and immediately started to converse about life at the front without giving the other a chance of asking whither they were bound.

The suspense was not of long duration, however, for in about half an hour's time, the destroyer slowed down and Desmond's host vanished. When he reappeared, it was to summon Desmond on deck.

They lay aside a mole by some steps cut in the solid concrete. Here Desmond's host took leave of him.

"There should be a car waiting for you up there," he said.

There on top of the mole, exposed to the keen blast of the wind, a large limousine was standing. A chauffeur, who looked blue with cold, got down from his seat as Desmond emerged from the stairs and touched his cap.

"Major Okewood?" he asked.

"That's my name!" said Desmond.

"If you'll get in, sir, we'll start at once!" the man replied.

Befogged and bewildered, Desmond entered the car, which cautiously proceeded along the breakwater, with glimpses of black water and an occasional dim light on either hand. They bumped over the railway–lines and rough cobblestones of a dockyard, glided through a slumbering town, and so gradually drew out into the open country where the car gathered speed and fairly raced along the white, winding road. Desmond had not the faintest idea of their whereabouts or ultimate destination. He was fairly embarked on the great adventure now, and he was philosophically content to let Fate have its way with him. He found himself wondering rather indolently what the future had in store.

The car slowed down and the chauffeur switched the headlights on. Their blinding glare revealed some white gate–posts at the entrance of a quiet country station. Desmond looked at his watch. It was half–past one. The car stopped at the entrance to the booking–office where a man in an overcoat and bowler was waiting.

"This way, Major, please," said the man in the bowler, and led the way into the dark and silent station. At the platform a short train consisting of an engine, a Pullman car and a brakesman's van stood, the engine under steam. By the glare from the furnace Desmond recognized his companion. It was Matthews, the Chief's confidential clerk.

Matthews held open the door of the Pullman for Desmond and followed him into the carriage. A gruff voice in the night shouted:

"All right, Charley!" a light was waved to and fro, and the special pulled out of the echoing station into the darkness beyond.

In the corner of, the Pullman a table was laid for supper. There was a cold chicken, a salad, and a bottle of claret. On another table was a large tin box and a mirror with a couple of electric lights before it. At this table was seated a small man with gray hair studying a large number of photographs.

"If you will have your supper, Major Okewood, sir," said Matthews, "Mr. Crook here will get to work. We've not got too much time."

The sea air had made Desmond ravenously hungry. He sat down promptly and proceeded to demolish the chicken and make havoc of the salad. Also he did full justice to the very excellent St. Estephe.

As he ate he studied Matthews, who was one of those undefinable Englishmen one meets in tubes and 'buses, who might be anything from a rate collector to a rat catcher. He had sandy hair plastered limply across his forehead, a small moustache, and a pair of watery blue eyes. Mr. Crook, who continued his study of his assortment of photographs without taking the slightest notice of Desmond, was a much more alert looking individual, with a shock of iron gray hair brushed back and a small pointed beard.

"Matthew's," said Desmond as he supped, "would it be indiscreet to ask where we are?"

"In Kent, Major," replied Matthews.

"What station was that we started from?"

"Faversham."

"And where are we going, might I inquire?"

"To Cannon Street, sir!"

"And from there?"

Mr. Matthews coughed discreetly.

"I can't really say, sir, I'm sure! A car will meet you there and I can go home to bed."

The ends sealed again! thought Desmond. What a man of caution, the Chief!

"And this gentleman here, Matthews?" asked Desmond, lighting one of the skipper's cigars.

"That, sir, is Mr. Crook, who does any little jobs we require in the way of make−up. Our expert on resemblances, if I may put it that way, sir, for we really do very little in the way of disguises. Mr. Crook is an observer of what I may call people's points, sir, their facial appearance, their little peculiarities of manner, of speech, of gait. Whenever there is any question of a disguise, Mr. Crook is called in to advise as to the possibilities of success. I believe I am correct in saying, Crook, that you have been engaged on the Major here for some time. Isn't it so?"

Crook looked up a minute from his table.

"That's right," he said shortly, and resumed his occupation of examining the photographs.

"And what's your opinion about this disguise of mine?" Desmond asked him.

"I can make a good job of you, Major," said the expert, "and so I reported to the Chief. You'll want to do your hair a bit different and let your beard grow, and then, if you pay attention to the lessons I shall give you, in a week or two, you'll be this chap here," and he tapped the photograph in his hand, "to the life."

So saying he handed Desmond the photograph. It was the portrait of a man about forty years of age, of rather a pronounced Continental type, with a short brown beard, a straight, rather well–shaped nose and gold–rimmed spectacles. His hair was cut en brosse, and he was rather full about the throat and neck. Without a word, Desmond stretched out his hand and gathered up a sheaf of other photos, police photos of Mr. Basil Bellward, front face and profile seen from right and left, all these poses shown on the same picture, some snapshots and various camera studies. Desmond shook his head in despair. He was utterly unable to detect the slightest resemblance between himself and this rather commonplace looking type of business man.

"Now if you'd just step into the compartment at the end of the Pullman, Major," said Crook, "you'll find some civilian clothes laid out. Would you mind putting them on? You needn't trouble about the collar and tie, or coat and waistcoat for the moment. Then we'll get along with the work."

The train rushed swaying on through the darkness. Desmond was back in the Pullman car in a few minutes arrayed in a pair of dark gray tweed trousers, a white shirt and black boots and socks. A cut–away coat and waistcoat of the same tweed stuff, a black bowler hat of rather an old–fashioned and staid pattern, and a black overcoat with a velvet collar, he left in the compartment where he changed.

He found that Crook had opened his tin box and set out a great array of grease paints, wigs, twists of tow of various colors, and a number of pots and phials of washes and unguents together with a whole battery of fine paint brushes. In his hand he held a pair of barber's clippers and the tips of a comb and a pair of scissors protruded from his vest pocket.

Crook whisked a barber's wrap round Desmond and proceeded, with clippers and scissors, to crop and trim his crisp black hair.

"Tst–tst" he clicked with his tongue. "I didn't realize your hair was so dark, Major. It'll want a dash of henna to lighten it."

The man worked with incredible swiftness. His touch was light and sure, and Desmond, looking at his reflection in the glass, wondered to see what fine; delicate hands this odd little expert possessed. Matthews sat and smoked in silence and watched the operation, whilst the special ran on steadily Londonwards.

When the clipping was done, Crook smeared some stuff on a towel and wrapped it round Desmond's head.

"That'll brighten your hair up a lot, sir. Now for a crepe beard just to try the effect. We've got to deliver you at Cannon Street ready for the job, Mr. Matthews and me, but you won't want to worry with this nasty messy beard once you get indoors. You can grow your own beard, and I'll pop in and henna it a bit for you every now and then."

There was the smart of spirit gum on Desmond's cheeks and Crook gently applied a strip of tow to his face. He had taken the mirror away so that Desmond could no longer see the effect of the gradual metamorphosis.

"A mirror only confuses me," said the expert, breathing hard as he delicately adjusted the false beard, "I've got this picture firm in my head, and I want to get it transferred to your face. Somehow a mirror puts me right off. It's the reality I want."

As he grew more absorbed in his work, he ceased to speak altogether. He finished the beard, trimmed the eyebrows, applied a dash of henna with a brush, leaning backwards continually to survey the effect. He sketched in a wrinkle or two round the eyes with a pencil, wiped them out, then put them in again. Then he fumbled in his tin box, and produced two thin slices of grey rubber.

"Sorry," he said, "I'm afraid you'll have to wear these inside your cheeks to give the effect of roundness. You've got an oval face and the other man has a round one. I can get the fullness of the throat by giving you a very low collar, rather open and a size too large for you."

Desmond obediently slipped the two slices of rubber into his mouth and tucked them away on either side of his upper row of teeth. They were not particularly uncomfortable to wear.

"There's your specs," said Crook, handing him a spectacle case, "and there's the collar. Now if you'll put on the rest of the duds, we'll have a look at you, sir."

Desmond went out and donned the vest and coat and overcoat, and, thus arrayed, returned to the Pullman, hat in hand.

Crook called out to him as he entered

"Not so springy in the step, sir, if you please. Remember you're forty–three years of age with a Continental upbringing. You'll have to walk like a German, toes well turned out and down on the heel every time. So, that's better. Now, have a look at yourself!"

He turned and touched a blind. A curtain rolled up with a click, disclosing a full length mirror immediately opposite Desmond.

Desmond recoiled in astonishment. He could scarcely credit his own eyes. The glass must be bewitched, he thought for a moment, quite overwhelmed by the suddenness of the shock. For instead of the young face set on a slight athletic body that the glass was wont to show him, he saw a square, rather solid man in ugly, heavy clothes, with a brown silky beard and gold spectacles. The disguise was baffling in its completeness. The little wizard, who had effected this change and who now stood by, bashfully twisting his fingers about, had transformed youth into middle age. And the bewildering thing was that the success of the disguise did not lie so much in the eternal adjuncts, the false beard, the pencilled wrinkles, as in the hideous collar, the thick padded clothes, in short, in the general appearance.

For the first time since his talk with the Chief at the United Service Club, Desmond felt his heart grow light within him. If such miracles were possible, then he could surmount the other difficulties as well.

"Crook," he said, "I think you've done wonders. What do you say, Matthews?"

"I've seen a lot of Mr. Crook's work in my day, sir," answered the clerk, "but nothing better than this. It's a masterpiece, Crook, that's what it is."

"I'm fairly well satisfied," the expert murmured modestly, "and I must say the Major carries it off very well. But how goes the enemy, Matthews?"

"It's half past two," replied, the latter, "we should reach Cannon Street by three. She's running well up to time, I think."

"We've got time for a bit of a rehearsal," said Crook. "Just watch me, will you please, Major, and I'll try and give you an impression of our friend. I've been studying him at Brixton for the past twelve days, day and night almost, you might say, and I think I can convey an idea of his manner and walk. The walk is a very important point. Now, here is Mr. Bellward meeting one of his friends. Mr. Matthews, you will be the friend!"

Then followed one of the most extraordinary performances that Desmond had ever witnessed. By some trick of the actor's art, the shriveled figure of the expert seemed to swell out and thicken, while his low, gentle voice deepened into a full, metallic baritone. Of accent in his speech there was none, but Desmond's ear, trained to foreigners' English, could detect a slight Continental intonation, a little roll of the "r's," an unfamiliar sound about those open "o's" of the English tongue, which are so fatal a trap for foreigners speaking our language. As he watched Crook, Desmond glanced from time to time at the photograph of Bellward which he had picked up from the table. He had an intuition that Bellward behaved and spoke just as the man before him.

Then, at Crook's suggestion, Desmond assumed the role of Bellward. The expert interrupted him continually.

"The hands, Major, the hands, you must not keep them down at your sides. That is military! You must move them when you speak! So and so!"

Or again:

"You speak too fast. Too... too youthfully, if you understand me, sir. You are a man of middle age. Life has no further secrets for you. You are poised and getting a trifle ponderous. Now try again!"

But the train was slackening speed. They were running between black masses of squalid houses. As the special thumped over the bridge across the river, Mr. Crook gathered up his paints and brushes and photographs and arranged them neatly in his black tin box.

To Desmond he said:

"I shall be coming along to give you some more lessons very soon, Major. I wish you could see Bellward for yourself: you are very apt at this game, and it would save us much time. But I fear that's impossible."

Even before the special had drawn up alongside the platform at Cannon Street, Crook and Matthews swung themselves out and disappeared. When the train stopped, a young man in a bowler hat presented himself at the door of the Pullman.

"The car is there, Mr. Bellward, sir!" he said, helping Desmond to alight. Desmond, preparing to assume his new role, was about to leave the carriage when a sudden thought struck him. What about his uniform strewn about the compartment where he had changed? He ran back. The compartment was empty. Not a trace remained of the remarkable scenes of their night journey.

"This is for you," said the young man, handing Desmond a note as they walked down the platform.

Outside the station a motor-car with its noisy throbbing awoke the echoes of the darkened and empty courtyard. Desmond waited until he was being whirled over the smooth asphalt of the City streets before he opened the letter.

He found a note and a small key inside the envelope.

"On reaching the house to which you will be conveyed," the note said, "you will remain indoors until further orders. You can devote your time to studying the papers you will find in the desk beside the bed. For the present you need not fear detection as long as you do not leave the house." Then followed a few rough jottings obviously for his guidance.

"Housekeeper, Martha, half blind, stupid; odd man, John Hill, mostly invisible, no risk from either. You are confined to house with heavy chill. Do not go out until you get the word."

Okewood of the Secret Service

The last sentence was twice underlined.

The night was now pitch–dark. Heavy clouds had come up and obscured the stars and a drizzle of rain was falling. The car went forward at a good pace and Desmond, after one or two ineffectual attempts to make out where they were going, was lulled by the steady motion into a deep sleep. He was dreaming fitfully of the tossing Channel as he had seen it but a few hours before when he came to his senses with a start. He felt a cold draught of air on his face and his feet were dead with cold.

A figure stood at the open door of the car. It was the chauffeur.

"Here we are, sir," he said.

Desmond stiffly descended to the ground. It was so dark that he could distinguish nothing, but he felt the grit of gravel under his feet and he heard the melancholy gurgle of running water. He took a step forward and groped his way into a little porch smelling horribly of mustiness and damp. As he did so, he heard a whirr behind him and the car began to glide off. Desmond shouted after the chauffeur. Now that he stood on the very threshold of his adventure, he wanted to cling desperately to this last link with his old self. But the chauffeur did not or would not hear, and presently the sound of the engine died away, leaving Desmond to the darkness, the sad splashing of distant water and his own thoughts.

And then, for one brief moment, all his courage seemed to ooze out of him. If he had followed his instinct, he would have turned and fled into the night, away from that damp and silent house, away from the ceaseless splashing of waters, back to the warmth and lights of civilization. But his sense of humor, which is very often better than courage, came to his rescue.

"I suppose I ought to be in the devil of a rage," he said to himself, "being kept waiting like this outside my own house! Where the deuce is my housekeeper? By Gad, I'll ring the place down!"

The conceit amused him, and he advanced further into the musty porch hoping to find a bell. But as he did so his ear caught the distant sound of shuffling feet. The shuffle of feet drew nearer and presently a beam of light shone out from under the door. A quavering voice called out:

"Here I am, Mr. Bellward, here I am, sir!"

Then a bolt was drawn back, a key turned, and the door swung slowly back, revealing an old woman, swathed in a long shawl and holding high in her hand a lamp as she peered out into the darkness.

"Good evening, Martha," said Desmond, and stepped into the house.

Save for Martha's lamp, the lobby was in darkness, but light was streaming into the hall from the half open door of a room leading off it at the far end. While Martha, wheezing asthmatically, bolted the front door, Desmond went towards the room where the light was and walked in.

It was a small sitting–room, lined with bookshelves, illuminated by an oil lamp which stood on a little table beside a chintz–covered settee which had been drawn up in front of the dying fire.

On the settee Nur–el–Din was lying asleep.

CHAPTER X. D. O. R. A. IS BAFFLED

When Barbara reached the Chief's ante–room she found it full of people. Mr. Marigold was there, chatting with Captain Strangwise who seemed to be just taking his leave; there was a short, fat, Jewish–looking man, very resplendently dressed with a large diamond pin in his cravat and a small, insignificant looking gentleman with a gray moustache and the red rosette of the Legion of Honor in his button–hole. Matthews came out of the Chief's room as Barbara entered the outer office.

"Miss Mackwayte," he said, "we are all so shocked and so very, sorry..."

"Mr. Matthews," she said hastily in a low voice, "never mind about that now. I must see the Chief at once. It is most urgent."

Matthews gesticulated with his arm round the room.

"All these people, excepting the officer there, are waiting to see him, Miss, and he's got a dinner engagement at eight..."

"It is urgent, Mr. Matthews, I tell you. If you won't take my name in, I shall go in myself!"

"Miss Mackwayte, I daren't interrupt him now. Do you know who's with him...?"

Strangwise crossed the room to where Barbara was standing.

"I can guess what brings you here, Miss Mackwayte," he said gently. "I hope you will allow me to express my condolences'...?"

The girl shrank back, almost imperceptibly, yet Strangwise, whose eyes were fixed on her pale face, noticed the spontaneous recoil. The sunshine seemed to fade out of his debonair countenance, and for a moment Barbara Mackwayte saw Maurice Strangwise as very few people had ever seen him, stern and cold and hard, without a vestige of his constant smile. But the shadow lifted as quickly as it had fallen. His face had resumed its habitually engaging expression as he murmured:

"Believe me, I am truly sorry for you!"

"Thank you, thank you!" Barbara said hastily and brushed past him. She walked straight across the room to the door of the Chief's room, turned the handle and walked in.

The room was in darkness save for an electric reading lamp on the desk which threw a beam of light on the faces of two men thrust close together in eager conversation. One was the Chief, the other a face that Barbara knew well from the illustrated papers.

At the sound of the door opening, the Chief sprang to his feet.

"Oh, it's Miss Mackwayte," he said, and added something in a low voice to the other man who had risen to his feet. "My dear," he continued aloud to Barbara, "I will see you immediately; we must not be disturbed now. Matthews should have told you."

"Chief," cried Barbara, her hands clasped convulsively together, "you must hear me now. What I have to say cannot wait. Oh, you must hear me!"

The Chief looked as embarrassed as a man usually looks when he is appealed to in a busy moment by an extremely attractive girl.

"Miss Mackwayte," he said firmly but with great courtesy, "you must wait outside. I know how unnerved you are by all that you have gone through, but I am engaged just now. I shall be free presently."

"It is about my father, Chief," Barbara said in a trembling voice, "I have found out what they came to get!"

"Ah!" said the Chief and the other man simultaneously.

"We had better hear what she has to say!" said the other man, "but won't you introduce me first?"

"This is Sir Bristowe Marr, the First Sea Lord," said the Chief, bringing up a chair for Barbara, "Miss Mackwayte, my secretary, Admiral!"

Then in a low impassioned voice Barbara told her tale of the package entrusted to her by Nur−el−Din and its disappearance from her bedroom on the night of the murder. As she proceeded a deep furrow appeared between the Chief's bushy eyebrows and he stared absently at the blotting−pad in front of him. When the girl had finished her story, the Chief said:

"Lambelet ought to hear this, sir: he's the head of the French Intelligence, you know. He's outside now. Shall we have him in? Miss Mackwayte shall tell her story, and you can then hear what Lambelet has to say about this versatile young dancer."

Without waiting for further permission, he pressed a bell on the desk and presently Matthews ushered in the small man with the Legion of Honor whom Barbara had seen in the ante−room.

The Chief introduced the Frenchman and in a few words explained the situation to him. Then he turned to Barbara:

"Colonel Lambelet speaks English perfectly," he said, "so fire away and don't be nervous!"

When she had finished, the Chief said, addressing Lambelet:

"What do you make of it, Colonel?"

The little Frenchman made an expressive gesture.

"Madame has become aware of the interest you have been taking in her movements, mon cher. She seized the opportunity of this meeting with the daughter of her old friend to get rid of something compromising, a code or something of the kind, qui sait? Perhaps this robbery and its attendant murder was only an elaborate device to pass on some particularly important report of the movements of your ships... qui sait?"

"Then you are convinced in your own mind, Colonel, that this woman is a spy?" The clear-cut voice of the First Sea Lord rang out of the darkness of the room outside the circle of light on the desk.

"Mail certainement!" replied the Frenchman quietly. "Listen and you shall hear! By birth she is a Pole, from Warsaw, of good, perhaps, even, of noble family. I cannot tell you, for her real name we have not been able to ascertain... parbleu, it is impossible, with the Boches at Warsaw, hein? We know, however, that at a very early age, under the name of la petite Marcelle, she was a member of a troupe of acrobats who called themselves The Seven Duponts. With this troupe she toured all over Europe. Bien! About ten years ago, she went out to New York as a singer, under the name of Marcelle Blondinet, and appeared at various second-class theatres in the United States and Canada. Then we lose track of her for some years until 1913, the year before the war, when the famous Oriental dancer, Nur-el-Din, who has made a grand success by the splendor of her dresses in America and Canada, appears at Brussels, scores a triumph and buys a fine mansion in the outskirts of the capital. She produces herself at Paris, Bordeaux, Lyons, Marseilles, Madrid, Milan and Rome, but her home in Brussels, always she returns there, your understand me, hein? La petite Marcelle of The Seven Duponts, Marcelle Blondinet of the cafe chantant, has blossomed out into a star of the first importance."

The Colonel paused and cleared his throat.

"To buy a mansion in Brussels, to run a large and splendid troupe, requires money. It is the men who pay for these things, you would say. Quite right, but listen who were the friends of Madame Nur−el−Din. Bischoffsberg, the German millionaire of Antwerp, von Wurzburg, of Berne... ah ha! you know that gentleman, mon cher?" he turned, chuckling, to the Chief who nodded his acquiescence; "Prince Meddelin of the German Embassy in Paris and administrator of the German Secret Service funds in France, and so on and so on. I will not fatigue you with the list. The direct evidence is coming now.

"When the war broke out in August, 1914, Madame, after finishing her summer season in Brussels, was resting in her Brussels mansion. What becomes of her? She vanishes."

"She told Samuel, the fellow who runs the Palaceum, that she escaped from Brussels!" interposed the Chief.

The Frenchman threw his hands above his head.

"Escaped, escaped? Ah, oui, par exemple, in a German Staff car. As I have told my colleague here," he went on, addressing the Admiral, "she escaped to Metz, the headquarters of the Army Group commanded by the... the... how do you say? the Prince Imperial?"

"The Crown Prince," rectified the Chief.

"Ah, oui,—the Crown Prince. Messieurs, we have absolute testimony that this woman lived for nearly two years either in Metz or Berlin, and further, that at Metz, the Crown Prince was a constant visitor at her house. She was one of the ladies who nearly precipitated a definite rupture between the Crown Prince and his wife. Mon Admiral," he went on, addressing the First Sea Lord again, that this woman should be at large is a direct menace to the security of this country and of mine. It is only this morning that I at length received from Paris the facts which I have just laid before you. It is for you to order your action accordingly!"

The little Frenchman folded his arms pompously and gazed at the ceiling.

"How does she explain her movements prior to her coming to this country" the First Sea Lord asked the Chief.

For an answer the Chief pressed the bell.

"Samuel, who engaged her, is outside. You shall hear her story from him," he said.

Samuel entered, exuding business acumen, prosperity, geniality. He nodded brightly to the Chief and stood expectant.

"Ah, Mr. Samuel," said the Chief, " I wanted to see you about Nur−el−Din. You remember our former conversation on the subject. Where did she say she went to when she escaped to Brussels?"

"First to Ostend," replied the music−hall proprietor, "and then, when the general exodus took place from there, to her mother's country place near Lyons, a village called Sermoise−aux−Roses."

"And what did she say her mother's name was?"

"Madame Blondinet, sir!"

The Frenchman rapped smartly on a little pocketbook which he had produced and now held open in his hand.

"There, is a Madame Blondinet who has a large farm near Sermoise−aux−Roses," he said, "and she has a daughter called Marcelle, who went to America."

"Why then...?" began the First Sea Lord.

"Attendez un instant!"

The Colonel held up a plump hand.

"Unfortunately for Madame Nur—el—Din, this Marcelle Blondinet spent the whole of her childhood, in fact, the whole of her life until she was nineteen years of age, on her mother's farm at a time when this Marcelle Blondinet was touring Europe with The Seven Duponts. The evidence is absolute. Mademoiselle here heard the dancer herself confirm it last night!"

"Thank you, Mr. Samuel," said the Chief, "we shan't require you any more. But I'm afraid your Nur—el—Din will have to break her contract with you."

"She's done that already, sir!" said Samuel ruefully.

The Chief sprang to his feet excitedly.

"Broken it already?" he cried. "What do you mean? Explain yourself! Don't stand there staring at me!"

Mr. Samuel looked startled out of his life.

"There was a bit of a row between her and the stage manager last night about her keeping the stage waiting again," he said; "and after lunch today she rang up to say she would not appear at the Palaceum to—night or any more at all! It's very upsetting for us; and I don't mind telling you, gentlemen, that I've been to my solicitors about it..."

"And why the blazes didn't you come and tell me?" demanded the Chief furiously.

"Well, sir, I thought it was only a bit of pique on her part, and I hoped to be able to talk the lady round. I know what these stars are!"

"You've seen her then?" the Chief snapped out.

"No, I haven't!" Mr. Samuel lamented. "I've been twice to the Nineveh—that's where she's stopping—and each time she was out!"

The Chief dismissed him curtly.

When the door had closed behind him, the Chief said to the First Sea Lord:

84

"This is where D.O.R.A. steps in, I think, sir!"

"Decidedly!" replied the Admiral. "Will you take the necessary steps"

The Chief nodded and pressed the bell. Matthews appeared.

"Anything from the Nineveh?" he asked.

"The lady has not returned, sir!"

"Anything from Gordon and Duff?"

"No, sir, nothing all day!"

The telephone on the desk whirred. The Chief lifted the receiver.

"Yes. Oh, it's you, Gordon? No, you can say it now: this is a private line."

He listened at the receiver for a couple of minutes. The room was very still.

"All right, come to the office at once!"

The Chief hung up the receiver and turned to the Admiral.

"She's given us the slip for the moment!" he said. "That was Gordon speaking. He and Duff have been shadowing our lady friend out of doors for days. She left the hotel on foot after lunch this afternoon with my two fellows in her wake. There was a bit of a crush on the pavement near Charing Cross and Duff was pushed into the roadway and run over by a motor–'bus. In the confusion Gordon lost the trail. He's wasted all this time trying to pick it up again instead of reporting to me at once."

"Zut!" cried the Frenchman.

CHAPTER XI. CREDENTIALS

The sight of Nur–el–Din filled Desmond with alarm. For a moment his mind was overshadowed by the dread of detection. He had forgotten all about Mr. Crook's handiwork in the train, and his immediate fear was that the dancer would awake and recognize him. But then he caught sight of his face in the mirror over the mantelpiece. The grave bearded man staring oddly at him out of the glass gave him a shock until he realized the metamorphosis that had taken place in his personality. The realization served instantly to still his apprehension.

Nur–el–Din lay on her side, one hand under her face which was turned away from the fire. She was wearing a big black musquash coat, and over her feet she had flung a tweed overcoat, apparently one of Mr. Bellward's from the hatstand in the hall. Her hat, a very dainty little affair of plain black velvet, was skewered with a couple of jewelled hatpins to the upholstery of the settee.

Desmond watched her for a moment. Her face looked drawn and tired now that her eyelids, with their long sweeping black lashes, were closed, shutting off the extraordinary luminosity of her eyes. As he stood silently contemplating her, she stirred and moaned in her sleep and muttered some word three or four times to herself. Desmond was conscious of a great feeling of compassion for this strangely beautiful creature. Knowing as he did of the hundred–eyed monster of the British Secret Service that was watching her, he found himself thinking how frail, how helpless, how unprotected she looked, lying there in the flickering light of the fire.

A step resounded behind him and old Martha shuffled into the room, carefully shading the lamp she still carried so that its rays should not fall on the face of the sleeper.

"I don't know as I've done right, sir," she mumbled, "letting the pore lady wait here for you like this, but I couldn't hardly help it, sir! She says as how she must see you, and seeing as how your first tellygram said you was coming at half–past nine, I lets her stop on!"

"When did she arrive" asked Desmond softly.

"About six o'clock," answered the old, woman. "Walked all the way up from Wentfield Station, too, sir, and that cold she was when she arrived here, fair blue with the cold she was, pore dear. D'reckly she open her lips, I sees she's a furrin' lady, sir. She asks after you and I tells her as how you are away and won't be back till this evening. 'Oh!' she says, I then I wait!' And in she comes without so much as with your leave or by your leave. She told me as how you knew her, sir, and were expecting to see her, most important, she said it was, so I hots her up a bit o' dinner. I hopes as how I didn't do wrong,, Mr. Bellward, sir!"

"Oh, no, Martha, not at all!" Desmond replied—at random. He was sorely perplexed as to his next move. Obviously the girl could not stay in the house. What on earth did she want with him? And could he, at any rate, get at the desk and read the papers of which the note spoke and which, he did not doubt, were the dossier of the Bellward case, before she awoke? They might, at least, throw some light on his relations with the dancer.

"She had her dinner here by the fire," old Martha resumed her narrative, "and about a quarter past nine comes your second tellygram, sir, saying as how you could not arrive till five o'clock in the morning."

Desmond glanced at the clock on the mantelpiece. The hands pointed to a quarter past five! He had lost all count of the time in his peregrinations of the night.

"I comes in here and tells the young lady as how you wouldn't be back last night, sir," the old woman continued, "and she says, 'Oh,' she says, 'then, where shall I go?' she says. 'Why don't you go home, my dear?' says I, 'and pop round and see the master in the morning,' I says, thinking the pore young lady lives about here. And then she tells me as how she come all the way from Lunnon and walked up from the station. As well you know, sir, the last train up leaves Wentfield Station at five minutes to nine, and so the pore young lady couldn't get back that night. So here she had to stop. I got the spare room ready for her and lit a nice fire and all, but she wouldn't go to bed not until she had seen you. I do hope as how I've not done wrong, sir. I says to Mr. Hill, I says..."

Desmond held up his hand to restrain her toothless babble. Nur–el–Din had stirred and was sitting up, rubbing her eyes. Then she caught sight of Desmond and scrambled rather unsteadily to her feet.

"Monsieur Bellward?" she said in French, "oh, how glad I am to see you!"

"All right, Martha," said Desmond, "see that the spare room is ready for this lady, and don't go to bed just yet. I shall want you to take this lady to her room."

The old woman hobbled away, leaving the two alone. As soon as the door had closed behind her, Nur–el–Din exclaimed:

"You know me; hein!"

Desmond bowed in the most correct Continental manner.

"Who does not know the charming Nur–el–Din?" he replied.

"No!" Nur–el–Din commanded with flashing eyes, "no, not that name! I am Madame Le Bon, you, understand, a Belgian refugee, from Termonde!"

Rather taken aback by her imperious manner, Desmond bowed again but said nothing.

"I received your letter," the dancer resumed, "but I did not answer it as I did not require your assistance. But now I wish your help. It is unfortunate that you were absent from home at the very time I counted upon your aid."

She flashed a glance at him as though awaiting an apology.

"I am extremely sorry," said Desmond, "if I had but known..."

Nur–el–Din nodded carelessly.

"I wish to pass the night here," she went on, "in fact, I may be here for several days. They are becoming inconvenient in London, you understand."

"But the theatre, your professional engagements?"

"Bah, I have left the theatre. I have had enough of these stupid English people... they know nothing of art!"

Desmond reflected a moment. Nur–el–Din's manner was most perplexing. What on earth could induce her to adopt this tone of condescension towards him? It nettled him. He resolved to try and find out on what it was based.

"I am only too happy to be of assistance to you," he said, "especially in view of the letter of introduction you sent me, but I must tell you plainly that what you ask is impossible."

"Impossible?" repeated Nur–el–Din, stamping her feet. "Impossible? Do you know what you are saying?"

"Perfectly," replied Desmond negligently. "Obviously, you must stay here for the rest of the night since you cannot return to London until the trains start running, but to stay here indefinitely as you propose to do is out of the question. People would talk!"

"Then it is your business to see that they don't!"

"Your letter of introduction came from one whom I am always anxious to oblige," Desmond went on. "but the service he is authorized to claim from me does not entitle him to jeopardize my other activities."

He drew a breath. It was a long shot. Would it draw her?

It did. Nur–el–Din fumbled in her bag, produced a leather pocket–book and from it produced a slip of paper folded in two.

"Read that!" she cried, "and then you shall apologize!"

Desmond took the paper. It was a sheet torn from a book of German military field messages. "Meldedienst" (Message Service) was printed in German at the top and there were blanks to be filled in for the date, hour and place, and at the bottom a printed form of acknowledgment for the recipient to sign.

In a large ostentatious, upright German handwriting was written what follows:

"To All Whom it May Concern.

"The lady who is the bearer of this, whose description is set out overleaf, is entitled to the full respect and assistance of the German forces on land and sea and in the air, wherever it may be. Her person and property are inviolate.

"Given At Our Headquarters at Metz "Friedrich Wilhelm "Kronprinz des "Deutschen Reiches."

Across the signature was the impress of a green stamp, lozenge–shaped, inscribed "Headquarters of the Fifth Army, General Staff, 21st September, 1914."

On the back of the slip was a detailed description of Nur–el–Din.

Desmond bowed and handed the paper back to its owner.

"Madame must accept my humble excuses," he murmured, hardly knowing what he was saying, so great was his surprise, "my house and services are at Madame's disposal!"

"The other letter was from Count Plettenbach, the Prince's A.D.C., whom I think you know!" added the dancer in a mollified voice as she replaced the slip of paper in its pocketbook and stowed it away in her hand–bag. Then, looking up archly at Desmond, she said:

"Am I so distasteful, then, to have in your house?"

She made a charming picture. Her heavy fur coat had fallen open, disclosing her full round throat, very brown against the V–shaped opening of her white silk blouse. Her mouth was a perfect cupid's bow, the upper lip slightly drawn up over her dazzlingly white teeth. Before Desmond could answer her question, if answer were needed, her mood had swiftly changed again. She put her hand out, a little brown hand, and laying it on his shoulder, looked up appealingly into his eyes.

"You will protect me," she said in a low voice, "I cannot bear this hunted life. From this side, from that, they, are closing in on me, and I am frightened, so very frightened. Promise you will keep me from harm!"

Desmond gazed down into her warm, expressive eyes helplessly. What she asked was impossible, he knew, but he was a soldier, not a policeman, he told himself, and under his breath he cursed the Chief for landing him in such a predicament. To Nur–el–Din he said gently:

"Tell me what has happened to frighten you. Who is hunting you? Is it the police?"

She withdrew her hand with a gesture of contempt.

"Bah!" she said bitterly. "I am not afraid of the police."

Then she sank into a reverie, her gaze fixed on the dying embers of the fire.

"All my life has been a struggle," she went on, after a moment, "first with hunger, then with men, then the police. I am used to a hard life. No, it is not the police!"

"Who is it, then" asked Desmond, completely nonplused.

Nur–el–Din let her eyes rest on his face for a moment.

"You have honest eyes," she said, "your eyes are not German... pardon me, I would not insult your race... I mean they are different from the rest of you. One day, perhaps, those eyes of yours may persuade me to answer your question. But I don't know you well enough yet!"

She broke off abruptly, shaking her head.

"I am tired," she sighed and all her haughty manner returned, "let the old woman show me to my room. I will take dejeuner with you at one o'clock."

Desmond bowed and stepping out into the hall, called the housekeeper. Old Martha shuffled off with the girl, leaving Desmond staring with vacant eyes into the fire. He was conscious of a feeling of exultation, despite his utter weariness and craving for sleep. This girl, with her queenly ways, her swiftly changing moods, her broad gusts of passion, interested him enormously. If she were the quarry, why, then, the chase were worth while! But the end? For a brief moment, he had a vision of that frail, clinging figure

91

swaying up against some blank wall before a file of levelled rifles.

Then again he seemed to see old Mackwayte lying dead on the landing of the house at Seven Kings. Had this frail girl done this unspeakable deed? To send her to the gallows or before a firing–squad—was this to be the end of his mission? And the still, small voice of conscience answered: " Yes! that is what you have come here to do! "

Old Martha came shuffling down the staircase. Desmond called to her, remembering that he did not yet know where his bedroom was.

"Will you light me up to my room, Martha?" he said, "I want to be sure that the sheets are not damp!"

So saying he extinguished the lamp on the table and followed the old woman upstairs.

CHAPTER XII. AT THE MILL HOUSE

Clad in a suit of Mr. Basil Bellward's pyjamas of elaborate blue–flowered silk, Desmond lay propped up in bed in Mr. Bellward's luxuriously fitted bedroom, sipping his morning coffee, and studying with absorbed interest a sheet of blue foolscap. A number of papers lay strewn about the eiderdown quilt. At the head of the bed a handsome Sheraton bureau stood open.

As the French say, Mr. Bellward had refused himself nothing. His bedroom was most tastefully furnished. The furniture was mahogany, every piece carefully chosen, and the chintz of curtains and upholstery was bright and attractive. A most elaborate mahogany wardrobe was fitted into the wall, and Desmond, investigating it, had found it to contain a very large assortment of clothes of every description, all new or nearly so, and bearing the name of a famous tailor of Cork Street. Folding doors, resembling a cupboard, disclosed, when open, a marble basin with hot water laid on, while a curtained door in the corner of the room gave access to a white tiled bathroom. Mr. Bellward, Desmond had reflected after his tour of the room on his arrival, evidently laid weight on his personal comfort; for the contrast between the cheerful comfort of his bedroom and the musty gloom of the rooms downstairs was very marked.

A bright log fire hissed on the open hearth and the room was pleasantly warm. Old Martha's coffee was excellent, and Desmond, very snug in Mr. Bellward's comfortable bed, noted with regret that the clock on the mantel–shelf marked a quarter to twelve. But then he thought of the tete–a–tete luncheon that awaited him at one o'clock and his face cleared. He didn't mind getting up so much after all.

He fell again to the perusal of the documents which he had found, as indicated in the note from headquarters, in the desk by the bed. They were enclosed in two envelopes, one large, the other small, both without any superscription. The large envelope enclosed Mr. Bellward 's dossier which consisted of a fairly detailed account of his private life, movements, habits and friends, and an account of his arrest. The small envelope contained Desmond's eagerly expected orders.

Desmond examined the papers in the large envelope first. From them he ascertained that the house in which he found himself was called The Mill House, and was situated two and a half miles from the station of Wentfield on the Great Eastern Railway in Essex. Mr. Bellward had taken the place some eight years before, having moved there from the Surrey hills, but had been wont to spend not more than two months in the year there. For the rest of the time he traveled abroad, usually passing the winter months on the Riviera, and the spring in Switzerland or Italy. The war had brought about a change in his habits, and Harrogate, Buxton and Bath had taken the place of the Continental resorts which he had frequented in peace time.

When in residence at The Mill House, Mr. Bellward had gone up to London nearly every morning, either walking or going by motor–cycle to the station, and not returning until dinner–time in the evening. Sometimes he passed the night in London, and on such occasions slept at a small hotel in Jermyn Street. His dossier included, a long and carefully compiled list of the people he knew in London, mostly men of the rich business set, stockbrokers, manufacturers, solicitors, and the like. Against every name was set a note of the exact degree of intimacy existing between Bellward and the man in question, and any other information that might serve Bellward's impersonator in good stead. Desmond laid this list aside for the moment, intending to study it more closely at his leisure.

Of intercourse with his neighbors in, the country, Mr. Bellward apparently had none. The Mill House stood in a lonely part of the country, remote from the more thickly populated centres of Brentwood and Romford, on the edge of a wide tract of inhospitable marshland, known as Morstead Fen, intersected by those wide deep ditches which in this part of the world are known as dykes. At this stage in the report there was a note to the effect that the rector of Wentfield had called twice at The Mill House but had not found Mr. Bellward at home, and that his visits had not been returned. There were also some opinions apparently culled locally regarding the tenant of the Mill House, set out something in this wise:—

"Landlord of the Red Lion, Wentfield: The gentleman has never been to the Red Lion, but sometimes orders my Ford car and always pays regularly.

"The Stationmaster at Wentfield: A gentleman who keeps himself to himself but very liberal with his money.

"Sir Marsham Dykes, of The Chase, Stanning: A damned unsociable churlish fellow.

"Mr. Tracy Wentfield, of the Channings, Home Green: A very rude man. He slammed the front door of the house in my face when I went to ask him for a contribution to our Cottage Hospital. It is not my habit to repeat idle gossip, but they do say he is a heavy drinker.

There was a lot more of this sort of thing, and Desmond turned from it with a smile to take up the account of Bellward's arrest. It appeared that, about a fortnight before, on the eve of the departure for France of a very large draft of troops, a telegram was handed in at the East Strand telegraph office addressed to Bellward. This telegram ran thus:

"Bellward, Bellward Hotel, Jermyn Street. "Shipping to you Friday 22,000 please advise correspondents. "Mortimer."

The authorities were unable to deliver this telegram gram as no such an hotel as the Hotel Bellward was found to exist in Jermyn Street. An examination of the address showed clearly that the sender had absent mindedly repeated the addressee's name in writing the name of the hotel. An advice was therefore addressed to the sender, Mortimer, at the address he had given on the back of the form, according to the regulations, to inform him that his telegram had not been delivered. It was then discovered that the address given by Mortimer was fictitious.

Suspicion being thus aroused, the telegram was forwarded to the Postal Censor's department whence it reached the Intelligence Authorities who promptly spotted the connection between the wording of the telegram and the imminent departure of the drafts, more especially as the dates tallied. Thereupon, Mr. Bellward was hunted up and ultimately traced by his correspondence to The Mill House. He was not found there, but was eventually encountered at his London hotel, and requested to appear before the authorities with a view to throwing some light on Mortimer. Under cross–examination Bellward flatly denied any knowledge of Mortimer, and declared that a mistake had been made. He cited various well known city men to speak for his bona–fides and protested violently against the action of the authorities in doubting his word. It was ultimately elicited that Bellward was of German birth and had never been naturalized, and he was detained in custody while a search was made at The Mill House.

The search was conducted with great discretion, old Martha being got out of the way before the detectives arrived and a careful watch being kept to avoid any chance of interruption. The search had the most fruitful results. Hidden in a secret drawer of the Sheraton desk in Bellward's bedroom, was found a most elaborate analysis of the movements of the transports to France, extremely accurate and right up to date. There was absolutely no indication, however, as to whence Bellward received his reports, and how or to whom he forwarded them. It was surmised that Mortimer was his informant, but an exhaustive search of the post office files of telegrams despatched showed no trace of any other telegram from Mortimer to Bellward save the one in the possession of the authorities. As for Mortimer, he remained a complete enigma.

That, summarised, was the gist of the story of Bellward's arrest. The report laid great stress on the fact that no one outside half a dozen Intelligence men had any knowledge (a) of Bellward being an unnaturalized German, (b) of his arrest."

Desmond's orders, which he reserved to the last ere short and to the point. They consisted of five numbered clauses.

"1. You will have a free hand. The surveillance of the house was withdrawn on your arrival and will not be renewed.

"2. You will not leave the house until further orders.

"3. You will keep careful note of any communication that may be made to you, whether verbal or in writing, of whatever nature it is. When you have anything to be forwarded, ring up 700 Slanning on the telephone and give Bellward's name. You will hand your report to the first person calling at the house thereafter asking for the letter for Mr. Elias.

"4. If help is urgently required, ring up 700 Stanning and ask for Mr. Elias. Assistance will be with you within 15 minutes after. This expedient must only be used in the last extremity.

"5. Memorize these documents and burn the lot before you leave the house."

"Handy fellow, Mr. Elias," was Desmond's commentary, as he sprang out of bed and made for the bathroom. At a quarter to one he was ready dressed, feeling very scratchy and uncomfortable about the beard which he had not dared to remove owing to Nur-el-Din's presence in the house. Before he left the bedroom, he paused a moment at the desk, the documents of the Bellward case in his hands. He had a singularly retentive memory, and he was loth to have these compromising papers in the house whilst Nur-el-Din was there. He took a quick decision and pitched the whole lot into the fire, retaining only the annotated list of Mr. Bellward's friends. This he placed in his pocket-book and, after watching the rest of the papers crumble away into ashes, went downstairs to lunch.

Nur-el-Din was in the drawing-room, a long room with two high windows which gave on a neglected looking garden. A foaming, churning brook wound its way through the garden, among stunted bushes and dripping willows, obviously the mill-race from which the house took its name. The drawing-room was a bare, inhospitable room, studded here and there with uncomfortable looking early Victorian armchairs swathed in dust-proof cloths. A fire was making an unsuccessful attempt to burn in the open grate.

Nur-el-Din turned as he entered the room. She was wearing a gray cloth tailor-made with a white silk, blouse and a short skirt showing a pair of very natty brown boots. By contrast with her ugly surroundings she looked fresh and dainty. Her eyes were bright and her face as smooth and unwrinkled as a child's.

"Bon jour," she cried gaily, "ah! but I am 'ungry! It is the air of the country! I love so the country!"

"I hope you slept well, Madame!" said Desmond solicitously, looking admiringly at her trim figure.

"Like a dead man," she replied with a little laugh, translating the French idiom. "Shall we make a leetle promenade after the, dejeuner? And you shall show me your pretty English country, voulez–vous? You see, I am dressed for le footing!"

She lifted a little brown foot.

They had a delightful luncheon together. Old Martha, who proved to be quite a passable cook, waited on them. There was some excellent Burgundy and a carafe of old brandy with the coffee. Nur–el–Din was in her most gracious and captivating mood. She had dropped all her arrogance of their last interview and seemed to lay herself out to please. She had a keen sense of humor and entertained Desmond vastly by her anecdotes of her stage career, some not a little risque, but narrated with the greatest bon–homie.

But, strongly attracted as he was to the girl, Desmond did not let himself lose sight of his ultimate object. He let her run on as gaily as she might but steadily, relentlessly he swung the conversation round to her last engagement at the Palaceum. He wanted to see if she would make any reference to the murder at Seven Kings. If he could only bring in old Mackwayte's name, he knew that the dancer must allude to the tragedy.

Then the unexpected happened. The girl introduce the old comedian's name herself.

"The only pleasant memory I shall preserve of the Palaceum," she said in French, "is my meeting with an old comrade of my youth. Imagine, I had not seen him for nearly twenty years. Monsieur Mackwayte, his name is, we used to call him Monsieur Arthur in the old days when I was the child acrobat of the Dupont Troupe. Such a charming fellow; and not a bit changed! He was doing a deputy turn at the Palaceum on the last night I appeared there! And he introduced me to his daughter! Une belle Anglaise! I shall hope to see my old friend again when I go back to London!"

Desmond stared at her. If this were acting, the most hardened criminal could not have carried it off better. He searched the girl's face. It was frank and innocent. She ran on about Mackwayte in the old days, his kindliness to everyone, his pretty wife, without a shadow of an attempt to avoid an unpleasant topic. Desmond began to believe that not only did the girl have nothing to do with the tragedy but that actually she knew nothing about it.

"Did you see the newspapers yesterday?" he asked suddenly.

"My friend," said Nur–el–Din, shaking her curls at him. "I never read your English papers. There is nothing but the war in them. And this war!"

She gave a little shudder and was silent.

At this moment old Martha, who had left them over their coffee and cigarettes, came into the room.

"There's a gentleman called to see you, sir!" she said to Desmond.

Desmond started violently. He was scarcely used to his new role as yet.

"Who is it, Martha?" he said, mastering his agitation.

"Mr. Mortimer!" mumbled the old woman in her tired voice, "at least that's what he said his name was. The gentleman hadn't got a card!"

Nur–el–Din sprang up from her chair so vehemently that she upset her coffee.

"Don't let him come in!" she cried in French.

"Did you say I was in?" Desmond asked the old housekeeper, who was staring at the dancer.

"Why, yes, sir," the woman answered.

Desmond made a gesture of vexation.

"Where is this Mr. Mortimer?" he asked

"In the library, sir!"

"Tell him I will be with him at once."

Martha hobbled away and Desmond turned to the girl.

"You heard what my housekeeper said? The man is here. I shall have to see him."

Nur–el–Din, white to the lips, stood by the table, nervously twisting a little handkerchief.

"Non, non," she said rapidly, "you must not see him. He has come to find me. Ah! if he should find out what I have done... you will not give me up to this man?"

"You need not see him," Desmond expostulated gently, "I will say you are not here! Who is this Mortimer that he should seek to do you harm?"

"My friend," said the dancer sadly, "he is my evil genius. If I had dreamt that you knew him I would never have sought refuge in your house."

"But I've never set eyes on the man in my life!" exclaimed Desmond.

The dancer shook her head mournfully at him.

"Very few of you have, my friend," she replied, "but you are all under his orders, nest–ce pas?"

Desmond's heart leaped. Was Mortimer's the guiding hand of this network of conspiracy?

"I've trusted you, Monsieur," Nur–el–Din continued in a pleading voice, "you will respect the laws of hospitality, and hide me from this man. You will not give me up! Promise it, my friend?"

Desmond felt strangely moved. Was this a callous murderess, a hired spy, who, with her great eyes brimming over with tears, entreated his protection so simply, so appealingly?

"I promise I will not give you up to him, Mademoiselle!" he said and hated himself in the same breath for the part he had to play. Then he left her still standing by the table, lost in thought.

Desmond walked through the hall to the room in which he had found Nur–el–Din asleep on his arrival. His nerves were strung up tight for the impending encounter with this Mortimer, whoever, whatever he was. Desmond did not hesitate on the threshold of the room. He quietly opened the door and walked in.

A man in a black and white check suit with white gaiters stood on the hearthrug, his hands tucked behind his back. He had a curiously young–old appearance, such as is found in professors and scientists of a certain type. This suggestion was probably heightened by the very strong spectacles he wore, which magnified his eyes until they looked like large colored marbles. He had a heavy curling moustache resembling that affected by the late Lord Randolph Churchill. There was a good deal of mud on his boots, showing that he had come on foot.

The two men measured one another in a brief but courteous glance. Desmond wondered what on earth this man's profession was. He was quite unable to place him.

"Mr. Bellward?" said Mortimer, in a pleasant cultivated voice, "I am pleased to have this opportunity of meeting you personally."

Desmond bowed and muttered something conventional. Mortimer had put out his hand but Desmond could not nerve himself to take it. Instead he pushed forward a chair.

"Thanks," said Mortimer sitting down heavily, "I've had quite a walk across the fen. It's pleasant out but damp! I suppose you didn't get my letter?"

"Which letter was that" asked Desmond.

"Why the one asking you to let me know when you would be back so that we might meet at last!"

Desmond shook his head.

"No," he said, "I didn't get that one. It must have gone astray. As a matter of fact," he added, "I only got back this morning."

"Oh, well then, I am fortunate in my visit," said Mortimer. "Did everything go off all right?"

"Oh, yes," Desmond hastened to say, not knowing what he was talking about, "everything went off all right."

"I don't in the least grudge you the holiday," the other observed, "one should always be careful to pay the last respects to the dead. It makes a good impression. That is so important in some countries!"

He beamed at Desmond through his spectacles.

"Was there anything left in your absence?" he asked, "no, there would be nothing; I suppose!"

Desmond took a firm resolution. He must know what the man was driving at.

"I don't know what you mean," he said bluntly.

"God bless my soul!" ejaculated Mortimer turning round to stare at him through his grotesque glasses. And then he said very deliberately in German:

"War niemand da?"

Desmond stood up promptly.

"What do you want with me?" he asked quietly, "and why do you speak German in my house?" Mortimer gazed at him blankly.

"Excellence, most excellent," he gasped. "I love prudence. My friend, where are your eyes?"

He put a large, firm hand up and touched the upper edge of the left lapel of his jacket. Desmond followed his gesture with his eyes and saw the other's first finger resting on the shiny glass head of a black pin. Almost instinctively Desmond imitated the gesture. His fingers came into contact with a glassheaded pin similarly embedded in the upper edge of the lapel of his own coat.

Then he understood. This must be the distinguishing badge of this confraternity of spies. It was a clever idea, for the black pin was practically invisible, unless one looked for it, and even if seen, would give rise to no suspicions. It had obviously escaped the notice of the Chief and his merry men, and Desmond made a mental resolve to rub this omission well into his superior on the first opportunity. He felt he owed the Chief one.

Mr. Mortimer cleared his throat, as though to indicate the conclusion of the episode. Desmond sat down on the settee.

"Nothing came while I was away!" he said.

"Now that you are back," Mortimer remarked, polishing his glasses with a bandanna handkerchief, "the service will be resumed. I have come to see you, Mr. Bellward," he went on, turning to Desmond, "contrary to my usual practice, mainly because I wished to confirm by personal observation the very favorable opinion I had formed of your ability from our correspondence. You have already demonstrated your discretion to me. If you continue to show that your prudence is on a level with your zeal, believe I shall not prove myself ungrateful."

So saying he settled his glasses on his nose again.

The action woke Desmond from a brown study. During the operation of wiping his spectacles, Mr. Mortimer had given Desmond a glimpse of his eyes in their natural state without the protection of those distorting glasses. To his intense surprise Desmond had seen, instead of the weak, blinking eyes of extreme myopia, a pair of keen piercing eyes with the clear whites of perfect health. Those blue eyes, set rather close together, seemed dimly familiar. Someone, somewhere, had once looked at him like that.

"You are too kind," murmured Desmond, grappling for the thread of the conversation.

Mortimer did not apparently notice his absentmindedness.

"Everything has run smoothly," he resumed, "on the lines on which we have been working hitherto, but more important work lies before us. I have found it necessary to select a quiet rendezvous where I might have an opportunity of conferring in person with my associates. The first of these conferences will take place very shortly. I count upon your attendance, Bellward!"

"I shall ,not fail you," replied Desmond. "But where is this rendezvous of yours, might I ask?"

Mortimer shot a quick glance at him.

"You shall know in good time," he answered drily. Then he added:

"Do you mind if I have a few words with Nur–el–Din before I go!"

The unexpected question caught Desmond off his guard.

"Nur–el–Din?" he stammered feebly.

"She is staying with you, I believe," said Mortimer pleasantly.

Desmond shook his head.

"There must be some mistake," he averred stoutly, "of course I know who you mean, but I have never met the lady. She is not here. What led you to suppose she was?"

But even as he spoke, his eyes fell on a black object which lay near his arm stretched out along the back of the settee. It was a little velvet hat, skewered to the upholstery of the settee by a couple of jewelled hat–pins. A couple of gaudy cushions lay between it and Mortimer's range of vision from the chair in which the latter was sitting. If only Mortimer had not spotted it already!

Desmond's presence of mind did not desert him. On the pretext of settling himself more comfortably he edged up another cushion until it rested upon the other two, thus effectively screening the hat from Mortimer's view even when he should get up.

"I wish she were here," Desmond added, smiling, "one could not have a more delightful companion to share one's solitude, I imagine."

103

"The lady has disappeared from London under rather suspicious circumstances;" Mortimer said, letting his grotesque eyes rest for a moment on Desmond's face, "to be quite frank with you, my dear fellow, she has been indiscreet, and the police are after her."

"You don't say!" cried Desmond.

"Indeed, it is a fact," replied the other, "I wish she would take you as her model, my dear Bellward. You are the pattern of prudence, are you not?"

He paused perceptibly and Desmond held his breath.

"She has very few reputable friends," Mortimer continued presently, "under a cloud as she is, she could hardly frequent the company of her old associates, Mowbury and Lazarro and Mrs. Malplaquet, you doubtless know whom I mean. I know she has a very strong recommendation to you, so I naturally thought—well, no matter!"

He rose and extended his hand.

"Au revoir, Bellward," he said, "you shall hear from me very soon. You've got a snug little place here, I must say, and everything in charming taste. I like your pretty cushions."

The blood flew to Desmond's face and he bent down, on pretense of examining the cushions, to hide his confusion.

"They aren't bad," he said, "I got them at Harrod's!"

He accompanied Mortimer to the front door and watched him disappear down the short drive and turn out of the gate into the road. Then feeling strangely ill at ease, he went back to join Nur-el-Din in the dining-room. But only the housekeeper was there, clearing the table.

"If you're looking for the young lady, sir," said old Martha, "she's gone out!"

"Oh!" said Desmond, with a shade of disappointment in his voice, "will she be back for tea?"

"She's not coming back at all," answered the old woman, "she told me to tell you she could not stop, sir. And she wouldn't let me disturb you, neither, sir."

"But did she leave no note or anything for me?" asked Desmond.

"No, sir," answered old Martha as she folded up the cloth.

Gone! Desmond stared gloomily out at the sopping garden with an uneasy feeling that he had failed in his duty.

CHAPTER XIII. WHAT SHAKESPEARE'S COMEDIES REVEALED

In a very depressed frame of mind, Desmond turned into the library. As he crossed the hall, he noticed how cheerless the house was. Again there came to him that odor of mustiness—of all smells the most eerie and drear—which he had noticed on his arrival. Somehow, as long as Nur–el–Din had been there, he had not remarked the appalling loneliness of the place.

A big log fire was blazing cheerfully in the grate, throwing out a bright glow into the room which, despite the early hour, was already wreathed in shadows. Wearily Desmond pulled a big armchair up to the blaze and sat down. He told himself that he must devote every minute of his spare time to going over in his mind the particulars he had memorized of Mr. Bellward's habits and acquaintanceships. He took the list of Bellward's friends from his pocket–book.

But this afternoon he found it difficult to concentrate his attention. His gaze kept wandering back to the fire, in whose glowing depths he fancied he could see a perfect oval face with pleading eyes and dazzling teeth looking appealingly at him.

Nur–el–Din! What an entrancing creature she was! What passion lurked in those black eyes of hers, in her moods, swiftly changing from gusts of fierce imperiousness to gentle airs of feminine charm! What a frail little thing she was to have fought her way alone up the ladder from the lowest rung to the very top! She must have character and grit, Desmond decided, for he was a young man who adored efficiency: to him efficiency spelled success.

But a spy needs grit, he reflected, and Nur–el–Din had many qualities which would enable her to win the confidence of men. Hadn't she half–captivated him, the would–be spy–catcher, already?

Desmond laughed ruefully to himself. Indeed, he mused, things looked that way. What would the Chief say if he could see his prize young man, his white–headed boy, sitting sentimentalizing by the fire over a woman who was, by her own confession, practically an accredited German agent? Desmond thrust his chin out and shook himself together. He would put the feminine side of Nur–el–Din out of his head. He must think of her henceforth only as a member of the band that was spotting targets for those sneaking, callous brutes of U–boat commanders.

He went back to the study of the list of Mr. Bellward's friends. But he found it impossible to focus his mind upon it. Do what he would, he could not rid himself of the sensation that he had failed at the very outset of his mission. He was, indeed, he told himself, the veriest tyro at the game. Here he had had under his hand in turn Nur–el–Din and Mortimer (who, he made no doubt, was the leader of the gang which was so sorely troubling the Chief), and he had let both get away without eliciting from either even as much as their address. By the use of a little tact, he had counted on penetrating something of the mystery enveloping the dancer and her relationship with the gang; for he thought he divined that Nur–el–Din was inclined to make him her confidant. With the information thus procured, he had hoped to get on to the track of the leader of the band.

But that ugly brute; Mortimer, with his goggle eyes, had spoiled everything. His appearance had taken Desmond completely by surprise: to tell the truth, it had thrown our young man rather off his guard. " If only I might have had a little longer acquaintance with my part," he reflected bitterly as $e sat by the fire, "I should have been better able to deal with that pompous ass!"

Afterwards, when thinking over the opening events of this extraordinary episode of his career, Desmond rather wondered why he had not followed Mortimer out of the house that afternoon and tracked him down to his hiding place. But, as a matter of fact, the idea did not occur to him at the time. His orders were positive not to leave the house, and he never even thought of breaking them—at any rate, not then.

His orders, also, it is true, were to report to headquarters any communication that might be made to him; but these instructions, at least as far as Nur−el−Din's and Mortimer's visits were concerned, he resolved to ignore.

For one thing, he felt angry with the Chief who, he argued rather irrationally, ought to have foreseen and prevented Mortimer thus taking him by surprise. The Chief liked secrets—well, for a change, he should be kept in the dark and the laugh would be on Desmond's side. For a few minutes after Mortimer's departure, Desmond had felt strongly inclined to go to the telephone which stood on the desk in the library and ring up Mr. Elias, as he should have done, but he resisted this impulse. Now, thinking things over in the firelight, he was glad he had refrained. He would ferret out for himself the exact part that Nur−el−Din and Mortimer were playing in this band of spies. Nothing definite had come of his interviews with them as yet. It would be time enough to communicate with Headquarters when he had something positive to report.

Then Desmond thrust the paper he had been studying back in his pocket−book and jumped up. He felt that the inaction was stifling him. He determined to go for a walk round the garden. That, at least, was in the spirit of his orders.

Remembering that he was supposed to be suffering from a chill he donned a heavy Ulster of Bellward's which was hanging in the hall and wound a muffler round his neck. Then cramming a soft cap on his head (he noted with satisfaction that Bellward's hats fitted him remarkably well) he opened the front door and stepped outside.

The rain had stopped, but the whole atmosphere reeled of moisture. Angry−looking, dirty−brown clouds chased each other across the lowering sky, and there was a constant sound of water, trickling and gurgling and splashing, in his ears.

An untidy−looking lawn with a few unkempt and overgrown rhododendron bushes dotted here and there ran its length in front of the house and terminated in an iron railing which separated the grounds from a little wood. A badly water−logged drive, green with grass in places, ran past the lawn in a couple of short bends to the front gate. On the other side the drive was bordered by what had once been a kitchen garden but was now a howling wilderness of dead leaves, mud and gravel with withered bushes and half a dozen black, bare and dripping apple trees set about at intervals. At the side of the house the kitchen garden stopped and was joined by a flower garden—at least so Desmond judged it to have been by a half ruined pergola which he had noticed from the drawing-room windows. Through the garden ran the mill-race which poured out of the grounds through a field and under a little bridge spanning the road outside.

Desmond followed the drive as far as the front gate. The surrounding country was as flat as a pancake, and in almost every field lay great glistening patches of water where the land had been flooded by the incessant rain. The road on which the house was built ran away on the left to the mist-shrouded horizon without another building of any kind in sight. Desmond surmised that Morstead Fen lay in the direction in which he was looking. To the right, Desmond caught a glimpse of a ghostly spire sticking out of some trees and guessed that this was Wentfield Church. In front of him the distant roar of a passing train showed where the Great Eastern Railway line lay.

More depressed than ever by the utter desolation of the scene, Desmond turned to retrace his steps to the house. Noticing a path traversing the kitchen garden, he followed it. It led to the back of the house, to the door of a kind of lean-to shed. The latch yielded on being pressed and Desmond entered the place.

He found himself in a fair-sized shed, very well and solidly built of pitch-pine, with a glazed window looking out on the garden, a table and a couple of chairs, and a large cupboard which occupied the whole of one side of the wall of the house against which the shed was built. In a corner of the shed stood a very good-looking Douglas motor-cycle, and on a nail ,on the wall hung a set of motor-cyclist's overalls. A few petrol cans, some full, some empty, stood against the wall.

Desmond examined the machine. It was in excellent condition, beautifully clean, the tank half full of spirits. A little dry sand on the tires showed that it had been used fairly recently.

"Old man Bellward's motor-bike that he goes to the station on," Desmond noted mentally. "But what's in the big cupboard, I wonder? Tools, I expect!"

Then he caught sight of a deep drawer in the table. It was half–open and he saw that it contained various tools and spare parts, neatly arranged, each one in its appointed place.

He went over to the cupboard and tried it. It was locked. Desmond had little respect for Mr. Bellward's property so he went over to the tool drawer and selected a stout chisel with which to burst the lock of the cupboard. But the cupboard was of oak, very solidly built, and he tried in vain to get a purchase for his implement. He leant his left hand against the edge of the cupboard whilst with his right he jabbed valiantly with the chisel.

Then an extraordinary thing happened. The whole cupboard noiselessly swung outwards while Desmond, falling forward, caught his forehead a resounding bang against the edge of the recess in which it moved. He picked himself up in a very savage frame of mind—a severe blow on the head is not the ideal cure for hypochondria—but the flow of objurgatives froze on his lips. For he found himself looking into Mr. Bellward's library.

He stepped into the room to see how the cupboard looked from the other side. He found that a whole section of bookshelves had swung back with the cupboard, in other words that the cupboard in the toolshed and the section of bookshelves were apparently all of one piece.

He carefully examined the walls on either side of the recess in the library to see how the mechanism worked. The bookshelves were open, made of mahogany, the sides elaborately carved with leaves and flowers. Desmond ran his hand down the perpendicular section immediately on the right of the recess. About halfway down—to be exact, it was in line with the fifth shelf from the floor—his fingers encountered a little knob which gave under pressure—the heart of a flower which released the section of bookshelves. Going back to the shed, Desmond examined the place against which his hand had rested as he sought to force the lock of the cupboard. As he expected, he found a similar catch let into the surface of the oak, but so cunningly inlaid that it could scarce be detected with the naked eye.

Before proceeding further with his investigations, Desmond softly turned the lock of the library door. He also shot forward a bolt he found on the inside of the door of the shed. He did not want to be interrupted by the housekeeper or the odd man.

Then he went back to the library and pulled the cupboard to behind him. It moved quite easily into place. He wanted to have a look at the bookshelves; for he was curious to know whether the cupboard was actually all of one piece with the section of bookshelves as it seemed to be. He was prepared to find that the books were merely library dummies, but no! He tried half a dozen shelves at random, and every book he pulled out was real.

Desmond was not easily baled, and he determined to scrutinize every shelf, of this particular section in turn. With the aid of one of those step–ladders folding into a chair which you sometimes see in libraries, he examined the topmost shelves but without result. He took down in turn Macaulay 's History of England, a handsome edition of the works of Swift, and a set of Moliere without getting any nearer the end of his quest.

The fourth shelf from the top was devoted to a library edition of Shakespeare, large books bound in red morocco. Desmond, who, by this time was getting cramp in the arms from stretching upwards and had made his hands black with dust, pulled out a couple of volumes at hazard from the set and found them real books like the rest.

"Oh, damn!" he exclaimed, and had half a mind to abandon the search and have a go with hammer and chisel at the cupboard in the shed. By this time it was almost dusk in the library, and Desmond, before abandoning the search, struck a match to have a final rapid glance over the shelves. The light showed him a curious flatness about the backs of the last six volumes of Shakespeare. He dropped the match and laid hold of a volume of the Comedies. It resisted. He tugged. Still it would not come. Exerting all his strength, he pulled, the gilt–lettered backs of the last six volumes came away in his hands in one piece and he crashed off the ladder to the ground.

This time he did not swear. He picked himself up quickly, lit the lamp on the table by the window, and brought it over to the bookcase. Where Shakespeare's Comedies had stood was now a gaping void with a small key stuck in a lock, above a brass handle. Desmond mounted on the steps again and eagerly turned the key. Then he grasped the handle and puled, the section of bookshelves swung back like a door, and he found himself face to face with a great stack of petrol cans. They lay in orderly piles stretching from the floor to the top of the bookshelves near the railing, several tiers deep. At a rough computation there must have been several hundred cans in the recess. And they were all full.

In a flash Desmond realized what his discovery signified. The motor–cycle in the shed without was the connecting link between Bellward and the man with whom he was co–operating in the organization. Under pretext of reading late in his library Bellward would send old Martha to bed, and once the house was quiet, sally forth by his secret exit and meet his confederate. Even when he was supposed to be sleeping in London he could still use the Mill House for a rendezvous, entering and leaving by the secret door, and no one a bit the wiser. In that desolate part of Essex, the roads are practically deserted after dark. Bellward could come and go much as he pleased on his motor–cycle. Were he stopped, he always had the excuse ready that he was going to—or returning from the station. The few petrol cans that Desmond had seen openly displayed in the shed without seemed to show that Bellward received a small quantity of spirit from the Petrol Board to take him to and from the railway.

The cache, so elaborately concealed, however, pointed to long journeys. Did Bellward undertake these trips to fetch news or to transmit it? And who was his confederate? Whom did he go to meet? Not Mortimer; for he had only, corresponded with Bellward. Nor was it Nur–el–Din; for she had never met Bellward, either.

Who was it, then?

CHAPTER XIV. BARBARA TAKES A HAND

"No luck, Mr. Marigold," said the Assistant Provost Marshal, "I'm sorry, but there it is! We've made every possible inquiry about this Private... er..." he glanced at the buff–colored leave pass in his hand, "... this Gunner Barling, but we can't trace him so far. He should have gone back to France the afternoon before the day on which you found his pass. But he hasn't rejoined his unit. He's been posted as an absentee, and the police have been warned. I'm afraid we can't do any more than that!"

The detective looked at the officer with mild reproach in his eyes.

"Dear, dear," he replied, "and I made sure you'd be able to trace him with that pass!"

He clicked his tongue against his teeth and shook his head.

"Dear, dear!" he said again.

"What's the feller been up to?" asked the A.P.M. Detectives have a horror of leading questions, and Mr. Marigold shrank visibly before the directness of the other's inquiry. Before replying, however, he measured the officer with his calm, shrewd eye. Mr. Marigold was not above breaking his own rules of etiquette if thereby he might gain a useful ally.

"Well, Captain Beardiston," he answered slowly,

I'll tell you because I think that you may be able to help me a little bit. It's part of your work to look after deserters and absentees and those sort o' folk, isn't it?"

The A.P.M. groaned.

"Part of my work?" he repeated, "it seems to be my whole life ever since I came back from the front."

"If you want to know what this young fellow has been up to," said Mr. Marigold in his even voice, "it's murder, if I'm not mistaken!"

"Murder?" echoed the other in surprise. "Why, not the Seven Kings murder, surely?"

The detective gave a brisk nod.

"That's it," he replied, "I'm in charge of that case, if you follow me. I found that pass in the front garden of the Mackwayte's house in Laleham Villas, half trodden into the earth of the flower–bed by a heavy boot, a service boot, studded with nails. There had been a lot of rain in the night, and it had washed the mosaic–tiled pathway up to the front door almost clean. When I was having a look round the garden, I picked up this pass, and then I spotted the trace of service boots, a bit faint, on the beds. You know the way the nails are set in the issue boots?"

The officer nodded:

"I ought to know that foot–print," he said. "It's all over the roads in northern France."

"We made inquiries through you," the detective resumed, "and when I found that this Gunner Barling, the owner of the pass, was missing, well, you will admit, it looked a bit suspicious."

"Still, you know," the A.P.M. objected, this man appears to have the most excellent character. He's got a clean sheet; he's never gone absent before. And he's been out with his battery almost since the beginning of the war."

"I'm not making any charge against him as yet," answered the detective, picking up his hat, "but it would interest me very much, very much indeed, Captain Beardiston, to have five minutes' chat with this gunner. And so I ask you to keep a sharp lookout for a man answering to his description, and if you come across him, freeze on to him hard, and give me a ring on the telephone."

"Right you are," said the officer, "I'll hold him for you, Mr. Marigold. But I hope your suspicions are not well−founded."

For a brief moment the detective became a human being.

"And so do I, if you want to know," he said. "One can forgive those lads who are fighting out there almost anything. I've got a boy in France myself!"

A little sigh escaped him, and then Mr. Marigold remembered "The Yard."

"I'll bid you good−day!" he added in his most official voice and took his leave.

He walked down the steps by the Duke of York's column and through the Horse Guards into Whitehall, seemingly busy with his own thoughts. A sprucely dressed gentleman who was engaged in the exciting and lucrative sport of war profiteering turned color and hastily swerved out towards the Park as he saw the detective crossing the Horse Guards' Parade. He was unpleasantly reminded of making the acquaintance of Mr. Marigold over a bucketshop a few years ago with the result that he had vanished from the eye of his friends for eighteen months. He congratulated himself on thinking that Mr. Marigold had not seen him, but he would have recognized his mistake could he but have caught sight of the detective's face. A little smile flitted across Mr. Marigold's lips and he murmured to himself:

"Our old friend is looking very prosperous just now. I wonder what he's up to?"

Mr. Marigold didn't miss much.

The detective made his way to the Chief's office. Barbara Mackwayte, in a simple black frock with white linen collar and cuffs, was at her old place in the ante-room. A week had elapsed since the murder, and the day before, Mr. Marigold knew, the mortal remains of poor old Mackwayte had been laid to rest. He was rather surprised to see the girl back at work so soon.

She did not speak to him as she showed him into the Chief, but there was a question lurking in her gray eyes.

Mr. Marigold looked at her and gravely shook his head.

"Nothing fresh," he said.

The Chief was unusually exuberant. Mr. Marigold found him surrounded, as was his wont, by papers, and a fearsome collection of telephone receivers. He listened in silence to Mr. Marigold's account of his failure to trace Barling.

"Marigold," he said, when the other had finished, "we must undoubtedly lay hold of this fellow. Let's see now... ah! I have it!"

He scribbled a few lines on a writing-pad and tossed it across to the detective.

"If your friend's innocent," he chuckled, "that'll fetch him to a dead certainty. If he murdered Mackwayte, of course he won't respond. Read it out and let's hear how it sounds!"

The Chief leaned back in his chair and lit a cigarette while the detective read out:

"If Gunner Barling, etcetera, etcetera, will communicate with Messrs. Blank and Blank, solicitors, he will hear of something to his advantage. Difficulties with the military can be arranged."

114

"But I say, sir," objected Mr. Marigold, "the military authorities will hardly stand for that last, will they?"

"Won't they, by Jove" retorted the Chief grimly. "They will if I tell 'em to. No official soullessness for me; thank you! And now, Marigold, just ask Matthews to fill in Barling's regimental number and all that and the name and address of the solicitors who do this kind of thing for us. And tell him we'll insert the ad. daily until further notice in the Mail, Chronicle, Daily News, Sketch, Mirror, Evening News..."

"And Star," put in Mr. Marigold who had Radical tendencies.

"The Star, too, by all means. That ought to cover the extent of your pal's newspaper reading, I fancy, eh, Marigold! Right!"

He held out a hand in farewell. But Mr. Marigold stood his ground. He was rather a slow mover, and there were a lot of things he wanted to discuss with the Chief.

"I was very sorry to see poor Major Okewood in the casualty list this morning, sir," he said. "I was going to ask you..."

"All terrible, terrible!" said the Chief. Then he added:

"Just tell Miss Mackwayte I want her as you go out, will you?"

The detective was used to surprises but the Chief still bowled him out occasionally. Before he knew what he was doing, Mr. Marigold found himself in the ante–room doing as he was bid.

As soon as her father's funeral was over; Barbara had insisted on returning to work. The whole ghastly business of the murder and the inquest that followed seemed to her like a bad dream which haunted her day and night. By tacit consent no one in the office had made any further allusion, to the tragedy. She had just slipped back into her little niche, prompt, punctual, efficient as ever.

"No, it's not for the letters," the Chief said to her as she came in with her notebook and pencil. "I'm going to give you a little trip down to the, country this afternoon, Miss

Mackwayte... to, Essex... the Mill House, Wentfield... you know whom it is you are to see, eh? I'm getting a little restless as we've had no reports since he arrived there. I had hoped, by this, to have been able to put him on the track of Nur–el–Din, but, for the moment, it looks as if we had lost the scent. But you can tell our friend all we know about the lady's antecedents—what we had from my French colleague the other day, you know? Let him have all the particulars about this Barling case—you know about that, don't you? Good, and, see here, try and find out from our mutual friend what he intends doing. I don't want to rush him... don't let him think that... but I should rather like to discover whether he has formed any plan. And now you get along. There's a good train about three which gets you down to Wentfield in just under the hour. Take care of yourself! See you in the morning!"

Pressing a bell with one hand and lifting up a telephone receiver with the other, the Chief immersed himself again in his work. He appeared to have forgotten Miss Mackwayte's very existence.

At a quarter to five that evening, Barbara unlatched the front gate of the Mill House and walked up the drive. She had come on foot from the station and the exercise had done her good. It had been a deliciously soft balmy afternoon, but with the fall of dusk a heavy mist had come creeping up from the sodden, low–lying fields and was spreading out over the neglected garden of Mr. Bellward's villa as Barbara entered the avenue.

The damp gloom of the place, however, depressed her not at all. She exulted in the change of scene and the fresh air; besides, she knew that the presence of Desmond Okewood would dispel the vague fears that had hung over her incessantly ever since her father's murder. She had only met him twice, she told herself when this thought occurred to her, but there was something bracing and dependable about him that was just the tonic she wanted.

A porter at the station, who was very intelligent as country porters go, had told her the way to the Mill House. The way was not easy to find for there were various turns to make but, with the aid of such landmarks as an occasional inn, a pond or a barn, given her by the friendly porter, Barbara reached her destination. Under the porch she pulled the handle of the bell, all dank and glistening with moisture, and heard it tinkle loudly somewhere within the house.

How lonely the place was, thought Barbara with a little shiver! The fog was growing thicker every minute and now seemed suspended like a vast curtain between her and the drive. Somewhere in the distance she heard the hollow gurgling of a stream. Otherwise, there was no sound.

She rang the bell again rather nervously and waited. In her bag she had a little torch–light (for she was a practical young person), and taking it out, she flashed it on the door. It presented a stolid, impenetrable oaken front. She stepped out into the fog and scanned the windows which were already almost lost to view. They were dark and forbidding.

Again she tugged at the bell. Again, with a groaning of wires, responded the hollow tinkle. Then silence fell once more. Barbara began to get alarmed. What had happened to Major Okewood? She had understood that there was no question of his leaving the house until the Chief gave him the word. Where, then, was he? He was not the man to disobey an order. Rather than believe that, she would think that something untoward had befallen him. Had there been foul play here, too?"

A sudden panic seized her. She grasped the bell and tugged and tugged until she could tug no more. The bell jangled and pealed and clattered reverberatingly from the gloomy house, and then, with a jarring of wires, relapsed into silence. Barbara beat on the door with her hands, for there was no knocker; but all remained still within. Only the dank mist swirled in ever denser about her as she stood beneath the dripping porch.

"This won't do!" said Barbara, pulling herself together. "I mustn't get frightened, whatever I do! Major Okewood is very well capable of defending himself. What's happened is that the man has been called away and the servants have taken advantage of his absence to go out! Barbara, my dear, you'll just have to foot it back to the station without your tea!"

She turned her back on the door and torch in hand, plunged resolutely into the fog–bank. The mist was bewilderingly thick. Still, by going slow and always keeping the gravel under her feet, she reached the front gate and turned out on the road.

Here the mist was worse than ever. She had not taken four paces before she had lost all sense of her direction. The gate, the railways, were gone. She was groping in a clinging pall of fog.

Her torch was worse than useless. It only illuminated swirling swathes of mist and confused her, so she switched it out. In vain she looked about her, trying to pick up some landmark to guide her. There was no light, no tree, no house visible, nothing but the dank, ghostly mist.

To some temperaments, Nature has no terrors. Barbara, to whose imagination an empty house at dusk had suggested all kinds of unimaginable fears, was not in the least frightened by the fog. She only hoped devoutly that a motor-car or a trap would not come along behind and run her down for she was obliged to keep to the road; the hard surface beneath her feet was her only guide.

She smiled over her predicament as she made her way along. She frequently found herself going off the road, more than once into patches of water, with the result that in a few minutes her feet were sopping. Still she forged ahead, with many vain halts to reconnoitre while the fog, instead of lifting, seemed to thicken with every step she took.

By this time she knew she was completely lost. Coming from the station there had been, she remembered, a cross-roads with a sign-board set up on a grass patch, about a quarter of a mile from the Mill House. She expected every minute to come upon this fork; again and again she swerved out to the left from her line of march groping for the sign-post with her hands but she never encountered it.

Few sounds came to break in upon the oppressive silence of the mist. Once or twice Barbara heard a train roaring along in the distance and, at one of her halts, her ear caught the high rising note of a motor engine a long way off. Except for these occasional reminders of the proximity of human beings. she felt she must be on a desert island instead of less than two score miles from London.

Her wrist watch showed her that she had walked for an hour when she heard a dog barking somewhere on the left of the road. Presently, she saw a blurred patch of radiance apparently on the ground in front of her. So deceptive are lights seen through a fog that she was quite taken aback suddenly to come upon a long low house with a great beam of light streaming out of the door.

The house was approached by a little bridge across a broad ditch. By the bridge stood a tall, massive post upon which a sign squeaked softly as it swayed to and fro. The inn was built round three sides of a square, the left–hand side being the house itself, the centre, the kitchen, and the right–hand side a tumble–down stable and some sheds.

The welcome blaze of light coming from the open door was very welcome to Barbara after her, long journey through the mist. She dragged her wet and weary feet across the little bridge and went up to the inn–door.

She stood for a moment at the entrance dazzled by the effect of the light on her eyes, which were smarting with the fog. She found herself looking into a long, narrow, taproom, smelling of stale beer and tobacco fumes, and lit by oil lamps suspended in wire frames from the raftered ceiling. The windows were curtained in cheerful red rep and the place was pleasantly warmed by a stove in one corner. By the stove was a small door apparently leading into the bar, for beside it was a window through which Barbara caught a glimpse of beer–engines and rows of bottles. Opposite the doorway in which she stood was another door leading probably to the back of the house. Down the centre of the room ran a long table.

The tap–room was empty when Barbara entered but as she sat down at the table, the door opposite opened, and a short, foreign–looking woman came out. She stepped dead on seeing the girl: Her face seemed familiar to Barbara.

"Good evening" said the latter, "I've lost my way in the fog and I'm very wet. Do you think I could have my shoes and stockings dried and get some tea? I..."

"A moment! I go to tell Meester Rass," said the woman with a very marked foreign accent and in a frightened kind of voice and slipped out by the way she came.

"Where have I met that woman before?" Barbara asked herself, as she crossed to tile stove to get warm. The woman's face seemed to be connected in her mind with something unpleasant, something she wanted to forget. Then a light dawned on her. Why, it was...

A shrill cry broke in upon her meditations, a harsh scream of rage. Barbara turned quickly and saw Nur–el–Din standing in the centre of the room. She was transfigured with passion. Her whole body quivered, her nostrils were dilated, her eyes flashed fire, and she pointed an accusing finger at Barbara.

"Ah! miserable!" she cried in a voice strangled with rage, "ah! miserable! Te voile enrol."

A cold chill struck at Barbara's heart. Wherever she went, the hideous spectre of the tragedy of her father seemed to follow her. And now Nur–el–Din had come to upbraid her with losing the treasure she had entrusted to her.

"Nur–el–Din," the girl faltered in a voice broken with tears.

"Where is it I Where is the silver box I gave into your charge? Answer me. Mais reponds, donc, canaille!"

The dancer stamped furiously with her foot and advanced menacingly on Barbara.

An undersized; yellow–faced man came quickly out of the small door leading from the bar and stood an instant, a helpless witness of the scene, as men are when women quarrel.

Nur–el–Din rapped out an order to him in a tongue which was unknown to Barbara. It sounded something like Russian. The man turned and locked the door of the bar, then stepped swiftly across the room and bolted the outer door.

Barbara recognized the threat that the action implied and it served to steady her nerves. She shrank back no longer but drew herself up and waited calmly for the dancer to reach her.

"The box you gave me," said Barbara very quietly, "was stolen from me by the person who... who murdered my father!"

Nur–el–Din burst into a peal of malicious laughter.

"And you?" she cried, "you are 'ere to sell it back to me, hein, or to get your blood money from your accomplice? Which is it?"

On this Barbara's self–control abandoned her.

"Oh, how dare you! How dare you!" she exclaimed, bursting into tears, "when that wretched box you made me take was the means of my losing the dearest friend I ever had!"

Nur−el−Din thrust her face, distorted with passion, into Barbara's. She spoke in rapid French, in a low, menacing voice.

"Do you think this play−acting will deceive me? Do you think I don't know the value of the treasure I was fool enough to entrust to your safe keeping? Grand Dieu! I must have been mad not to have remembered that no woman could resist the price that they were willing to pay for it! And to think what I have risked for it! Is all my sacrifice to have been in vain?"

Her voice rose to a note of pleading and the tears started from her eyes. Her mood changed. She began to wheedle.

"Come, ma petite, you will help me recover my little box, n'est−ce pas? You will find me generous. And I am rich, I have great savings. I can..."

Barbara put up her hands and pushed the dancer away from her.

"After what you have said to me to−night," she said, "I wouldn't give you back your box even if I had it."

She turned to the man.

"Will you tell me the way to the nearest station" she went on, "and kindly open that door!"

The man looked interrogatively at Nur−el−Din who spoke a few words rapidly in the language she had used before. Then she cried to Barbara:

"You stay here until you tell me what you have done with the box!"

Barbara had turned to the dancer when the latter spoke so that she did not notice that the man had moved stealthily towards her. Before she could struggle or cry out, a hand as big as a spade was clapped over her mouth, she was seized in an iron grip and half−dragged, half−carried out of the taproom through the small door opposite the front entrance.

The door slammed behind them and Barbara found herself in darkness. She was pushed round a corner and down a flight of stairs into some kind of cellar which smelt of damp straw. Here the grip on her mouth was released for a second but before she could utter more than a muffled cry the man thrust a handkerchief into her mouth and effectually gagged her. Then he tied her hands and feet together with some narrow ropes that cut her wrists horribly. He seemed to be able to see in the dark for, though the place was black as pitch, he worked swiftly and skillfully. Barbara felt herself lifted and deposited on a bundle of straw. In a little she heard the man's heavy foot–step on the stair, there was a crash as of a trap–door falling to, the noise of a bolt. Then Barbara fainted.

CHAPTER XV. MR. BELLWARD IS CALLED TO THE TELEPHONE

A knocking at the door of the library aroused Desmond from his cogitations. He hastened to replace the volumes of Shakespeare on their shelf and restore all to its former appearance. Then he went to the door and opened it. Old Martha stood in the hall.

"If you please, sir," she wheezed, "the doctor's come!"

"Oh," said Desmond, rather puzzled, "what doctor?"

"It's not Dr. Haines from the village, Mr. Bellward, sir," said the housekeeper, "It's a genel'man from Lunnon!"

Then Desmond remembered Crook's promise to look him up and guessed it must be he. He bade Martha show the doctor in and bring tea for two.

Desmond's surmise was right. The old woman ushered in Crook, looking the very pattern of medical respectability, with Harley Street written all over him from the crown of his glossy top–hat to the neat brown spats on his feet. In his hand he carried a small black bag.

"Well," he said, surveying Desmond, "and how do we find ourselves to–day? These chills are nasty things to shake off, my dear sir!"

"Oh, stow that!" growled Desmond, who was in little mood for joking.

"Voice inclined to be laryngeal," said Crook putting down his hat and bag on a chair, "we shall have to take care of our bronchial tubes! We are not so young as we were!"

"You can drop all that mumming, Crook!" snapped Desmond irascibly.

"Voice rotten," replied Crook calmly surveying him through his pince-nez. "Really, Major—I should say, Mr. Bellward—you must take more pains than that. You are talking to me exactly as though I were a British Tommy. Tut, tut, this will never do, sir! You must talk thicker, more guttural-like, and open the vowels well."

He had dropped his jesting manner altogether and spoke with the deep earnestness of the expert airing his pet topic. He was so serious that Desmond burst out laughing. It must be said, however, that he laughed as much like a German as he knew how. This appeared to mollify Crook who, nevertheless, read him a long lecture against ever, for a moment, even when alone, quitting the role he was playing. Desmond took it in good part; for he knew the soundness of the other's advice.

Then old Martha brought' tea, and over the cups and saucers Crook gave Desmond a budget of news. He told of the warrant issued for the arrest of Nur-el-Din and of the search being made for her.

Desmond heard the news of Nur-el-Din's disappearance from London with some consternation. He began to realize that his failure to detain Nur-el-Din that afternoon might have incalculable consequences. Sunk in thought, he let Crook run on. He was wondering whether he ought to give him a message for the Chief, telling him of Nur-el-Din's visit and of her flight on the arrival of Mortimer.

Now, Desmond had a good deal of pride, and like most proud people, he was inclined to be obstinate. To confess to the Chief that he had let both Nur-el-Din and Mortimer slip through his fingers was more than he could face. He could not bear to think that the Chief might believe him capable of failure, and take independent measures to guard against possible mistakes. Also, in his heart of hearts, Desmond was angry with the Chief. He thought the latter had acted precipitately in getting out a warrant for Nur-el-Din's arrest before he, Desmond, had had time to get into the skin of his part.

So Desmond heard Crook out and made no comment. When the other asked him if he had anything to tell the Chief, he shook his head. He was not to know then the consequences which his disobedience of orders was destined to have. If he had realized what the result of his obstinacy would be, he would not have hesitated to send a full report by Crook—and this story might never have been written!

But if youth followed reason instead of impulse, the world would stand still. Desmond was still at an age at which a man is willing to take on anything and anybody, and he was confident of bringing his mission to a successful conclusion without any extraneous aid. So Crook, after changing Desmond's make–up and giving him a further rehearsal of his role, packed up his pots and paints and brushes in his black bag and returned to London with "nothing to report" as the communiques say.

He repeated his visit every day for the next four days. Crook's arrival each afternoon was the only break in the monotony of a life which was rapidly becoming unbearable to Desmond's mercurial temperament. He found himself looking forward to the wizened little man's visits and for want of better employment, he threw himself wholeheartedly into the study of his role under the expert's able direction. Desmond's beard had sprouted wonderfully, and Crook assured him that, by about the end of the week, the tow substitute, which Desmond found a most unmitigated nuisance, would be no longer necessary. He also showed his pupil how to paint in the few deft lines about the eyes which completed the resemblance between Bellward and his impersonator.

The time hung terribly heavily on Desmond's hands. He had long since memorized and destroyed the list of Mr. Bellward's friends. Every morning he spent at least an hour before the mirror in his bedroom working up the role. With every day he felt more confident of himself; with every day he grew more anxious to go to London, and, taking the bull by the horns, boldly visit one of Mr. Bellward's acquaintances and test the effect of his disguise.

But no orders came from Headquarters to release him from his confinement. Moreover, no word arrived from Nur–el–Din nor did Mortimer send any message or call again at the Mill House. The silence of the two conspirators made Desmond uneasy. Suppose Mortimer, who, he felt sure, had caught him out lying about Nur–el–Din's presence in the house at the time of his visit, had grown suspicious! What if Nur–el–Din had succeeded in making good her escape to the Continent? He had had his chance of laying hold of both suspects and he had failed. Would that chance come again?

Desmond doubted it. Every morning he awoke long before the dawn and lay awake until daylight, his mind racked by these apprehensions. He chafed bitterly at his inaction and he plied Crook with questions as to whether he had any orders for him. Each time Crook replied in the negative.

In the library Desmond found an Ordnance map of Essex. His military training had given him a good schooling in the use of maps, and he spent many hours studying the section of the country about the Mill House, seeking to impress it upon his mind against future emergencies.

He was surprised to find how remote the Mill House lay from other habitations. Between it and Wentfield station, once Wentfield village was passed, there were only a few lonely farms; but to the south there was an absolutely uninhabited tract of fen traversed by the road running past the front gate of the Mill House. The Mill House was duly marked on the map; with a little blue line showing the millrace which Desmond traced to its junction with one of the broad dykes intersecting Morstead Fen. The only inhabited house to the south of the Bellward villa appeared to be a lonely public house situated on the far edge of the fen, a couple of hundred yards away from the road. It was called "The Dyke Inn."

One afternoon—it was the fifth day after Desmond's arrival at Bellward's—Mr. Crook announced that this was to be his last visit.

"I go abroad to–night, Mr. Bellward," he said (he always insisted on addressing Desmond by his assumed name), "a little job o' work in Switzerland; at Berne, to be precise. Urgent, you might call it, and really, sir, you've made so much progress that I think I can safely leave you. And I was to say that you will be able to go out very soon now."

"Good!" exclaimed Desmond, rubbing his hands together. "And you think I'll do, Crook, eh?"

Crook rubbed his nose meditatively.

"I'll be quite frank with you, Mr. Bellward," he said: "With a superficial acquaintance, even with an intimate friend, if he's as unobservant as most people are, you'll pass muster.

125

But I shouldn't like to guarantee anything if you were to meet, say, Mrs. Bellward, if the gentleman has got a wife, or his mother. Keep out of a strong light; don't show your profile more than you can help, and remember that a woman is a heap more observant than a man.

"That's my advice to you, sir. And now I'll take my leave! You won't want that tow beard any more after to–day."

That night Desmond slept well and did not awake until the sunshine was streaming in between the Venetian blinds in his bedroom. He felt keen and vigorous, and he had an odd feeling that something was going to happen to him that day.

It was a delicious morning, the air as balmy as spring. As he brushed his hair in front of the window, Desmond saw the peewits running about in the sunshine on the fields by the road. He made an excellent breakfast and then, lighting a pipe, opened the Times which lay folded by his plate.

He turned first, as was his daily habit, to the casualty list. There it was! Under the names of the "Killed in Action," he read: "Okewood, Major D. J. P.," followed by the name of his regiment. It gave him an odd little shock, though he had looked for the announcement every day; but the feeling of surprise was quickly followed by one of relief. That brief line in the casualty list meant the severing of all the old ties until he had hunted down his quarry.

Now he was ready to start.

He spent the morning in the garden. Here, for the first time, he met Mr. Hill, the odd man, who, on seeing him, became intensely busy picking up handfuls of leaves and conveying them to a fire which was smouldering in a corner. Desmond essayed to enter into conversation with him but the man was so impenetrably deaf that Desmond, tiring of bawling, "It's a fine day!" in Mr. Hill's ear, left him and strolled over to the shed where the motor–cycle was stored. Here he amused himself for more than an hour in taking the machine to pieces and putting it together again. He satisfied himself that the bike was in working order and filled up the tank. He had an idea that this means of conveyance might come in useful.

The day was so mild that he lunched by the open window with the sunshine casting rainbows can the tablecloth through the wine–glasses. He was just finishing his coffee when the housekeeper came in and told him he was wanted on the telephone.

Desmond sprang from his chair with alacrity. His marching orders at last! he thought, as he hurried across the hall to the library.

"Hullo!" he cried as he picked up the receiver.

"Is that Mr. Bellward?" answered a nasal voice.

"Bellward speaking!" said Desmond, wondering who had called him up. The voice was a man's but it was not the abrupt clear tones of the Chief nor yet Mr. Matthews' careful accents.

"Madame Le Bon wishes to see you!"

Madame Le Bon? thought Desmond. Why, that was the name that Nur–el–Din had given him. "I am Madame Le Bon, a Belgian refugee," she had said.

"Do you know whom I mean?" the voice continued.

"Certainly," replied Desmond. "You will come alone. Otherwise, Madame will not see you. You understand? If you do not come alone, you will waste your time!"

"Where are you speaking from?" Desmond asked.

"If you will turn to the left on leaving your front gate," the voice resumed, "and follow the road, a messenger will meet you and take you to the lady."

"But..." Desmond began.

"Will you come at once? And alone?" the nasal voice broke in sharply.

Desmond took a moment's thought. To go was to disobey orders; not to go was to risk losing a second chance of meeting Nur–el–Din. To telephone to 700 Stanning for assistance would bring a hornets' nest about his ears; yet he might only see the dancer if he went alone. He lost no time in making up his mind. The Chief must allow him latitude for meeting emergencies of this kind. He would go.

"I will come at once," said Desmond.

"Good," said the voice and the communication ceased.

Somewhere aloft there sits a sweet little cherub whose especial job is to look after the headstrong. It was doubtless this emissary of providence that leant down from his celestial seat and whispered in Desmond's ear that it would be delightful to walk out across the fen on this sunny afternoon. Desmond was in the act of debating whether he would not take the motor–bike, but the cherub's winning way clinched it and he plumped for walking.

In the hall he met the housekeeper who told him she wanted to go into Stanning to do some shopping that afternoon. Desmond told her that he himself was going out and would not be back for tea. Then, picking a stout blackthorn out of the hallstand, he strode down the drive and out into the road.

It was still beautifully fine, but already the golden sunshine was waning and there were little wisps and curls of mist stealing low along the fields. Desmond turned to the left, on leaving the Mill House, as he was bid and saw the road running like a khaki ribbon before him into the misty distance.

Swinging his stick, he strode on rapidly. The road was neglected, broken and flinty and very soft. After he had gone about a mile it narrowed to pursue its way between two broad ditches lined with pollard willows and brimful of brown peaty water. By this time he judged, from his recollection of the map, that he must be on Morstead Fen. An interminable waste of sodden, emerald green fields, intersected by ditches, stretched away on either hand.

He had walked for half an hour when he made out in the distance a clump of trees standing apart and seemingly in the middle of the fields. Then in the foreground he descried a gate. A figure was standing by it.

As he approached the gate he saw it was a small boy. On remarking the stranger, the urchin opened the gate and without looking to right or left led off down the road towards the clump of trees: Desmond followed at his leisure.

As they neared the trees, the low red roof of a house detached itself. By this time the sun was sinking in a smear of red across a delicately tinted sky. Its dying rays held some glittering object high up on the side of the house.

At first Desmond thought it was a window, but presently the light went out, kindled again and once more vanished. It was too small for a window, Desmond decided, and then, turning the matter over in his mind, as observant people are accustomed to do even with trifles, he suddenly realized that the light he had seen was the reflection of the sun on a telescope or glasses.

They were now within a few hundred yards of the house. The road had made a right angle turn to the left, but the diminutive guide had quitted it and struck out along a very muddy cart track. Shading his eyes, Desmond gazed at the house and presently got a glimpse of a figure at a window surveying the road through a pair of field glasses. Even as he looked, the figure bobbed down and did not reappear.

"They want to be sure I'm alone," thought Desmond, and congratulated himself on having had the strength of mind to break his orders.

The cart–track led up to a little bridge over a ditch. By the bridge stood a tall pole, on the top of which was a blue and gold painted sign–board inscribed, "The Dyke Inn by J. Rass." The urchin led him across the bridge and up to the door of the inn.

An undersized, yellow–faced man, wearing neither collar nor tie, came to the door as they approached. Although of short stature, he was immensely broad with singularly long arms. Altogether he had something of the figure of a gorilla, Desmond thought on looking at him.

The man put a finger up and touched his forelock.

"Madame Le Bon is upstairs waiting for you!" he said in a nasal voice which Desmond recognized as that he had heard on the telephone. "Please to follow me!"

He led the way across a long low tap-room through a door and past the open trap-door of a cellar to a staircase. On the first landing, lit by a window looking out on a dreary expanse of fen, he halted Desmond.

"That's her room," he said, pointing to a door opposite the head of the staircase, half a dozen steps up, and so saying, the yellow-faced man walked quickly downstairs and left him. Desmond heard his feet echo on the staircase and the door of the tap-room slam.

He hesitated a moment. What if this were a trap? Suppose Mortimer, growing suspicious, had made use of Nur-el-Din to lure him to an ambush in this lonely place? Why the devil hadn't he brought a revolver with him?

Then Desmond's Irish blood came to his rescue. He gave his head a little shake, took a firm hold of his stick which was a stoutish sort of cudgel and striding boldly up to the door indicated, tapped.

"Entrez!" said a pretty voice that made Desmond's heart flutter.

CHAPTER XVI. THE STAR OF POLAND

The room in which Desmond found Nur-el-Din was obviously the parlor of the house. Everything in it spoke of that dreary period in art, the middle years of the reign of Victoria the Good. The wall-paper, much mildewed in places, was an ugly shade of green and there were dusty and faded red curtains at the windows and draping the fireplace. Down one side of the room ran a hideous mahogany sideboard, almost as big as a railway station buffet, with a very dirty tablecloth. The chairs were of mahogany, upholstered in worn black horsehair and there were two pairs of fly-blown steel engravings of the largest size on the wall. In the centre of the apartment stood a small round table, covered with a much stained red tablecloth and there was a door in the corner.

The dainty beauty of Nur-el-Din made a very forlorn picture amid the unmatched savagery of this English interior. The dancer, who was wearing the same becoming gray tweed suit in which Desmond had last seen her, was sitting sorrowfully at the table when Desmond entered. At the sight of him she sprang up and ran to meet him with

130

outstretched hands.

"Ah!" she cried, "comme je suis heureuse de vows voir! It is good of you to come!"

And then, without any warning, she burst into tears and putting her hands on the man's shoulders, hid her head against his chest and sobbed bitterly.

Desmond took one of her hands, small and soft and warm, and gently disengaged her. His mind was working clearly and rapidly. He felt sure of himself, sure of his disguise; if this were an exhibition of woman's wiles, it would find him proof; on that he was resolved. Yet, dissolved in tears as she was, with her long lashes glistening and her mouth twitching pitifully, the dancer seemed to touch a chord deep down in his heart.

"Come, come," said Desmond gutturally, with a touch of bonhomie in his voice in keeping with his ample girth, "you mustn't give way like this, my child! What's amiss? Come, sit down here and tell me what's the matter."

He made her resume her seat by the table and pulled up one of the horsehair chairs for himself. Nur—el—Din wiped her eyes on a tiny lace handkerchief, but continued to sob and shudder at intervals.

"Marie, my maid," she said in French in a broken voice, "joined me here to—day. She has told me of this dreadful murder!"

Desmond stiffened to attention. His mind swiftly reverted to the last woman he had seen cry, to Barbara Mackwayte discovering the loss of the package entrusted to her charge by the woman who sat before him.

"What murder?" he asked, striving to banish any trace of interest from his voice. He loathed the part he had to play. The dancer's distress struck him as genuine.

"The murder of Monsieur Mackwayte," said Nur—el—Din, and her tears broke forth anew.

"I have read of this in the newspapers," said Desmond. "I remember you told me he was a friend of yours."

131

Briefly, with many sobs, the dancer told him of the silver box which she had entrusted to Barbara Mackwayte's charge.

"And now," she sobbed, "it is lost and all my sacrifice, all my precautions, have been in vain!"

"But how?" asked Desmond. "Why should you think this box should have been taken? From what I remember reading of this case in the English newspapers there was a burglary at the house, but the thief has been arrested and the property restored. You have only to ask this Miss—what was the name? ah! yes, Mackwayte for your box and she will restore it!"

"No, no!" Nur–el–Din answered wearily, "you don't understand. This was no burglary. The man who murdered Monsieur Arthur murdered him to get my silver box."

"But," objected Desmond, "a silver box! What value has a trifling object like that? My dear young lady, murder is not done for a silver box!"

"No, no," Nur–el–Din repeated, "you don't understand! You don't know what that box contained!"

Then she relapsed into silence, plucking idly at the shred of cambric she held between her fingers.

Already dusk was falling and the room was full of shadows. The golden radiance of the afternoon had died and eerie wraiths of fog were peering–in at the window.

Desmond held his peace. He felt he was on the threshold of a confession that might rend the veil of mystery surrounding the murder at Seven Kings. He stared fixedly at the ugly red tablecloth, conscious that the big eyes of the girl were searching his face.

"You have honest eyes," she said presently. "I told you that once before... that night we met.at your house... do you remember? Your eyes are English. But you are a German, hein?"

"My mother was Irish," said Desmond and felt a momentary relief that, for once, he had been able to speak the truth.

"I want a friend," the girl resumed wearily, "someone that I can trust. But I look around and I find no one. You serve the German Empire, do you not?"

Desmond bowed.

"But not the House of Hohenzollern?" the girl cried, her voice trembling with passion.

"I am not of the Emperor's personal service, if that is what you mean, madame," Desmond returned coldly.

"Then, since you are not altogether an iron Prussian," Nur−el−Din resumed eagerly, "you can differentiate. You can understand that there is a difference between working for the cause of Germany and for the personal business of her princes."

"But certainly," answered Desmond, "I am not an errand boy nor yet a detective. I regard myself as a German officer doing his duty on the front. We have many fronts besides the Western and the Eastern. England is one.

"Ah," exclaimed the girl, clasping her hands together and looking at him with enraptured eyes, "I see you understand! My friend, I am much tempted to make a confidant of you!"

Desmond looked at her but did not speak. Again he felt that silence was now his only role. He tried hard to fix his mind on his duty; but the man in him was occupied with the woman who looked so appealingly at him.

"... but if I do," the girl went on and her voice was hurried and anxious, "you must swear to me that you will respect my confidence, that you will not betray me to the others and that you will, if need be, protect me."

Seeing that Desmond remained silent, she hastened to add:

"Believe me, what I ask you to do is not in opposition to your duty. My friend, for all my surroundings, I am not what I seem. Pate has drawn me into the system of which you form part; but, believe me, I know nothing of the service to which you and Mortimer and the rest belong!"

She spoke with painful earnestness and in a tone so mournful that Desmond felt himself profoundly moved. "If only she is not acting!" he thought, and sought to shake himself free from the spell which this girl seemed able to cast about him at will.

"Promise me that you will respect my confidence and help me!" she said and held out her hand.

Desmond's big hand closed about hers and he felt an odd thrill of sympathy with her as their hands met.

"I promise!" he said and murmured to himself something very like a prayer that he might not be called upon to redeem his word.

She let her eyes rest for a moment on his.

"Be careful!" she urged warningly, while the ghost of a smile flitted across her face. "Very soon I may call upon you to make good your words!"

"I promise!" he repeated—and his eyes never left hers.

"Then," she cried passionately, "find out who has stolen for the Crown Prince the Star of Poland at the price of the life of a harmless old man!"

"The Star of Poland!" repeated Desmond. "What is the Star of Poland"

The girl drew herself up proudly and there was a certain dignity about her manner as she answered.

"I am a Pole," she said, "and to us Poles, the Star of Poland has stood for centuries as a pledge of the restoration of our long-lost kingdom. It was the principal jewel of the Polish Coronation sword which vanished many hundreds of years ago—in the thirteenth century, one of my compatriots once told me—and it was one of the most treasured national possessions in the Chateau of our great king, John Sobieski at Villanoff, outside

Warsaw. My friend, I am not religious, and since my childhood I have renounced the ancient faith of my fathers, but, when I think of the extraordinary chain of circumstances by which this treasure came into my possession, I almost believe that God has chosen me to restore this gem to the King of an independent Poland.

"Four years ago I was in the United States, a very humble dancer in vaudeville of the third or fourth class. When I was appearing at Columbus, Ohio, I met a German, a man who had been an officer in the Prussian Guard but had come to grief and had been forced to emigrate.

"This man's name was Hans von Schornbeek. Like so many German officers who go to America, in his time he had been everything—waiter, lift–man, engine–driver and heaven knows what else, but when I met him he was apparently well–off. It was only later on that I knew he was one of your principal secret agents in America.

"He praised my talents highly and offered to furnish the capital to start me as an Oriental dancer with a large company of my own. There was only one condition attaching to his offer, a condition, ma foi! which was not disagreeable to me. It was that, after six months tour in the States and Canada, I should go to Brussels and settle down there in a house that Herr von Schornbeek would present me with.

"Mon ami, in those days, I understood nothing at all of diplomacy. I knew only that I was often hungry and that I had a little talent which, were it given a chance, might keep me from want. Herr von Schornbeek fulfilled his promises to me. I had my company, I did my tour of America and Canada with great success and finally I came to Europe and made my debut at Brussels.

"I knew Brussels already from the old days. As a half–starved, unhappy child with a troupe of acrobats, I had often appeared there. But now I came to Brussels as a conqueror. A beautiful villa in the suburb of Laeken was ready to receive me and I found that a large credit had been opened in my name at one of the principal banks so that I could keep open house.

"I think I scarcely realized then the role that I was destined to fill by the German Secret Service. In all my life before, I had never been happy, I had never ceased to struggle for my bare existence, I had never had pretty clothes to wear, and motor–cars and servants of my own."

She paused and glanced around her. The room was almost dark; the fog outside hung like a veil before the window.

"Light the lamp!" she begged, "I do not like the dark!"

Desmond struck a match and kindled an oil lamp, which stood on the sideboard.

"Ah! my friend," the girl resumed. "I took my fill of life with both hands. The year was 1913. Now I know that I was one of the German agents for the penetration of Belgium in preparation of what was coming. My mission was to make friends among the Belgians and the French and the cosmopolitan society of Brussels generally, and invite them to my house where your people were waiting to deal with them.

"My pretty villa became the rendezvous for half the rascals of Europe, men and women, who used to meet there with all kinds of mysterious Germans. Sometimes there was a scandal. Once a Belgian Colonel was found shot in the billiard–room; they said it was suicide and the thing was hushed up, but dame! now that I know what I know...

"Enfin! I shut my eyes to it all... it was none of my business... and I revelled in my robes, my dancing, my new life of luxury!

"And then the war came. I was at Laeken, resting after a visit to Rome. There was a lot of talk about the war amongst the people who came to my house, but I did not see how it could affect me, an artiste, and I never read the newspapers. My German friends assured me that, in a little while, the German army would be at Brussels; that, if I remained quietly at home, all would be well. They were very elated and confident, these German friends of mine. And rightly; for within a few weeks the Germans entered the city and a General quartered himself in my villa. It was he who brought the Crown Prince to see me.

"Mon cher, you know this young man and his reputation. I am not excusing myself; but all my life had been spent up to then in the bas–fonds of society. I had never known what it was to be courted and admired by one who had the world at his feet. Parbleu! one does not meet a future Emperor every day!

"Enfin! the Prince carried me with him back to Metz, where he had his headquarters. He was very epris with me, but you know his temperament! No woman can hold him for more than a few weeks, vain and weak and arrogant as he is. But pardon! I was forgetting that you are a good German. I fear I offend your susceptibilities..."

Desmond laughed drily.

"Madame," he said, "I hope I have preserved sufficient liberty of judgment to have formed my own opinion about our future sovereign. Most Germans have..."

"Alors," she broke in fiercely, her voice shaking with passion, "you know what an ignoble canaille is this young man, without even enough decency of feeling to respect the troops of whom he has demanded such bloody sacrifices. At Metz we were near enough to the fighting to realize the blood and tears of this war. But the Prince thought of nothing, but his own amusement. To live as he did, within sound of the guns, with parties every night, women and dancing and roulette and champagne suppers—bah! c'etait trop fort! It awakened in me the love of country which lies dormant in all of us. I wanted to help my country, lest I might sink as low as he..."

"One day the Prince brought a young officer friend of his to dine with me. This officer had come from the Eastern front and had been present at the capture of Warsaw. After dinner he took a leather case out of his pocket and said to the Prince: "I have brought your Imperial Highness a little souvenir from Poland!" As he spoke he touched a spring and the case flew open, displaying an enormous diamond, nearly as big as the great Orloff diamond which I have seen at Petrograd, surrounded by five other brilliants, the whole set like a star.

"'The Star of Poland,' said the young officer (the Prince called him 'Erich;' I never heard his full name), 'it comes from the long–lost Coronation sword of the Polish kings. I took it for your Imperial Highness from the Chateau of John Sobieski at Villanoff.

"I could not take my eyes off the gem. As the Prince held it down under the lamp to study it, it shone like an electric light. I had met many of my fellow countrymen in America and I had often heard of this jewel, famous in our unhappy history.

"The Prince, who was gay with champagne, laughed and said:

"'These lousy Poles will have no further use for this pretty trinket, thanks to our stout German blows, will they, Erich?'

"And his friend replied:

"'We'll give them a nice new German constitution instead, your Imperial Highness!'

"The Prince, as I have said, was very merry that night. He let me take the jewel from its case and hold it in my hands. Then I fastened it in my hair before the mirror and turned to show myself to the Prince and his companion.

"'Donnerwetter! said Willie. 'It looks wonderful in your hair, Marcelle!'

"Then, as if struck by a sudden thought, he cried:

"'Erich! What do you say, Marcelle is a Pole. She shall have the Star of Poland and wear it in memory of me!'

"The other thought this a famous idea, and so the jewel passed into my hands. That same evening I resolved that it should be a sacred duty on my part to keep it in safety until I could hand it back to the lawful sovereign of an independent Poland.

"I was very unhappy at Metz until the Star of Poland came to comfort me. When I was alone, I used to take it from its case and feast my eyes upon it. I made many attempts to get away, but the Prince would never let me go, though he had long since tired of me and I was merely one of his harem of women. Pfui!"

She gave an exclamation of disgust.

"It was the Crown Princess who eventually came to my rescue," she continued. "Long–suffering wife as she is, the stories that came to her ears from Metz were such that she went to the Emperor and declared that she would insist upon a divorce. There was a great scandal. The Prince's headquarters were moved and at length I got my release.

"I had no money. This was a detail which the Prince overlooked. But I wanted to resume my stage work, so, with great difficulty, through the influence of the Prince, I obtained a passport to Holland and from there got across to England.

"I had hoped to turn my back once and for all on my connection with the Prince. But your German Secret Service had been warned about me. The Imperial Authorities were obviously afraid that I might tell tales out of school. Scarcely had I arrived in London when a man who called himself Bryan Mowbury, but who looked and spoke like a German, came to see me and said he had been instructed to 'look after me.' What that meant, I was soon to discover. In a very few days I found that I was under the supervision of your Secret Service here. In fact, Mowbury gave me to understand that any indiscretion on my part as to my stay at Metz would result in my immediate denunciation to the English police as a spy.

"My friend, I had no alternative. I am not German; I am not English; I am a Pole. I have good friends in Germany, I have good friends in England, and their quarrels are not mine. I held my peace about the past and submitted to the incessant watch which Mowbury and his friends kept on my movements.

"And then one day I had a letter. It was from Count Plettenbach, the Crown Prince's aide–de–camp, as I knew by the hand–writing, for it was signed with an assumed name. In this letter the Count, 'on behalf of a mutual friend,' as he put it, requested me to hand back to a certain Mr. Mortimer, his accredited representative, 'Erich's present.' There were cogent reasons, it was added, for this unusual request.

"I sent no reply to that letter, although an address in Switzerland was given to which an answer might be despatched. I was resolved, come what may, not to part with the Star of Poland. When Mortimer came, five days later, I told him the jewel was not mine to hand over, that it was part of the regalia of Poland and that I would never give it up.

"Mortimer replied that the German and Austrian Governments had decided to restore the independence of Poland, that probably an Austrian Archduke would be made king and that it was essential that the Star of Poland should be restored in order to include it in the regalia for the Coronation. But I knew what this Austro–German kingdom of Poland was to be, a serf state with not a shadow of that liberty for which every Pole is longing. Since I have been in England, I have kept in touch with the Polish political organizations in this country. Rass, as he calls himself, the landlord of this inn, is one of the most prominent of the Polish leaders in England.

"Mortimer reasoned with me in vain and finally went away empty–handed. But he did not abandon hope. Four successive attempts were made to get the jewel away from me. Twice my apartments at the Nineveh Hotel were rifled; once my dressing–room at the theatre was entered and searched whilst I was on the stage. But I wore the jewel day and night in a little bag suspended by a chain from my neck and they never got it from me.

"Two days before I came down to your house—it was the day before the murder—I was hustled by a group of men as I came out of the theatre. Fortunately the stage–door keeper came up unexpectedly and the men made off. But the encounter frightened me, and I resolved to break my contract with the Palaceum and bury myself down here in the country.

"But somehow Mortimer learnt of my intention. The next night—it was the night of the murder—he came to the theatre and warned me against trying to elude his vigilance by flight. I have never forgotten his words.

"'I can afford to wait,' he said, 'for I shall get what I want: I always do. But you have chosen to set yourself against me and you will bitterly repent it!'"

As though the recollection proved too much for her, Nur–el–Din broke off her narrative and covered her face with her hands.

"And do you think that Mortimer did this murder?" asked Desmond gently.

Wearily the girl raised her head.

"Either he or one of his accomplices, of whom this girl is one!" she answered.

"But why not have put the jewel in a bank or one of the safe deposits? Surely it was risky to have entrusted it to a girl of whom you knew nothing"

"My friend,", said the dancer, "I was desperate. Mortimer sees and knows all. This unexpected meeting with the daughter of my old friend seemed at the moment like a heaven–sent chance to place the jewel, unknown to him, in safe hands. I felt that as long as I carried it on me, my life was in constant danger. It was only to–day, when I heard of the murder, that it dawned on me how indiscreet I had been. I might have guessed, since

Miss Mackwayte knew Mortimer—"

"Miss Mackwayte knows Mortimer?" echoed Desmond in stupefaction.

"But certainly," replied Nur–el–Din. "Was it not I myself—" She broke off suddenly with terror in her eyes.

"Ah, no!" she whispered. "It is enough. Already I have said too much..."

Desmond was about to speak when the door opened and a foreign–looking maid, whom Desmond remembered to have seen in the dancer's dressing–room, came in. She went swiftly to her mistress and whispered something in her ear.

The dancer sprang to her feet.

"A little moment... you will excuse me..." she cried to Desmond and ran from the room. The maid followed her, leaving Desmond alone.

Presently, the sound of Nur–el–Din's voice raised high in anger struck on his ears. He stole softly to the door and opened it. Before him lay the staircase deserted. He tiptoed down the stairs to the first landing and listened. The murmur of voices reached him indistinctly from the room below. Then he heard Nur–el–Din crying out again in anger.

He craned his ear over the well of the staircase, turning his face to the window which stood on the landing. The window gave on a small yard with a gate over which a lamp was suspended and beyond it the fen now swathed in fog. The dancer's maid stood beneath the lamp in earnest conversation with a man in rough shooting clothes who held a gun under his arm. As Desmond looked the man turned his head so that the rays of the lamp fell full upon his face. To his unspeakable consternation and amazement, Desmond recognized Strangwise.

CHAPTER XVII. MR. BELLWARD ARRANGES A BRIDGE EVENING

Oblivious of the voices in the room below, Desmond stood with his face pressed against the glass of the window. Was Strangwise staying at "The Dyke Inn"? Nothing was more probable; for the latter had told him that he was going to spend his leave shooting in Essex, and Morstead Fen must abound in snipe and duck.

But he and Strangwise must not meet. Desmond was chary of submitting his disguise to the other's keen, shrewd eyes. Strangwise knew Nur-el-Din: indeed, the dancer might have come to the inn to be with him. If he recognized Desmond and imparted his suspicions to the dancer, the game world be up; on the other hand, Desmond could not take him aside and disclose his identity; for that would be breaking faith with the Chief. There was nothing for it, he decided, but flight.

Yet how could he get away unobserved? There was no exit from the staircase by the door into the tap-room where Nur-el-Din was, and to go through the tap-room was to risk coming face to face with Strangwise.

So Desmond remained where he was by the window and watched. Presently, the woman turned and began to cross the yard, Strangwise, carrying his gun, following her. Desmond waited until he heard a door open somewhere below and then he acted.

Beside the window ran an old lead water-pipe which drained the roof above his head. On a level with the sill of the landing below, this pipe took a sharp turn to the left and ran diagonally down to a tall covered-in water-butt that stood on the fiat roof of an outhouse in the little yard.

Desmond raised the window very gently and tested the pipe with his hand. It seemed rather insecure and shook under his pressure. With his eye he measured the distance from the sill to the pipe; it was about four feet. Desmond reckoned that, if the pipe would hold, by getting out of the window and hanging on to the sill, he might, by a pendulum-like motion, gain sufficient impulse to swing his legs across the diagonally-running pipe, then transfer his hands and so slide down to the outhouse roof.

He wasted no time in debating the chances of the pipe collapsing under his weight. All his life it had been his practice to take a risk, for such is the Irish temperament—if the object to be attained in any way justified it; and he was determined to avoid at all costs the chance of a meeting with Strangwise. The latter had probably read the name of

Okewood in that morning's casualty list, but Desmond felt more than ever that he distrusted the man, and his continued presence in the neighborhood of Nur–el–Din gravely preoccupied him.

He stood a moment by the open window and listened. The murmur of voices went on in the taproom, but from another part of the house he heard a deep laugh and knew it to be Strangwise's. Trusting to Providence that the roof of the outhouse would be out of sight of the yard door, Desmond swung his right leg over the window–sill and followed it with the other, turning his back on the yard. The next moment he was dangling over the side of the house.

Then from the yard below he heard Strangwise call:

"Rufus! Rufus!"

A heavy footstep sounded on the flags. Desmond remained perfectly still. The strain on his arms was tremendous. If Strangwise should go as far as the gate, so as to get clear of the yard, he must infallibly see that figure clinging to the window–sill.

"Where the devil is that doggy" said Strangwise. Then he whistled, and called again:

"Rufus! Rufus!"

Desmond made a supreme effort to support the strain on his muscles. The veins stood out at his temples and he felt the blood singing in his ears. Another minute and he knew he must drop. He no longer had the power to swing himself up to the window ledge again.

A bark rang out in the courtyard, followed by the patter of feet. Desmond heard Strangwise speak to the dog and reenter the house. Then silence fell again. With a tremendous effort Desmond swung his legs athwart the pipe, gripped it with his right hand, then his left, and very gently commenced to let himself down. The pipe quivered beneath his weight, but it held fast and in a minute he was standing on the roof of the outhouse, cautiously peering through the dank fog that hung about the yard.

Screening himself from view behind the tall waterbutt, he reconnoitred the back of the inn. The upper part of the house was shrouded in darkness, but a broad beam of light from a half–open door and a tall window on the ground floor cleft the pall of fog. The window showed a snug little bar with Strangwise standing by the counter, a glass in his hand. As Desmond watched him, he heard a muffled scream from somewhere within the house. Strangwise heard it too, for Desmond saw him put his glass down on the bar and raise his head sharply. There followed a dull crash from the interior of the inn and the next moment the yellow–faced man, whom Desmond judged to be Rass, stepped into the circle of light inside the window. He said something to Strangwise with thumb jerked behind him, whereupon the latter clapped him, as though in approval, on the shoulder, and both hurried out together.

Puzzled though he was by the scene he had just witnessed, Desmond did not dare to tarry longer. The roof of the outhouse was only some ten feet from the ground, an easy drop. He let himself noiselessly down and landing on his feet without mishap, darted out of the yard gate. As he did so, he heard the inn door open and Strangwise's voice cry out:

"Who's that?"

But Desmond heeded not. He dashed out upon the fen. Before he had gone a dozen paces the fog had swallowed up inn and all. Out of the white pall behind him he heard confused shouts as he skirted swiftly round the house and reached the road.

Once he had gained the freedom of the highway; Desmond breathed again. The dense fog that enveloped him, the hard road beneath his feet, gave him a sense of security that he had missed as long as he was in the atmosphere of that lonely, sinister place. He struck out at a good pace for home, intent upon one thing, namely, to send an immediate summons for help to surround the Dyke Inn and all within it. Nur–el–Din, it was clear, whether a spy or no (and Desmond believed her story), was the only person who could throw any light on the mysterious circumstances surrounding old Mackwayte's murder. Besides, her arrest would safeguard her against further machinations on the part of Mortimer, though Desmond suspected that the latter, now that he had secured the jewel, would leave the dancer in peace. As for Strangwise, it would be for him to explain as best he could his continued association with a woman for whose arrest a warrant had been issued.

Desmond let himself in with his key. The housekeeper had returned and was laying the dinner–table. In the library the curtains were drawn and a fire burned brightly in the grate. The room looked very snug and cosy by contrast with the raw weather outside.

Desmond shut and locked the door and then went to the telephone at the desk. "Ring up 700 Stanning"—he repeated his instructions to himself "and ask for Mr. Elias. Assistance'll be with you within fifteen minutes afterwards."

By the clock on the mantelpiece it was a quarter to seven. If aid arrived promptly, with a car they could be at the Dyke Inn by a quarter past seven.

The telephone gave no sign of life. Desmond impatiently jerked the receiver hook up and down. This time, at least, he would not fail, he told himself. Before he went to bed that night Nur–el–Din, her maid, Rass, and if needs be, Strangwise (who needed a lesson to teach him discretion), should be in custody.

Still no reply.

"Hullo! Hullo!" cried Desmond, depressing the hook repeatedly. "Hullo, Exchange!"

But there was no answer. Then it struck Desmond that the line was dead: his ear detected none of that busy whirr which is heard in the telephone when one is waiting to get a number.

He spent five minutes in vain attempts to obtain a reply, then abandoned the endeavor in disgust.

"I shall have to take the motor–bike and go over to Stunning," he said to himself, "how I shall find my way there in this fog, the Lord only knows! And I don't know whom to apply to when I get there. The police–station, I suppose!"

He unlocked the door and rang for Martha.

"I have to go over to Stunning, Martha," he said, "I will try and be back for dinner at eight!"

He had no intention of accompanying the party to the Dyke Inn. He must preserve his incognito until Mortimer, the main quarry, had been run down.

He filled his case from the box of cigarettes on the table and thrust a box of matches into his pocket to light his head-lamp. Then, taking a cap from the hat-stand, he opened the front door. Even as he did so a big open car slowed down throbbing outside the porch. A man sprang out and advanced into the light streaming from the front door into the eddying mist. It was Mortimer.

"Fortune," thought Desmond, "has broken her rule. She has given me a second chance! "

"Well met, Bellward!" cried Mortimer, blinking at the other through his thick glasses. "Tut, tut! What a night! You were never going out, I swear."

Already Desmond had decided in his mind the course of action he would pursue. For the moment he must let the party at the Dyke Inn slide in favor of the bigger catch. He must slip away later and have another try at the telephone and if it were still out of order, he must endeavor to overpower Mortimer and then go for assistance himself. On a night like this it was useless to think of employing a half-blind old dolt like Martha to take a message. As for the odd man, he lived at Wakefield, and went away at dusk every evening.

So Desmond muttered some plausible lie about wanting to have a look at the weather and cordially invited Mortimer in.

"You will stay for dinner" he said.

"Gladly," replied the other, sinking with aunt into the settee. "And I should be glad if we might dine early."

Desmond raised his eyebrows.

"... Because," Mortimer resumed, "I have ventured to ask a few friends round here to... to have an evening at bridge. Doubtless, you have cards, eh?"

Desmond pointed to a card-table standing in the corner with several packs of cards and markers. Then he rang and told the housekeeper that they would dine as soon as possible.

"The coming fortnight," said Mortimer, tucking his napkin into his collar as they sat at the dinner table, "is pregnant with great events. No less than ten divisions are, I understand, to be transferred to the other side. I have waited to communicate with you until I had confirmation of this report. But now that the matter has been decided, it only remains for us to perfect our arrangements for communicating these plans to our friends beyond the North Sea. Therefore, I thought a friendly bridge evening at the hospitable home of our dear colleague Bellward would be in place."

He smiled affably and bent over his soup–plate.

"I shall be delighted to receive our friends," Desmond replied, "a glass of sherry?"

"Thank you," said Mortimer.

"I shall have to provide a few refreshments," said Desmond. "May I ask how many guests I may expect?"

Mortimer reckoned on his fingers.

"Let's see," he answered, "there's Max, that's one, and Madame Malplaquet, that's two. No. 13 and Behrend makes four and myself, five!"

"And Madame Nur–el–Din?" queried Desmond innocently, but inwardly quaking at his rashness.

Mortimer genially shook a finger at him.

"Sly dog!" he chuckled, "you're one too many for me in that quarter, I see! I know all about your tete–a–tete with our charming young friend this afternoon!"

Desmond felt the blood rush to his face. He thought of Nur–el–Din's words: "Mortimer sees and knows all." He picked up his sherry glass and drained it to cover his confusion.

"... It was hardly gallant of you to bolt so suddenly and leave the lady!" Mortimer added.

How much did this uncanny creature know?

Without waiting for him to reply, Mortimer went on.

"I suppose she told you a long story of my persecution, eh, Bellward? You needn't shake your head. I taxed her with it and she admitted as much."

"I had no idea that you were staying at the Dyke Inn!" said Desmond at a venture.

"My friend," replied Mortimer, lowering his voice, "your fair charmer is showing a decided inclination to make a nuisance of herself. I have had to keep an eye on her. It's been a very serious inconvenience to my plans, I can assure you. But you haven't answered my question. What sent you away in such a hurry this afternoon? and in so romantic a fashion? By the window, was it not?"

Through sheer apprehension, Desmond was now keyed up to a kind of desperate audacity. The truth is sometimes a very effective weapon in the game of bluff, and Desmond determined to employ it.

"I saw someone I didn't want to meet," he replied.

"Ah!" said Mortimer, "who was that, I wonder? The Dyke Inn could hardly be described as a frequented resort, I imagine!"

The entry of old Martha to change the plates prevented Desmond from replying. He used the brief respite to review the situation. He would tell Mortimer the truth. They were man to man now and he cared nothing even if the other should discover the fraud that had been practised upon him. Come what might, Mortimer, dead or alive, should be delivered up to justice that night.

The housekeeper left the room and Desmond spoke.

"I saw an officer I knew in the courtyard," he said.

"Oh, Strangwise, I suppose!" said Mortimer carelessly. "There's nothing to fear from him, Bellward. He's of the beef and beer and no brains stamp of British officer. But how do you know Strangwise?"

"I met him at the Nineveh Hotel in town one night," replied Desmond. "I don't care about meeting officers, however, and that's a fact!"

Mortimer looked at him keenly for a brief instant. "What prudence!" he cried. "Bellward, you are the very model of what a secret agent should be! This pheasant is delicious!"

He turned the conversation into a different channel but Desmond could not forget that brief searching look. His mind was in a turmoil of half–digested facts, of semi–completed deductions. He wanted to go away somewhere alone and think out this mystery and disentangle each separate web of this baffling skein of intrigue.

He must focus his attention on Mortimer and Nur–el–Din. If Mortimer and Strangwise were both staying at the Dyke Inn, then they were probably acquainted. Strangwise knew Nur–el–Din, too, knew her well; for Desmond remembered how familiarly they had conversed together that night in the dancer's dressing–room at the Palaceum. Strangwise knew Barbara Mackwayte also. Nur–el–Din had introduced them, Desmond remembered, on that fateful night when he had accompanied Strangwise to the Palaceum. Strange, how he was beginning to encounter the man Strangwise at every turn in this sinister affair.

And then, with a shock that struck him like a blow in the face, Desmond recalled Barbara's parting words to him in the taxi. He remembered how she had told him of seeing Nur–el–Din's face in the mirror as the dancer was talking to Strangwise that night at the Palaceum, and of the look of terror in the girl's eyes. Nur–el–Din was terrified of Mortimer; for so much she had admitted to Desmond that very afternoon; she was terrified of Strangwise, too, it seemed, of this Strangwise who, like Mortimer, kept appearing at every stage of this bewildering affair. What confession had been on Nur–el–Din's lips when she had broken off that afternoon with the cry:

"Already I have said too much!"

Thereafter Desmond's eyes were never long absent from Mortimer's face, scrutinizing each feature in turn, the eyes, set rather close together, grotesquely shielded by the thick spectacles, the narrow cheeks, the rather cynical mouth half hidden by the heavy, drooping moustache, the broad forehead broken by a long lock of dark hair brushed out flat in a downward direction from an untidy, unkempt crop.

They talked no more of Strangwise or of Nur–el–Din. The rest of dinner was passed in conversation of a general order in which Mr. Mortimer showed himself to great advantage. He appeared to be a widely traveled, well–read man, with a fund of dry, often rather grim humor. And all the time Desmond watched, watched, unobtrusively but unceasingly, looking out for something he was confident of detecting through the suave, immobile mask of this brilliant conversationalist.

Skillfully, almost imperceptibly, Desmond edged the talk on to the war. In this domain, too, Mortimer showed himself a man of broad views, of big, comprehensive ideas. Towards the strategy and tactics of the two sides, he adopted the attitude of an impartial onlooker, but in his comments he proved himself to have a thorough grasp of the military situation. He talked freely and ably of such things as tanks, the limited objective in the attack and the decentralization of responsibility in the field.

Encouraged by his volubility, for he was a man who delighted in conversation, Desmond gradually gave the talk a personal turn. But willing as Mortimer showed himself to discuss the war generally, about his personal share he was as mute as a fish. Try as he would Desmond could get nothing out of him. Again and again, he brought the conversation round to personal topics; but every time his companion contrived to switch it back to general lines.

At last Desmond risked a direct question. By this time a pint of Pommery and Greno was tingling in his veins and he felt he didn't care if the roof fell in.

"Ever since Nur–el–Din told me yon were of the Crown Prince's personal service," he said, "I have been devoured with curiosity to know what you were doing before you came to England. Were you at Metz with his Imperial Highness? Did you see the assault at Verdun? Were you present at the capture of the Fort of Douaumont?" '

Mortimer shook his head, laughing, and held up a deprecating hand.

"Professional discretion, my dear fellow, professional discretion!" he retorted. "You know what it is!"

Then lowering his voice, he added:

"Between ourselves the less said about my connection with Master Willie the better. Our colleagues are already restless at what they consider my neglect of my professional work. They attribute it to the wiles of Nur–el–Din. They may if they like and I don't propose to disillusion them. You understand, Bellward?"

His voice was commanding and he bent his brows at Desmond, who hastened to protest that his discretion in the matter would be absolute.

When they had had their coffee and Mortimer was contentedly puffing one of Bellward's excellent double Coronas, Desmond rose from the table.

"If you will excuse me a minute," he said, "I will just go across to the library and see if my housekeeper has put all in order for our guests!"

Instantly Mortimer got up from the table.

"By all means," he said, and emptied his glass of brandy, "so, I will come with you!"

Mortimer meant to stick to him, thought Desmond; that was evident. Then an idea struck him. Why should he not telephone in Mortimer's presence? To ask for Mr. Elias was in no way incriminating and if help came promptly, Mortimer could be secured and the other spies pounced upon in their turn as they arrived.

Therefore, as soon as they reached the library, Desmond walked over to the desk and picked up the telephone receiver from its hook.

"Excuse me," he said to Mortimer, "I had forgotten I had to ring up Stanning!"

"Oh, dear," said Mortimer from his place on the hearth rug where he was warming his coat tails in front of the fire, "isn't that unfortunate? I wish I had known! Tut, tut, how annoying for you!"

The telephone seemed quite dead.

"I don't understand!" said Desmond to Mortimer. "What's annoying?"

"The telephone, my dear Bellward,"—Mortimer spoke in a pompous voice—"the telephone is the symbol of the age in which we live, the age of publicity but also of indiscretion. It is almost as indiscreet to have a telephone in your house as to keep a diary. Therefore, in view of our little party here this evening, to prevent us from being disturbed in any way, I took the liberty of... of severing the connection... temporarily, mind you, only temporarily; it shall be restored as soon as we break up. I have some small acquaintance with electrical engineering."

Desmond was silent. Disappointment had deprived him for the moment of the power of speech. It was to be man to man then, after all. If he was to secure Mortimer and the rest of the gang that night, he must do it on his own. He could not hope for aid. The prospect did not affright him. If Mortimer could have seen the other's eyes at that moment he might have remarked a light dancing in them that was not solely of Messrs. Pommery and Greno's manufacture.

"If I had known you wanted to use the instrument, my dear fellow," Mortimer continued in his bland voice, "I should certainly have waited until you had done your business!"

"Pray don't mention it," replied Desmond, "you do well to be prudent, Mr. Mortimer!"

Mortimer shot a sudden glance at him. Desmond met it with a frank, easy smile.

"I'm a devil for prudence myself!" he observed brightly.

CHAPTER XVIII. THE GATHERING OF THE SPIES

Action, or the promise of action, always acted on Desmond Okewood like a nerve tonic. His visit to the inn, followed by the fencing with Mortimer at dinner, had galvanized his nerves jaded with the inaction of the preceding days. He averted his eyes from the future, he put the past resolutely away. He bent his whole attention on the problem immediately before him—how to carry off the role of Bellward in front of four strangers, one of whom, at least, he thought, must know the man he was impersonating; how to extract as much information as possible about the gang and its organization before uncovering his hand; finally, how to overpower the four men and the one woman when the moment had come to strike.

Mortimer and he were in the library. By Desmond's direction old Martha had put out two bridge tables and cards. A tantalus stand with siphons and glasses, an assortment of different colored liqueurs in handsome cut–glass carafes and some plates of sandwiches stood on a side–table. At Mortimer's suggestion Desmond had told the housekeeper that, once the guests had arrived, she might go to bed.

The library was very still. There was no sound except for the solemn ticking of the clock on the mantelpiece or the occasional rustle of the evening paper in Mortimer's hand as he stood in front of the fire. Desmond was sitting on the settee, tranquilly smoking, studying Mortimer and thinking out the problem before him.

He measured Mortimer with his eye. The latter was a bigger man than Desmond in every way and Desmond suspected that he was even stronger than he looked. Desmond wondered whether he should try and overpower him then and there. The other was almost certain to carry a revolver, he thought, while he was unarmed. Failure, he knew, would ruin everything. The gang would disperse to the four winds of heaven while as for Mr. Bellward—well, he would certainly be "for it," as the soldiers say.

No, he must hold his hand until the meeting had taken place. This was the first conference that Mortimer had summoned, and Desmond intended to see that it should be the last. But first he meant to find out all there was to know about the working of the gang.

He resolved to wait and see what the evening would bring forth. The telephone was "a washout": the motor–cycle was now his only chance to summon aid for he knew it was hopeless to think of tackling single–handed odds of four to one (to say nothing of the lady in the case). It must be his business to make an opportunity to slip away on the motor–bike to Stanning. Ten minutes to get there, five minutes to deliver his message at the police station (if the Chief's people made their headquarters there), and ten minutes to get back if they had a car. Could he leave the meeting for 25 minutes without arousing suspicions? He doubted it; but it must be. There was no other way. And then with a shock that made him cold with fear he remembered Mortimer's motor–car.

If, during his absence, anything occurred to arouse their suspicions, the whole crowd could pile into the car and be away long before Desmond could be back with help. The fog had lifted and it was a clear night outside. The car would have to be got rid of before he left the house, that was all about it. But how? A means to that end must also be discovered as the evening progressed. By the way, what had Mortimer done with his car?

A very faint throbbing somewhere outside answered Desmond's unspoken question.

Mortimer flung aside his paper.

"Isn't that a car?" he asked, "that'll be they. I sent Max to Wentfield station to meet our friends!"

There was the sound of voices, of bustle in the hall. Then the door opened and a man came in. Desmond had a brief moment of acute suspense. Was he supposed to know him?

He was a short, ugly fellow with immensely broad shoulders, a heavy puffy face, a gross, broad nose, and a tooth-brush moustache. He might have been a butcher to look at. In the top edge of his coat lapel, he wore a small black pin with a glass head.

"Well, Max," said Mortimer. "Have you brought them all?"

The man was mustering Desmond with a suspicious, unfriendly stare.

"My friend, Bellward!" said Mortimer, clapping Desmond on the shoulder. "You've heard of Bellward, Max!"

And to Desmond's surprise he made some passes in the air.

The man's mien underwent a curious change. He became cringing; almost overawed.

"Reelly," he grunted, "reelly now! You don't siy! Glad to know yer, mister, I'm shore!"

He spoke with a vile snuffing cockney accent, and thrust out his hand to Desmond. Then he added to Mortimer:

"There's three on 'em. That's the count, ain't it? I lef' the car outside on the drive!"

At this moment two more of the guests entered: One was a tall, emaciated looking man of about fifty who seemed to be in the last stages of consumption; the other a slightly built young fellow with a shock of black hair brushed back and an olive complexion. He wore pince—nez and looked like a Russian revolutionary. They, too, wore the badge of the brotherhood—the black pin in the coat lapel.

"Goot efening, Mr. Mortimer," said the tall man in a guttural voice, "this is Behrend"—he indicated the young man by his side—"you haft not meet him no?"

Then, leaving Behrend to shake hands with Mortimer, he literally rushed at Desmond and shook him by the hand exactly as though he were working a pump handle.

"My tear Pellward," he cried, "it is a hondred year since I haf see you, not? And how are the powers!"

He lowered his voice and gazed mysteriously at him.

Desmond, at a loss what to make of this extraordinary individual, answered at random:

"The powers? Still fighting, I believe!"

The tall man stared open—mouthed at him for a moment. Then, clapping his hands together, he burst into a high—pitched cackle of laughter.

"A joke," he yelled, "a mos' excellent joke! I must tell this to Minna. My vriend, I haf not mean the great Powers."

He looked dramatically about him, then whispered:

"I mean, the oggult!"

Desmond, who was now quite out of his depth, wagged his head solemnly at the other as though to indicate that, his occult powers were something not to be lightly mentioned. He had no fear of the tall man, at any rate. He placed him as a very ordinary German, a common type in the Fatherland, simple—minded, pedantic, inquisitive,, and a prodigious bore withal but dangerous, for of this stuff German discipline kneads militarists.

155

But the door opened again to admit the last of the guests. A woman entered. Desmond was immediately struck by the contrast she presented to the others, Mortimer with his goggle eyes and untidy hair, Max, gross and bestial, Behrend, Oriental and shifty, and the scarecrow figure of the tall man.

Despite her age, which must have been nearly sixty, she still retained traces of beauty. Her features were very regular, and she had a pair of piercing black eyes of undimmed brightness. Her gray hair was tastefully arranged, and she wore a becoming black velvet gown with a black lace scarf thrown across the shoulders. A white silk rose was fastened to her bodice by a large black pin with a glass head.

Directly she appeared, the tall man shouted to her in German.

"Sag' mal, Minna..." he began.

Mortimer turned on him savagely.

"Hold your tongue, No. 13," he cried, "are you mad? What the devil do you mean by it? You know the rules!"

By way of reply, "No. 13" broke into a regular frenzy of coughing which left him gasping for breath.

"Pardon! I haf' forgot!" he wheezed out between the spasms.

The woman went over to Mortimer and put out tier gloved hand.

"I am Mrs. Malplaquet," she said in a pleasant voice. "And you are Mr. Mortimer, I think!"

Mortimer bowed low over her hand.

"Madame, I am charmed to meet one of whom I have heard nothing but praise," he said.

"Verry pretty!" replied Mrs. Malplaquet smiling. "They tell me you have a great way with the ladies, my dear sir!"

"But," she went on, "I am neglecting our host, my dear Mr. Bellward. How are you, my friend? How well you are looking... so young... so fresh! I declare you seem to have got five years younger!"

The keen black eyes searched Desmond's face. He felt horribly uncomfortable. The woman's eyes were like gimlets boring right into him. He suddenly felt that his disguise was a poor one. He remembered Crook's warning to be wary of women, and he inwardly quailed.

"I am so glad to meet you again!" he murmured. He didn't like Mrs. Malplaquet's eyes. They assorted strangely with the rest of her gentle and refined appearance. They were hard and cruel, those black eyes. Thy put him in mind of a snake.

"It is so long since I've seen you," she said, "that positively your voice seems to have changed."

"That's because I have a cold," said Desmond.

"Fiddlesticks!" retorted the lady, "the timbre is quite different! Bellward, I believe you're in love! Don't tell me you've been running after that hank of hair that Mortimer is so devoted to!" She glanced in Mortimer's direction, but that gentleman was engaged in earnest conversation with Behrend and the tall man.

"Whom do you meant" asked Desmond.

"Where are your eyes, man?" rapped out Mrs. Malplaquet. "The dancer woman, of course, Nur–el–what–do–you–call–it. There's the devil of a row brewing about the way our friend over there is neglecting us to run after the minx. They're getting sharp in this country, Bellward—I've lived here for forty years so I know what I'm talking about—and we can't afford to play any tricks. Mortimer will finish by bringing destruction on every one of us. And I shall tell him so tonight. And so will No. 13! And so will young Behrend! You ought to hear Behrend about it!"

Mrs. Malplaquet began to interest Desmond. She was obviously a woman of refinement, and he was surprised to find her in this odd company. By dint of careful questioning, he ascertained the fact that she lived in London, at a house on Campden Hill. She seemed to know a good many officers, particularly naval men.

"I've been keeping my eyes open as I promised, Bellward," she said, "and I believe I've got hold of a likely subject for you—a submarine commander he is, and very psychic. When will you come and meet him at my house?"

Mortimer's voice, rising above the buzz of conversation, checked his reply.

"If you will all sit down," he said, "we'll get down to business."

Despite all distractions, Desmond had been watching for this summons. He had marked down for himself a chair close to the door. For this he now made, after escorting Mrs. Malplaquet to the settee where she sat down beside Behrend. Max took the armchair on the left of the fireplace; while No. 13 perched himself grotesquely on a high music–stool, his long legs curled round the foot. Mortimer stood in his former position on the hearth, his back to the fire.

A very odd–looking band! Desmond commented to himself but he thought he could detect in each of the spies a certain ruthless fanaticism which experience taught him to respect as highly dangerous. And they all had hard eyes!

When they were seated, Mortimer said:

"About the 14th of this month the British Admiralty will begin the work of shipping to France ten divisions of American troops now training in this country. The most extraordinary precautions are being taken to complete this huge undertaking with success. It seems to me that the moment has come for us to demonstrate the efficiency of our new organization."

He looked round at his audience but no one said a word. Desmond felt very distinctly that there was a hostile atmosphere against Mortimer in that room.

"I asked you to come here to–night," Mortimer went on, "to discuss the plans for sending prompt and accurate information regarding the movements of these transports to the other side. I warn you that this time our mode of procedure will have to be radically different from the methods we have pursued on former occasions. To expend our energies in

158

collecting information at half a dozen different ports of war will be waste of time. The direction of the whole of this enterprise lies in the hands of one man at the Admiralty."

Behrend, who had struck Desmond as a rather taciturn young man, shook his head dubiously.

"That makes things very difficult," he remarked.

"Wait," replied Mortimer. "I agree, it is very difficult, the more so as I have reason to believe that the authorities have discovered the existence of our organization."

Mrs. Malplaquet and Behrend turned to one another simultaneously.

"What did I say?" said Behrend.

"I told you so," said the lady.

"Therefore," Mortimer resumed, "our former activities on the coast will practically be paralyzed. We shall have to confine our operations to London while Max and Mr. Behrend here will be entrusted with the task of getting the news out to our submarines."

No. 13 broke in excitedly.

"Vork in London, vork in London!" he cried. "It is too dangerous, my vriend. Vot do I know of London? Portsmouth" (he called it Portsmouse), Sout'ampton, the Isle of Vight... good... it is my province. But, London... it is senseless!"

Mortimer turned his gig–lamps on the interrupter.

"You will take your orders from me as before," he said quietly.

Behrend adjusted his pince–nez.

"No. 13 is perfectly right," he remarked, "he knows his territory, and he should be allowed to work there."

"You, too," Mortimer observed in the same calm tone as before, "will take your orders from me!"

With a quick gesture the young man dashed his long black hair out of his eyes.

"Maybe," he replied, "but only as long as I feel sure that your orders are worth following.

"Do you dare..." began Mortimer, shouting.

"... At present," the other continued, as though Mortimer had not spoken. "I don't feel at all sure that they are."

The atmosphere was getting a trifle heated, thought Desmond. If he judged Mortimer aright, he was not the man to let himself be dictated to by anybody. He was wondering how the scene would end when suddenly something caught his eye that took his mind right away from the events going forward in the room.

Opposite him, across the library, was a French window across which the curtains had been drawn. One of the curtains, however, had got looped up on a chair so that there was a gap at the bottom of the window showing the pane.

In this gap was a face pressed up against the glass. To his astonishment Desmond recognized the weather–beaten features of the odd man, Mr. John Hill. The face remained there only for a brief instant. The next moment it was gone and Desmond's attention was once more claimed by the progress of the conference.

"Do I understand that you refuse to serve under we any longer?" Mortimer was saying to Behrend, who had risen from the settee and stood facing him.

"As long as you continue to behave as you are doing at present," replied the other, "you may understand that!"

Mortimer made a quick dive for his pocket. In an instant Max had jumped at him and caught his arm.

"Don't be a fool!" he cried, "for Gawd's sake, put it away, carn't yer? D 'you want the 'ole ruddy plice abart our ears?"

"I'll have no disobedience of orders," roared Mortimer, struggling with the other. In his fist he had a big automatic pistol. It was a prodigious weapon, the largest pistol that Desmond had ever seen.

"He threatened him, he threatened him!" screamed No. 13 jumping about on his stool.

"Take it away from him, Max, for Heaven's sake!" cried the lady.

Everybody was talking at once. The noise was so loud that Desmond wondered whether old Martha would hear the din. He sat in his chair by the door, a silent witness of the scene. Then suddenly, at the height of the hubbub, he heard the faint humming of a motor–car. It lasted for perhaps thirty seconds, then gradually died away.

"What did it mean?" he asked himself. The only living being he knew of outside was John Hill, the odd man, whose face he had just seen; the only car was Mortimer's. Had the odd man gone off in Mortimer's car? He was thankful to note that, in the din, none save him seemed to have heard the car.

By this time Mortimer had put up his pistol and Mrs. Malplaquet was speaking. Her remarks were effective and very much to the point. She upbraided Mortimer with his long and mysterious absences which she attributed to his infatuation for Nur–el–Din and complained bitterly of the dancer's imprudence in consorting openly with notorious folk like Lazarro and Bryan Mowbury.

"I went to the girl myself," she said, "and begged her to be more circumspect. But Madame would not listen to advice; Madame was doubtless sure of her position with our revered leader, and thought she could reject the friendly counsel of one old enough to be her mother. Behrend and Max and No. 13 there—all of us—are absolutely agreed that we are not going on with this sort of thing any longer. If you are to remain in charge of our organization, Mr. Mortimer, we want to know where you are to be found and how you spend your time. In short, we want to be sure that you are not playing a game that most of us have at different times played on subordinate agents... I mean, that when the crisis comes, we fall into the trap and you walk away. You had better realize once and for all

161

that we are too old hands for that sort of trick."

Here Max took up the thread. "Mrs. Malplaquet had put it very strite, so she 'ad, and wot he wanted to know was what Mortimer 'ad to siy?"

Mortimer was very suave in his reply; a bad sign, thought Desmond, for it indicated that he was not sure of himself. He was rather vague, spoke about a vitally important mission that he had had to fulfil but which he had now brought to a successful conclusion, so that he was at length free to devote his whole attention once more to the great task in hand.

Behrend brought his fist crashing down on the arm of the settee.

"Words, words," he cried, "it won't do for me. Isn't there a man in the room besides me? You, Bellward, or you, Max, or you, No.13? Haven't you got any guts any of You? Are you going to sit here and listen to the soft soap of a fellow who has probably sent better men than himself to their death with tripe of this kind? It may do for you, but by the Lord, it won't do for me!"

Mortimer cleared his throat uneasily.

"Our host is silent," said Mrs. Malplaquet, "what does Mr. Bellward think about it?"

Desmond spoke up promptly.

"I think it would be very interesting to hear something further about this mission of Mortimer's," he observed:

Mortimer cast him a glance of bitter malice.

"Well," he said, after a pause, "you force my hand. I shall tell you of this mission of mine and. I shall show you the evidence, because it seems essential in the interests of our organization. But I assure you I shall not forget this want of confidence you have shown in me; and I shall see that you don't forget it, either!"

As he spoke, he glared fiercely at Desmond through his glasses.

162

"Let's hear about the precious mission," jeered Behrend, "let's see the evidence. The threats'll keep!"

Then Mortimer told them of how the Star of Poland came into Nur–el–Din's possession, and of the Crown Prince's embarrassment when the German authorities claimed it for the regalia of the new Kingdom of Poland.

"The Crown Prince," he said, "summoned me to him in person and gave me the order to make my way to England immediately and recover the gem at all costs and by any means. Did I whine or snivel about being sent to my death as some of you were doing just now? No! That is not the way of the Prussian Guard..."

The Prussian Guard?" cried No. 13 in an awed voice. "Are you also of the Prussian Guard, comrade?"

He had risen from his seat and there was something almost of majesty about his thin, ungainly figure as he drew himself to his full height.

"Ay, comrade, I was," replied Mortimer.

"Then," cried No. 13, "you are..."

"No names, comrade," warned Mortimer, "no names, I beg!"

"No names, no names!" repeated the other and relapsed into his seat in a reverie.

"How I got to England," Mortimer continued, "matters nothing; how I fulfilled my mission is neither here nor there. But I recovered the gem and the proof..."

He thrust a hand into the inner pocket of his coat and plucked out a white paper package sealed up with broad red seals.

Desmond held his breath. It was the white paper package, exactly as Barbara had described.

"Look at it well, Behrend," said Mortimer, holding it up for the young man to see, "it cost me a man's life to get that. If it had sent twenty men to their death, I should have had it just the same!"

Mrs. Malplaquet clapped her hands, her eyes shining.

"Bravo, bravo!" she exclaimed, "that's the spirit! That's the way to talk, Mortimer!"

"Cut it out," snarled Behrend, "and let's see the goods!"

All had left their seats and were gathered in a group about Mortimer as he began to break the gleaming red wag seals. One by one he burst them, the white paper slipped off and disclosed... a box of cigarettes.

Mortimer stood gazing in stupefaction at the gaudy green and gold lettering of the box. Then, running his thumb-nail swiftly along the edge of the box, he broke the paper wrapping, the box burst open and a shower of cigarettes fell to the ground.

"So that's your Star of Poland, is it?" cried Behrend in a mocking voice.

"Wot 'ave yer done wiv' the sparklers, eh?" demanded Max, catching Mortimer roughly by the arm.

But Mortimer stood, aimlessly shaking the empty box in front of him, as though to convince himself that the gem was not there. Behrend fell on his knees and raked the pile of cigarettes over and over with his fingers.

"Nothing there!" he shouted angrily, springing to his feet. "It's all bluff! He's bluffing to the end! See, he doesn't even attempt to find his famous jewel! He knows it isn't there!"

But Mortimer paid no heed. He was staring straight in front of him, a strangely woe-begone figure with his thatch of untidy hair and round goggle eyes. Then the cigarette box fell to the floor with a crash as Mortimer's hands dropped, with, a hopeless gesture, to his sides.

"Barbara Mackwayte!" he whispered in a low voice, not seeming to realize that he was speaking aloud, "so that's what she wanted with Nur–el–Din!"

Desmond was standing at Mortimer's elbow and caught the whisper. As he heard Mortimer speak Barbara's name, he had a sudden premonition that his own unmasking was imminent, though he understood as little of the purport of the other's remark as of the pile of cigarettes lying on the carpet. As Mortimer turned to look at him, Desmond nerved himself to meet the latter's gaze. But Mortimer's face wore the look of a desperate man. There was no recognition in his eyes.

Not so with Desmond. Perhaps the bitterness of his disappointment had made Mortimer careless, perhaps the way in which he had pronounced Barbara's name struck a familiar chord in Desmond's memory. The unkempt hair brushed down across the forehead, the thick glasses, the heavy moustache still formed together an impenetrable mask which Desmond's eyes failed to pierce. But now he recalled the voice. As Mortimer looked at him, the truth dawned on Desmond and he knew that the man standing beside him was Maurice Strangwise, his comrade–in–arms in France.

At that very moment a loud crash rang through the room, a cold blast of damp air came rushing in and the lamp on the table flared up wildly, flickered an instant and went out, leaving the room in darkness save for the glow of the fire.

A deep voice cried:

"May I ask what you are all doing in my house?"

The secret door of the bookshelves had swung back and there, framed in the gaping void, Desmond saw the dark figure of a man.

CHAPTER XIX. THE UNINVITED GUEST

There are moments in life when the need for prompt action is so urgent that thought, decision and action must be as one operation of the brain. In the general consternation following on the dramatic appearance of this uninvited guest, Desmond had a brief respite in which to think over his position.

Should he make a dash for it or stay where he was and await developments?

Without a second's hesitation; he decided on the latter course. With the overpowering odds against him it was more than doubtful whether he could ever reach the library door. Besides, to go was to abandon absolutely all hope of capturing the gang; for his flight would warn the conspirators that the game was up. On the other hand, the new−comer might be an ally, perhaps an emissary of the Chief's. The strange behavior of the odd man had shown that something was afoot outside of which those in the library were unaware. Was the uninvited guest the deus ex machina who was to help him, Desmond, out of his present perilous fix?

Meanwhile the stranger had stepped into the room, drawing the secret door to behind him. Desmond heard his heavy step and the dull thud of the partition swinging into place. The sound seemed to break the spell that hung over the room.

Mortimer was the first to recover his presence of mind. Crying out to No. 13 to lock the door leading into the hall, he fumbled for a moment at the table. Desmond caught the noise of a match being scratched and the next moment the library was again bathed in the soft radiance of the lamp.

Picking up the light, Mortimer strode across to the stranger.

"What do you want here" he demanded fiercely, "and who the devil..."

He broke off without completing his sentence, drawing back in amazement. For the rays of the lamp fell upon the pale face of a stoutish, bearded man, veering towards middle age standing in front of Mortimer. And the face was the face of the stoutish, bearded man, veering towards middle age, who stood in the shadow a few paces behind Mortimer. Each man was a complete replica of the other, save that the face of the new arrival was thin and haggard with that yellowish tinge which comes from long confinement.

As Mortimer staggered back, the uninvited guest recoiled in his turn. He was staring fixedly across the room at his double who met his gaze firmly, erect, tense, silent. The others looked in sheer stupefaction from one to the other of the two Mr. Bellwards. For nearly a minute the only sound in the room was the deep ticking of the clock, counting away the seconds separating him from eternity, Desmond thought.

It was Mrs. Malplaquet who broke the silence. Suddenly her nerves snapped under the strain, and she screamed aloud.

"A—ah!" she cried, "look! There are two of them! No, no, it can't be!"

And she sank half fainting on the sofa.

Behrend whipped out a pistol from his hip pocket and thrust it in Mortimer's face.

"Is this another of your infernal surprise packets?" he demanded fiercely.

All the spies seemed on a sudden to be armed, Desmond noted, all, that is, save Mrs. Malplaquet who lay cowering on the settee. Mortimer had pulled out his super–Mauser; No. 13, who was guarding the door, had a revolver in his hand, and Behrend, as has been stated, was threatening Mortimer with his Browning.

Now Max advanced threateningly into the room, a long seaman's knife in his hand..

"Put that blarsted shooting–iron awiy!" he snarled at Mortimer, "and tell us wot's the little gime, will yer! Come on, egpline!"

With absolute self–possession Mortimer turned from the stranger to Desmond.

"I think it is up to the twins to explain," he said almost nonchalantly, "suppose we hear what this gentleman, who arrived so surprisingly through the book–shelves, has to say?"

Though threatened with danger from two sides, from the gang and possibly, as far as he knew, from the stranger, Mortimer was perfectly calm. Desmond never admired Maurice Strangwise more than in that moment. All eyes now turned questioningly towards the new arrival. As for Desmond he drew back as far as he dared into the shadow. He knew he was in the direst peril; but he was not afraid for himself. He was crushed to the ground by the sickening feeling that he was going to be beaten, that the gang were going to slip through his fingers after all... and he was powerless to prevent it.

He guessed at once what had happened. Bellward must have escaped from custody; for there was no disguise about this pale, flustered creature who had the cowed look of a hunted man in his eyes. He must have come to the Mill House to get his motorcycle; for he surely would have known that the villa would be the first place to which the police would follow him up.

Desmond saw a little ray of hope. If—it was a very big if—Bellward's flight were discovered promptly, the police might be expected to reach the Mill House very soon behind him. Bellward must have come straight there; for he had not even taken the very elementary precaution of shaving off his beard. That made Desmond think that he must have escaped some time that evening after the barbers' shops were closed.

With thumping heart, with bated breath, he waited for what was to come. In a very little while, he told himself, the truth must come out. His only chance was to try and bluff his way out of this appalling dilemma and above all, at all costs—this was the essential fact which, he told himself, he must keep steadfastly before his eyes—not to lose sight of Mortimer whatever happened.

Bellward's voice—and its tones showed Desmond what an accomplished mime Crook had been—broke the silence.

"I have nothing to explain," he said, turning from the sofa where he had been exchanging a few words in an undertone with Mrs. Malplaquet, "this is my house. That is sufficient explanation for my presence here, I imagine. But I confess I am curious to know what this person"—he indicated Desmond—"is doing in my clothes, if I mistake not, giving what I take to be a very successful impersonation of myself."

Then Desmond stepped boldly out of the shadow into the circle of light thrown by the lamp.

"I don't know what you all think," he said firmly, but it seems to me singularly unwise for us to stand here gossiping when there is a stranger amongst us. I fail to understand the motive of this gentleman in breaking into my house by my private door, wearing my clothes, if I am to believe my eyes; but I clearly realize the danger of admitting strangers to a gathering of this kind."

"Quite right," agreed Behrend, nodding his head in assent.

"You have had one singular surprise to–night already," Desmond resumed, "in the matter of the jewel which our respected leader was about to show us: if you recollect, our friend was only prevented from giving us the explanation which he certainly owed us over his little hoax by the arrival, the most timely arrival, of his confederate..."

"Confederate?" shouted Mortimer, "what the devil do you mean by that?"

"Yes, confederate," Desmond repeated. "Max, Behrend, Mrs. Malplaquet, all of you, look at this wretched fellow"—he pointed a finger of scorn at Bellward—"trembling with fright at the role that has been thrust upon him, to force his way into our midst, to give his accomplice the tip to clear out before the police arrive."

"Stop!" exclaimed Mortimer, raising his pistol. Behrend caught his hand.

"We'll hear you in a minute!" he said.

"Let him finish!" said Mrs. Malplaquet, and there was a certain ominous quietness in her tone that startled Desmond.

As for Bellward, he remained silent, with arms folded, listening very intently.

"Doubtless, this double of mine," continued Desmond in a mocking voice, "is the bearer of the Star of Poland, the wonderful jewel which has required our beloved leader to devote so much of his time to a certain charming lady. Bah! are you going to let a man like this," and he pointed to Mortimer disdainfully with his hand, "a man who puts you in the fighting line while he amuses himself in the rear, are you going to let this false friend, this bogus spy, cheat you like this? My friends, my advice to you, if you don't want to have another and yet more disagreeable surprise, is to make sure that this impudent imposter is not here for the purpose of selling us all!"

He raised his voice until it rang through the room, at the same time looking round the group at the faces of the spies to see how his harangue had worked upon their feelings. Max and Behrend, he could see, were on his side; No. 13 was obviously, undecided; Mortimer and Bellward were, of course, against him; Mrs. Malplaquet sat with her hands in her lap, her eyes cast down, giving no sign.

"It's high time..." Mortimer began violently but Mrs. Malplaquet put up her hand and checked him.

"Better hear Bellward!" she said softly.

"I know nothing of what has been taking place in my absence," he said, "either here or outside. I only know that I escaped from the escort that was taking me back from Scotland Yard to Brixton Prison this evening and that the police are hard on my track. I have delayed too long as, it is. Every one of us in this room, with the exception of the traitor who is amongst us"—he pointed a finger in denunciation at Desmond—"is in the most imminent peril as long as we stay here. The rest of you can please yourselves. I'm off!"

He turned and pressed the spring. The book shelves swung open. Behrend sprang forward.

"Not so fast," he cried. " Yon don't leave this room until we know who you are!"

And he covered him with his pistol.

"Fool!" exclaimed Bellward who had stopped on the threshold of the secret door, "do you want to trap the lot of us! Tell him, Minna," he said to Mrs. Malplaquet, "and for Heaven's sake, let us be gone!"

Mrs. Malplaquet stood up.

"This is Basil Bellward," she said, "see, he's wearing the ring I gave him, a gold snake with emerald eyes! And now," she cried, raising her voice shrilly, "before we go, kill that man!"

And she pointed at Desmond.

Bellward had seized her by the arm and was dragging her through the opening in the shed when a shrill whistle resounded from the garden. Without any warning Mortimer swung round and fired point–blank at Desmond. But Desmond had stooped to spring at the other and the bullet went over his head. With ears singing from the deafening report of the pistol in the confined space, with the acrid smell of cordite in his nostrils, Desmond leapt at Mortimer's throat, hoping to bear him to the ground before he could shoot again. As he sprang he heard the crash of glass and a loud report. Someone cried out sharply "Oh!" as though in surprise and fell prone between him and his quarry; then he stumbled and at the same time received a crashing blow on the head. Without a sound he dropped to the ground across a body that twitched a little and then lay still.

* * * * * *

Somewhere in the far, far distance Desmond heard a woman crying—long drawn-out wailing lamentations on a high, quavering note. He had a dull, hard pain in his head which felt curiously stiff. Drowsily he listened for a time to the woman's sobbing, so tired, so curiously faint that he scarcely cared to wonder what it signified. But at last it grated on him by its insistency and he opened his eyes to learn the cause of it.

His bewildered gaze fell upon what seemed to him a gigantic, ogre–like face, as huge, as grotesque, as a pantomime mask. Beside it was a light, a brilliant light, that hurt his eyes.

Then a voice, as faint as a voice on a long distance telephone, said:

"Well, how are you feeling?"

The voice was so remote that Desmond paid no attention to it. But he was rather surprised to hear a voice reply, a voice that came from his own lips, curiously enough:

"Fine!"

So he opened his eyes again to ascertain the meaning of this phenomenon. This time the ogre–like face came into focus, and Desmond saw a man with a tumbler in his hand bending over him.

"That's right," said the man, looking very intently at him, "feel a bit better, eh? Got a bit of a crack, what? Just take a mouthful of brandy... I've got it here!"

Desmond obediently swallowed the contents of the glass that the other held to his lips. He was feeling horribly weak, and very cold. His collar and shirt were unbuttoned, and his neck and shoulders were sopping wet with water. On his ears still fell the wailing of the woman.

"Corporal," said the man bending over him, "just go and tell that old hag to hold her noise! She'll have to go out of the house if she can't be quiet!"

Desmond opened his eyes again. He was lying on the settee in the library. A tall figure in khaki, who had been stirring the fire with his boot, turned at the doctor's summons and left the room. On the table the lamp was still burning but its rays were neutralized by the glare of a crimson dawn which Desmond could see flushing the sky through the shattered panes of the French window. In the centre of the floor lay a long object covered by a tablecloth, beside it a table overturned with a litter of broken glass strewn about the carpet.

The woman's sobbing ceased. The corporal came back into the room.

"She'll be quiet now, sir," he said, "I told her to get you and the gentlemen a cup o' tea."

Then, to Desmond, he said:

"Nasty ding you got, sir! My word, I thought they'd done for you when I come in at the winder!"

The telephone on the desk tingled sharply. The door opened at the same moment and a shabby little old man with sandy side whiskers and moleskin trousers came briskly in.

His appearance had a curious effect on the patient on the settee. Despite the doctor's restraining hand, he struggled into a sitting position, staring in bewilderment at the shabby old man who had gone straight to the telephone and lifted the receiver. And well might Desmond stare; for here was Mr. John Hill, the odd man, talking on the telephone. And his voice...

"Well?" said the man at the telephone, curtly.

"Yes, speaking. You've got her, eh? Good. What's that? Well, that's something. No trace of the others? Damn!"

He slammed down the receiver and turned to face the settee.

"Francis!" cried Desmond.

And then he did a thing highly unbecoming in a field officer. He burst into tears.

CHAPTER XX. THE ODD MAN

Desmond and Francis Okewood sat in the dining–room of the Mill House finishing an excellent breakfast of ham and eggs and coffee which old Martha had prepared for them.

Francis was still wearing Mr. John Hill's greasy jacket and moleskins, but the removal of the sandy whiskers and a remarkable wig, consisting of a bald pate with a fringe of reddish hair, had gone far to restore him to the semblance of his former self.

Desmond was feeling a good deal better. His head had escaped the full force of the smashing blow dealt at him by Strangwise with the butt of his pistol. He had instinctively put up his arm to defend his face and the thickly padded sleeve of Bellward's jacket had broken the force of the blow. Desmond had avoided a fractured skull at the price of an appalling bruise on the right forearm and a nasty laceration of the scalp.

Francis had resolutely declined to enlighten him as to the events of the night until both had breakfasted. After despatching the corporal of military police to hurry the housekeeper on with the breakfast, Francis had taken his brother straight to the dining–room, refusing to let him ask the questions which thronged his brain until they had eaten and drunk. Only when all the ham and eggs had disappeared, did Francis, lighting one of Mr. Bellward's cigars, consent to satisfy his brother's curiosity.

"It was only yesterday morning," he said, "that I landed at Folkstone from the Continent. How I got the Chief's message recalling me and how I made my escape through the Turkish lines to Allenby's headquarters is a long story which will keep. The Chief had a car waiting for me at Folkstone and I reached London in time to lunch with him. We had a long talk and he gave me carte blanche to jump into this business now, when and where I thought I could best help you."

Desmond smiled bitterly.

"The Chief couldn't trust me to make good on my own, I suppose," he said.

"The Chief had a very good idea of the character of the people you had to deal with, Des.," retorted Francis, "and he was a trifle apprehensive that the role you were playing might lead to complications, supposing the gang were to see through your impersonation. He's a wonderful man, that, Des., and he was dead right—as he always is."

"But how?" asked Desmond. "Did the crowd spot me?"

"No," answered the other; "but it was your disguise which was responsible for the escape of Strangwise—"

"What?" cried Desmond. "He's escaped after all!"

Francis nodded.

"Yes," he said, "got clear away and left no trace. Wait a minute and you shall hear! When I have told my story, you shall tell yours and between us, we'll piece things together!

"Well, when I left the Chief yesterday, I came down here. The description of Mr. John Hill, your odd man, rather tickled my fancy. I wanted badly to get at you for a quiet chat and it seemed to me that if I could borrow Mr. Hill's appearance for a few hours now and then I might gain access to you without rousing any suspicion. You see, I knew that old Hill left here about dusk every afternoon, so I guessed the coast would be clear.

"Clarkson's fitted me out with the duds and the make-up and I got down to Wentfield by half-past six. The fog was so infernally thick that it took me more than an hour to get here on foot. It must have been close on eight o'clock when I pushed open your front gate. I thought of going boldly into the kitchen and asking for you, but, fortunately, I decided to have a preliminary prowl round the place. Through a chink in the curtains of the library I saw you and a stranger talking together. The stranger was quite unknown to me; but one thing about him I spotted right off. I saw that he was disguised; so I decided to hang about a bit and await developments.

"I loafed around in the fog for about half an hour. Then I heard a car coming up the drive. I hid myself in the rhododendron bush opposite the front door and saw two men and a woman get out. They hurried into the house, so that I didn't have a chance of seeing their faces. But I got a good, glimpse of the chauffeur as he bent down to turn out the headlights. And, yes, I knew him!"

"Max, they called him," said Desmond.

"His name was Mirsky when last I saw him," answered Francis, "and mine was Apfelbaum, if you want to know. He was a German agent in Russia and as ruthless and unscrupulous a rascal as you'll find anywhere in the German service. I must say I never thought he'd have the nerve to show his face in this country, though I believe he's a Whitechapel Jew born and bred. However, there he was and the sight of his ugly mug told me that something was doing. But like a fool I decided to hang on a bit and watch, instead of going right off in that car and fetching help from Stanning."

"It was just as well you waited," said Desmond, "for if you'd gone off at once they must have heard the car and the fat would have been in the fire straight away!"

And he told Francis of the loud dispute among the confederates in the library, the noise of which had effectually covered the sound of the departing ear.

Francis laughed.

"From my observation post outside," he said, "I could only see you, Des, and that blackguard, Mug, as you two were sitting opposite the window. I couldn't see more than the feet of the others. But your face told me the loud voices which reached me even outside meant that a crisis of some sort was approaching, so I thought it was time to be up and doing. So I sneaked round to the front of the house, got the engine of the car going and started off down the drive.

"I had the very devil of a job to get to Stanning. Ever since you've been down here, the Chief has had special men on duty day and night at the police–station there. I didn't dare stop to light the head–lamps and as a result the first thing I did was to charge the front gate and get the back wheel so thoroughly jammed that it took me the best part of twenty minutes to get the blooming car clear. When at last I got to the station, I found that

175

Matthews, the Chief's man, you know, had just arrived by car from London with a lot of plain–clothes men and some military police. He was in the very devil of a stew. He told me that Bellward had escaped, that the Chief was out of town for the night and ungetatable, and that he (Matthews) had come down on his own to prevent the gaff being blown on you and also to recapture Mr. Bellward if he should be mad enough to make for his old quarters.

"I told Matthews of the situation up at the Mill House. Neither of us was able to understand why you had not telephoned for assistance—we only discovered later that the telephone had been disconnected—but I went bail that you were up against a very stiff proposition. I told Matthews that, by surrounding the house, we might capture the whole gang.

"Matthews is a cautious cuss and he wanted a good deal of persuading, so we lost a lot of time. In the end, he wouldn't take my advice to rush every available man to the scene, but only consented to take two plainclothes men and two military police. He was so precious afraid of upsetting your arrangements. The Chief, it appears, had warned everybody against doing that. So we all piled into the car and I drove them back to the Mill House.

"This time I left the car at the front gate and we went up to the house on foot. We had arranged that Matthews and one of the military police, both armed, should stay and guard the car, while the two plainclothes men and the other military policeman, the corporal here, should accompany me to the house. Matthews believed my yarn that we were only going to 'investigate.' What I intended to do in reality was to round up the whole blessed lot.

"I put one of the plain–clothes men on the front door and the other round at the back of the house. Their orders were to stop anybody who came out and at the same time to whistle for assistance. The corporal and I went to our old observation post outside the library window.

"The moment I glanced into the room I knew that matters had reached a climax. I saw you—looking pretty blue, old man—facing that woman who seemed to be denouncing you. Max stood beside you with a pistol, and beside him was our friend, Mortimer, with a regular whopper of an automatic. Before I had time to move, the plain–clothes man at the back of the house whistled. He had found the secret door with Bellward and the woman coming out of it.

Then I saw Mortimer fire point—blank at you. I had my gun out in a second, but I was afraid of shooting, for fear of hitting you as you went for the other man.

"But the corporal at my side wasn't worrying much about you. Just as you jumped he put up his gun and let fly at Mortimer with a sense of discrimination which does him infinite credit. He missed Mortimer, but plugged Max plumb through the forehead and my old friend dropped in his tracks right between you and the other fellow. On that we hacked our way through the French window. The corporal found time to have another shot and laid out a tall, odd—looking man..."

"No. 13," elucidated Desmond.

"... When we got inside we found him dead across the threshold of the door leading into the hall. Behrend we caught hiding in a brush cupboard by the back stairs. As for the others—"

"Gone?" queried Desmond with a sudden sinking at his heart.

Francis nodded.

"We didn't waste any time getting through that window," he said, "but the catch was stiff and the broken glass was deuced unpleasant. Still, we were too late. You were laid out on the floor; Mortimer, Bellward and the lady had made their lucky escape. And the secret door showed us how they had gone..."

"But I thought you had a man posted at the back?"

"Would you believe it? When the shooting began, the infernal idiot must rush round to our assistance, so, of course, Mortimer and Co., nipping out by the secret door, got clear away down the drive. But that is not the worst. Matthews gave them the car!"

"No!" said Desmond incredulously.

"He did, though," answered Francis. "Mind you, Mortimer had had the presence of mind to throw off his disguise. He presented himself to Matthews as Strangwise. Matthews knows Strangwise quite well: he has often seen him with the Chief.

"'My God, Captain Strangwise,' says Matthews, as the trio appeared, 'What's happened?'

"'You're wanted up at the house immediately, Matthews,' says Strangwise quite excitedly. 'We're to take the car and go for assistance.'

"Matthews had a look at Strangwise's companions, and seeing Bellward, of course, takes him for you. As for the lady, she had a black lace muffler wound about her face.

"'Miss Mackwayte's coming with us, Matthews,' Strangwise says, seeing Matthews look at the lady. That removed the last of any lurking suspicions that old Matthews might have had. He left the military policeman at the gate and tore off like mad up the drive while Strangwise and the others jumped into the car and were away before you could say 'knife.' The military, policeman actually cranked up the car for them!

"When Matthews burst into the library with the story of you and Strangwise and Miss Mackwayte having gone off for help in our only car, I knew we had been sold. You were there, knocked out of time on the floor, in your disguise as Bellward, so I knew that the man with Strangwise was the real Bellward and I consequently deduced that Strangwise was Mortimer and consequently the very man we had to catch.

"We were done brown. If we had had a little more time to think things out, we should have found that motor–bike and I would have gone after the trio myself. But my first idea was to summon aid. I tried to telephone without success and then we found the wire cut outside. Then I had the idea of pumping Behrend. I found him quite chatty and furious against Mortimer, whom he accused of having sold them. He told us that the party would be sure to make for the Dyke Inn, as Nur–el–Din was there.

"By this time Strangwise and his party had got at least an hour clear start of us. I had set a man to repair the telephone and in the meantime was thinking of sending another on foot to Stanning to fetch one of our cars. Then I found the motor–bike and despatched one of the military policemen on it to Stanning.

"In about half an hour's time he was back with a car in which were Gordon and Harrison and some more military police. I put Matthews in charge of the party and sent them off to the Dyke Inn, though I felt pretty sure we were too late to catch the trio. That was really the reason I stayed behind; besides, I wanted to look after you. I got a turn when I saw you spread out all over the carpet, old man, I can tell you."

Desmond, who had listened with the most eager attention, did not speak for a minute. The sense of failure was strong upon him. How he had bungled it all!

"Look here," he said presently in a dazed voice, "you said just now that Matthews mistook Mrs. Malplaquet for Miss Mackwayte. Why should Matthews think that Miss Mackwayte was down here? Did she come down with you?"

Francis looked at him quickly.

"That crack on the head makes you forget things," he said. "Don't you remember Miss Mackwayte coming down here to see you yesterday afternoon Matthews thought she had stayed on..."

Desmond shook his head.

"She's not been here," he replied I'm quite positive about that!"

Francis sprang to his feet.

"Surely you must be mistaken," he said in tones of concern. "The Chief sent her down yesterday afternoon on purpose to see you. She reached Wentfield Station all right; because the porter told Matthews that she asked him the way to the Mill House."

An ominous foreboding struck chill at Desmond's heart. He held his throbbing head for an instant. Someone had mentioned Barbara that night in the library but who was it? And what had he said?

Ah! of course, it was Strangwise. "So that's what she wanted with Nur-el-Din!" he had said;

179

Desmond felt it all coming back to him now. Briefly he told Francis of his absence from the Mill House in response to the summons from Nur–el–Din, of his interview with the dancer and her story of the Star of Poland, of his hurried return just in time to meet Mortimer, and of Mortimer's enigmatical reference to the dancer in the library that night.

Fancis looked graver and graver as the story proceeded. Desmond noted it and reproached himself most bitterly with his initial failure to inform the Chief of the visits of Nur–el–Din and Mortimer to the Mill House. When he had finished speaking, he did not look at Francis, but gazed mournfully out of the window into the chilly drizzle of a sad winter's day.

"I don't like the look of it at all, Des," said his brother shaking his head, "but first we must make sure that there has been no misunderstanding about Miss Mackwayte. You say your housekeeper was already here when you came back from the Dyke Inn. She may have seen her. Let's have old Martha in!"

Between fright, bewilderment and indignation at the invasion of the house, old Martha was, if anything, deafer and more stupid than usual. After much interrogation they had to be satisfied with her repeated assertion that "she 'adn't seen no young lady" and allowed her to hobble back to her kitchen.

The two brothers stared at one another blankly. Francis was the first to speak. His eyes were shining and his manner was rather tense.

"Des," he asked; "what do you make of it? From what Strangwise let fall in the library here tonight, it seems probable that Miss Mackwayte, instead of coming here to see you as she was told—or she may have called during your absence—went to the Dyke Inn and saw Nur–el–Din. The muffed cry you heard at the inn suggests foul play to me and that suspicion is deepened in my mind by the fact that Matthews found Nur–el–Din at the Dyke Inn, as he reported to me by telephone just now; but he says nothing about Miss Mackwayte. Des, I fear the worst for that poor girl if she has fallen into the hands of that gang!"

Desmond remained silent for a moment. He was trying to piece things together as best as his aching head would allow. Both Nur–el–Din and Strangwise were after the jewel. Nur–el–Din believed that afternoon that Strangwise had it, while Strangwise, on discovering his loss, had seemed to suggest that Barbara Mackwayte had recovered it.

"Either Strangwise or Nur–el–Din, perhaps both of them," said Desmond, "must know what has become of Miss Mackwayte."

And he explained his reasoning to Francis. His brother nodded quickly.

"Then Nur–el–Din shall tell us," he answered sternly.

"They've arrested her?" asked Desmond with a sudden pang.

"Yes," said Francis curtly. But too late to prevent a crime being committed. When Matthews and his party arrived. they found Nur–el–Din in the very act of leaving the inn. The landlord, Rass, was lying dead on the floor of the tap–room with a bullet through the temple. That looks to me, Des, as though Nur–el–Din had recovered the jewel!"

"But Rass is a compatriot of hers," Desmond objected.

"But he was also an inconvenient witness of her dealings with Strangwise," retorted Francis. "If either Nur–el–Din or Strangwise have regained possession of the Star of Poland, Des, I fear the worst for Barbara Mackwayte. Come in!"

The corporal stood, saluting, at the door.

"Mr. Matthews on the telephone, sir!"

Francis hurried away, leaving Desmond to his thoughts, which were not of the most agreeable. Had he been wrong in thinking Nur–el–Din a victim? Was he, after all, nothing but a credulous fool who had been hoodwinked by a pretty woman's play–acting? And had he sacrificed Barbara Mackwayte to his obstinacy and his credulousness?

Francis burst suddenly into the room.

Des," he cried, "they've found Miss Mackwayte's hat on the floor of the tap–room... it is stained with blood..."

Desmond felt himself growing pale:

"And the girl herself," he asked thickly, "what of her?"

Francis shook his head.

"Vanished," he replied gravely. "Vanished utterly.

Desmond," he added, "we must go over to the Dyke Inn at once!"

CHAPTER XXI. THE BLACK VELVET TOQUE

Across Morsted Fen the day was breaking red and sullen. The brimming dykes, fringed with bare pollards, and the long sheets of water spread out across the lush meadows, threw back the fiery radiance of the sky from their gleaming surface. The, tall poplars about the Dyke Inn stood out hard and clear in the ruddy light; beyond them the fen, stretched away to the flaming horizon gloomy and flat and desolate, with nothing higher than the stunted pollards visible against the lurid background.

Upon the absolute silence of the scene there presently broke the steady humming of a car. A great light, paled by the dawn, came bobbing and sweeping, along the road that skirted the fen's edge. A big open car drew up by the track and branched, off to the inn. Its four occupants consulted together for an instant and then alighted. Three of them were in plain clothes; the other was a soldier. The driver was also in khaki.

"They're astir, Mr. Matthews," said one, of the plain clothes men, pointing towards the house, "see, there's a light in the inn!"

They followed the direction of his finger and saw a beam of yellow light gleaming from among the trees.

"Get your guns out, boys!" said Matthews. "Give them a chance to put their hands up, and if they don't obey, shoot!"

Very swiftly but very quietly, the four men picked their way over the miry track to the little bridge leading to the yard in front of the inn. The light they had remarked shone from the inn door, a feeble, flickering light as of an expiring candle.

Matthews, who was leading, halted and listened. Everything was quite still. Above their head the inn sign groaned uneasily as it was stirred by the fresh morning breeze.

"You, Gordon," whispered Matthews to the man behind him—they had advanced in Indian file—"take Bates and go round to the back. Harrison will go in by the front with me."

Even as he spoke a faint noise came from the interior of the house. The four men stood stock-still and listened. In the absolute stillness of the early morning, the sound fell distinctly on their ears. It was a step—a light step—descending the stairs.

Gordon and the soldier detached themselves from the party as Matthews and the other plain clothes man crossed the bridge swiftly and went up to the inn door. Hardly had Matthews got his foot on the stone step of the threshold than, a piercing shriek resounded from the room quite close at hand. The next minute a flying figure burst out of the door and fell headlong into the arms of Matthews who was all but overbalanced by the force of the impact.

He closed with the figure and grappled it firmly. His arms encountered a frail, light body, shaking from head to foot, enveloped in a cloak of some soft, thick material.

"It's a woman!" cried Matthews.

"It's Nur-el-Din!" exclaimed his companion in the same breath, seizing the woman by the arm.

The dancer made no attempt to escape. She stood with bowed head, trembling violently, in a cowering, almost a crouching posture.

Harrison, who had the woman by the arm, had turned her head so that he could see her face. She was deathly pale and her black eyes were wide open, the pupils dilated. Her teeth were chattering in her head. She seemed incapable of speech or motion.

183

"Nur–el–Din?" exclaimed Matthews in accents of triumph. "Bring her in, Harrison, and let's have a look at her!"

But the woman recoiled in terror. She arched her body stiff, like a child in a passion, and strained every muscle to remain where she was cowering by the inn–door.

"Come on, my girl," said the man not unkindly, "don't you 'ear wot the Guv'nor sez! In you go!"

Then the girl screamed aloud.

"No, no!" she cried, "not in that house! For the love of God, don't take me back into that room! Ah! For pity's sake, let me stay outside! Take me to prison but not, not into that house again!"

She half fell on her knees in the mire, pleading, entreating, her body shaken by sobs.

Then Harrison, who was an ex–Guardsman and a six–footer at that, plucked her off her feet and carried her, still struggling, still imploring with piteous cries, over the threshold into the house: Matthews followed behind.

The shutters of the tap–room were still closed. Only a strip of the dirty floor, strewn with sawdust, was illuminated by a bar of reddish light from the daybreak outside. On the table a candle, burnt down to the socket of its brass candlestick, flared and puttered in a riot of running wag. Half in the bar of daylight from outside, half in the darkness beyond the open door, against which the flickering candlelight struggled feebly, lay the body of a yellow–faced, undersized man with a bullet wound through the temple.

Without effort Harrison deposited his light burden on her feet by the table. Instantly, the girl fled, like some frightened animal of the woods, to the farthest corner of the room. Here she dropped sobbing on her knees, rocking herself to and fro in a sort of paroxysm of hysteria. Harrison moved quickly round the table after her; but he was checked by a cry from Matthews who was kneeling by the body.

"Let her be," said Matthews, "she's scared of this and no wonder! Come here a minute, Harrison, and see if you know, this chap!"

184

Harrison crossed the room and looked down at the still figure. He whistled softly.

"My word!" he said, "but he copped it all right, sir! Ay, I know him well enough! He's Rass, the landlord of this pub, that's who he is, as harmless a sort of chap as ever was! Who did it, d'you think, sir?"

Matthews, who had been going through the dead man's pockets, now rose to his feet.

"Nothing worth writing home about there," he said half aloud. Then to Harrison, he added

"That's what we've got to discover... hullo, who's this?"

The door leading from the bar to the tap–room was thrust open. Gordon put his head in.

"I left Bates on guard outside, sir," he said in answer to an interrogatory glance from Matthews, "I've been all over the ground floor and there's not a soul here..."

He checked himself suddenly.

"God bless my soul!" he exclaimed, his eyes on the figure crouching in the corner, "you don't mean to say you've got her? A pretty dance she led Dug and myself! Well, sir, it looks to me like a good night's work!".

Matthews smiled a self–satisfied smile.

"I fancy the Chief will be pleased," he said, "though the rest of 'em seem to have given us the slip. Gordon, you might take a look upstairs—that door in the corner leads to the upper rooms, I fancy whilst I'm telephoning to Mr. Okewood. He must know about this without delay. You, Harrison, keep an eye on the girl!"

He went through the door leading into the bar, and they heard him speaking on the telephone which hung on the wall behind the counter. He returned presently with a white tablecloth which he threw over the prostrate figure on the floor.

Then he turned to the dancer.

"Stand up," he said sternly, "I want to speak to you."

Nur-el-Din cast a frightened glance over her shoulder at the floor beside the table where Rass lay. On seeing the white pall that hid him from view, she became somewhat reassured. She rose unsteadily to her feet and stood facing Matthews.

"In virtue of the powers conferred upon me by the Defence of the Realm Acts, I arrest you foil espionage... Matthews rolled off in glib, official gabble the formula of arrest ending with the usual caution that anything the prisoner might say might be used against her at her trial. Then he said to Harrison:

"Better put them on her, Harrison!"

The plain clothes man took a pace forward and touched the dancer's slender wrists, there was a click and she was handcuffed.

"Now take her in there," said Matthews pointing to the bar. "There's no exit except by this room. And don't take your eyes off her. You understand? Mr. Okewood will be along presently with a female searcher."

"Sir!" said the plain clothes man with military precision and touched the dancer on the shoulder. Without a word she turned and followed him into the bar.

Gordon entered by the door at the end of the room.

"I'd like you to have a look upstairs, sir," he said to Matthews, "there's not a soul in the house, but somebody has been locked up in one of the rooms. The door is still locked but one of the panels has been forced out. I think you ought to see it!"

The two men passed out of the tap-room together, and mounted the stairs. On the landing Matthews paused a moment to glance out of the window on to the bleak and inhospitable fen which was almost obscured from view by a heavy drizzle of rain.

"Brr!" said Mr. Matthews, "what a horrible place!"

Looking up the staircase from the landing, they could see that one of the panels of the door facing the head of the stairs had been pressed out and lay on the ground. They passed up the stairs and Matthews, putting one arm and his head through the opening, found himself gazing into that selfsame ugly sitting room where Desmond had talked with Nur–el–Din.

A couple of vigorous heaves burst the fastening of the door. The sitting–room was in the wildest confusion. The doors of the sideboard stood wide with its contents scattered higgledy–piggledy on the carpet. A chest of drawers in the corner had been ransacked, some of the drawers having been taken bodily out and emptied on the floor.

The door leading to the inner room stood open and showed that a similar search had been conducted there as well. The inner room proved to be a bare white–washed place, very plainly furnished as a bedroom. On the floor stood a small attache case, and beside it a little heap of miscellaneous articles such as a woman would take away with her for a weekend, a crepe–de–chine nightdress, a dainty pair of bedroom slippers and some silver–mounted toilet fittings. From these things Matthews judged that this had been Nur–el–Din's bedroom.

The two men spent a long time going through the litter with which the floor in the bedroom and sitting room was strewed. But their labors were vain, and they turned their attention to the remaining rooms, of which there were three.

The first room they visited, adjoining Nur–el–Din's bedroom, was scarcely better than an attic. It contained in the way of furniture little else than a truckle–bed, a washstand, a table and a chair. Women's clothes were hanging on hooks behind the door. The place looked like a servant's bedroom.

They pursued their search. Across the corridor two rooms stood side by side. One proved to be Rass's. His clothes lay about the room, and on a table in the corner, where writing materials stood, were various letters and bills made out in his name.

The other room had also been occupied; for the bed was made and turned back for the night and there were clean towels on the washstand. But there was no clue as to its occupant save for a double–barreled gun which stood in the corner. It had evidently been recently used; for fresh earth was adhering to the stock and the barrel, though otherwise clean, showed traces of freshly–burnt powder.

There being nothing further to glean upstairs, the two men went down to the tap–room again. As Matthews came through the door leading from the staircase his eye caught a dark object which lay on the floor under the long table. He fished it out with his stick.

It was a small black velvet toque with a band of white and black silk flowers round it. In one part the white flowers were besmeared with a dark brown stain.

Matthews stared at the little hat in his hand with puckered brows. Then he called to Gordon.

"Do you know that hat?" he asked, holding it up for the man to see.

Gordon shook his head.

"I might have seen it," he replied, "but I don't take much account of such things, Mr. Matthews, being a married man..."

"Tut, tut," fussed Matthews, "I think you have seen it. Come, think of the office for a minute!"

"Of the office?" repeated Gordon. Then he exclaimed suddenly:

"Miss Mackwayte!"

"Exactly," answered Matthews, "it's her hat, I recall it perfectly. She wore it very often to the office. Look at the blood on it!"

He put the hat down on the table and ran into the bar where Nur–el–Din. sat immobile on her chair, wrapped in a big overcoat of some soft blanket cloth in dark green, her chin sunk on her breast.

Matthews called up the Mill House and asked for Francis Okewood. When he mentioned the finding of Barbara Mackwayte's hat, the dancer raised her head and cast a frightened glance at Matthews. But she said nothing and when Matthews turned from the telephone to go back to the tap–room she had resumed her former listless attitude.

Matthews and Gordon made a thorough search of the kitchen and back premises without finding anything of note. They had just finished when the sound of a car outside attracted their attention. On the road beyond the little bridge outside the inn Francis and Desmond Okewood were standing, helping a woman to alight. Francis was still wearing his scarecrow–like apparel, while Desmond, with his beard and pale face and bandaged head, looked singularly unlike the trim Brigade Major who had come home on leave only a week or so before.

Matthews went out to meet them and, addressing the woman—a brisk–looking person–as Mrs. Butterworth, informed her that it was shocking weather. Then he led the way into the inn.

The first thing that Desmond saw was the little toque with the brown stain on its flowered band lying on the table. Francis picked it up, turned it over and land it down again.

Where did you find it?" he asked Matthews. The latter informed him of the circumstances of the discovery. Then Francis, sending the searcher in to Nur–el–Din in the bar, pointed to the body on the floor.

"Let's have a look at that!" he said.

Matthews removed the covering and the three men gazed at the set face of the dead man. There was a clean bullet wound in the right temple. Matthews showed the papers he had taken off the body and exchanged a few, words in a low tone with Francis. There is something about the presence of death which impels respect whatever the circumstances.

Five minutes later Mrs. Butterworth came out of the bar. In her hands she held a miscellaneous assortment of articles, a small gold chain purse, a pair of gloves, a gold cigarette case, a tiny handkerchief, and a long blue envelope. She put all the articles down on the tables save the envelope which she handed to Francis.

"This was in the lining of her overcoat, sir," she said.

Francis took the envelope and broke the seal. He drew out half a dozen sheets of thin paper, folded lengthwise. Leisurely he unfolded them, but he had hardly glanced at the topmost sheet than he turned to the next and the next until he had run through the whole bunch. Desmond, peering over his shoulder, caught a glimpse of rows of figures, very neatly set out in a round hand and knew that he was looking at a message in cipher code.

The door at the end of the tap-room was flung open and a soldier came in quickly.

He stopped irresolute on seeing the group.

"Well, Bates," said Matthews.

"There's a woman lying dead in the cellar back yonder," said the man, jerking his thumb over his shoulder.

"The cellar?" cried Matthews.

"Yes, sir... I think you must ha' overlooked it."

Francis, Desmond and Matthews exchanged a brief glance. A name was on the lips of each one of them but none dared speak it. Then, leaving Harrison and Mrs. Butterworth with Nur-el-Din, the three men followed the soldier and hurriedly quitted the room.

CHAPTER XXII. WHAT THE CELLAR REVEALED

On opening the door at the farther end of the tap-room they saw before them a trap-door standing wide with a shallow flight of wooden steps leading to the darkness below. Bates pointed with his foot to a square of linoleum which lay on one side.

"That was covering the trap," he said, "I wouldn't ha' noticed nothing out of the ordinary myself only I slipped, see, and kicked this bit o' ilecloth away and there was the ring of the trap staring me in the face, as you might say. Show us a light here, Gordon!"

Gordon handed him an electric torch. He flashed it down the stair. It fell upon something like a heap of black clothes huddled up at the foot of the ladder.

"Is it Miss Mackwayte?" whispered Francis to his brother. "I've never seen her, you know!"

"I can't tell," Desmond whispered back, "until I see her face."

He advanced to descend the ladder but Matthews was before him. Producing an electric torch from his pocket, Matthews slipped down the stair with Gordon close behind. There was a pause, so tense that it seemed an eternity to Desmond, as he waited half-way down the ladder with the musty smell of the cellar in his nostrils. Then Matthews cried:

"It's not her!"

"Let me look!" Gordon broke in. Then Desmond heard him exclaim.

"It's Nur-el-Din's French maid! It's Marie... she's been stabbed in the back!"

Desmond suddenly felt rather sick. This progress from one deed of violence to another revolted him. The others crowded into the cellar; but he did not follow them. He remained at the top of the trap, leaning against the wall, trying to collect his thoughts.

Barbara Mackwayte was now his sole preoccupation. If anything had happened to her,—it was through his fault alone; for he began to feel sure she must have come to the Mill House in his absence. What then had become of her? The blood-stained toque pointed to foul play. But if they had murdered her, what had they done with the body?

His thoughts flew back to his interview with Nur-el-Din upstairs on the previous afternoon. He remembered the entrance of the maid and the dancer's hurried exit. Might not Marie have come to tell her that Barbara Mackwayte was below asking for her? It was very shortly after this interruption that, crouching on the roof of the shed, he had heard that muffled cry from the house and seen Rass enter the bar and speak with Strangwise. He had seen, too, the maid, Marie, in earnest conversation with Strangwise by the back gate on the fen. Had both Marie and Rass been in league with Strangwise against the dancer? And had Nur-el-Din discovered their treachery? His mind refused to follow these deductions to their logical sequence; for, black as things looked against Nur-el-Din, he could not bring himself to believe her a murderess.

But now there were footsteps on the ladder. They were all coming out of the cellar again. As soon as Francis saw Desmond's face, he caught his brother by the arm and said:

"The open air for you, my boy! You look as if you'd seen a ghost! I should have remembered all you've gone through!"

He walked him quickly through the tap–room and out through the inn door into the yard.

The rain had ceased and the sun was making a brave attempt to shine through the, clouds. The cold air did Desmond good and after a turn or two in the yard, arm in arm with Francis, he felt considerably better.

"Where is Miss Mackwayte?" he asked.

"Des," said his brother, " I don't know and I don't want to cross–examine Nur–el–Din in there until I have reasoned out some theory which will fit Miss Mackwayte in her place in this horrible affair. The men have gone to search the outhouses and precincts of the inn to see if they can find any traces of her body. but I don't think they will find anything. I believe that Miss Mackwayte is alive."

"Alive?" said Desmond.

"The blood on that toque of hers might have been Rass's. There is a good deal of blood on the floor. You see, I still think Miss Mackwayte's safety depends on that jewel not being recovered by either Strangwise or Nur–el–Din. Strangwise, we know, has lost the jewel and there is no trace of it here: moreover, we know that, as late as yesterday afternoon, Nur–el–Din did not have it. Therefore, she cannot have sent it away! I am inclined to believe, too, that Strangwise, before going over to the Mill House last night, carried off Miss Mackwayte somewhere with the aid of Rass and Marie, who were evidently his accomplices, in order to find out from her where the jewel is concealed..."

"But Miss Mackwayte cannot know what has become of it," objected Desmond.

"Maybe not," retorted his brother, "but both Strangwise and Nur–el–Din know that the jewel was originally entrusted to her charge. Nur–el–Din did not, it is true, tell Miss Mackwayte what the silver box contained but the latter may have found out, at least the

192

dancer might suppose so; while Strangwise might think the same. Therefore, both Strangwise and Nur–el–Din had an interest in detaining Miss Mackwayte, and I think Strangwise forestalled the dancer. When Nur–el–Din discovered it, both Rass and her maid paid the penalty of their betrayal."

They walked once up and down the yard before Desmond replied.

"Francis," he said, "you remember Nur–el–Din's story—I told it to you just as I had it from her."

"Perfectly," answered his brother.

"Well," Desmond went on deliberately, "I think that story gives us the right measure of Nur–el–Din's, character. She may be vain, she may be without morals, she may be weak, she may be an adventuress, but she's not a murderess. If anything, she's a victim!"

Francis laughed shortly.

"Victim be damned!" he cried. "Man alive," he went on, "how can you talk such nonsense in face of the evidence, with this bloody–minded woman's victims hardly cold yet? But, horrible as these murders are, the private squabbles of this gang of spies represent neither your interest nor mine in this case. For us the fact remains that Nur–el–Din, besides being a monster of iniquity, is the heart and soul and vitals of the whole conspiracy!"

Jaded and nervous, Desmond felt a quick sting of resentment at his brother's tone. Why should Francis thus lay down the law to him about Nur–el–Din? Francis knew nothing of the girl or her antecedents while he, Desmond, flattered himself that he had at least located the place she occupied in this dark conspiracy. And he cried out vehemently:

"You're talking like a fool! I grant you that Nur–el–Din has been mixed up with this spy crowd; but she herself stands absolutely apart from the organization..."

"Half a minute!" put in Francis, "aren't you forgetting that blue envelope we took off her just now?"

"What about it?" asked Desmond sharply.

"Merely this; the cipher is in five figure groups, addressed to a four figure group and signed by a six figure group..."

"Well?"

"That happens to be the current secret code of the German Great General Staff. If you were to tap a German staff message out in France to–day, ten to one it would be in that code. Curious coincidence, isn't it?"

When one is angry, to be baffled in argument does not have a sedative effect as a rule. If we were all philosophers it might; but being merely human beings, cold reason acts on the inflamed temperament as a red rag is said to affect a bull.

Desmond, sick with the sense of failure and his anxiety about Barbara, was in no mood to listen to reason. The, cold logic of his brother infuriated him mainly because Desmond knew that Francis was right.

"I don't care a damn for the evidence," vociferated Desmond; "It may look black against Nur–el–Din; I daresay it does; but I have met and talked to this girl and. I tell you again that she is not a principal in this affair but a victim!"

"You talk as if you were in love with the woman!" Francis said mockingly.

Desmond went rather white.

"If pity is a form of love," he replied in a low voice, "then I am, for God knows I never pitied any woman as I pity Nur–el–Din! Only you, I suppose," he added bitterly, "are too much of the policeman, Francis, to appreciate anything like that!" Hot tempers run in families and Francis flared up on the instant.

"I may be a policeman, as you say," he retorted, but I've got enough sense of my duty, I hope, not to allow sentimentality to interfere with my orders!"

It was a shrewd thrust and it caught Desmond on the raw.

"I'm sick of arguing here," he said hotly, "if you're so mighty clever, you'd better shoot Nur–el–Din first and arrest Strangwise afterwards. Then you'll find out which of us two is right!"

He turned on his heel and started for the little bridge leading out onto the fen.

Francis stood still a moment watching him, then ran after him. He caught up with Desmond as the latter reached the bridge.

"Desmond!" he said, pleadingly.

"Oh, go to hell!" retorted the other savagely, whereupon Francis turned his back on him and walked back to the inn.

A car had stopped by the bridge and a man was getting out of it as Desmond moved towards the fen. The next moment he found himself face to face with the Chief.

The Chief's face was hard and cold and stern. There was a furrow between his eyes which deepened when he recognized Desmond.

"Well," he said curtly, "and where is my secretary?"

"I don't know," Desmond faltered.

"Why are you here, then?" came back in that hard, uncompromising voice.

Desmond was about to reply; but the other checked him.

"I know all you have to say," he resumed, "but no excuse you can offer can explain away the disappearance of Miss Mackwayte. Your orders were formal to remain at home. You saw fit to disobey them and thereby, maybe, sent Miss Mackwayte to her death. No!" he added, seeing that Desmond was about to expostulate, "I want to hear nothing from you. However obscure the circumstances of Miss Mackwayte's disappearance may be, one fact is perfectly clear, namely, that she went to the Mill House, as she was ordered and you were not there. For no man or woman in my service ever dares to disobey an order I have given."

"Chief..." Desmond broke in, but again that inexorable voice interposed.

"I will hear nothing from you," said the Chief, "it is a rule of mine never to interfere with my men in their work or to see them until their mission has been successfully completed. When you have found Miss Mackwayte I will hear you but not before!"

Desmond drew himself up.

"In that case, sir," he said stiffly, "I will bid you good morning. And I trust you will hear from me very soon again!"

He walked over to one of the cars waiting outside the inn, spoke a word to the driver and got in. The driver started the engine and presently the car was bumping slowly along the muddy track to the main road.

The Chief stood looking after him.

"Well," he murmured to himself. "I soaked it into him pretty hard; but he took it like a brick. I do believe he'll find her yet!"

He shook his head sagely and continued on hid way across the yard.

CHAPTER XXIII. MRS. MALPLAQUET GOES DOWN TO THE CELLAR

In the age of chivalry woman must have been built of sterner stuff than the girl of to-day. At least, we read in medieval romance of fair ladies who, after being knocked down by a masterful suitor and carried off across his saddle bow thirty or forty miles, are yet able to appear, cold but radiantly beautiful, at the midnight wedding and the subsequent marriage feast.

But this is a romance of the present day, the age of nerves and high velocity. Barbara Mackwayte, strong and plucky as she was, after being half throttled and violently thrown into the cellar of the Dyke Inn, suddenly gave way under the strain and conveniently evaded facing the difficulties of her position by fainting clear away.

The precise moment when she came out of her swoon she never knew. The cellar was dark; but it was nothing compared to the darkness enveloping her mind. She lay there on the damp and mouldy straw, hardly able, scarcely wanting, to move, overwhelmed by the extraordinary adventure which had befallen her. Was this to be the end of the pleasant trip into the country on which she had embarked so readily only a few hours before? She tried to remember that within twenty miles of her were policemen and taxis and lights and all the attributes of our present day civilization; but her thoughts always returned, with increasing horror, to that undersized yellow–faced man in the room above, to the face of Nur–el–Din, dark and distorted with passion.

A light shining down the cellar stairs drew her attention to the entrance. The woman she had already seen and in whom she now recognized Marie, the dancer's maid, was descending, a tray in her hand. She placed the tray on the ground without a word, then went up the stairs again and fetched the lamp. She put the lamp down by the tray and, stooping, cut the ropes that fastened Barbara's hands and feet.

"So, Mademoiselle," she said, drawing herself erect with a grunt, "your supper: some tea and meat!"

She pulled a dirty deal box from a corner of the cellar and put the tray upon it. Then she rose to her feet and sat down. The maid watched Barbara narrowly while she ate a piece of bread and drank the tea.

"At least," thought Barbara to herself, "they don't mean to starve me!"

The tea was hot and strong; and it did her good. It seemed to clear her faculties, too; for her brain began to busy itself with the problem of escaping from her extraordinary situation.

"Mademoiselle was a leetle too clevaire," said the maid with an evil leer,—she would rob Madame, would she? She would play the espionne, hein? Eh bien, ma petite, you stay 'ere ontil you say what you lave done wiz ze box of Madame!"

"Why do you say I have stolen the box?" protested Barbara, "when I tell you I know nothing of it. It was stolen from me by the man who killed my father. More than that I don't know. You don't surely think I would conspire to kill" her voice trembled—"my

197

father, to get possession of this silver box that means nothing to me!"

Marie laughed cynically.

"Ma foi," she cried, "when one is a spy, one will stop at nothing! But tiers, here is Madame!"

Nur-el-Din picked her way carefully down the steps, the yellow-faced man behind her. He had a pistol in his hand. The dancer said something in French to her maid who picked up the tray and departed.

"Now, Mademoiselle," said Nur-el-Din, "you see this pistol. Rass here will use it if you make any attempt to escape. You understand me, hein? I come to give you a las' chance to say where you 'ave my box..."

Barbara looked at the dancer defiantly.

"I've told you already I know nothing about it. You, if any one, should be better able to say what has become of it..."

"Quoi?" exclaimed Nur-el-Din in genuine surprise, "comment?"

"Because," said Barbara, " a long black hair—one of your hairs—was found adhering to the straps with which I was fastened!"

"Tiens!" said the dancer, her black eyes wide with surprise, "tiens!"

She was silent for a minute, lost in thought. The man, Rass, suddenly cocked his ear towards the staircase and said something to Nur-el-Din in the same foreign tongue which Barbara had heard them employ before.

The dancer made a gesture, bidding him to be silent.

"He was at my dressing-table that night;" she murmured in French, as though to herself, "then it was he who did it!"

She spoke rapidly to Barbara.

"This man who tied you up... you didn't see him?"

Barbara shook her head.

"I could see nothing; I don't even know that it was a man. He seized me so suddenly that in the dark I could distinguish nothing... it might have been a woman... yourself, for instance, for all I know!"

Nur–el–Din clasped her hands together.

"It was he, himself, then," she whispered, I might have known. Yet he has not got it here!"

Heavy footsteps resounded in the room above. Rass cried out something swiftly to the dancer, thrust the pistol into her hands, and dashed up the ladder. The next moment there was a loud report followed by the thud of a heavy body falling. Somewhere in the rooms above a woman screamed.

Nur–el–Din's hands flew to her face and the pistol crashed to the ground. Two men appeared at the head of the cellar stairs. One was Strangwise, in uniform, the other was Bellward.

"They're both here!" said Strangwise over his shoulder to Bellward.

"Ah, thank God, you've come!" cried Barbara, running to the foot of the ladder.

Strangwise brushed past her and caught Nur–el–Din by the arm.

"Run her upstairs," he said quickly to Bellward who had followed behind him, " and lock her in her room. I've seen to the rest. You, Miss Mackwayte," he added to Barbara, "you will come with us!"

Barbara was staring in fascination at Bellward. She had never believed that any disguise could be so baffling, so complete; Major Okewood, she thought, looked like a different man.

But Bellward had grasped the dancer by the two arms and forced her up the stairs in front of him. Nur–el–Din seemed too overcome with terror to utter a sound.

"Oh, don't be so rough with her, Major Okewood!" entreated Barbara, "you'll hurt her!"

She had her back turned to Strangwise so she missed the very remarkable change that came over his features at her words.

"Okewood," he whispered but too low for the girl to distinguish the words, "Okewood? I might have guessed! I might have guessed!" Then he touched Barbara lightly on the shoulder.

"Come," he said, "we must be getting upstairs. We have much to do!"

He gently impelled her towards the ladder up which Bellward and Nur–el–Din had already disappeared. At the top, he took the lead and conducted Barbara into the taproom. A single candle stood on the table, throwing a wan light into the room. Rass lay on his back in the centre of the floor, one hand doubled up under him, one knee slightly drawn up.

Barbara started back in horror.

"Is he... is he..." she stammered, pointing at the limp still form.

Strangwise nodded.

"A spy!" he said gravely, "we were well rid of him. Go over there in the corner where you won't see it. Stay!" he added, seeing how pale the girl had become, "you shall have some brandy!"

He produced a flask and measured her out, a portion in the cup. Suddenly, the door leading from the bar opened and a woman came into the room. Her black velvet dress, her gray hair and general air of distinction made her a bizarre figure in that squalid room lit by the guttering candle.

"Time we were off!" she said to Strangwise, "Bellward's just coming down!"

"There's the maid..." began Strangwise, looking meaningly at Barbara.

The woman in black velvet cast a questioning glance at him.

Strangwise nodded.

"I'll do it," said the woman promptly, "if you'll call her down!"

Strangwise went to the other door of the tap–room and called:

"Marie!"

There was a step outside and the maid came in, pale and trembling.

"Your mistress wants you; she is downstairs in the cellar," he said pleasantly.

Marie hesitated an instant and surveyed the group.

"Non, non," she said nervously, "je n'veux pas descendre!"

Strangwise smiled, showing his teeth.

"No need to be frightened, ma fille," he replied. "Madame here will go down with you!" and he pointed to the woman in black velvet.

This seemed to reassure the maid and she walked across the room to the door, the woman following her. As the latter passed Strangwise he whispered a word in her ear.

"No, no," answered the other, "I prefer my own way," and she showed him something concealed in her hand.

The two women quitted the room together, leaving Strangwise and Barbara alone with the thing on the floor. Strangwise picked up a military great–coat which was hanging over the back of a chair and put it on, buttoning it all the way up the front and turning up the collar about the neck. Then he crammed a cap on his head and stood listening intently.

A high, gurgling scream, abruptly checked, came through the open door at the farther end of the room.

Barbara sprang up from the chair into which she had sunk.

"What was that" she asked, whispering.

Strangwise did not reply. He was still listening, a tall, well set–up figure in the long khaki great–coat.

"But those two women are alone in the cellar," exclaimed Barbara, "they are being murdered! Ah! what was that?"

A gentle thud resounded from below.

A man came in through the door leading from the bar:

He had a fat, smooth–shaven face, heavily jowled.

"All ready, Bellward?" asked Strangwise carelessly.

Barbara stared at the man thus addressed. She saw that he was wearing the same clothes as the man who had come down into the cellar with Strangwise but the beard was gone. And the man she saw before her was not Desmond Okewood.

Without waiting to reason out the metamorphosis, she ran towards Bellward.

"They're murdering those two women down in the cellar," she cried, "oh, what has happened? Won't you go down and see?"

Bellward shook her off roughly.

"Neat work!" said Strangwise.

"She's a wonder with the knife!" agreed the other.

Barbara stamped her foot.

"If neither of you men have the courage to go down," she cried, "then I'll go alone! As for you, Captain Strangwise, a British officer..."

She never finished the sentence. Strangwise caught her by the shoulder and thrust the cold barrel of a pistol in her face.

"Stay where you are!" he commanded. "And if you scream I shoot!"

Barbara was silent, dumb with horror and bewilderment, rather than with fear. A light shone through the open door at the end of the tap–room and the woman in black velvet appeared, carrying a lamp in her hand She was breathing rather hard and her carefully arranged gray hair was a little untidy; but she was quite calm and self–possessed.

"We haven't a moment to lose!" she said, putting the lamp down on the table and blowing it out.

"Bellward, give me my cloak!"

Bellward advanced with a fur cloak and wrapped it about her shoulders.

"You are the perfect artiste, Minna," he said.

"Practise makes perfect!" replied Mrs. Malplaquet archly.

Strangwise had flung open the door leading to the front yard. A big limousine stood outside.

"Come on," he said impatiently, "don't stand there gossiping you two!"

Then Barbara revolted.

"I'll not go!" she exclaimed, "you can do what you like but I'll stay where I am! Murderers..."

"Oh," said Strangwise wearily, "bring her along, Bellward!"

Bellward and the woman seized the girl one by each arm and dragged her to the car. Strangwise had the door open and between them they thrust her in. Bellward and the woman mounted after her while Strangwise, after starting the engine, sprang into the driving–seat outside. With a low hum the big car glided forth into the cold, starry night.

From the upper floor of the Dyke Inn came the sound of a woman's terrified sobs. Below there reigned the silence of death.

CHAPTER XXIV. THE TWO DESERTERS

Desmond drove to Wentfield Station in an angry and defiant mood. He was incensed against Francis, incensed against the Chief, yet, if the truth were told, most of all incensed against himself.

Not that he admitted it for a moment. He told himself that he was very hardly used. He had undergone considerable danger in the course of discharging a mission which was none of his seeking, and he had met with nothing but taunts from his brother and abuse from the Chief.

"I wash my hands of the whole thing," Desmond declared, as he paced the platform at Wentfield waiting for his train. "As Francis is so precious cocksure about it all, let him carry on in my place! He's welcome to the Chief's wiggings! The Chief won't get me to do his dirty work again in a hurry! That's flat!"

Yet all the while the little gimlet that men call conscience was patiently drilling its way through the wall of obduracy behind which Desmond's wounded pride had taken cover. Rail as he would against his hard treatment at the hands of the Chief, he knew perfectly well that he could never wash his hands of his mission until Barbara Mackwayte had been brought back into safety. This thought kept thrusting itself forward into the foreground of his mind; and he had to focus his attention steadfastly on his grievances to push it back again.

But we puny mortals are all puppets in the hands of Fate. Even as the train was bearing Desmond, thus rebellious, Londonwards, Destiny was already pulling the strings which was to force the "quitter" back into the path he had forsaken. For this purpose Fate had donned the disguise of a dirty–faced man in a greasy old suit and a spotted handkerchief in lieu of collar... but of him presently.

On arriving at Liverpool Street, Desmond, painfully conscious of his unkempt appearance, took a taxi to a Turkish bath in the West End. There his first care was to submit himself to the hands of the barber who, after a glance at his client's bandaged head, muddy clothes and shaggy beard, coughed ominously and relapsed into a most unbarber–like reserve.

Desmond heard the cough and caught the look of commiseration on the man's face.

"I rather think I want a shave!" he said, weakly. "I rather think you do, sir!" replied the man, busy with his lather.

"... Had a nasty accident," murmured Desmond, "I fell down and cut my head..."

"We're used to that here, sir," answered the barber, "but the bath'll make you as right as, rain. W'y we 'ad a genel'man in 'ere, only lars' week it was, as 'adn't been 'ome for five days and nights and the coat mos tore off 'is back along with a bit of turn–up 'e'd 'at one o' them night clubs. And drunk I... w'y 'e went to bite the rubber, so they wos tellin' me! But, bless you, 'e 'ad a nice shave and a couple of hours in the bath and a bit of a nap; we got him his clothes as was tore mended up fine for 'im and 'e went 'ome as sober as a judge and as fresh as a daisy!"

Desmond had it in his mind to protest against this material interpretation of his disreputable state; but the sight in the mirror of his ignominiously scrubby and battered appearance silenced him. The barber's explanation was as good as any, seeing that he himself could give no satisfactory account of the circumstances which had reduced him to his sorry pass. So Desmond held his peace though he felt constrained to reject the barber's offer of a pick–me–up.

From the shaving saloon, Desmond sent a messenger out for some clothes, and for the next three hours amused himself by exhausting the resources of the Turkish bath. Finally, about the hour of noon, he found himself, considerably refreshed, swathed in towel, reposing on a couch, a cup of coffee at his elbow and that morning's Daily Telegraph spread out before him.

Advertisements, so the experts say, are printed on the front and back of newspapers in order to catch the eye of the indolent, on the chance that having exhausted the news, they may glance idly over the front and back of the paper before laying it aside. So Desmond, before he even troubled to open his paper, let his gaze wander down the second column of the front page whence issue daily those anguishing appeals, mysterious messages, heart–rending entreaties and barefaced begging advertisements which give this column its characteristic name.

There his eye fell on an advertisement couched in the following terms:

"If Gunner Martin Barling, 1820th Battery, R.F.C., will communicate with Messrs. Mills &Cheyne, solicitors 130 Bedford Row, W. C., he will hear of something to his advantage. Difficulties with the military can be arranged."

Desmond read this advertisement over once and then, starting at the beginning, read it over again. Gunner Barling... the name conjured up a picture of a jolly, sun–burned man, always very spick and span, talking the strange lingo of our professional army gleaned from India, Aden, Malta and the Rock, the type of British soldier that put the Retreat from Mons into the history books for all time.

Advertisements like this; Desmond reflected dreamily, meant legacies as a rule; he was glad of it, for the sake of Barling whom he hadn't seen since the far–away days of Aldershot before the war.

"Buzzer" Barling was the brother of one Private Henry Barling who had been Desmond's soldier–servant. He derived the nickname of "Buzzer" from the fact that he was a signaller. As the vicissitudes of service had separated the two brothers for many years, they had profited by the accident of finding themselves at the same station to see as much of one another as possible, and Desmond had frequently come across the gunner at his quarters in barracks. Henry Barling had gone out to France with Desmond but a sniper in the wood at Villers Cotterets had deprived Desmond of the best servant and the truest friend he had ever had Now here was Henry's brother cropping up again. Desmond hoped that "Buzzer" Barling would see the advertisement, and half asleep, formed a mental resolve to cut out the notice and send it to the gunner who, he felt glad to think, was still alive. The rather curiously worded reference to difficulties with the military must mean, Desmond thought, that leave could be obtained for Martin Barling to come home and collect his legacy.

At this point the Daily Telegraph fell to the ground and Desmond went off to sleep. When he awoke, the afternoon hush had fallen upon the bath. He seemed to be the only occupant of the cubicles. His clothes which had arrived from the shop during his slumbers, were very neatly laid out on a couch opposite him.

He dressed himself leisurely. The barber was quite right. The bath had made a new man of him. Save for a large bump on the back of his head he was none the worse for Strangwise's savage blow. The attendant having packed Bellward's apparel in the suit–case in which Desmond's clothes had come from the club, Desmond left the suit–case in the man's charge and strolled out into the soft air of a perfect afternoon. He had discarded his bandage and in his well fitting blue suit and brown boots he was not recognizable as the scrubby wretch who had entered the bath six hours before.

Desmond strolled idly along the crowded streets in the sunshine. He was rather at a loss as to what his next move should be. Now that his mental freshness was somewhat restored, his thoughts began to busy themselves again with the disappearance of Barbara Mackwayte. He was conscious of a guilty feeling towards Barbara. It was not so much the blame he laid upon himself for not being at the Mill House to meet her when she came as the sense that he had been unfaithful to the cause of her murdered father.

Now that he was away from Nur–el–Din with her pleading eyes and pretty gestures, Desmond's thoughts turned again to Barbara Mackwayte. As he walked along Piccadilly, he found himself contrasting the two women as he had contrasted them that night he had met them in Nur–el–Din's dressing room at the Palaceum. And, with a sense of shame; he became aware of how much he had succumbed to the dancer's purely sensual influence; for away from her he found he could regain his independence of thought and action.

The thought of Barbara in the hands of that woman with the cruel eyes or a victim to the ruthlessness of Strangwise made Desmond cold with apprehension. If they believed the girl knew where the jewel had disappeared to, they would stop at nothing to force a confession from her; Desmond was convinced of that. But what had become of the trio?

In vain he cast about him for a clue. As far as he knew, the only London address that Strangwise had was the Nineveh; and he was as little likely to return there as Bellward was to make his way to his little hotel in Jermyn Street. There remained Mrs. Malplaquet who, he remembered, had told him of her house at Campden Hill.

For the moment, Desmond decided, he must put both Strangwise and Bellward out of his calculations. The only direction in which he could start his inquiries after Barbara Mackwayte pointed towards Campden Hill and Mrs. Malplaquet.

The delightful weather suggested to his mind the idea of walking out to Campden Hill to pursue his investigations on the spot. So he made his way across the Park into Kensington Gardens heading for the pleasant glades of Notting Hill. In the Bayswater Road he turned into a postoffice and consulted the London Directory. He very quickly convinced himself that among the hundreds of thousands of names compiled by Mr. Kelly's indefatigable industry Mrs. Malplaquet's was not to be found. Neither did the street directory show her as the tenant of any of the houses on Campden Hill.

I don't know that there is a more pleasant residential quarter of London than the quiet streets and gardens that straggle over this airy height. The very steepness of the slopes leading up from the Kensington High Street on the ono side and from Holland Park Avenue on the other effectually preserves the atmosphere of old-world languor which envelops this retired spot. The hill, with its approaches so steep as to suggest to the imaginative the pathway winding up some rock-bound fastness of the Highlands, successfully defies organ-grinders and motor-buses and other aspirants to the membership in the great society for the propagation of street noises. As you near the summit, the quiet becomes more pronounced until you might fancy yourself a thousand leagues, instead of as many yards, removed from the busy commerce of Kensington or the rather strident activity of Notting Hill.

So various in size and condition are the houses that it is as though they had broken away from the heterogeneous rabble of bricks and mortar that makes up the Royal Borough of

Kensington, and run up in a crowd to the summit of the hill to look down contemptuously upon their less fortunate brethren in the plain. On Campden Hill there are houses to suit all purses and all tastes from the vulgar mansion with its private garden to the little one–story stable that Art (which flourishes in these parts) and ten shillings worth of paint has converted into a cottage.

For half an hour Desmond wandered in a desultory fashion along the quiet roads of natty houses with brightly painted doors and shining brass knockers. He had no definite objective; but he hoped rather vaguely to pick up some clue that might lead him to Mrs. Malplaquet's. He walked slowly along surveying the houses and scrutinizing the faces of the passers–by who were few and far between, yet without coming any nearer the end of his search.

It was now growing dusk. Enthroned on the summit of the hill the water–tower stood out hard and clear against the evening sky. Desmond, who hid lost his bearings somewhat in the course of his wanderings, came to a full stop irresolutely, where two streets crossed, thinking that he would retrace his footsteps to the main–road on the chance of picking up a taxi to take him back to town. He chose one of the streets at random; but it proved to be a crescent and brought him back practically to the spot he had started from. Thereupon, he took the other and followed it up, ignoring various side–turnings which he feared might be pitfalls like the last: But the second road was as bad as the first. It was a cul de sac and brought Desmond face to face with a blank wall.

He turned and looked about him for somebody of whom to ask the way. But the street was entirely deserted. He seemed to be on the very summit of the hill; for all the roads were a–tilt. Though the evening was falling fast, no light appeared in any of the houses and the street lamps were yet unlit. Save for the distant bourdon of the traffic which rose to his ears like the beating of the surf, the breeze rustling the bushes in the gardens was the only sound.

Desmond started to walk back slowly the way he had come. Presently, his eyes caught the gleam of a light from above a front door. When he drew level with it, he saw that a gas–jet was burning in the fanlight over the entrance to a neat little two–story house which stood by itself in a diminutive garden. As by this time he was thoroughly sick of wandering aimlessly about, he went up to the neat little house and rang the bell.

A maid–servant in a cap and apron who seemed to be drawn to the scale of the house, such an insignificant little person she was, opened the door.

"Oh, sir," she exclaimed when she saw him, "was it about the rooms?"

And she pointed up at the fan–light where, for the first time, Desmond noticed a printed card with the inscription–:

"Furnished Rooms to Let."

The servant's unexpected question put an idea into Desmond's head. He could not return to the club, he reflected, since he was supposed to be killed in action. Why not take a room in this house in the heart of the enemy's country and spend some days on the watch for Mrs. Malplaquet or for any clue that might lead him to her?

So Desmond answered, yes, it was about the rooms he had come.

Promising that she would tell "the missus," the little servant showed him into a tiny sitting–room, very clean and bright, with blue cretonne curtains and a blue carpet and an engraving of "King Cophetua and The Beggar Maid" over the mantelpiece. Directly you came into the room, everything in it got up and shouted "Tottenham Court Road."

Then the door opened and, with a great tinkling and rustling, a stoutish, brisk–looking woman sailed in. The tinkling proceeded frown the large amount of cheap jewelry with which she was adorned; the rustling from a black and shiny glace silk dress. With every movement she made the large drops she wore in her ears chinked and were answered by a melodious chime from the charm bangles she had on her wrists.

She measured Desmond in a short glance and his appearance seemed to please her for she smiled as she said in rather a mincing voice:

"My (she pronounced it 'may') maid said you wished to see the rooms!"

Desmond intimated that such was his desire.

"Pray be seated," said the little woman: "You will understand, I'm sure, that ay am not in the habit of taking in paying guests, but may husband being at the front, ay have a bedroom and this sitting–room free and ay thought..."

She stopped and looked sharply at Desmond.

"You are an officer, I think" she asked.

Desmond bowed.

"May husband is also an officer," replied the woman, "Captain Viljohn–Smythe; you may have met him. No? Of course, had you not been of commissioned rank, ay should not..."

She trailed off vaguely.

Desmond inquired her terms and surprised her somewhat by accepting them on the spot.

"But you have not seen the bedroom!" protested Mrs. Viljohn–Smythe.

"I will take it on trust," Desmond replied, "and here," he added, pulling out his note–case, "is a week's rent in advance. I'll go along now and fetch my things. By the way," he went on, "I know some people here at Campden Hill but very foolishly, I've mislaid the address. Malplaquet... Mrs. Malplaquet. Do you happen to know her house"

"Ay know most of the naice people living round about here," replied the lady, "but for the moment, ay cannot recollect... was it one of the larger houses on the hill, do you know?"

"I'm afraid I don't know," said Desmond. "You see, I've lost the address!"

"Quayte!" returned Mrs. Viljohn–Smythe. "Ay can't say ay know the name!" she added.

However, she consented to consult the handmaiden, who answered to the name of Gladays, as to Mrs. Malplaquet's address, but she was as ignorant as her mistress.

Promising to return in the course of the evening with his things and having received exact instructions as to the shortest way to Holland Park Avenue, Desmond took his leave. He felt that he had embarked on a wild goose chase; for, even if the fugitives had made their way to Mrs. Malplaquet's (which was more than doubtful) he imagined they would take care to lie very low so that his chances of coming across any of them were of the most meager.

Following the directions he had received, he made his way easily back to the main road. He halted under a street–lamp to catch the eye of any passing taxi which might happen to be disengaged. A dirty faced man in a greasy old suit and a spotted handkerchief knotted about his throat came slouching along the pavement, keeping close to the wall. On catching sight of Desmond's face by the light of the lamp, he stopped irresolutely and then advanced slowly towards him.

"Excuse me, sir!" he said falteringly.

Desmond looked round at the sound of the man's voice and seeing a typical street loafer, asked the fellow to get him a taxi.

"It is Captain Okewood," said the loafer, "you don't remember me, sir?"

Desmond looked at the dirty, rather haggard face with its unshaven chin and shook his head.

"I don't think I do," he answered, "though you seem to know my name!"

The vagrant fumbled in his pocket for a minute and extracting a scrap of paper, unfolded it and held it out to Desmond.

"That's me, sir!" he said, "and, oh, sir! if you would kindly help me with a word of good advice, just for old times' sake, I'd be very grateful!"

Desmond took the scrap of paper which the man tendered and held it so as to catch the rays of the lamp. It was a fragment torn from a newspaper. He had hardly set eyes on the cutting than he stretched out his hand to the vagrant.

"Why, Gunner Barling, " he cried, "I didn't know you! How on earth do you come to be in this state?"

The man looked shamefacedly down on the ground.

"I'm a deserter, sir!" he said in a low voice.

"Are you, by George?" replied Desmond, "and now I come to think of it, so am I!"

CHAPTER XXV. TO MRS. MALPLAQUET'S

Clasping Barbara's wrist in a bony grip, Mrs. Malplaquet sat at the girl's side in the back seat of the limousine whilst Bellward placed himself on the seat opposite. The car was powerfully engined; and, once the cart track up to the inn was passed and the main road reached, Strangwise opened her out.

By the track leading to the inn the high road made a right angle turn to the right. This turn they took, leaving the Mill House away in the distance to the left of them, and, after skirting the fen for some way and threading a maze of side roads, presently debouched on a straight, broad road.

Dazed and shaken by her experiences, Barbara lost all count of time, but after running for some time through the open country in the gray light of dawn, they reached the edge of those long tentacles of bricks and mortar which London thrusts out from her on every side. The outer fringes of the metropolis were still sleeping as the great car roared by. The snug " High Streets," the red brick "Parades," and "Broadways," with their lines of houses with blinds drawn, seemed to have their eyes shut, so blank, so somnolent was their aspect.

With their lamps alight, the first trams were gliding out to begin the new day, as the big car swiftly traversed the eastern suburbs of London. To Barbara, who had had her home at Seven Kings, there was something familiar about the streets as they flickered by; but her powers of observation were dulled, so great was the sense of helplessness that weighed her down.

High–booted scavengers with curious snake–like lengths of hose on little trolleys were sluicing the asphalt as the limousine snorted past the Mansion House into Poultney and Cheapside. The light was growing clearer now; the tube stations were open and from time to time a motor–bus whizzed by.

Barbara stirred restlessly and Mrs. Malplaquet's grip on her wrist tightened.

"Where are you taking me?" the girl said.

Mrs. Malplaquet spoke a single word.

"Bellward!" she said in a gentle voice; but it was a voice of command.

Bellward leaned forward.

"Look at me, Miss Mackwayte!" he said.

There was a curious insistence in his voice that made Barbara obey. She struggled for a moment against the impulse to do his bidding; for some agency within her told her to resist the summons. But an irresistible force seemed to draw her eyes to his. Bellward did not move. He simply leaned forward a little, his hands on his knees, and looked at her. Barbara could not see his eyes, for the light in the car was still dim, but inch by inch they captured hers.

She looked at the black outline of his head and instantly was conscious of a wave of magnetic power that transmitted itself from his will to hers. She would have cried out, have struggled, have sought to break away; but that invisible dance held her as in a vice. A little gasp broke from her lips; but that was all.

"So!" said Bellward with the little sigh of a man who has just accomplished some bodily effort, "so! you will keep quiet now and do as I tell you. You understand?"

No reply came from the girl. She had thrust her head forward and was gazing fixedly at the man. Bellward leaned towards the girl until his stubbly hair actually touched her soft brown curls. He was gazing intently at her eyes.

He was apparently well satisfied with his inspection, for he gave a sigh of satisfaction and turned to Mrs. Malplaquet.

"She'll give no more trouble now!" he remarked airily.

"Ah! Bellward," sighed Mrs. Malplaquet, "you're incomparable! What an undefeatable combination you and I would have made if we'd met twenty years sooner!"

And she threw him a coquettish glance.

"Ah, indeed!" returned Bellward pensively. "But a night like this makes me feel twenty years older, Minna. He's a daredevil, this Strangwise. Imagine going back to that infernal inn when the police might have broken in on us any minute. But he is a determined chap. He doesn't seem to know what it is to be beaten. He wanted to make sure that Nur–el–Din had not recovered the jewel from him, though he declares that it has never left him day or night since he got possession of it. He fairly made hay of her room back at the inn there."

"Well," said Mrs. Malplaquet rather spitefully, "he seems to be beaten this time. He hasn't found his precious Star of Poland."

"No," answered the man reflectively, but I think he will!"

Mrs. Malplaquet laughed shrilly.

"And how, may I ask? From what Strangwise told me himself, the thing has utterly vanished. And he doesn't seem to have any clue as to who has taken it!"

"Perhaps not," replied Bellward, who appeared to have a high opinion of Strangwise, "but, like all Germans, our friend is thorough. If he does not see the direct road, he proceeds by a process of elimination until he bits upon it. He did not expect to find the jewel in Nur–el–Din's room; he told me as much himself, but he searched because he is thorough in everything. Do you know why he really went back to the Dyke Inn?"

"Why?" asked Mrs. Malplaquet.

"To secure our young friend here," answered Bellward with a glance at Barbara.

Mrs. Malplaquet made a little grimace to bid him to be prudent in what he said before the girl.

"Bah!" the man laughed, "you understand nothing of what we are saying, do you?" he said, addressing Barbara.

The girl moved uneasily.

"I understand nothing of what you are saying," she replied in a strained voice.

"This girl was the last person to have the jewel before Strangwise," Bellward said, continuing his conversation with Mrs. Malplaquet, and she is employed at the Headquarters of the Secret Service. Strangwise was satisfied that nobody connected him with the theft of the silver box which Nur–el–Din gave to this girl until our young lady here appeared at the Dyke Inn yesterday afternoon. Nur–el–Din played his game for him by detaining the girl. Strangwise believes—and I must say I agree with him—that probably two persons know where the Star of Poland is. One is this girl..."

"The other being the late Mr. Bellward?" queried Mrs. Malplaquet.

"Precisely. The late Mr. Bellward or Major Desmond Okewood!" said Bellward. "Between him and this girl here I think we ought to be able to recover Strangwise's lost property for him!"

"But you haven't got Okewood yet!" observed the lady in a mocking voice.

The man looked evilly at her, his heavy, fat chin set square.

"But we shall get him, never fear. With a little bird–lime as attractive as this—"

He broke off and jerked his head in the direction of Barbara.

"... I shall do the rest!" he added.

"Ah!"

Mrs. Malplaquet drew a deep sigh of admiration.

"That's a clever idea. He is so ruse, this Strangwise. You are quite right, Bellward, he never admits himself beaten. And he never is! But tell me," she added, "what about Nur–el–Din? They'll nab her, eh?"

"Unless our British friends are even more inefficient than I believe them to be, they most certainly will," he replied.

"And then?"

Bellward shrugged his shoulders and spread wide his hands.

"A little morning ceremony at the Tower," he answered, "unless these idiotic English are too sentimental to execute a woman..."

The car was running down the long slope to Paddington Station. It drew up at the entrance to the booking office, and Strangwise, springing from the driver's seat, flung open the door.

"Come on!" he cried, "we must look sharp or we'll miss our train!"

He dragged a couple of bags off the roof and led the way into the station. In the booking–hall he inquired of a porter what time the express left for Bath, then went to the ticket office and took four first–class tickets to that place. Meanwhile, the car remained standing empty in the carriageway.

Strangwise led his little party up some stairs and across a long bridge, down some stairs and up some stairs again, emerging, finally, at the Bakerloo Tube Station. There he despatched Bellward to fetch a taxi.

Taxis are rare in the early hours of the morning in war–time and Bellward was gone fully twenty minutes. Strangwise fidgeted continually, drawing out his watch repeatedly and casting many anxious glances this way and that.

217

His nervous demeanor began to affect Mrs. Malplaquet, who had linked her arm affectionately in Barbara's. The girl remained absolutely apathetic. Indeed, she seemed almost as one in a trance.

"Aren't we going to Bath?" at length demanded Mrs. Malplaquet of Strangwise.

"Don't ask questions!" snapped the latter.

"But the car?" asked the lady.

"Hold your tongue!" commanded the officer; and Mrs. Malplaquet obeyed.

Then Mr. Bellward returned with the news that he had at last got a taxi. Strangwise turned to Bellward.

"Can Minna and the girl go to Campden Hill alone?" he asked. "Or will the girl try and break away, do you think?"

Bellward held up his hand to enjoin silence.

"You will go along with Mrs. Malplaquet," he said to Barbara in his low purring voice, "you will stay with her until I come. You understand?"

"I will go with Mrs. Malplaquet!" the girl replied in the same dull tone as before.

"Upon my word," exclaimed Mrs. Malplaquet, you might have told me that we were going to my own place..."

But Strangwise shut her up.

"Bellward and I will come on by tube... it is safer," he said, "hurry, hurry! We must all be under cover by eight o'clock... we have no time to lose!"

CHAPTER XXVI. THE MAN IN THE SUMMER-HOUSE

The hour of the theatre rush was long since over and its passing had transformed the taxi-drivers from haughty autocrats to humble suppliants. One taxi after another crawled slowly past the street corner where Desmond had stood for over an hour in deep converse with Gunner Barling, but neither flaunting flag nor appealingly uplifted finger attracted the slightest attention from the athletic-looking man who was so earnestly engaged in talk with a tramp. But at last the conversation was over; the two men separated and the next taxi passing thereafter picked up a fare.

At nine o'clock the next morning Desmond appeared for breakfast in his sitting-room at Santona Road; for such was the name of the street in which his new rooms were situated. When he had finished his meal, he summoned Gladys and informed her that he would be glad to speak to Mrs. Viljohn-Smythe. That lady having duly answered the summons, Desmond asked whether, in consideration of terms to be mutually agreed upon, she could accommodate his soldier servant. He explained that the last-named was of the most exemplary character and threw out a hint of the value of a batman for such tasks as the cleaning of the family boots and the polishing of brass or silver.

The landlady made no objections and half an hour later a clean and respectable-looking man arrived whom Desmond with difficulty recognized as the wretched vagrant of the previous evening. This was, indeed, the Gunner Barling he used to know, with his smooth-shaven chin and neat brown moustache waxed at the ends and characteristic "quiff" decorating his brow. And so Desmond and his man installed themselves at Santona Road.

The house was clean and comfortable, and Mrs. Viljohn-Smythe, for all her "refaynement," as she would have called it, proved herself a warm-hearted, motherly soul. Desmond had a small but comfortably furnished bedroom at the top of the house, on the second floor, with a window which commanded a view of the diminutive garden and the back of a row of large houses standing on the lower slopes of the hill. So precipitous was the fall of the ground, indeed, that Desmond could look right into the garden of the house backing on Mrs. Viljohn-Smythe's. This garden had a patch of well-kept green sward in the centre with a plaster nymph in the middle, while in one corner stood a kind of large summer-house or pavilion built on a slight eminence, with a window looking into Mrs. Viljohn–Smythe's' back garden.

In accordance with a plan of action he had laid down in his mind, Desmond took all his meals at his rooms. The rest of the day he devoted to walking about the streets of Campden Hill and setting on foot discreet inquiries after Mrs. Malplaquet amongst the local tradespeople.

For three or four days he carried out this arrangement without the slightest success. He dogged the footsteps of more than one gray–haired lady of distinguished appearance without lighting upon his quarry. He bestowed largesse on the constable on point duty, on the milkman and the baker's young lady; but none of them had ever heard of Mrs. Malplaquet or recognized her from Desmond's description.

On the morning of the fourth day Desmond returned to lunch, dispirited and heart–sick. He had half a mind to abandon his quest altogether and to go and make his peace with the Chief and ask to be sent back to France. He ate his lunch and then, feeling that it would be useless to resume his aimless patrol of the streets, lit a cigar and strolled out into the little back–garden.

It was a fine, warm afternoon, and already the crocuses were thrusting their heads out of the neat flower–beds as if to ascertain whether the spring had really arrived. There was, indeed, a pleasant vernal scent in the air.

"A fine day!" said a voice.

Desmond looked up. At the open window of the summerhouse of the garden backing on Mrs. Viljohn–Smythe's, his elbows resting on the pitch–pine frame, was a middle–aged man. A cigarette was in his mouth and from his hands dangled a newspaper. He had a smooth–shaven, heavily–jowled face and a large pair of tortoise–shell spectacles on his nose.

Desmond remembered to have seen the man already looking out of a window opposite his on one of the upper floors of the house. In reply to a casual inquiry, Mrs. Viljohn–Smythe had informed him that the house was a nursing home kept by a Dr. Radcombs, a nerve specialist.

"It is quite like spring!" replied Desmond, wondering if this were the doctor. Doctors get about a good deal and Dr. Radcombe might be able to tell him something about Mrs. Malplaquet.

"I think we have seen one another in the mornings sometimes," said the heavily–fowled man, "though I have noticed that you are an earlier riser than I am. But when one is an invalid—"

"You are one of Dr. Radcombe's patients, then!" said Desmond.

"I am," returned the other, "a great man, that, any dear sir. I doubt if there is his equal for diagnosis in the kingdom."

"He has lived here for some years, I suppose?"

"Oh yes!" answered the man, "in fact, he is one of the oldest and most–respected residents of Kensington, I believe!"

"I am rather anxious to find some friends of mine who live about here," Desmond remarked, quick to seize his opportunity, "I wonder whether your doctor could help me..."

"I'm sure he could," the man replied, "the doctor knows everybody..."

"The name—" began Desmond, but the other checked him.

"Please don't ask me to burden my memory with names," he protested. "I am here for a complete rest from over–work, and loss of memory is one of my symptoms. But look here; why not come over the wall and step inside the house with me? Dr. Radcombe is there and will, I am sure, be delighted to give you any assistance in his power!"

Desmond hesitated.

"Really," he said, "it seems rather unconventional. Perhaps the doctor would object..."

"Object" said the heavily–fowled man, "tut, tut, not at all. Come on, I'll give you a hand up!"

He thrust out a large, white hand. Desmond was about to grasp it when he saw gleaming on the third finger a gold snake ring with emerald eyes—the ring that Mrs. Malplaquet had given Bellward. He was about to draw back but the man was too quick for him. Owing to the slope of the ground the window of the summer–house was on a level with Desmond's throat. The man's two hands shot out simultaneously. One grasped Desmond's wrist in a steel grip whilst the other fastened itself about the young man's throat, squeezing the very breath out of his body. It was done so quickly that he had no time to struggle, no time to shout. As Bellward seized him, another arm was shot out of the window. Desmond felt himself gripped by the collar and lifted, by a most amazing effort of strength, bodily over the wall.

His brain swimming with the pressure on his throat, he struggled but feebly to recover his freedom. However, as Desmond was dropped heavily on to the grass on the other side of the wall, Bellward's grip relaxed just for a second and in that instant Desmond made one desperate bid for liberty. He fell in a crouching position and, as he felt Bellward loosen his hold for a second with the jerk of his victim's fall, Desmond straightened himself up suddenly, catching his assailant a violent blow with his head on the point of the chin.

Bellward fell back with a crash on to the timber flooring of the pavilion. Desmond heard his head strike the boards with a thud, heard a muttered curse. He found himself standing in a narrow lane, less than three feet wide, which ran between the garden wall and the summer–house; for the pavilion, erected on a slight knoll surrounded by turf, was not built against the wall as is usually the case with these structures.

In this narrow space Desmond stood irresolute for the merest fraction of a second. It was not longer; for, directly after Bellward had crashed backwards, Desmond heard a light step reverberate within the planks of the summerhouse. His most obvious course was to scramble back over the wall again into safety, in all thankfulness at having escaped so violent an attack. But he reflected that Bellward was here and that surely meant that the others were not far off. In that instant as he heard the stealthy footstep cross the floor of the summer–house, Desmond resolved he would not leave the garden until he had ascertained whether Barbara Mackwayte was there.

Desmond decided that he would stay where he was until he no longer heard that footstep on the planks within; for then the person inside the summer–house would have reached the grass at the door. Desmond remembered the arm which had shot out beside Bellward at the window and swung him so easily off his feet. He knew only one man capable of achieving that very respectable muscular performance; for Desmond weighed every ounce of twelve stone. That man was Maurice Strangwise.

As soon as the creaking of the timbers within ceased, Desmond moved to the left following the outer wall of the pavilion. On the soft green sward his feet made no sound. Presently he came to a window which was let in the side of the summerhouse opposite the window from which Bellward had grappled with him. Raising his eyes to the level of the sill, Desmond took a cautious peep. He caught a glimpse of the face of Maurice Strangwise, brows knit, nostrils dilated, the very picture of venomous, watchful rancor.

Strangwise had halted and was now looking back over the wall into Mrs. Viljohn–Smythe's back garden. Was it possible, Desmond wondered, that he could believe that Desmond had scrambled back over the wall? Strangwise remained motionless, his back now fully turned to Desmond, peering into the other garden.

The garden in which the summer–house stood was oblong in shape and more than twice as broad as it was long. The pavilion was not more than forty yards from the back entrance of the house. Desmond weighed in his mind the possibility of being able to dash across those forty yards, the turf deadening the sound of his feet, before Strangwise turned round again. The entrance to the back of the house was through a door in the side of the house, to which two or three wrought–iron steps gave access. Once he had gained the steps Desmond calculated that the side of the house would shelter him from Strangwise's view. He turned these things over in his mind in the twinkling of an eye; for all his life he had been used to quick decision and quick action. To cover those forty yards across the open in one bound was, he decided, too much to risk; for he must at all costs gain access to the house and discover, if possible, whether Barbara Mackwayte were confined within, before he was caught.

Then his eye fell on the plaster nymph in the middle of the grass. She was a stoutly–built female, life–size, standing upon a solid–looking pedestal fully four feet broad. Desmond measured the distance separating him from the nymph. It was not more than twenty yards at the outside and the pedestal would conceal him from the eyes of Strangwise if the latter should turn round before he had made his second bound and reached the steps at the side of the house.

He peeped through the window again. Strangwise stood in his old attitude gazing over the garden wall. Then Desmond acted. Taking long strides on the points of his toes, he gained the statue and crouched down behind it. Even as he started, he heard a loud grunt from the inside of the summerhouse and from his cover behind the nymph saw Strangwise turn quickly and enter the summerhouse. On that Desmond sprang to his feet again, heedless of whether he was seen from the house, ran lightly across the grass and reached the steps at the side of the house.

The door stood ajar.

He stood still on the top step and listened for a moment. The house was wrapped in silence. Not a sign of life came from within.

But now he heard voices from the garden and they were the voices of two angry men, raised in altercation. As he listened, they drew nearer.

Desmond tarried no longer. He preferred the unknown perils which that silent house portended to the real danger advancing from the garden. He softly pushed the door open and slipped into the house.

CHAPTER XXVII. THE RED LACQUER ROOM

The side–door led into a little white passage with a green baize door at the end. A staircase, which from its white–washed treads, Desmond judged to be the back stairs, gave on the passage. Calculating that the men in the garden would be certain to use the main staircase, Desmond took the back stairs which, on the first lauding, brought him face to face with a green baize door, similar in every respect to that on the floor below.

He pushed this door open and listened. Hearing nothing he passed on through it. He found himself in a broad corridor on to which gave the main staircase from below and its continuation to the upper floors. Three rooms opened on to this corridor, a large drawing–room, a small study and what was obviously the doctor's consulting room, from the operating table and the array of instruments set out in glass cases. The rooms were empty and Desmond was about to return to the back stairs and proceed to the next floor when his attention was caught by a series of framed photographs with which the walls of the corridor were lined.

These were groups of doctors taken at various medical congresses. You will find such photographs in many doctors' houses. Below each group were neatly printed the names of the persons therein represented. Anxious to see what manner of man was this Doctor Radcombe in whose house spies were apparently at liberty to consort with impunity, Desmond looked for his name.

There it was—Dr. A. J. Radcombe. But, on looking at the figure above the printed line, what was his astonishment to recognize the angular features and drooping moustache of "No. 13"!

There was no possible mistake about it. The photographs were excellent and Desmond had no difficulty in identifying the eccentric–looking German in each of them. So this was Mrs. Malplaquet's house, was it? A nursing–home run by "No. 13," who in addition to being a spy, would seem to have been a nerve specialist as well. In this guise, no doubt, he had made trips to the South of England which had gained for him that intimate acquaintance with Portsmouth and Southsea of which he had boasted at the gathering in the library. In this capacity, moreover, he had probably met Bellward whose "oggult" powers, to which "No. 13" had alluded, seem to point to mesmerism and kindred practices in which German neurasthenic research has made such immense progress.

Pondering over his surprising discovery, Desmond pursued his way to the floor above. Here, too, was a green baize door which opened on to a corridor. Desmond walked quickly along it, glancing in, as he passed, at the open doors of two or three bedrooms. Just beyond where the staircase crossed the corridor were two doors, both of which were closed. The one was a white door and might have been a bathroom; the other was enameled a brilliant, glossy red.

The second floor was as silent and deserted as the corridor below. But just as Desmond passed the head of the main staircase he heard the sound of voices. He glanced cautiously down the well of the stairs and saw Strangwise and Bellward talking together. Bellward was on the stairs while Strangwise stood in the corridor.

"It's our last chance," Strangwise was saying.

"No, no," Bellward replied heatedly, " I tell you it is madness. We must not delay a minute. For Heaven's sake, leave the girl alone and let's save ourselves."

"What?" cried Strangwise, "and abandon Minna!"

"Minna is well able to look after herself," answered Bellward in a sulky voice, "it's a question of sauve qui peat now... every man for himself!"

"No!" said Strangwise firmly, "we'll wait for Minna, Bellward. You exaggerate the danger. I tell you I was at the garden wall within a few seconds of our friend laying you out, and I saw no sign of him in his garden. It was a physical impossibility for him to have got over the wall and back into the house in the time. And in his garden there's nowhere to hide. It's as bare as the Sahara!"

"But, good Heavens!" cried Bellward, throwing his hands excitedly above his head, "the man can't dissolve into thin air. He's gone back to the house, I tell you, and the police will be here at any minute. You know he's not in our garden; for you searched every nook and corner of it yourself. Okewood may be too clever for you, Strangwise; but he's not a magician!"

"No," said Strangwise sternly, he is not." And he added in a low voice:

"That's why I am convinced that he is in this house!"

Desmond felt his heart thump against his ribs.

Bellward seemed surprised for he cried quickly:

"What? Here?"

Strangwise nodded.

"You stand here gossiping with that man loose in the house?" exclaimed Bellward vehemently, "why the next thing we know the fellow will escape us again!"

"Oh, no, he won't" retorted the other. "Every window on the ground floor is barred... this is a home for neurasthenics, you know, and that is sometimes a polite word for a lunatic, my friend... and the doors, both front and back are locked. The keys are here!"

Desmond heard a jingle as Strangwise slapped his pocket.

"All the same," the latter went on, "it is as well to be prepared for a sudden change of quarters. That's why I want you to finish off the girl at once. Come along, we'll start now..."

"No, no!" declared Bellward. "I'm far too upset. You seem to think you can turn me on and off like you do the gas!"

"Well, as you like," said Strangwise, "but the sooner we clear up this thing the better. I'm going to see if our clever young friend has taken refuge in the servants' quarters upstairs. He's not on this floor, that's certain!"

Desmond drew back in terror. He heard the green baize door on the floor below swing back as Strangwise went out to the back stairs and Bellward's heavy step ascended the main staircase. There was something so horribly sinister in that firm, creaking tread as it mounted towards him that for the moment he lost his head. He looked round wildly for a place of concealment; but the corridor was bare. Facing him was the red enamel door. Boldly he turned the handle and walked in, softly closing the door behind him.

It was as though he had stepped into another world. The room in which he found himself was a study in vivid red emphasized by black. Red and black; these were the only colors in the room. The curtains, which were of black silk, were drawn, though it was not yet dark outside, and from the ceiling was suspended a lamp in the shape of a great scarlet bowl which cast an eerie red light on one of the most bizarre apartments that Desmond had ever seen.

It was a lacquer room in the Chinese style, popularized by the craze for barbaric decoration introduced by Bakst and the Russian Ballet into England. The walls were enameled the same brilliant glossy red as the door and hung at intervals with panels of magnificent black and gold lacquer work. The table which ran down the centre of the room was of scarlet and gold lacquer like the fantastically designed chairs and the rest of the furniture. The heavy carpet was black.

Desmond did not take in all these details at once; for his attention was immediately directed to a high-backed armchair covered in black satin which stood with its back to the door. He stared at this chair; for, peeping out above the back, making a splash of deep golden brown against the black sheen of the upholstery, was a mass of curls... Barbara Mackwayte's hair.

As he advanced towards the girl, she moaned in a high, whimpering voice:

"No, no, not again! Let me sleep! Please, please, leave me alone!"

Desmond sprang to her side.

"Barbara!" he cried and never noticed that he called her by her Christian name.

Barbara Mackwayte sat in the big black armchair, facing the black-curtained window. Her face was pale and drawn, and there were black circles under her eyes. There was a listless yet highly-strung look about her that you see in people who habitually take drugs.

She heeded not the sound of his voice. It was as though he had not spoken. She only continued to moan and mutter, moving her body about uneasily as a child does when its sleep is disturbed by nightmares. Then, to his inexpressible horror, Desmond saw that her feet were bound with straps to the legs of the chair. Her arms were similarly tethered to the arms of the chair, but her hands had been left free.

"Barbara!" said Desmond softly, you know me! I'm Desmond Okewood! I've come to take you home!"

The word "home" seemed to catch the girl's attention; for now she turned her head and looked at the young man. The expression in her eyes, wide and staring, was horrible; for it was the look of a tortured animal.

Desmond was bending to unbind the straps that fastened Barbara's arms when he heard a step outside the door. The curtains in front of the window were just beside him. They were long and reached to the floor. Without a second's hesitation he slipped behind them and found himself in the recess of a shallow bow window.

The bow window was in three parts and the central part was open wide at the bottom. It gave on a little balcony which was in reality the roof of a bow window of one of the rooms on the floor below. Desmond promptly scrambled out of the window and letting himself drop on to the balcony crouched down blow the sill.

A door opened in the room he had just left. He heard steps moving about and cupboards opened and shut. Then, there was the sound of curtains being drawn back and a voice said just above him:

"He's not here! I tell you the fellow's not in the house! Now perhaps you'll believe me!"

The balcony was fairly deep and it was growing dusk; but Desmond could scarcely hope to escape detection if Bellward, for he had recognized his voice, should think of leaning out of the window and looking down upon the balcony. With his coat collar turned up to hide the treacherous white of his linen, Desmond pressed himself as close as possible against the side of the house and waited for the joyful cry that would proclaim that he had been discovered. There was no possible means of escape; for the balcony stood at an angle of the house with no windows or water–pipes anywhere within reach, to give him a foothold, looking out on an inhospitable and gloomy area.

Whether Bellward, who appeared bent only on getting away from the house without delay, examined the balcony or not, Desmond did not know; but after the agony of suspense had endured for what seemed to him an hour, he heard Strangwise say:

"It's no good, Bellward! I'm not satisfied! And until I am satisfied that Okewood is not here, I don't leave this house. And that's that!"

Bellward swore savagely.

"We've searched the garden and not found him: we've ransacked the house from top to bottom without result. The fellow's not here; but by God, he'll be here presently with a bunch of police, and then it'll be too late! For the last time, Strangwise, will you clear out?"

There was a moment's pause. Then Desmond heard Strangwise's clear, calm voice.

"There's a balcony there... below the window, I mean."

"I've looked," replied Bellward, "and he's not there. You can see for yourself!"

The moment of discovery had arrived. To Desmond the strain seemed unbearable and to alleviate it, he began to count, as one counts to woo sleep. One! two! three! four! He heard a grating noise as the window was pushed further up. Five! six! seven! eight!

"Strange!"

Strangwise muttered the word just above Desmond's head. Then, to his inexpressible relief, he heard the other add:

"He's not there!"

And Desmond realized that the depth of the balcony had saved him. Short of getting out of the window, as he had done, the others could not see him.

The two men returned to the room and silence fell once more. Outside on the damp balcony in the growing darkness Desmond was fighting down the impulse to rush in and stake all in one desperate attempt to rescue the girl from her persecutors. But he was learning caution; and he knew he must bide his time.

Some five minutes elapsed during which Desmond could detect no definite sound from the red lacquer room except the occasional low murmur of voices. Then, suddenly, there came a high, quavering cry from the girl.

Desmond raised himself quickly erect, his ear turned so as to catch every sound from the room. The girl wailed again, a plaintive, tortured cry that seemed to issue forth unwillingly from her.

"My God!" said Desmond to himself, "I can't stand this!"

His head was level with the sill of the window which was fortunately broad. Getting a good grip on the rough cement with his hands, he hoisted himself up on to the sill, by the sheer force of his arms alone, sat poised there for an instant, then very lightly and without any noise, clambered through the window and into the room. Even as he did so, the girl cried out again.

"I can't! I can't!" she wailed.

Every nerve in Desmond 's body was tingling with rage. The blood was hotly throbbing against his temples and he was literally quivering all over with fury. But he held himself in check. This time he must not fail. Both those men were armed, he knew. What chance could he, unarmed as he was, have against them? He must wait, wait, that they might not escape their punishment.

Steadying the black silk curtains with his hands, he looked through the narrow chink where the two panels met. And this was what he saw.

Barbara Mackwayte was still in the chair; but they had unfastened her arms though her feet were still bound. She had half–risen from her seat. Her body was thrust forward in a strained, unnatural attitude; her eyes were wide open and staring; and there was a little foam on her lips. There was something hideously deformed, horribly unlife–like about her. Though her eyes were open, her look was the look of the blind; and, like the blind, she held her head a little on one side as though eager not to miss the slightest sound.

Bellward stood beside her, his face turned in profile to Desmond. His eyes were dilated and the sweat stood out in great beads on his forehead and trickled in broad lanes of moisture down his heavy cheeks. He was half–facing the girl and every time he bent towards her, she tugged and strained at her bonds as though to follow him.

"You say he has been here. Where is he? Where is he? You shall tell me where he is."

Bellward was speaking in a strange, vibrating voice. Every question appeared to be a tremendous nervous effort. Desmond, who was keenly sensitive to matters psychic, could almost feel the magnetic power radiating from the man. In the weird red light of the room, he could see the veins standing out like whipcords on the back of Bellward's hands.

231

"Tell me where he is? I command you!"

The girl wailed out again in agony and writhed in her bonds. Her voice rose to a high, gurgling scream.

"There!" she cried, pointing with eyes staring, lips parted, straight at the curtains behind which Desmond stood.

CHAPTER XXVIII. AN OFFER FROM STRANGWISE

Desmond sprang for the window; but it was too late. Strangwise who had not missed a syllable of the interrogatory was at the curtains in a flash. As he plucked the hangings back, Desmond made a rush for him; but Strangwise, wary as ever, kept his head and, drawing back, jabbed his great automatic almost in the other's face.

And then Desmond knew the game was up.

Barbara had collapsed in her chair. Her face was of an ivory pallor and she seemed to have fallen back into the characteristic hypnotic trance. As for Bellward, he had dropped on to a sofa, a loose mass, exhausted but missing nothing of what was going forward, though, for the moment, he seemed too spent to take any active part in the proceedings. In the meantime Strangwise, his white, even teeth bared in a quiet smile, was very steadily looking at his prisoner.

"Well, Desmond," he said at last, "here's a pleasant surprise! I thought you were dead!"

Desmond said nothing. He was not a coward as men go; but he was feeling horribly afraid just then. The deviltry of the scene he had just witnessed had fairly unmanned him. The red and black setting of the room had a suggestion of Oriental cruelty in its very garishness. Desmond looked from Strangwise, cool and smiling, to Bellward, gross and beastly, and from the two men to Barbara, wan and still and defenceless. And he was afraid.

Then Bellward scrambled clumsily to his feet, plucking a revolver from his inside pocket as he did so.

"You sneaking rascal," he snarled, "we'll teach you to play your dirty tricks on us!"

He raised the pistol; but Strangwise stepped between the man and his victim.

"Kill him!" cried Bellward, "and let's be rid of him once and for all!"

"What" said Strangwise. "Kill Desmond? Ah, no, my friend, I don't think so!"

And he added drily:

"At least not quite yet!"

"But you must be mad," exclaimed Bellward, toying impatiently with his weapon, "you let him escape through your fingers before! I know his type. A man like him is only safe when he's dead. And if you won't..."

"Now, Bellward," said Strangwise not budging but looking the other calmly in the eye, "you're getting excited, you know."

But Bellward muttered thickly:

"Kill him! That's all I ask. And let's get out of here! I tell you it isn't safe! Minna can shift for herself!" he added sulkily.

"As she has always done!" said a voice at the door. Mrs. Malplaquet stood there, a very distinguished looking figure in black with a handsome set of furs.

"But who's this?" she asked, catching sight of Desmond, as she flashed her beady black eyes round the group. Of Barbara she took not the slightest notice. Desmond remarked it and her indifference shocked him profoundly.

"Of course, you don't recognize him!" said Strangwise. "This is Major Desmond Okewood, more recently known as Mr. Basil Bellward!"

The woman evinced no surprise.

"So!" she said, "I thought we'd end by getting him. Well, Strangwise, what are we waiting for? Is our friend to live for ever"

"That's what I want to know!" bellowed Bellward savagely.

"I have not finished with our friend here!" observed Strangwise.

"No, no," cried Mrs. Malplaquet quickly, Strangwise, "you've had your lesson. You've lost the jewel and you're not likely to get it back unless you think that this young man has come here with it on him. Do you want to lose your life, the lives of all of us, as well? Come, come, the fellow's no earthly good to us! And he's a menace to us all as long as he's alive!"

"Minna," said Strangwise, "you must trust me. Besides..." he leaned forward and whispered something in her ear. "Now," he resumed aloud, "you shall take Bellward downstairs and leave me to have a little chat with our friend here."

To Bellward he added:

"Minna will tell you what I said. But first," he pointed to Barbara who remained apparently lifeless in her chair, "bring her round. And then I think she'd better go to bed."

"But what about the treatment to–night" asked Mrs. Malplaquet.

Strangwise smiled mysteriously.

"I'm not sure that any further treatment will be required," he said.

In the meantime, Bellward had leaned over the girl and with a few passes of his hand had brought her back to consciousness. She sat up, one hand pressed to her face, and looked about her in a dazed fashion. On recognizing Desmond she gave a little cry.

"Take her away!" commanded Strangwise.

Bellward had unfastened the ropes binding her feet, and he and Mrs. Malplaquet between them half–dragged, half–lifted the girl (for she was scarcely able to walk) from the room.

When the door had closed behind them, Strangwise pointed to a chair and pulled out his cigarette case. "Sit down, Desmond," he said, "and let's talk. Will you smoke?"

He held out his case. A cigarette was the one thing for which Desmond craved. He took one and lit it. Strangwise sat down on the other side of a curiously carved ebony table, his big automatic before him.

"I guess you're sharp enough to know when you're beaten, Desmond," he said. "You've put up a good fight and until this afternoon you were one up on me. I'll grant you that. And I don't mind admitting that you've busted up my little organization—for the present at any rate. But I'm on top now and you're in our power, old man."

"Well," replied Desmond shortly, "what are you going to do about it?"

"I'm going to utilize my advantage to the best I know how," retorted Strangwise, snapping the words, "that's good strategy, isn't it, Desmond? That's what Hamley and all the military writers teach, isn't it? And I'm going to be frank with you. I suppose you realize that your life hung by a thread in this very room only a minute ago. Do you know why I intervened to save you?"

Desmond smiled. All his habitual serenity was coming back to him. He found it hard to realize that this old brother officer of his, blowing rings of cigarette smoke at him across the table, was an enemy.

"I don't suppose it was because of the love you bear me," replied Desmond.

And he rubbed the bump on his head.

Strangwise noted the action and smiled.

"Listen here," he resumed, planking his hands down on the table and leaning forward, "I'm ready and anxious to quit this spying business. It was only a side line with me anyway. My main object in coming to this country was to recover possession of that diamond star. Once I've got it back, I'm through with England..."

"But not with the army," Desmond broke in, "thank God, we've got a swift way with traitors in this country!"

"Quite so," returned the other, "but you see, my friend, the army hasn't got me. And I have got you! But let us drop talking platitudes," he went on. "I'm no great hand at driving a bargain, Desmond—few army men are, you know—so I won't even attempt to chaffer with you. I shall tell you straight out what I am ready to offer. You were given the job of breaking up this organization, weren't you?"

Desmond was silent. He was beginning to wonder what Strangwise was driving at.

"Oh, you needn't trouble to deny it. I never spotted you, I admit, even when the real Bellward turned up: that idea of putting your name in the casualty list as 'killed' was a masterstroke; for I never looked to find you alive and trying to put it across me. But to return to what I was saying—your job was to smash my little system, and if you pull it off, it's a feather in your cap. Well, you've killed two of my people and you've arrested the ringleader."

"Meaning Behrend?" asked Desmond.

"Behrend be hanged! I mean Nur–el–Din!"

"Nur–el–Din was not the ringleader," said Desmond, "as well you know, Strangwise!"

"Your employers evidently don't share your views, Desmond," he replied, "all the documents were found on Nur–el–Din!"

"Bah!" retorted Desmond, "and what of it? Mightn't they have been planted on her in order to get her arrested to draw the suspicion away from the real criminal, yourself?"

Strangwise laughed a low, mellow laugh.

"You're devilish hard to convince," he remarked. "Perhaps you'll change your mind about it when I tell you that Nur–el–Din was sentenced to death by a general court–martial yesterday afternoon."

The blow struck Desmond straight between the eyes. The execution of spies followed hard on their conviction, he knew. Was he too late?

"Has... has she... has the sentence already been carried out?" he asked hoarsely.

Strangwise shrugged his shoulders.

"My information didn't go as far as that!" he replied. "But I expect so. They don't waste much time over these matters, old man! You see, then," he continued, "you've got the ringleader, and you shall have the other two members of the organization and save your own life into the bargain if you will be reasonable and treat with me."

Desmond looked straight at him; and Strangwise averted his eyes.

"Let me get this right," said Desmond slowly. "You let me go free—of course, I take it that my liberty includes the release of Miss Mackwayte as well—and in addition, you hand over to me your two accomplices, Bellward and the Malplaquet woman. That is your offer, isn't it? Well, what do you want from me in exchange?"

"The Star of Poland!" said Strangwise in a low voice.

"But," Desmond began. He was going to add "I haven't got it," but checked himself in time. Why should he show his hand?

Strangwise broke in excitedly.

"Man," he cried, "it was grandly done. When first I discovered the gem, I opened the package in which the silver box was wrapped and took the jewel from its case to make sure that it was there. Then I sealed it up again, silver box and all, with the firm intention that no other hand should break the seals but the hand of His Imperial Highness the Crown Prince when I reported to him that I had fulfilled my mission. So you will understand that I was loth to open it to satisfy those blockheads that evening at the Mill House.

"I carried the package on me night and day and I could hardly believe my eyes when I discovered that a box of cigarettes had been substituted for the silver casket containing the jewel. I then suspected that Barbara Mackwayte, in collusion with Nur–el–Din, whom she had visited at the Dyke Inn that evening, had played this trick on me. But before I escaped from the Mill House I picked up one of the cigarettes which fell from the box when I broke the seals. Ah! There you made a slip, Desmond. When I looked at the cigarette I found it was a 'Dionysus'—your own particular brand—why, I have smoked dozens of them with you in France. The sight of the familiar name reminded me of you and then I remembered your unexpected visit to me at the Nineveh when I was packing up to go away on leave the evening you were going back to France. I remembered that I had put the package with the jewel on my table for a moment when I was changing my tunic. Your appearance drove it out of my head for the time, and you utilized the chance to substitute a similar package for mine. It was clever, Desmond, 'pon my word it was a stroke of genius, a master coup which in my country would have placed you at the very top of the tree in the Great General Staff!"

Desmond listened to this story in amazement. He did not attempt to speculate on the different course events would have taken had he but known that the mysterious jewel which had cost old Mackwayte his life, had been in his, Desmond's, possession from the very day on which he had assumed the guise and habiliments of Mr. Bellward. He was racking his brains to think what he had done with the box of cigarettes he had purchased at the Dionysus shop on the afternoon of the day he had taken the leave train back to France.

He remembered perfectly buying the cigarettes for the journey. But he didn't have them on the journey; for the captain of the leave boat had given him some cigars as Desmond had nothing to smoke. And then with a flash he remembered. He had packed the cigarettes in his kit—his kit which had gone over to France in the hold of the leave boat? And to think that there was a 100,000 pound jewel in charge of the M.L.O. at a French port!

The idea tickled Desmond's sense of humor and he smiled.

"Come," cried Strangwise, "you've heard my terms. This jewel, this Star of Poland, it is nothing to you or your Government. You restore it to me and I won't even ask you for a safe conduct back to Germany. I'll just slide out and it will be as if I had never been to England at all. As for my organization, you, Desmond Okewood, have blown it sky–high!"

He stretched out his hand to Desmond as though he expected the other to produce the gem from his pocket. But Desmond rose to his feet and struck the hand contemptuously on one side. The smile had vanished from his face.

"Are you sure that is all you have to say to me?" he asked.

Strangwise had stood up as well.

"Why, yes!" he said, "I think so!"

"Well, then," said Desmond firmly, "just listen to me for a moment! Here's my answer. You've lost the jewel for good and all, and you will never get it back. Your offer to betray your accomplices to me in exchange for the Star of Poland is an empty one; for your accomplices will be arrested with you. And lastly I give you my word that I shall make it my personal duty to see that you are not shot by clean–handed British soldiers, but strung up by the neck by the common hangman—as the murderer that you are!"

Strangwise's face underwent an extraordinary change. His suavity vanished, his easy smile disappeared and he looked balefully across the table as the other fearlessly confronted him.

"If you are a German, as you seem to be," Desmond went on, "then I tell you I shall never have guessed it until this interview between us. But a man who can murder a defenceless old man and torture a young girl and then propose to sell his pals to a British officer at the price of that officer's honor can only be a Hun! And you seem to be a pretty fine specimen of your race!"

Strangwise mastered his rising passion by an obvious effort; but his face was evil as he spoke.

"I put that Malplaquet woman off by appealing to her avarice," he said, "I've promised her and Bellward a thousand pounds apiece as their share of my reward for recovering the jewel. I only have to say the word, Okewood, and your number's up! And you may as well know that Bellward will try his hand on you before he kills you. If that girl had known where the Star of Poland was, Bellward would have had it out of her! Three times a day he's put her into the hypnotic sleep. I warn you, you won't like the interrogatory!"

239

The door flew open and Bellward came in. He went eagerly to Strangwise.

"Well, have you got it!" he demanded.

"Have you anything further to say, Desmond?" asked Strangwise. "Perhaps you would care to reconsider your decisions"

Desmond shook his head

"You've had my answer!" he said doggedly.

"Then, my friend," said Strangwise to Bellward, "after dinner you shall try your hand on this obstinate fool. But first we'll take him upstairs."

He was close beside Desmond and as he finished speaking he suddenly caught him by the throat and forced him back into the chair to which Barbara had been tethered. To struggle was useless, and Desmond suffered them to bind his arms and feet to the arms and legs of the chair. Then the two men picked him up, chair and all, and bore him from the room upstairs to the third floor. There they carried him into a dark room where they left him, turning the key in the lock as they went away.

CHAPTER XXIX. DOT AND DASH

For a long time after the retreating footsteps of Strangwise and Bellward had died away, Desmond sat listless, preoccupied with his thoughts. They were somber enough. The sinister atmosphere of the house, weighing upon him, seemed to deepen his depression.

About his own position he was not concerned at all. This is not an example of unselfishness it is simply an instance of the force of discipline which trains a man to reckon the cause as everything and himself as naught. And Desmond was haunted by the awful conviction that he had at length reached the end of his tether and that nothing could now redeem the ignominious failure he had made of his mission.

He had sacrificed Barbara Mackwayte; he had sacrificed Nur-el-Din; he had not even been clever enough to save his own skin. And Strangwise, spy and murderer, had escaped and was now free to reorganize his band after he had put Barbara and Desmond out of the way.

The thought was so unbearable that it stung Desmond into action. Strangwise should not get the better of him, he resolved, and he had yet this brief interval of being alone in which he might devise some scheme to rescue Barbara and secure the arrest of Strangwise and his accomplices. But how?

He raised his head and looked round the room. The curtains had not been drawn and enough light came into the room from the outside to enable him to distinguish the outlines of the furniture. It was a bedroom, furnished in rather a massive style, with some kind of thick, soft carpet into, which the feet sank.

Desmond tested his bonds. He was very skillfully tied up. He fancied that with a little manipulation he might contrive to loosen the rope round his right arm, for one of the knots had caught in the folds of his coat. The thongs round his left arm and two legs were, however, so tight that he thought he had but little chance of ridding himself of them, even should he get his right arm free; for the knots were tied at the back under the seat of the chair in such a way that he could not reach them.

He, therefore, resigned himself to conducting operations in the highly ridiculous posture in which he found himself, that is to say, with a large arm-chair attached to him, rather like a snail with its house on its back. After a certain amount of maneuvering he discovered that, by means of a kind of slow, lumbering crawl, he was able to move across the ground. It might have proved a noisy business on a parquet floor; but Desmond moved only a foot or two at a time and the pile carpet deadened the sound.

They had deposited him in his chair in the centre of the room near the big brass bedstead. After ten minutes' painful crawling he had reached the toilet table which stood in front of the window with a couple of electric candles on either side of the mirror. He moved the toilet table to one side, then bumped steadily across the carpet until he had reached the window. And then he gave a little gasp of surprise.

He found himself looking straight at the window of his own bedroom at Mrs. Viljohn-Smythe's. There was no mistaking it. The electric light was burning and the curtains had not yet been drawn. He could see the black and pink eiderdown on his bed and the black lining of the chintz curtains. Then he remembered the slope of the hill. He must be in the room from which he had seen Bellward looking out.

The sight of the natty bedroom across the way moved Desmond strangely. It seemed to bring home to him for the first time the extraordinary position in which he found himself, a prisoner in a perfectly respectable suburban house in a perfectly respectable quarter of London, in imminent danger of a violent death.

He wouldn't give in without a struggle. Safety stared him in the face, separated only by a hundred yards of grass and shrub and wall. He instinctively gripped the arms of the chair to raise himself to get a better view from the window, forgetting he was bound. The ropes cut his arms cruelly and brought him back to earth.

He tested again the thongs fastening his right arm. Yes! they were undoubtedly looser than the others. He pulled and tugged and writhed and strained. Once in his struggles he crashed into the toilet table and all but upset one of the electric candles which slid to the table's very brink and was saved, as by a miracle, from falling to the floor. He resumed his efforts, but with less violence. It was in vain. Though the ropes about his right arm were fairly loose, the wrist was solidly fastened to the chair, and do what he would, he could not wrest it free. He clawed desperately with his fingers and thumb, but all in vain.

In the midst of his struggles he was arrested by the sound of whistling. Somebody in the distance outside was whistling, clearly and musically, a quaint, jingling sort of jig that struck familiarly on Desmond's ear. Somehow it reminded him of the front. It brought with it dim memory of the awakening to the early morning chill of a Nissen hut, the smell of damp earth, the whirr of aircraft soaring through the morning sky, the squeak of flutes, the roll of drums... why, it was the Grand Reveille," that ancient military air which every soldier knows.

He stopped struggling and peered cautiously out into the dusk. The time for darkening the windows must be at hand, he thought, for in most of the houses the blinds were already drawn. Here and there, however, an oblong of yellow light showed up against the dark mass of the houses on the upper slopes of the hill. The curtains of his bedroom at Mrs. Viljohn−Smythe's were not yet drawn and the light still burned brightly above the bed.

The whistling continued with occasional interruptions as though the whistler were about some work or other. And then suddenly "Buzzer" Barling, holding something in one hand and rubbing violently with the other, stepped into the patch of light between the window and the bed in Desmond's bedroom.

Desmond's heart leaped within him. Here was assistance close at hand. Mechanically he sought to raise his hand to open the window, but an agonising twinge reminded him of his thongs. He swiftly reviewed in his mind the means of attracting the attention of the soldier opposite. Whatever he was going to do, he must do quickly; for the fact that people were beginning to darken their windows showed that it must be close on half–past six, and about seven o'clock, Barling, after putting out Desmond's things, was accustomed to go out for the evening.

Should he shout? Should he try and break the window? Desmond rejected both these suggestions. While it was doubtful whether Barling would hear the noise or, if he heard it, connect it with Desmond, it was certain that Strangwise and Bellward would do both and be upon Desmond without a moment's delay.

Then Desmond's eye fell upon the electric candle which had slid to the very edge of the table. It was mounted in a heavy brass candle–stick and the switch was in the pedestal, jutting out over the edge of the table in the position in which the candle now stood. The candle was clear of the mirror and there was nothing between it and the window. Desmond's brain took all this in at a glance. That glance showed him that Providence was being good to him.

A couple of jerks of the chair brought him alongside the table. Its edge was practically level with the arms of the chair so that, by getting into the right position, he was able to manipulate the switch with his fingers. And then, thanking God and the Army Council for the recent signalling course he had attended, he depressed the switch with a quick, snapping movement and jerked it up again, sending out the dots and dashes of the Morse code.

"B–A–R–L–I–N–G" he spelt out, slowly and laboriously, it is true; for he was not an expert.

As he worked the switch, he looked across at the illuminated window of the room in which Barling stood, with bent head, earnestly engaged upon his polishing.

"B–a–r–l–i–n–g–ack–ack–ack–B–a–r–l–i–n–g–ack–ack–ack"

The light flickered up and down in long and short flashes. Still "Buzzer" Barling trilled away at the "Grand Reveille" nor raised his eyes from his work.

Desmond varied the call:

"O–K–E–W–O–O–D T–O B–A–R–L–I–N–G" he flashed.

He repeated the call twice and was spelling it out for the third time when Desmond saw the "Buzzer" raise his head.

The whistling broke off short.

"0–k–e–w–o–o–d t–o B–a–r–l–i–n–g" flickered the light.

The next moment the bedroom opposite was plunged in darkness. Immediately afterwards the light began to flash with bewildering rapidity. But Desmond recognized the call.

"I am ready to take your message," it said.

"S–t–r–a–n–g–w–i–s–e h–a–s g–o–t m–e ack–ack–ack," Desmond flashed back, "f–e–t–c–h h–e–l–p a–t o–n–c–e ack–ack–ack: d–o–n–t r–e–p–l–y; ack–ack–ack; s–e–n–d o–n–e d–o–t o–n–e d–a–s–h t–o s–h–o–w y–o–u u–n–d–e–r–s–t–a–n–d ack–ack–ack!"

For he was afraid lest the light flashing from the house opposite might attract the attention of the men downstairs.

He was very slow and he made many mistakes, so that it was with bated breath that, after sending his message, he watched the window opposite for the reply.

It came quickly. A short flash and a long one followed at once. After that the room remained in darkness. With a sigh of relief Desmond, as quietly as possible, manoeuvred the dressing–table back into place and then jerked the chair across the carpet to the position where Strangwise and Bellward had left him in the middle of the floor:

It was here that the two men found him, apparently asleep, when they came up half–an–hour later. They carried him down to the red lacquer room again.

"Well, Desmond!" said Strangwise, when their burden had been deposited on the floor under the crimson lamp.

"Well, Maurice?" answered the other.

Strangwise noticed that Desmond had addressed him by his Christian name for the first time since he had been in the house and his voice was more friendly when he spoke again.

"I see you're going to be sensible, old man," he said. "Believe me, it's the only thing for you to do. You're going to give up the Star of Poland, aren't you?"

"Oh, no, Maurice, I'm not," replied Desmond in a frank, even voice. "I've told you what I'm going to do. I'm going to hand you over to the people at Pentonville to hang as a murderer. And I shouldn't be at all surprised if they didn't run up old Bellward there alongside of you!"

Strangwise shook his head at him.

"You are very ill–advised to reject my offer, Desmond," he said, "for it simply means that I can do nothing more for you. Our friend Bellward now assumes the direction of affairs. I don't think you can realize what you are letting yourself in for. You appear to have been dabbling in Intelligence work. Perhaps it would interest you to hear something about this, our latest German method for extracting Accurate information from reluctant or untruthful witnesses. Bellward, perhaps you would enlighten him."

Bellward smiled grimly.

"It is a blend," he explained glibly, "of that extreme form of cross–examination which the Americans call 'the third degree' and hypnotic treatment. Many people, as you are doubtless aware, are less responsive to hypnotic influence than others. An intensified course of the third degree and lack of sleep renders such refractory natures extraordinarily susceptible to mesmeric treatment. It prepares the ground as it were!"

Bellward coughed and looked at Desmond over his tortoise–shell spectacles which he had put on again.

"The method has had its best results when practised on women," he resumed. "Our people in Holland have found it very successful in the case of female spies who come across the Belgian frontier. But some women—Miss Barbara, for example—seem to have greater powers of resistance than others. We had to employ a rather drastic form of the third degree for her, didn't we, Strangwise?"

He laughed waggishly.

"And you'll be none too easy either," he added.

"You beasts," cried Desmond, "but just you wait, your turn will come!"

"Yours first, however," chuckled Bellward. "I rather fancy you will think us beasts by the time we have done with you, my young friend!"

Then he turned to Strangwise.

"Where's Minna?" he asked.

"With the girl."

"Is the girl sleeping?"

Strangwise nodded.

"She wanted it," he replied, "no sleep for four days... I tell you it takes some constitution to hold out against that!"

"Well," said Bellward, rubbing the palms of his hands together, "as we're not likely to be disturbed, I think we'll make a start!"

He advanced a pace to where Desmond sat trussed up, hand and foot, in his chair. Bellward's eyes were large and luminous, and as Desmond glanced rather nervously at the face of the man approaching him, he was struck by the compelling power they seemed to emit.

Desmond bent his head to avoid the insistent gaze. But in a couple of quick strides Bellward was at his side and stooping down, had thrust his face right into his victim's. Bellward's face was so close that Desmond felt his warm breath on his cheek whilst those burning eyes seemed to stab through his closed eyelids and steadily, stealthily, draw his gaze.

Resolutely Desmond held his head, averted. All kinds of queer ideas were racing through his brain, fragments of nursery rhymes, scenes from his regimental life in India, memories of the front, which he had deliberately summoned up to keep his attention distracted from those merciless eyes, like twin search–lights pitilessly playing on his face.

Bellward could easily have taken Desmond by the chin and forced his face up until his eyes came level with the other's. But he offered no violence of any kind. He remained in his stooping position, his face thrust forward, so perfectly still that Desmond began to be tormented by a desire to risk a rapid peep just to see what the mesmerist was doing.

He put the temptation aside. He must keep his eyes shut, he told himself. But the desire increased, intensified by the strong attraction radiating from Bellward, and finally Desmond succumbed. He opened his eyes to dart a quick glance at Bellward and found the other's staring eyes, with pupils distended, fixed on his. And Desmond felt his resistance ebb. He tried to avert his gaze; but it was too late. That basilisk glare held him fast.

With every faculty of his mind he fought against the influence which was slowly, irresistibly, shackling his brain. He laughed, he shouted defiance at Bellward and Strangwise, he sang snatches of songs. But Bellward never moved a muscle. He seemed to be in a kind of cataleptic trance, so rigid his body, so unswerving his stare.

The lights in the room seemed to be growing dim. Bellward's eyeballs gleamed redly in the dull crimson light flooding the room. Desmond felt himself longing for some violent shock that would disturb the hideous stillness of the house. His own voice was sounding dull and blunted in his ears. What was the use of struggling further? He might as well give up...

A loud crash, the sound of a door slamming, reechoed through the house. The room shook. The noise brought Desmond back to his senses and at the same time the chain binding him to Bellward snapped. For Bellward started and raised his head and Strangwise sprang to the door. Then Desmond heard the door burst open, there was the deafening report of a pistol, followed by another, and Bellward crashed forward on his knees with a sobbing grunt. As Desmond had his back to the door he could see nothing of what was taking place, but some kind of violent struggle was going on; for he heard the smash of glass as a piece of furniture was upset.

Then suddenly the room seemed full of people. The thongs binding his hands and feet fell to the ground. "Buzzer" Barling stood at his side.

CHAPTER XXX. HOHENLINDEN TRENCH

A man broke quickly away from the throng of people pressing into the room. It was Francis. The Chief and Mr. Marigold were close at his heels.

"Des," cried Francis, "ah! thank God! you are all right!"

Desmond looked in a dazed fashion from one to the other. The rapid transition from the hush of the room to the scene of confusion going on around him had left him bewildered. His glance traveled from the faces of the men gathered round his chair to the floor. The sight of Bellward, very still, hunched up with his face immersed in the thick black carpet, seemed to recall something to his mind.

"Barbara!" he murmured in a strained voice.

"She's all right!" replied his brother, "we found her on the bed in a room on the floor below sleeping the sleep of the just. The woman's vanished, though. I'm afraid she got away! But who's this?"

He pointed to "Buzzer" Barling who stood stiffly at attention beside Desmond's chair.

"Ay, who are you, young fellow" repeated Mr. Marigold coming up close to the soldier. "Ask him!" said Desmond, raising his arm, "he knows!"

The group around the door had broken up. Strangwise, his wrists handcuffed together, his hair dishevelled and his collar torn, stood there between two plain clothes men. And at him Desmond pointed.

Strangwise was staring at the straight, square figure of the gunner, awkwardly attired in one of Desmond's old suits. Berling's frank, honest eyes returned the other's gaze unflinchingly. But Strangwise was obviously taken aback, though only for the moment. The flush that mounted to his cheek quickly died down, leaving him as cool and impassive as ever.

"Do you know this man!" the Chief, asked sternly, addressing Strangwise.

"Certainly," retorted Strangwise, "it's Gunner Barling, one of the Brigade signallers!"

Mr. Marigold gave a keen glance at the soldier.

"So you're Barling, eh?" he muttered as though talking to himself, "ah! this is getting interesting!"

"Yes," said Desmond, "this is Gunner Barling. Have a good look at him, Strangwise. It is he who summoned these gentlemen to my assistance. It is he who's going to tell them who and what you are!"

Turning to the Chief he added with a touch of formality: "May Gunner Barling tell his story, sir?"

"By all means," replied the Chief. "I am all attention. But first let this fellow be removed."

And beckoning to two of his men; he pointed to the body of Bellward.

"Is he dead" asked Desmond.

The Chief shook his head.

"He drew a bead on one of my men as we came in," he answered, "and got a bullet through the chest for his pains. We'll have to cure him of this gunshot wound so as to get him ready to receive another!"

He laughed a grim dry laugh at his little joke.

"Now, Barling," said Desmond, when Bellward had been borne away, "I want you to tell these gentlemen the story of the raid on the Hohenlinden trench."

Barling glanced rather self–consciously about him. But the look of intense, almost nervous watchfulness on the face of Maurice Strangwise seemed to reassure him. And when he spoke, he spoke straight at Strangwise.

"Well," he said, "Major Okewood here, what I used to know along of my brother being his servant, says as how you gentlemen'll make it all right about my stoppin' absent if I tells you what I know about this orficer. Tell it I will and gladly; for it was all along of him that I spoiled a clean sheet of eighteen years' service, gentlemen.

"When we was down Arras way a few months ago the infantry was a–goin' to do a raid, see? And the Captain here was sent along of the infantry party to jine up a lineback to the 'tillery brigade headquarters. Well, he took me and another chap, name o' Macdonald—Bombardier he was—along with him as signallers.

"This was a daylight raid, d'ye see, gentlemen? Our chaps went over at four o'clock in the afternoon. They was to enter a sort o' bulge in the German front line wot they called Hohenlinden Trench, bomb the Gers. out o' that, push on to the support line and clear out that and then come back. The rocket to fetch 'em home was to go up forty minutes after they started.

"Well, me and Mac—that's the Bombardier—went over with th' officer here just behind the raiding party. O' course Fritz knew we was comin' for it was broad daylight, and that clear you could see for miles over the flats. First thing we knew Fritz had put down a roarin', tearin' barrage, and we hadn't gone not twenty yards before ole Mac. cops one right on the nut; about took his head off, it did. So me and the captain we goes on alone and drops all nice and comfortable in the trench, and I starts getting my line jined up.

"It was a longish job but I got the brigade line goin' at last. Our chaps had cleared out the front line and was off down the communication trenches to the support. What with machine-guns rattlin' and bombs a-goin' off down the trench and Fritz's barrage all over the shop the row was that awful we had to buzz every single word.

"There was a bit of a house like, a goodish way in front, X farm, they called it, and presently the Brigade tells the Captain, who was buzzin' to them, to register B battery on to the farm.

"'I can't see the farm nohow from here,' sez the Captain. I could see it as plain as plain, and I pointed it out to him. But no! he couldn't see it.

"'I'll crawl out of the trench a bit, gunner,' sez he to me, 'you sit tight,' he sez, 'I'll let you know when to follow!'"

"With that he up and out o' the trench leavin' me and the instruments behind all among the dead Gers., and our lads had killed a tidy few. It was pretty lonely round about were I was; for our chaps had all gone on and was bombin' the Gers., like they was a lot o' rabbits, up and down the support line.

"I followed the Captain with me eye, gentlemen, and I'm blessed if he didn't walk straight across the open and over the support trench. Then he drops into a bit of a shell-hole and I lost sight of him. Well, I waited and waited and no sign of th' orficer. The rocket goes up and our lads begin to come back with half a dozen Huns runnin' in front of them with their hands up. Some of the chaps as they passed me wanted to know if I was a-goin' to stay there all night! And the Brigade buzzin' like mad to talk to the Captain.

"I sat in that blessed trench till everybody had cleared out. Then, seeing as how not even the docket had brought th' orficer back, I sez to myself as how he must ha' stopped one.

So I gets out of the trench and starts crawling across the top towards the place where I see the Captain disappear. As I got near the support line the ground went up a little and then dropped, so I got a bit of a view on to the ground ahead. And then I sees the Captain here!"

Buzzer Barling stopped. All had listened to his story with the deepest interest, especially Strangwise, who never took his eyes off the gunner's brown face. Some men are born story–tellers and there was a rugged picturesqueness about Barling's simple narrative which conjured up in the minds of his hearers the picture of the lonely signaller cowering in the abandoned trench among the freshly slain, waiting for the officer who never came back.

"It's not a nice thing to have to say about an orficer," the gunner presently continued, "and so help me God, gentlemen, I kep' my mouth shut about it until... until..."

He broke off and looked quickly at Desmond.

"Keep that until the end, Barling," said Desmond, "finish about the raid now!"

"Well, as I was sayin', gentlemen, I was up on a bit of hillock near Fritz's support line when I sees the Captain here. He was settin' all comfortable in a shell–hole, his glases in his hand, chattin' quite friendly like with two of the Gers. officers, I reckoned they was, along o' the silver lace on their collars. One was wearin' one o' them coal–scuttle helmets, t'other a little flat cap with a shiny peak. And the Captain here was a–pointin' at our lines and a–wavin' his hand about like he was a–tellin' the two Fritzes all about it, and the chap in the coal–scuttle hat was a–writin' it all down in a book."

Barling paused. He was rather flushed and his eyes burned brightly in his weather–beaten face.

"Eighteen year I done in the Royal Regiment," he went on, and his voice trembled a little, "and me father a battery sergeant–major before me, and I never thought to see one of our orficers go over to the enemy. Fritz was beginnin' to come back to his front line: I could see their coal–scuttle hats a–bobbin' up and down the communication trenches, so I crawled back the way I come and made a bolt for our lines.

"I meant to go straight to the B.C. post and report wot I seen to the Major. But I hadn't the heart to, gentlemen, when I was up against it. It was an awful charge to bring against an orficer, d'you see? I told myself I didn't know but what the Captain hadn't been taken prisoner and was makin' the best of it, w'en I see him, stuffin' the Fritzes up with a lot o' lies. And so I jes' reported as how th' orficer 'ad crawled out of the trench and never come back. And then this here murder happened..."

Mr. Marigold turned to the Chief.

"If you remember, sir," he said, "I found this man's leave paper in the front garden of the Mackwayte's house at Laleham Villas, Seven Kings, the day after the murder. There are one or two questions I should like to put..."

"No need to arsk any questions," said Barling. "I'll tell you the whole story meself, mister. I was on leave at the time, due to go back to France the next afternoon. I'd been out spending the evenin' at my niece's wot's married and livin' out Seven Kings way. Me and her man wot works on the line kept it up a bit late what with yarnin' about the front an' that and it must a' been nigh on three o'clock w'en I left him to walk back to the Union Jack Club where I had a bed.

"There's a corfee–stall near their road and the night bein' crool damp I thought as how a nice cup o' corfee'd warm me up afore I went back to the Waterloo Bridge Road. I had me cup o' corfee and was jes' a–payin' the chap what has the pitch w'en a fellow passes by right in the light o' the lamp on the stall. It was th' orficer here, in plain clothes—shabby–like he was dressed—but I knew him at once.

"'Our orficers don't walk about these parts after midnight dressed like tramps,' I sez to meself, and rememberin' what I seen at the Hohenlinden Trench I follows him..."

"Just a minute!"

The Chief's voice broke in upon the narrative.

"Didn't you know, Barling, hadn't you heard, about Captain Strangwise's escape from a German prisoners of war camp?"

"No, sir!" replied the gunner.

"There was a good deal about it in the papers."

"I've not got much eddication, sir," said Barling, "that's w'y I never took the stripe and I don't take much account of the newspapers an' that's a fact!"

"Well, go on!" the Chief bade him.

"It was pretty dark in the streets and I follered him along without his seeing me into the main−road and then down a turnin'..."

"Laleham Villas," prompted Mr. Marigold.

"I wasn't payin' much attention to were he was leadin' me," said Barling, "what I wanted to find out was what he was up to! Presently he turned in at a gate. I was closer up than I meant to be, and he swung in so sudden that I had to drop quick and crouch behind the masonry of the front garden wall. My leave pass must a' dropped out o' my pocket and through the railin's into the garden.

"Well, the front door must a' been on the jar for th' orficer here just pushes it open and walks in, goin' very soft like. I crep' in the front gate and got as far as the door w'ich was a−standin' half open. I could 'ear the stair creakin' under 'im and I was just wonderin' whether I should go into the house w'en I hears a bang and wi' that someone comes aflyin' down the stairs, dodges through the front hall and out at the back. I see him come scramblin' over the back gate and was a−goin' to stop him thinkin' it was th' orficer here w'en I sees it is a tubby little chap, not big like the Captain. And then it come over me quite sudden−like that burglary and murder had been done in the house and wot would I say if a p'liceman come along? So I slipped off and went as hard as I could go back to the old Union Jack Club.

"The next mornin' I found I'd lost me leave paper. I was afraid to go and report it in case it had been picked up, and they'd run me in for this murder job. That's how I come to desert, gentlemen, and spoilt a eighteen years' conduct sheet without a entry over this murderin' spy here!"

254

Gunner Barling broke off abruptly as though he had committed himself to a stronger opinion than discipline would allow. It was the Chief who broke the silence following the termination of the gunner's story.

"Strangwise," he said, "hadn't you better tell us who you are?"

"He's an officer of the Prussian Guard," Desmond said, "and he was sent over here by the German secret service organization in the United States to get a commission in the British Army. When a good man was wanted to recover the Star of Poland for the Crown Prince, the secret service people in Berlin sent word to Strangwise (who was then serving with the gunners in France) to get himself captured. The German military authorities duly reported him a prisoner of war and then let him 'escape' as' the easiest and least suspicious means of getting him back to London!"

The Chief smiled genially.

"That's a dashed clever idea," he observed shrewdly, "'pon my word, that's bright! That's very bright! I should like to compliment the man who thought of that!"

"Then you may address your compliments to me, Chief," said Strangwise.

The Chief turned and looked at him.

"I've met many of your people in my time, Strangwise," he said, "but I don't know you! Who are you?"

Strangwise laughed.

"Ask Nur–el–Din, " he said, "that is to say, if you haven't shot her yet!"

"And if we have?" asked the Chief.

Desmond sprang tip.

"It isn't possible!" he cried. "Why, the woman's a victim, not a principal! Chief..."

"What if we have?" asked the Chief again.

A curious change had come over the prisoner. His jaunty air had left him and there was an apprehensive look in his eyes.

"I would have saved her if I could have," Strangwise said, "but she played me false over the jewel. She imperiled the success of my mission. You English have no idea of discipline. To us Prussian officers an order stands above everything else. There is nothing we would not sacrifice to obey our orders. And my order was to recover the Star of Poland for His Imperial Highness the Crown Prince, Lieutenant Colonel in the Regiment to which I have the honor to belong, the First Regiment of Prussian Foot Guards. But Nur–el–Din plotted with our friend here and with that little fool upstairs to upset my plans, and I had no mercy on her. I planted those documents in her dress—or rather Bellward did—to draw suspicion away from me. I thought you English would be too flabby to execute a woman; but I reckoned on you putting the girl away for some years to come. I would have shot her as I shot Rass if..." His voice trembled and he was silent.

"If what?" asked the Chief.

"If she hadn't been my wife," said Strangwise.

CHAPTER XXXI. THE 100,000 KIT

It was a clear, crisp morning with a sparkle of frost on jetty and breakwater. The English Channel stretched flashing like a living sheet of glass to the filmy line marking the coast of France, as serene and beautiful in its calm as it is savage and cruel in its anger. It was high tide; but only a gentle murmur came from the little waves that idly beat upon the shore in front of the bungalow.

A girl lay in a deck chair on the verandah, well wrapped up against the eager air. But the fresh breeze would not be denied and, foiled by the nurse's vigilance of its intents against the patient, it revenged itself by blowing havoc among the soft brown curls which peeped out from under the girl's hat.

She turned to the man at her side.

"Look!" she said, and pointed seawards with her finger.

A convoy of vessels was standing out to sea framed in the smoke–blurs of the escorting destroyers. Ugly, weatherbeaten craft were the steamers with trails of smoke blown out in the breeze behind them. They rode the sea's highway with confidence, putting their trust in the unseen power that swept the road clear for them.

"Transports, aren't they?" asked the man.

But he scarcely looked at the transports. He was watching the gleam of the sun on the girl's brown hair and contrasting the deep gray of her eyes with the ever–changing hues of the sea.

"Yes," replied the girl. "It's the third day they've gone across! By this time next week there'll be ten fresh divisions in France. How secure they look steaming along! And to think they owe it all to you!"

The man laughed and flushed up.

"From the strictly professional standpoint the less said about me the better," he said.

"What nonsense you talk!" cried the girl. "When the Chief was down to see me yesterday, he spoke of nothing but you. 'They beat him, but he won out!' he said, 'they shook him off but he went back and found 'em!' He told me it was a case of grit versus violence—and grit won. In all the time I've known the Chief, I've never heard him talk so much about one man before. Do you know," Barbara went on, looking up at Desmond, "I think you've made the Chief feel a little bit ashamed of himself. And that I may tell you is a most extraordinary achievement!"

"Do you think you're strong enough to hear some news?" asked Desmond after a pause.

"Of course," replied the girl. "But I think I can guess it. It's about Strangwise, isn't it?"

Desmond nodded.

"He was shot yesterday morning," he replied. "I'm glad they did it in France. I was terrified lest they should want me to go to it."

"Why?" asked the girl with a suspicion of indignation in her voice, "he deserved no mercy."

"No," replied Desmond slowly, "he was a bad fellow—a Prussian through and through. He murdered your poor father, he shot Rass, he instigated the killing of the maid, Marie, he was prepared to sacrifice his own wife even, to this Prussian God of militarism which takes the very soul out of a man's body and puts it into the hands of his superior officer. And yet, and yet, when one has soldiered with a man, Barbara, and roughed it with him and been shelled and shot at with him, there seems to be a bond of sympathy between you and him for ever after. And he was a brave man, Barbara, cruel and unscrupulous, I admit, but there was no fear in him, and I can't help admiring courage. I seem to think of him as two men—the man I soldiered with and the heartless brute who watched while that beast Bellward..."

He broke off as a spasm of pain crossed the girl's face. "I shall remember the one and forget the other," he concluded simply.

"Tell me," said the girl suddenly, "who was Strangwise?"

"After he was arrested and just before they were going to take him off," Desmond said, "he asked to be allowed to say a word privately to the Chief. We were all sent away and he told the Chief his real name. He thought he was going to be hanged, you see, and while he never shrank from any crime in the fulfilment of his mission, he was terrified of a shameful death. He begged the Chief to see that his real name was not revealed for the disgrace that his execution would bring upon his family. Curiously Prussian attitude of mind, isn't it?"

"And what did the Chief say?"

"I don't know; but he was mighty short with him, I expect."

"And what was Strangwise's real name?"

"When he told us that Nur–el–Din was his wife, I knew at once who he was. His name is Hans von Schornbeek. He was in the Prussian Foot Guards, was turned out for some reason or other and went to America where, after a pretty rough time, he was taken on by the German secret service organization. He was working for them when he met Nur–el–Din. They were married out there and, realizing the possibilities of using her as a decoy in the secret service, he sent her to Brussels where the Huns were very busy getting ready for war. He treated her abominably; but the girl was fond of him in her way and even when she was in fear of her life from this man she never revealed to me the fact that he was Hans von Schornbeek and her husband."

Barbara sat musing for a while, her eyes on the restless sea.

"How strange it is," she said, "to think that they are all dispersed now... and the transports are sailing securely to France. Two were killed at the Mill House, Behrend committed suicide in prison, Bellward died in hospital, Mrs. Malplaquet has disappeared, and now Strangwise has gone. There only remains..."

She cast a quick glance at Desmond but he was gazing seaward at the smoke of the transports smudging the horizon.

"What are they going to do with Nur–el–Din?" she asked rather abruptly.

"Didn't the Chief tell you?" said Desmond.

"He only asked me what I had to say in the matter as I had had to suffer at her hands. But I told him I left the matter entirely to him. I said I took your point of view that Nur–el–Din was the victim of her husband..."

"That was generous of you, Barbara," Desmond said gently.

She sighed.

"Daddy knew her as a little girl," she answered, "and he was so pleased to see her again that night. She never had a chance. I hope she'll get one now!"

"They're going to intern her, I believe," said Desmond, "until the end of the war; they could do nothing else, you know. But she will be well looked after, and I think she will be safer in our charge than if she were allowed to remain at liberty. The German Secret Service has had a bad knock, you know. Somebody has got to pay for it!"

"I know," the girl whispered, "and it frightens me."

"You poor child!" said Desmond, "you've had a rough time. But it's all over now. And that reminds me, Barney is coming up for sentence to-day; they charged him with murder originally; but Marigold kept on getting him remanded until they were able to alter the charge to one of burglary. He'll probably get two years' hard labor, Marigold says."

"Poor Barney!" said Barbara, "I wish they would let him go free. All these weeks the mystery of poor Daddy's death has so weighed upon my mind that now it has been cleared up I feel as though one day I might be happy again. And I want everybody to be happy, too!"

"Barbara," said Desmond and took her hand.

Barbara calmly withdrew it from his grasp and brushed an imaginary curl out of her eye.

"Any news of your hundred thousand pound kit?" she asked, by way of turning the conversation.

"By Jove," said Desmond, "there was a letter from Cox's at the club this morning but I was so rushed to catch my train that I shoved it in my pocket and forgot all about it. I wrote and asked them weeks ago to get my kit back from France. Here we are!"

He pulled a letter out of his pocket, slit open the envelope and took out a printed form. Barbara, propping herself up with one hand on his shoulder, leaned over him to read the communication. This is what she read.

"We are advised," the form ran, "that a Wolseley valise forwarded to you on the 16th inst. from France has been lost by enemy action. We are enclosing a compensation form which..."

But neither troubled to read further.

"Gone to the bottom, by Jove!" cried Desmond. "But isn't it strange," he went on, "to think of the Star of Poland lying out there on the bed of the Channel? Well, I'm not so sure that it isn't the best place for it. It won't create any further trouble in this world at least!"

"Poor Nur–el–Din!" sighed the girl.

They sat awhile in silence together and watched the gulls circling unceasingly above the receding tide.

"You're leaving here to–morrow then?" said Desmond presently.

Barbara nodded

"And going back to your work with the Chief?"

Barbara nodded again.

"It's not good enough," cried Desmond. "This is no job for a girl like you, Barbara. The strain is too much; the risks are too great. Besides, there's something I wanted to say..."

Barbara stopped him.

"Don't say it!" she bade him.

"But you don't know what I was going to say!" he protested.

Barbara smiled a little happy smile.

"Barbara..." Desmond began.

Her hand still rested on his shoulder and he put his hand over hers. For a brief moment she let him have his way.

Then she withdrew her hand.

"Desmond," she said, looking at him with kindly eyes, "we both have work to do..."

"We have," replied the man somberly, "and mine's at the front!"

The girl shook her head.

"No!" she said. "Henceforward it's where the Chief sends you!"

Desmond set his jaw obstinately.

"I may have been a Secret Service agent by accident," he answered, "but I'm a soldier by trade. My place is in the fighting–line!"

"The Secret Service has its fighting–line, too," Barbara replied, "though the war correspondents don't write about it. It never gets a mention in despatches, and Victoria Crosses don't come its way. The newspapers don't publish its casualty list, though you and I know that it's a long one. A man slips quietly away and never comes back, and after a certain lapse of time we just mark him off the books and there's an end of it. But it's a great service; and you've made your mark in it. The Chief wants men like you. You'll have to stay!"

Desmond was about to speak; but the girl stopped him. "What do you and I matter," she asked, "when the whole future of England is at stake! If you are to give of your best to this silent game of ours, you must be free with no responsibilities and no ties, with nothing that will ever make you hesitate to take a supreme risk. And I never met a man that dared more freely than you!"

"Oh, please..." said Desmond and got up.

He stood gazing seawards for a while.

Then he glanced at his watch.

"I must be going back to London," he said. "I have to see the Chief at four this afternoon. And you know why!"

The girl nodded.

"What will you tell him?" she asked. "Will you accept his offer to remain on in the Secret Service?"

Desmond looked at her ruefully.

"You're so eloquent about it," he said slowly, "that I think I must!"

Smiling, she gave him her hand. Desmond held it for an instant in his.

Then, without another word, he turned and strode off towards the winding white road that led to the station.

Barbara watched him until a turn in the road hid him from her sight. Then she pulled out her handkerchief.

"Good Heavens, girl!" she said to herself, I believe you're crying!"